Insatiable

OTHER BOOKS BY ALLISON HOBBS

Pandora's Box

Dangerously in Love

Double Dippin'

Insatiable

ALLISON HOBBS

STREBOR BOOKS
NEW YORK LONDON TORONTO SYDNEY

Published by
SBI
Strebor Books
P.O. Box 6505
Largo, MD 20792
http://www.streborbooks.com

Originally published in trade paperback in 2004.

Cover Design: www.mariondesigns.com

ISBN 0-7432-9607-9
LCCN 2003116578

First Strebor Books mass market paperback edition June 2006

10 9 8 7 6 5 4 3 2

Manufactured in the United States of America

For information regarding special discounts for bulk purchases, please contact Simon & Schuster Special Sales at 1-800-456-6798 or business@simonandschuster.com

Dedication

This is dedicated to my forever friend, Karen Dempsey Hammond. Thank you so much for your patience, love, and concern throughout the writing of this novel.

Acknowledgments

Shari Reason, my daughter in spirit. I know you sacrificed a lot to make it to my numerous book signings last year. I thank you from the bottom of my heart.

Aletha Dempsey, you are truly an angel. Thanks for the support during those dark days last November. On a brighter note, thanks for all the good food you served at your pool parties last summer. Big congratulations on the opening of Bubba and Skye's Soul To Go restaurant.

A very special thanks to LisaMarie Heyward and all the members of the Philly African American Book Club. You ladies are a class act; thanks for your support.

Shakira Abdullah, I'm privileged to call you a friend. Thanks for keeping it real.

I'd like to take this opportunity to thank some of the people who were supportive of my first novel in their own special way: My little cuz, Salima Jones, Vincent and Renee Waters, Verdell and Sylvia Hicks, Stacey Long, Frances Lacey, Verna Bailey, Jane Atland, Camillah Carey, Elizabeth Green, Jessica Johnson,

Vanessa Brown, Tammy Kirkland, Lisa Butler, Barbara Harris, Rhonda Jones, Rita Randolph, Pauline Johnson, Ann Durante, and Nelson Maldonado.

Finally, I'm grateful to my new extended family, The Strebor Family: Charmaine Parker, the best publicist/editor in the world. Thank you Destiny Wood for all your help during the numerous Strebor events and special thanks for rescuing me as I wandered around the parking garage looking for my rental car. It's been an honor to work with the Strebor authors: Darrien Lee (Good looking out in New Orleans), Tina Brooks McKinney (I've gotta get you a set of pom-poms, girl), D.V. Bernard, Keith Lee Johnson, Shelley Halima, Harold Turley, Nane Quartay, Laurinda Brown, JDaniels, Jonathan Luckett, V. Anthony Rivers, Rique Johnson, and William Fredrick Cooper.

And last but certainly not least, Zane.

Chapter One

Terelle Chambers tried to carry her daughter Markeeta the two blocks to the bus stop but after trudging along for only half a block, she had to stop.

"You have to walk for a little while, Keeta. Mommy can't carry you and this big ol' turkey, too."

Squirming and trying to cling to her mother, two-year-old Markeeta whimpered as she felt herself being lowered to the pavement.

Markeeta's eyes bulged with disbelief and then clouded with tears. Her mouth, wide-open, was silent for a few seconds. Then there was a tremendous wail. Markeeta stubbornly withheld the tiny hand that her mother reached for. "Come on, give me your hand, Keeta," Terelle demanded. Markeeta shrieked again. "Shh. Be quiet. I'll pick you up in a minute."

The turkey was a Thanksgiving gift from her employer a fifteen-pound freebie that she should have left at work and picked up tomorrow while Markeeta was at the day care center. But tomorrow was her day off, and she did not feel like being anywhere near that back-breaking job.

Besides, she had plans for tomorrow. The people from the prison were coming by in the morning to interview her; they wanted to see if her apartment was suitable for Marquise to reside in for the six months he'd be on house arrest.

She and Markeeta had been living with her grandmother, but when she found out Marquise would soon be released from prison, Terelle started working doubles at the nursing home where she was a nursing assistant. It took close to three months of overtime to put together the money for the apartment.

It hadn't been easy. In fact, it had been downright grueling. She and Markeeta had to get up every morning at five. After dropping her daughter off at the day care center (which, thankfully was in walking distance from her grandmother's house) she took the bus and the subway to the nursing home and worked the first shift until three. During her lunch break on the second shift, she'd rush back to the day care center, pick up Markeeta and rush her to her grandmother's. Terelle would have to listen to Gran bitch and moan for at least five minutes before racing back to work. The second shift ended at eleven. Dog-tired, she'd make it home around midnight and start preparing for the next day.

Knocked low too many times to count, Terelle's life had never been easy.

But things were going to be different now. Marquise was coming home!

Terelle straightened up the shoulder that was dipped and aching from the weight of the turkey. Rejuvenated by thoughts of Marquise, she swooped up Markeeta with her other arm—an arm already laden with her own shoulderbag and her daughter's diaper bag. Kissing her daughter's tear-soaked cheek, Terelle determinedly race-walked to the bus stop.

✿✿✿

At home, sitting in her highchair, Markeeta munched happily on animal crackers. Terelle shed her nursing uniform and slipped into an old pair of sweat pants and tee shirt. Brand-new Baby Phat jeans and a sweater hung in the closet—gifts from her best friend, Saleema. The expensive designer clothing would not be worn until Marquise came home. She was petite and blessed with an hourglass figure most black men revered. With her tiny waistline, round hips, thick shapely legs, and Hottentot-protruding buttocks, Terelle looked spectacular in the jeans. Marquise was going to love looking at her booty in those jeans.

She'd been merely simulating living during Marquise's absence—just going through the motions. She took care of Markeeta, handled her household, and helped her grandmother and her mother, but life wouldn't really begin until Marquise came home.

Marquise was a changed man. Their lives would

change, he had promised. He said he wanted to get married; he was ready to be a family man. His daughter, he said, was going to have two parents loving and caring for her, and Terelle was going to have a man that she could depend on. From now on, he said, he was going to do his part and Terelle would never again have to hold it down alone. He wanted her to go back to school. No more working doubles, no more lugging Markeeta around on public transportation. They were going to get a car. Nothing fancy. A little hooptie to start off with.

Jail house promises. That's what Saleema had to say about Marquise's pledges of honor. But Terelle knew better; she knew her man's heart. Marquise was tired of the streets; he was ready to settle down. Terelle didn't care what Saleema or anyone else thought about Marquise.

Terelle let out a sigh. She was so tired. Tired of being lonely, tired of struggling to take care of Markeeta alone, tired of juggling bills. And she was sick and tired of dealing with her mother's issues—her unending problems. Her mother, Cassandra Chambers, had been on and off drugs for most of Terelle's life. At present, Cassandra was clean. She'd been clean for three months, the longest time ever.

The phone rang.

"Hello," Terelle sang the word, anticipating the computerized voice instructing her to press "1" to accept a collect call from Marquise.

"Hey, Terelle," her mother said drearily.

Terelle wanted to slam down the phone. She wanted

to talk to Marquise; she wasn't in the mood to listen to her mother's depressing conversation. "Hey, Mom," she said in a fake cheerful voice that implied that her mother's call was welcome.

"How's Keeta?"

Terelle smiled over at her daughter who was making a mess with the animal cookies. "She's doing good, Mom. I'm trying to hype her up about her daddy coming home." Terelle's smile widened.

"How you expect Keeta to be excited about somebody she don't hardly even know."

"She knows her father!" Terelle snapped. "I've been taking her to see him for two years. And she talks to him on the phone practically every day."

"So what! Talking baby talk to a voice on the phone ain't the same as being raised by her father. Marquise been in jail since before Keeta was born. It's gonna take a while before she really thinks of him as her daddy."

Terelle could feel her face burning with anger. "There you go. Why you always badmouthin' Marquise? It ain't like you got room to talk."

Inflamed, Terelle began pacing around the kitchen, holding the phone with one hand and rubbing her temple with the other. "You're in rehab now and I'm happy for you. But I don't think I'm ever going to forget how you neglected me. After all you put me through—three different foster homes—you should be glad I still call you Mom."

"Why you tryin' to upset me, Terelle? I thought we

said we was gonna leave the past where it belongs and move forward. Ain't that what you promised when I made it through the detox program?"

"Which time, Mom? You been in so many programs I stopped countin' a long time ago."

"Forget it, Terelle. I thought we could have a decent conversation for a change, but all you want to do is bring up the past and make me feel worse than I already feel. I'm doing the best I can, you know. Living in this depressing place with all these funky women... All these rules and regulations they make you put up with is ridiculous. You gotta be in at a certain time. Can't go nowhere alone. Gotta ask somebody if you can use the phone. Shit, I might as well be in jail. I'm getting sick of this dumb shit." Cassandra paused, as if waiting for Terelle to utter a sound of understanding. Terelle's silence encouraged Cassandra to produce more evidence of her mistreatment at the rehabilitation group home. "Do you realize three other women sleep in my bedroom? Uh-huh, that's right. We only have two beds and they got us in there four deep! Now, that's some bullshit and you know it. Ain't no such thing as privacy around here. I don't know how much longer I can put up with this crap."

"What are you saying, Mom?" Terelle's mouth was pursed.

"I'm saying...I'm thinking about making some changes. That's what I'm saying!"

Terelle's shoulders slumped. "You made it through three whole months. You gotta be strong. One step at a time! That's the name of the program 'cause that's what you gotta do." Terelle paused. "Right, Mom?"

"Wrong! I ain't taking no more steps."

"What? You just gonna give up? Go back on drugs?"

"Hell no. But now that you got your own place, I don't see why I can't come stay with you? I could do the outpatient thing. They got plenty of outpatient programs right there in Southwest Philly. There's a place near 56th & Greenway. Shit, I could walk there from your place..."

Terelle's head was pounding. "Mom, you're not ready for Outpatient. You need to stay where you are for the amount of time they say you need to be there." She used a placating tone that seemed to give her mother more determination.

"No way! These crazy people talkin' 'bout it takes a year to get on your feet. I'm not staying here for no damn year. I can get a job—help you pay rent..."

"No! You're staying in the program until you can stand on your own feet. You've been doing drugs since that shit first hit the streets—since I was seven years old. How you think three months gonna straighten out your life? It's gonna take a minute before you're ready to live drug-free on the outside. Them rules and things are for your own good."

Cassandra emitted a loud, "Humph!"

"Seriously, Mom. You can't expect to just start working and following real rules when you've been living by your own rules for all these years."

"Terelle, I ain't callin' you for no lecture. Can I stay there or not?"

"No! I'm trying to get things together for me and Keeta."

"And Marquise," Cassandra added, spitting out the name.

"Yeah, and Marquise. What's wrong with that?"

"Everything's wrong with that. You wanna make a way for that nothin' nigga but you don't wanna do shit for me—your own flesh and blood."

Her mother was wearing her down. "I'm not trying to put anybody before you, Mom." Terelle sighed and switched the phone to her other ear. She looked up at the kitchen clock. It was time for Marquise to call. "There's a place in my heart that belongs to you, there's a place for Keeta, and there's a place for Marquise."

Cassandra was hopeful until Marquise's name was included.

"Time!" shouted a woman in the house where Cassandra lived. The voice was deliberately commanding, loud, and ugly. But, desperately wanting to get off the phone with her mother, Terelle was grateful that the unpleasant woman possessed the authority to terminate the telephone conversation.

"See what I mean?" Cassandra's voice rose. "That was the house manager. She loves telling me what to do. Look, I gotta get off the phone. I'll call you tomorrow. Kiss Keeta for me."

Terelle checked the time again. Damn. She'd probably missed Marquise's call. She wished she still had call-waiting, but someone from the sheriff's department had called to inform her that she would have to take all the features off her phone in order for them to install a monitor on her phone line. This monitor would allow them to keep track of Marquise's whereabouts while he was on house arrest.

With eyes bouncing from the kitchen clock to the phone, she scooped canned spaghetti into a bowl for Markeeta's dinner and set the microwave for forty seconds. Shit! Why'd she allow her mother to guilt-trip her into staying on the phone. Feeling discouraged, Terelle placed the bowl in front of her daughter and began mindlessly stirring the sauce and noodles with a fork bearing Elmo's image at the tip. Lost in her thoughts, she didn't notice that Markeeta was leaning forward with her mouth open, hungrily awaiting the first mouthful. She gave her daughter the fork.

The phone finally made a sound. Terelle snatched it off the base in the middle of the first ring.

"What's crackin', babe," Marquise said in his slow sexy way.

"Marquise! How'd you get through without calling collect?"

"Your line was busy so I had to call my man, Jalil. He hit you with his three-way."

"Thanks, Jalil," Terelle offered.

"He ain't on the phone; he just hit you up and laid the phone down."

"Oh."

"So, why were you on the phone? You know what time I call."

"I'm sorry, Quise. My mom called. Depressed as usual about her situation. I was trying to keep her spirits up."

Marquise didn't respond. Terelle was not surprised. There was bad blood between Marquise and her mother and she didn't know why.

"So, you hear anything yet?" Marquise asked.

"Yeah. Some people are supposed to come over tomorrow to interview me and check out the apartment building."

"Check it out for what?"

"I don't know. I guess to make sure there's no drug traffic going on in the building. Didn't they talk to you about the procedure?"

"I ain't heard shit. I'm locked up, remember? They do all their communicatin' with you."

"I meant your lawyer. Didn't he mention something about the process?"

"That dickhead! He's on the county payroll. He don't tell me nothin." Marquise was getting worked up.

"I know. I know. Well, don't get all hyped. I'm sure I'll have some news for you tomorrow."

"Good news, I hope. 'Cause I'm about sick of bein'

jerked around by the system. The black man can't get a break..."

✿✿✿

Terelle quickly interjected soothingly, "Don't worry, baby. It's gonna be over soon. We're on our way to a brand new life." How had the tables turned, she wondered? Instead of receiving the comfort she needed, she was playing the role of comforter to Marquise—calming and reassuring him.

"Yo, Quise!" Jalil's discarnate voice startled Terelle. "My mom gotta use the phone, dawg."

"Okay, man. I'll be off in a minute. Terelle, let me hollah at my baby girl for a sec."

Terelle aligned the phone to Markeeta's mouth and ear. "Say hi to Daddy, Keeta."

Before Markeeta could begin to formulate one word, Terelle heard the blaring dial tone. Jalil had disconnected them; he probably didn't want his mom to find out he had accepted a collect call. Damn! She had really needed to talk to Marquise. She was lonely and needed to hear him tell her how much he loved and missed her. She was sick of living off phone calls. Expensive phone calls. Ten minutes of communicating with her man cost her fifteen dollars a day...a lot of chips for a woman with a salary of only nine dollars an hour. Terelle had calculated that after taxes, she had to work about two and a half hours for ten minutes of phone time with her man. But hearing his voice was worth every dime.

Chapter Two

The image on the computer monitor was too small. Kai Montgomery clicked a button and enlarged it. Much better. There she was—wearing her million-dollar smile. She scrolled down and smiled at the stethoscope that dangled between her bare breasts. Her beautiful luscious melons, according to Dr. Kenneth Harding, the owner of the stethoscope and the brilliant white lab coat Kai wore in the photograph. There was no denying that it was his jacket. His name, embroidered in bright red letters, attested to that fact.

Kai put photo paper in the printer and clicked print. This photo was sure to knock the smug smiles off the faces of Dr. and Mrs. Kenneth Harding. How dare he leave for vacation without telling her? And, having to be told the news by his secretary was the lowest blow of all. Kai wallowed in self-righteous indignation and preparing the photograph did little to assuage her injured ego. Just whom did he think he was dealing with? Surely he didn't place her in the same category with the many grateful dull-witted women with whom he had dallied in the past—women who considered him the prize?

She was the prize, dammit, and Dr. Kenneth Harding with his rarely hard—mostly flaccid—premature ejaculating little dick should have been honored to be in her presence, let alone her bed. The nerve of that bastard!

Kai walked over to the living room window of her twenty-sixth-floor apartment and stared. Annoyed and feeling exposed by the view she usually enjoyed, she yanked the drapes closed. Throwing on workout attire, she slammed out of her apartment, planning to take out her frustration on the beanbag in her apartment building's fitness center. Later, when her mind was more settled, she'd focus her concentration on the most effective way to deliver the goods: FedEx, snail mail, or maybe she'd have it hand-delivered. She'd figure it out later, she told herself as she absently pushed for the elevator and stepped in. Deep in thought, she ignored the other passengers. She considered sprinkling the package with anthrax for good measure. No! That would be overkill. Kai burst out laughing, taking great delight in her wicked sense of humor. Her unexpected laughter caused the passengers to jump in startled unison.

Attempting to calm herself and control her public outbursts, Kai decided that the unimpeachable photographic evidence of the good doctor's infidelity would be more than enough to rock the lily-white utopian world of Dr. and Mrs. Harding.

Chapter Three

The alleged culinary delights scrawled on the chalkboard menu in the cafeteria left Terelle unenthused: chicken tenders, hot dogs, cream of mushroom soup, peas, and mashed potatoes. Don, the cheerful attendant who served the food, patiently waited for her decision. She shook her head and moved toward the salad bar. Nothing appealing there either. If you didn't get your salad on Monday, you were shit outta luck. It was Wednesday and everything looked wilted and sickly. The bowl containing fake seafood salad looked contaminated. Terelle continued to push her empty tray and stopped at the deli section. She ordered a turkey sandwich on whole wheat, chips, and a soda. There was a long line behind her. The sandwich maker was also the cashier and until the sandwich was made, the line did not move.

Melanie, who worked in the laundry department, motioned Terelle over to her table. Terelle didn't feel like listening to Melanie talk a mile a minute; she needed solitude to try to work out some of her problems, but not wanting to appear rude, she reluctantly joined her co-worker.

"Hey, Melanie. Your hair looks nice," Terelle said, indicating Melanie's short blonde weave.

"Thanks. Girl, how come you don't do nothin' with all that long pretty hair you got?"

"I'll get around to it one day. For now, pulling it back into a ponytail is easier."

"You ain't gonna catch a man that way," Melanie added, winking.

"Whatever," Terelle said, shrugging

Melanie knew damn well that Terelle's man was in jail. She had probably heard that Marquise was getting out soon and wanted details straight from the source.

But Terelle didn't have any details. Those house arrest people didn't tell her jack shit. They said Marquise was on a waiting list. The only thing keeping him and Terelle apart was the availability of a monitor. As soon as one of those black boxes became available Marquise would be released immediately. The word *immediately* should have made Terelle feel good, but it didn't. She felt panicked because without a definite release date she couldn't even ask for the time off from work. What would happen, she'd asked, if they released Marquise and she wasn't home? She was told that they'd call first and if she weren't home, Marquise's box would be assigned to someone else. She hastily gave them the number to the nurses' station on her unit, and assured the prison interviewers that she'd leave work the instant Marquise was released.

"What? Don't tell me you finally stopped waiting for that guy you was messin' wit…the one in jail."

"Girl, I'm just chillin'," Terelle said, without really giving up any information.

Realizing that her half-ass sleuthing wasn't going to work, Melanie changed the subject. "Guess who got fired?"

Disinterested, Terelle lifted one brow. The latest victim of the nursing home's swift and ever-swinging ax was juicy gossip to most employees, but Terelle was absorbed by her own personal dilemma.

"Malik," Melanie offered.

"Who's that?"

"You know…the guy who works in Dietary."

"I don't know anybody named Malik." She really didn't care either. She hoped Melanie's lunch break would soon end.

"Yes, you do," Melanie insisted. Big guy—bald head. You know 'em. He stays wearing a new pair of Tims. Thinks he's all dat.

"Oh, yeah," Terelle said halfheartedly.

"Girl, you ain't gonna believe what his ass was doing?"

Terelle cocked her head to the side.

Melanie looked around the room and then leaned forward. "Girl, he was selling drugs to the young adult residents."

"You know you're lying," Terelle said, laughing despite herself.

"I swear! They got him on tape. His dumb ass should know they got cameras all over the place."

"What was he selling—crack?"

"No. I heard he was selling weed. And check this out…he been stealing them little cups off the med cart. You know…them little plastic cups they put the pills in?"

Terelle nodded. "Stealing them for what?"

"Girl, he was selling the older residents shots of cheap liquor for a dollar a cup. "You know most of those old people—the women and the men—most of 'em been alcoholics since back in the day."

"How do you know? You work in Laundry; you don't read their charts."

"And you're just a nursing assistant; you don't read the charts either, but you hear things, don't you? Well, so do I. Ain't no secrets in this place."

Obviously miffed, Melanie looked at the big institutional clock on the wall, pushed back her chair and was positioned in a half-stand when the new social worker walked in. Melanie sat back down. "You like her?" she whispered with a sneer.

"I don't know her."

"She don't speak to none of the black people. I can't stand bitches like her that be hatin' their own kind."

"That's her business; I don't give a shit." Terelle wanted to be alone.

"Just lettin' you know before you start acting all Joe friendly with her."

"Thanks," Terelle said. Her tone was flat.

Leaving the lunchroom, Melanie mixed in with other uniform-wearing women. The uniforms, a rainbow of colors with every department in the nursing home represented by a different shade: royal blue for Housekeeping, light blue for Laundry, beige for Dietary, green for Recreation, brown for Plant Operations, and the nursing staff wore a variety of cheery pastel-colored scrubs.

When the social worker came into Terelle's field of vision, she zoomed in on her name badge. *Kai Montgomery*. Tall, model thin and exotically beautiful, Kai oozed with self-confidence. Terelle took notice of Kai's chin-length hair. Fashionably coiffed light-brown ringlets with subtle blonde highlights framed her face. *Nice*.

Terelle had always felt ill at ease around women like Kai. Kai wore a gray cashmere sweater and slacks. Expensive-looking jewelry hung from her neck and dangled from her wrists. Her black and gray suede pumps looked like they cost a bundle, too. Terelle looked down critically at her own shapeless nursing uniform and beat-up sneakers and felt extremely unattractive and poor. Looking up, she watched with great interest as Kai placed a cup of soup on her tray. No crackers. With her back now facing Terelle, the social worker glided toward the cashier. She extracted money from a classy thin leather wallet.

Someone had told her that social workers didn't make much money. Well, someone lied because this social worker definitely had it going on. Maybe she should reconsider that eighteen-month licensed nursing program she was going to sign up for and look into becoming a social worker?

Stabbed by feelings of inadequacy, Terelle looked down when Kai turned around.

Kai left the lunchroom with her soup. Apparently averse to mingling with the support staff, many of the professional staff preferred to eat in their offices. Terelle bit into her sandwich. Deep in thought, she chewed without much enjoyment.

She tried to cheer herself up with thoughts of Marquise, but couldn't. Tomorrow was Thanksgiving—the third Thanksgiving without him. Christmas, she hoped, would be different. It had to be. She was scared, always broke, tired and very lonely. Massaging both temples, she lowered her head.

Chapter Four

I have a migraine, mother! My head feels like it's about to explode. Please stop interrogating me!"

"This is not an interrogation, darling. I'm concerned. Your father will be extremely upset," Miranda Montgomery said on the other end of the telephone.

"Upset about what? My migraine or that my seat will be empty, ruining your picture-perfect Thanksgiving dinner."

"There's no need for sarcasm, dear. What's gotten into you?"

"How many times do I have to say it: I...have... a...headache!" Kai screamed the last word.

"Well, it's no wonder you have a headache. You're so filled with animosity. Displaced animosity, I might add."

"Is that what your therapist told you, Mother?"

"I have to go, Kai. Please be sure to call your father. He deserves to hear from you."

"Does he deserve to hear from me because he pays my rent?"

"Among other things...," Miranda said sarcastically,

and then cleared her throat. "You should call and wish him a happy Thanksgiving because he's your father."

"So they say," Kai commented cruelly.

"I have to go, Kai." Miranda managed to sound unruffled, but Kai knew she had struck a nerve. Her lips curved into a satisfied smile. God, she hated her parents.

They said she used to be a happy child, but she had only vague memories of happy times. Unhappy memories were quite vivid and haunted her. She recalled how her mother had cut her hair into a misshapen, lopsided Afro, causing classmates at the predominantly white elementary school she attended to point and ask obnoxious questions about her heritage.

"Is Kai black?" Eric Raymond, one of her first-grade classmates, asked Mrs. Pauley, their teacher. Mrs. Pauley turned pale with embarrassment. "I'm not really sure, Eric, but that is an inappropriate question to ask and we shouldn't..."

"Are you black, Kai?" Eric interrupted.

"I don't think so," Kai muttered, examining her hands.

"Then why do you have hair like black people?" the little boy wanted to know.

Kai was silent for a moment and then shrugged helplessly.

Later that day, Kai tearfully told her mother what had happened. "Am I black?" she asked, her voice filled with fear.

Her mother admitted that she was adopted and yes...

she was part black, but Kai's color didn't matter. That she was dearly loved by both her parents was the only thing that mattered, her mother had told her.

Being told that she was different made her feel less valuable than her parents. She blamed her mother. In her naïve, young mind, her true heritage would have remained a secret had her mother not cut her hair in that dreadful Afro.

But her mother had felt she had no choice for unfortunately, Kai's hair had become more wild and unmanageable every day. Sarah, the black housekeeper, usually combed Kai's hair a few times a week. But Kai was in school now and her hair required daily upkeep. Miranda Montgomery didn't possess the skills nor was she inclined to comb through Kai's tangled mane day after day. Miranda's solution was to chop it off.

Years later, Kai would tell her own therapist that she felt her mother had disfigured her the day she cut her hair.

Her hatred for her father began during her teens. She, a privileged young lady from Radnor, was doing volunteer work (a mandatory school project) in the impoverished city of Chester, Pennsylvania. The residents of Chester were accustomed to white volunteers from the Main Line but never a black volunteer. The few blacks living in Radnor had long ago distanced themselves from their country cousins and wouldn't dream of venturing into the "wilds" of Chester to lend a helping hand.

Kai's presence in Chester puzzled the residents. She

was obviously biracial, but assumed the attitude and dialect of a white girl. She was there to do her civic duty for the downtrodden blacks, and there was no recognition or sign of kinship in her eyes.

Folks scratched their heads, trying to figure her out. *Her last name is Montgomery, huh? Don't that name sound familiar?* Then old Miss Celestine, a historian of sorts, recalled the white doctor. *The liberal. You know, the one who used to volunteer at the clinic a few days a week?* Memories were refreshed. Tongues began to wag. *The one who knocked up that black girl and then adopted the baby? It was a baby girl, wasn't it? Uh-huh, she'd be about Kai's age by now. Hmmm! What happened to the mother? Don't know. She wasn't from 'round here anyway. Didn't she run off with some musician? Uh-huh, that's right. Never heard from again.*

The gossip and speculations soon reached Kai's ears; the seeds of suspicion were firmly planted. "How do you disown your own child?" Kai asked her father, years later when she finally mustered the nerve. "You say you adopted me because you love me, but I think you were motivated by guilt. So…if you have nothing to hide, let me see the adoption papers. My birth records. Be honest; tell me who I really am."

"Your birth records are sealed. Let's leave it that way," her father said, ending the subject.

Screaming how much she hated her coldblooded lying-ass parents, Kai had pounded up the stairs to her bedroom and slammed the door. The subject was never mentioned again. Her parents never knew the degree of hurt nor the burning shame Kai felt regarding her heritage.

Chapter Five

The turkey was baked to perfection, but Terelle didn't attempt to make the macaroni and cheese; it never turned out right, so Aunt Bennie (short for Benita) brought her delicious baked macaroni and cheese. Aunt Bennie lost points, however, when she tried to pass off a tub of canned Glory collards as homemade.

"Addin' some smoked turkey to canned food don't make it homemade," Gran complained. "And I still don't see why we had to have Thanksgiving dinner in this cramped-up little apartment. Had me walkin' up all those stairs…It's a wonder my heart didn't just up and explode." Gran scowled as she sized up the small kitchen, the even smaller dining area and living room.

"Mom, you know Terelle doesn't want to miss Marquise's call," Aunt Bennie explained.

"Oh, God!" Terelle glared at her aunt, chastising her with her eyes for bringing up Marquise's name. Aunt Bennie shrugged; her expression asked: *what did I do?*

Gran looked over her glasses at the phone suspiciously. "Terelle, you still payin' for that boy to call you collect? You had to work overtime to pay for all those calls while you was livin' with me. And don't think I don't know about all those expensive boots and sneakers and things you was sending him. What the hell he need that stuff for anyhow? He's in jail! Don't they have to wear them orange jumpsuits?"

"Gran, why you worrying about what I do...as long as I take care of Keeta..."

"Hmph! Lord, you 'bout as dumb as they come," Gran interrupted. "Look at you! Out here struggling with a child, all on your own, and you mean to tell me you're still lettin' that boy run up your phone bill?"

"Let's eat." Terelle began scooping collards on Gran's plate. Best to stuff Gran's mouth with food before she really became agitated and started aiming cuss words as sharp as an ax in Terelle's direction. It didn't matter that Markeeta was present. Once Gran got started, it wouldn't matter if Christ himself were present at the table.

Looking guilty, Aunt Bennie busied herself with the task of slicing the turkey.

"Don't give me no dark meat, 'cause I don't like no dark meat," Gran grumbled.

"I know, I know. Calm down, Mom," Aunt Bennie said.

"How can I calm down? My oldest child is a damn drug addict..."

"Cassy's in recovery, Mom..."

"My granddaughter is working like a mule to take care

of a man in jail, and my youngest daughter is a goddamn bulldagger," Gran barked. Aunt Bennie's mouth opened in wide protest.

"It's Thanksgiving, Gran. Please stop!" Terelle pleaded. "Aunt Bennie's not gay."

"I ain't said nothing about gay. I said she's a bulldagger. She ain't foolin' me with her mannish self—walking around in her bedroom wearing men's boxer shorts. It's probably my own damn fault for giving her that nickname." Gran sighed heavily, then went on, "At the time, I thought it was a cute way to shorten up Benita. But if I knew then what I know now..."

"How you gonna tell me what I am? Lots of women wear boxers nowadays."

There was pain in Aunt Bennie's eyes that Terelle took no pleasure in witnessing. If her aunt was actually gay, she needed to come out of the closet; hiding her sexual orientation was obviously a heavy burden.

"That's bullshit," Gran grumbled. "Do you wear men's underwear, Terelle?"

"No, but..."

"But, nothing. Where's her husband? Where's her children? Where's her damn boyfriend? She ain't got none of that because she's too busy bumpin' coochies with other women."

Aunt Bennie's wounded expression tugged at Terelle's heart. "Gran! Don't be saying that nasty stuff around Keeta."

"Don't think I'm forgetting about you, neither. You's a damn fool. Why you allowin' that boy to take advantage of you like that? Keeta's my only hope of something decent coming out of this family. But with the daddy she got...I doubt if that's possible."

"Stop talking about Marquise, right in front of Keeta. That ain't right, Gran."

"Sooner or later Keeta's gonna learn the truth—might as well be sooner. And Terelle, you should be 'shamed of yourself for stickin' by a man who done got your mother all messed up on drugs."

"Marquise..." Terelle struggled to get the words out. "He didn't do that to my mother. Me and Marquise were kids when my mother started messin' with that stuff." She looked at Aunt Bennie for confirmation, but her aunt, still nursing the injuries sustained from Gran's attack, gazed at Terelle with unfocused eyes.

"Yeah, and when he grew up, he made sure your mother stayed on that junk, now didn't he?"

Her grandmother was working her nerves. Terelle became silent as she prepared Markeeta's plate. She knew that if she didn't keep her mouth shut, her grandmother's temper was liable to rise up and whirl around the kitchen like a hurricane. The dinner had turned into a disaster. If she was lucky, Gran would gobble down her food, try to belch, complain of heartburn and insist upon leaving immediately.

It was partly true—she had invited them over

because she didn't want to miss Marquise's call; she also wanted to show off her new apartment. But, it didn't matter. Gran hadn't said one word of praise. Her comments about the apartment were all negative. Her ornery grandmother loved making everybody miserable. She'd been mean as a snake for as long as Terelle could remember.

She picked at her food, her mind replaying what Gran had said about her being a fool and she was getting more pissed by the minute. Gran had her nerve—raising her own two children in a speakeasy. Terelle's mother had told her that she'd learned how to pour the right brand of liquor based on the color of the bottle before she could read. And pouring from the wrong bottle meant an encounter with Gran's wrath. Gran had one hellish temper. Terelle's mother and Aunt Bennie still bore the scars of that temper. Beatings with razor straps, ironing cords, broom handles—whatever Gran could get her hands on. Terelle figured if Aunt Bennie was actually a lesbian, then it was probably due to her being molested by one of Gran's drunken customers. But that was kept quiet because the man was supposed to be somebody important—somebody politically connected. Her mother's drug addiction and poor parenting skills could probably be blamed on Gran, too. Gran was no model parent—that was for sure.

It had taken Marquise a long time to grow up and

face his responsibilities but now that he was ready, she was going to do everything in her power to help pull him along. She didn't mind working a little overtime to pay for the calls. That was a small thing. She worked for her money and didn't ask anybody for anything. Marquise was her future, and if holding her man up until he could do better classified her as a fool, then she was glad to be one.

Chapter Six

"This is Kai Montgomery. Has Dr. Harding returned from vacation?" Kai asked, confident that her professional tone would persuade the receptionist at Dr. Harding's posh Bala Cynwyd office to impart the information.

"Yes, Ms. Montgomery, he's back. But he won't be in the office until late this afternoon. He's at the nursing home this morning. Would you care to leave a message?"

"No thanks. I'll call him there." Kai hung up. Bewildered, she wound a lock of hair around her finger. The bastard was right here in the facility and hadn't bothered to call her. She angrily punched the numbers to his pager and after inputting her extension, slammed the phone into its cradle.

The wait was excruciating. Patting her foot impatiently, and twirling her hair until it became tangled around her finger, Kai grimaced when she began to feel a dull throbbing in her left temple, the prelude to an oncoming migraine.

Eight minutes later the phone rang; Kai yanked the receiver from the cradle on the first ring.

"I can't believe..."

"Miss Montgomery?" The voice did not belong to Kenneth. Kai regularly received calls from relatives of nursing home residents on her caseload and, unfortunately for her, the call was from a client's family member.

"Yes, this is Kai Montgomery. How can I help you?" She didn't try to disguise her annoyance.

"This is Emma...uh, Emma Randolph. Irving Randolph's wife...," the woman stammered.

"Yes, what can I do for you, Mrs. Randolph?"

"Well, you see, I have the receipt here for some socks I bought my husband. I bought—let me see now... Yeah, I bought twelve pairs of those heavy thermal socks. And they wasn't cheap. I got the receipt right here. Socks don't cost what they used to. Was a time when..."

Kai's long sigh of exasperation caused the woman to pause.

"Now I was there last night—and when I visit Irving I always check his closet and drawers to make sure all his things..."

"How many pairs of socks are missing, Mrs. Randolph?"

"Well...all of them. He ain't got none of them new socks. The onliest ones left in his drawer is..."

Onliest! Kai sucked her teeth and groaned, certain she had now heard it all.

"Bring in the receipt and you'll be reimbursed."

"I can get all my money back?"

"Yes." Kai hissed.

"Okay, I'm gonna take your word. 'Cause the last time I..."

"Mrs. Randolph, I have another call," she said, wishing she did. Where the hell was Kenneth?

"When should I bring it in? Will you be in your office tomorrow mornin'? See, I ain't got nobody to bring me there today..."

"Take the receipt to the Finance Department on the first floor. Listen, I have to go." Kai slammed down the phone.

Swiveling in her chair and twirling her hair mercilessly, Kai pondered making a trip to the second-floor office of Dr. Harding, but decided against it. That would be a wasted trip. Kenneth was rarely in his office. More than likely he was making rounds, which included bullshitting with the nurses and the unit clerks. A mental picture of tall, blond, solidly built Kenneth working his charm shot across Kai's mind and through her heart. Wasn't it bad enough that he had snuck off on a vacation with his wife; why did he have to disrespect her even more by not answering her page? Maybe she should call the receptionist and have her overhead page the good doctor. *No! The hell with paging!*

Awash in rage, Kai stood. She'd comb the facility floor by floor until she found the smiling pompous bastard! And if he didn't stop whatever he was doing the moment he spotted her, God help him because she would not be held accountable for the violence and mayhem that would ensue.

Distracted by the delicious reverie of doing bodily harm to Dr. Kenneth Harding, Kai was startled by the muted sound of her cell phone. The phone was in her purse, which was locked in the bottom desk drawer. Kai scrambled for her office keys. *Why the hell is he calling on my cell phone?* She'd put her office extension on his pager. Always cautious, always careful to cover his tracks—or so he thought—because he fucked up royally when he left his lab coat and stethoscope unattended while he slept at her apartment.

The phone had stopped ringing by the time Kai had unlocked the drawer and retrieved it from her purse. *Oh, how I despise him!* She gazed at the phone, waiting for the word *message* to pop up. When it did, she quickly punched the numbers to hear what Kenneth had to say.

"Hello, Kai. Look, I'm here at the nursing home, but I've been pretty busy all morning. I'll be leaving shortly—uh, I have a lunch engagement. A business lunch. But, I'll call you tonight. You have a pleasant and productive day."

The call ended and a computerized voice asked Kai if she wished to save or delete the message. Angrily, she pressed the button that would erase Kenneth's smug indifference. She rooted through some files, and pulled out the manila envelope that contained the photo of her wearing Kenneth's lab coat. She took a moment to examine the image gazing back at her and smiled approvingly at her handiwork. She grabbed her purse and her new lavender suede coat and bolted from the office.

Moving swiftly, Kai didn't so much as glance or utter a greeting to her coworkers or the elderly nursing home residents who cluttered the corridor. She impatiently navigated around an old man who ambled along with the assistance of a rolling walker. Passing him, she picked up speed, but began muttering curse words when she had to slow down to squeeze between an abandoned laundry cart and a white-haired woman who self-propelled her wheelchair at an agonizingly slow pace.

"Social worker, social worker," the woman called in a raspy voice. "Can I make a phone call? I have to call my mother."

Kai did not slow her stride or look back. She completely ignored the eighty-five-year-old woman who had long- and short-term memory problems. The woman's mother was long dead and Kai had no time for validation therapy or reality orientation; she had pressing business to attend to.

Her path finally clear, Kai hurried toward the double set of elevators. Mindful that germs were everywhere and on everything inside the nursing home, she carefully covered her hands with lavender leather gloves before pressing the arrow pointing down. The scowl that distorted her facial features gradually changed into an expression of amusement. Gloved fingers gaily tapped the manila envelope that was tucked under her arm, and she wondered if driving to the FedEx office at Eighth and Spring Garden during her lunch break was productive enough for Dr. Harding. She'd pay anything to witness the expression of the good doctor's wife when she received the package.

Yes, the thought of Mrs. Harding unveiling the damning photograph was providing Kai with an exceptionally pleasant and productive day!

Chapter Seven

The height of fashion, Saleema stepped inside Terelle's Kingsessing Avenue apartment draped from head to toe in leather and fur: fox head wrap; cream- colored leather coat with a big fox collar; chocolate leather pants with an outside slit that was trimmed in a light-colored fur; and two-toned chocolate and cream leather ankle boots. "Ta-da," she sang, announcing her entrance with outstretched arms before striking a dramatic pose. She and Terelle burst into laughter. Both could recall the days when Saleema's wardrobe was selected from huge plastic bags donated by the neighborhood Baptist church. Saleema had come a long way.

"Where's Keeta?"

"Sleep, thank God. And please don't wake her up."

"Girl, you gonna scream when you see all the phat shit I bought Keeta for Christmas. And I ain't wrapping none of it, 'cause I want all her gear spread out and displayed under the tree. I went to the toddler department in Strawbridge's and went buck wild. My girl is gonna be rockin' designer everything: shoes, undershirts, dresses, coats, jackets, jeans, hoodies—everything. And I found her the cutest little Timberlands at Footlocker in the Gallery. I ain't finished yet. I'm gonna put Keeta's cute little butt in some Baby Phat jeans. Couldn't find none in her size in Philly, but somebody told me I could find them in New York." Saleema gazed at Terelle thoughtfully. "I ain't even got started on her toys yet; I'll probably get her toys in New York, too."

"Keeta don't need nothin' else, Saleema," Terelle said in weak protest.

"Hmph. My godbaby ain't gonna be looking like no ragamuffin. She gonna stay fly just like me."

"I gotta give you your props; you really look good, Saleema. Where you on your way to? You gotta be on your way to someplace fly like P. Diddy's club in New York—you look too good to be hanging in Philly." Terelle paused to touch the butter-soft leather coat. "Where'd you get your coat?"

"Saks," Saleema said proudly. "You know I live in that store. All the money I spend up in there, they need to give a sistah some stock."

"What size is it? A three?" Terelle frowned.

"Naw, I'm in a size five now. Good living—eating good, girl."

"I get mad just thinking about all those fly clothes you don't even wear. So just keep on eating, girl,"

Terelle said playfully. "Come on up to my size so I can rock some of your gear."

"Hell no, I ain't putting on another pound. Bad for business. You better come on down to my size."

"Chile, Marquise would flip if I lost weight. He loves seeing my hips filling out a size ten."

Saleema's eyes became slits. "Marquise ain't got room to be flippin' about nothin'—not with all the debt he got you in. Thank God Keeta got me for a godmother. If I didn't come through, her little butt would be wearing clothes from Wal-Mart—her feet would be all squeezed up in some Payless shoes."

"Don't go there, Saleema. And I'm not in debt."

"Hmph. No? Then you livin' above your means paying the phone company damn near a dub a day just to talk to a nigga. And now that you ain't got no nighttime babysitter, I know you can't work no more overtime. So, how you still payin' for his calls? I sure hope you don't let that nigga get your phone cut off."

"Saleema!" Terelle said sharply. "His name is Marquise—not *That Nigga!* My mother, my grandmother, all of my so-called friends...everybody thinks it's their right to make me feel bad about my relationship with Marquise. But you're supposed to be my girl—ever since the first grade. If anybody understands me and knows how I feel, it's supposed to be you."

"You're right," Saleema said, looking contrite. Her smile appeared pained. "My bad. I just get so mad when

I think about all that nigga—I mean, Marquise done put you through. I just don't wanna see you get hurt no more."

"I got this, Saleema. I know what I'm doing. Trust me. I know what I'm doing."

Saleema nodded in agreement, but her sorrowful eyes contradicted the movement of her head. "I gotta go," she said as she checked her Fendi link watch. "And...to answer your question, I'm meeting one of my regulars in a half-hour. Remember Dave, the white trick from Swarthmore? We met at Pandora's Box—now I see him on the outside."

"The one who bought you the platinum necklace?"

"No, that's Ralph. I don't fuck with him like that no more. He got too possessive."

"Girl, be careful. You know I worry about you hanging around with all those freakish white men you meet at work. If you have to do that kind of work, why don't you just see them at Pandora's? At least it's safe there."

"Safe!" Saleema snorted. "The manager got popped a couple years ago by two knuckleheads and you think Pandora's Box is safe?"

"You know what I mean. Didn't the owner beef up security after that?"

"Yeah, right. That bitch put in a Brinks alarm system to protect her money. But we ain't no safer than we was before."

"So why do you work somewhere that's so dangerous?"

"The world is dangerous. I take my chances. Shit, I could get robbed steppin' outta my truck coming here to see you. The way niggas be foaming at the mouth... checkin' out Jezzy...it's a wonder ain't nobody tried to jack me for my ride."

Jezzy was the nickname Saleema had given her white Ford Expedition. The vanity plate read: JEZEBEL.

"Look, Pandora's be keepin' my pockets full, but I ain't always in the mood to be breakin' that bitch off. I'm not tryin' to give the owner half my dough every time I get a session. Gabrielle already got a Rolls-Royce and a mansion. I'm still tryin' to get mine, ya dig?"

"No. I worry about you, Saleema. Another thing, why are all your customers white? They the ones who be doin' all that weird shit. Don't you date any of the black men that come through?"

"Hmph! Niggas be gettin' into some wild shit, too. What about them two snipers down South. Uh-huh! Anyway, brothas ain't feelin' me. They don't want my black ass. All they wanna do is git wit them high-yella bitches; I'm too dark and too thin for niggas so I stick with the muthafuckers who appreciate this chocolate candy bar." Saleema swiveled and smoothed her hands from her fur hat down to her leather pants. "The white man loves to pay my rent and the note on my truck. And I loves to let 'em."

"Just be careful, okay?"

"I'm straight. Let some nut even think about comin'

at me all crazy...I'd whoop so much ass, that muthafucker would be beggin' for mercy. But, then again, knowin' how twisted them tricks can be, he might enjoy the ass whoopin' I put on 'em, and then I'd have to charge him extra," Saleema said, shoulders shaking with laughter.

"All right, Saleema. I know you think you all gangsta, but how your little ass gonna stop a man from hurting you?"

Saleema winked. "I never leave home without my piece. No baby, my piece goes wherever I go. I ain't playing with these dumb ass niggas or crackas. Let somebody try to come at me or try to jack my ride and I'm gonna blast that pussy without even blinkin'."

"Whatchu sayin'? You gotta gun?"

"Uh-huh."

"I don't believe it."

Saleema unzipped her Fendi bag and revealed a small silver gun.

"Damn, it's kinda cute—pretty," Terelle admitted in awe. "Never thought I'd see a pretty gun."

Saleema extended the hand holding the gun. "Wanna hold it?" she asked devilishly.

Terelle backed up. "Hell no, you know I don't mess with guns. Too scared."

Saleema shook her head in pity. "You'd get over that fear right quick if your life or Keeta's life was at stake."

"I won't have to protect us; that's Marquise's job,"

Terelle said with pride. "When Marquise gets home, I'm just gonna sit back and let him handle things."

"I'd like to know how he gonna protect somebody, walking around with a damn bracelet around his ankle?" Saleema burst out laughing and Terelle, despite herself, laughed, too. "How far can he go with that thing keepin' check on his movements? If a nigga dragged you outta the front door, what Marquise gonna do? Huh?"

Terelle shrugged, looking amused. "I guess he gonna have to chase a nigga down."

"Won't that black box start squealing if he tries to leave this apartment?"

"Girl, I don't know. I think a red light will come on if he goes out of range. But under special circumstances, like him having to defend me, I'm sure he won't get in any trouble."

"Please! Who you think is gonna believe he left the apartment to defend your honor? They'll lock that ass up so quick..." Saleema paused in thought and didn't finish the sentence. "Then, they'll turn around and make him serve the rest of his back time."

"Damn, Saleema." Terelle was no longer feeling amused. "How we go from my fear of guns to you disrespecting Marquise for the second time since you been here?"

"My bad," Saleema said with a snicker. "Seriously. I'm sorry." Saleema kissed Terelle's cheek.

"I gotta go. Dave keeps a thick wad in his pocket." She gestured the thickness by stretching her thumb and index finger. "Cash, credit cards...the whole nine. And I don't want him to even think about peeling off one dollar before I get there." Saleema pulled out her car keys and a narrow bank envelope. "Here, here's a little something to put on that phone bill."

"Saleema, you don't have to..."

"Hush, girl. Just like you said...we go back to elementary school and I know your proud ass like I know the back of my hand. You'd go hungry before you'd ask anybody to help you."

Instead of responding, Terelle looked down at the kitchen tiles.

"By the way, when did they say Marquise can come home?"

"Any day. That's all they've been telling me. They're waiting for a monitor to free up. Those damn people got my life on hold—for real."

"Don't worry. Quise will be home raising hell before you know it. Give me a call tomorrow, okay?"

Nodding, Terelle opened the door for her friend. "Thanks, Saleema," Terelle's voice cracked. "I mean it. Thanks." Her body sagged, giving her a world-weary appearance.

Saleema kissed at the air. "Smooches. I'll talk to you tomorrow."

"Okay," Terelle said in a whisper and closed the door.

She treaded to the living room, placed the unopened envelope on the coffee table and flopped down on the futon.

She tried to choke back the tears, but couldn't. Saleema was so good to her, but she was so tired of being a charity case. She ached for Marquise—for his support—his strong shoulders to lean on. Tears spilled over as she curled up on the futon to wait for Marquise's call.

Chapter Eight

Her cell phone rang during her workout at the gym. Drenched in perspiration, she dismounted the stair climber, threw a towel around her neck and went to a quiet corner near the entrance where reception would be better.

"Have you lost your mind completely?" Kenneth boomed.

"Is something wrong, Kenneth?" Kai asked innocently, as she rubbed the towel over her damp hair.

"I should have never gotten involved with you. You're beyond unstable but so beautifully packaged, who would have guessed you're psychotic?"

"Would you mind telling me what you're talking about?"

"Don't feign innocence, Kai. It's beneath you and extremely insulting to me. That little stunt of yours didn't work. My wife never opened that damn package. I did!"

Kai felt instantly deflated.

"And you can rest assured that I won't give you

another opportunity to wreak havoc upon my home life. We're finished, Kai. Do you hear me? Finished!"

"Kenneth, I don't know what..."

"Stop it, Kai. Please. You're a dangerous, deranged young woman," he said slowly. "You're in desperate need of professional help and I swear I'll press charges if you ever harass..."

"You'll press charges, will you?" she exclaimed in a voice so loud it surprised her. "Did it ever occur to you that I could file sexual harassment charges against you, Dr. Harding?" Her voice was now a soft whisper. "The last time I checked, you're the one in a position of authority at the nursing home; I'm just a lowly social worker, so tell me who would be judged as being in the best position to harass whom?"

"If you feel you were harassed, then by all means, sue me. Your claims won't stand up in a court of law. We started our personal relationship long before you began employment at the nursing home. So be my guest; initiate litigation and see how quickly your case is dismissed."

Kai grinned at the telephone. "You can use that reverse psychology on one of the little nursing dimwits who think so highly of you. I'm definitely going to file charges and Kenneth, darling—I'm definitely going to win. And throughout the procedure, I'm going to have a grand old time exposing your sexual deviancy in front of your wife and colleagues," Kai taunted.

Dr. Harding snorted. "Your threats bore me almost as much as you do."

Kai winced.

"Grow up, Kai; stop this juvenile behavior. It's so unbecoming. And I reiterate—get yourself some help, kiddo."

"*Kiddo!*" Kai spat, deeply offended. "Is my behavior as unbecoming as your behavior when I have to put up with your futile efforts in keeping your limp dick from slipping out of my pussy?" Kai's voice grew louder. "You want me to grow up? Why don't you try growing a dick that can stay hard? And I strongly recommend that you get *yourself* some goddamn help for your chronic erectile dysfunction." She was so angry, screaming and sputtering, she was barely coherent. "I should sue you for being such an abominably bad fuck." Then in a calm tone, she added, "See you in court, Doc." She clicked off the cell phone.

But, despite her haughty tone and below-the-belt jabs, Kai was shaken. She'd gone too far this time. Said things she couldn't take back. Kenneth did have erection problems, but not all the time. Why did she stoop to attacking his manhood? She didn't want to lose Kenneth. She loved him—well at least needed him. Acceptance and validation by the wealthy, prominent, blue-eyed, and blond-haired Dr. Harding was very necessary to her self-esteem as well as reinforcing her connection to her Caucasian heritage.

She just wanted to teach him a lesson—show him how much his dishonesty and lack of attention upset her. She'd never dreamed he'd actually end the relationship.

Why would he be interested in keeping that wilting and matronly wife of his when he could have her? She'd seen his wife; the woman's beauty and figure (if she'd ever possessed such attributes) had obviously dissipated years ago. The old girl had seen better days and was now falling apart. And neither makeup nor a trillion visits to the hair salon was going to change her frumpy image. It was absolutely ludicrous for Kenneth to even want to remain attached to his dowdy wife.

Despite the discouraging developments, she knew one thing with certainty: she wouldn't think of allowing Kenneth to dump her over a silly little photograph or a few thoughtless words. She'd invested entirely too much time to just roll over and bow out gracefully for the sake of his stupid marriage. No, she was not giving up Dr. Kenneth Harding.

She'd think of some clever maneuver that would immediately rectify this disastrous situation.

Her mind drifted back to that night—a night of unusually good sex with Dr. Kenneth Harding. Kenneth's typical post-sexual behavior was to hold and cuddle with Kai for a few obligatory moments and then dash to the shower, dress and leave. But that night, he'd fallen asleep. As he slept, she had photographed herself nude beneath his lab coat.

She had intended to surprise him with the photo—

a sexy keepsake for his eyes only. But, he'd slept so deeply, Kai couldn't resist the opportunity of snooping in his archaic daily planner and then jotting down pertinent information. For the life of her, she didn't know why he hadn't upgraded to a Palm Pilot. If she'd had a copy machine handy, she'd have photocopied his itinerary for the entire year. Funny, there was no mention of his Caribbean vacation—that week had been left blank. Didn't matter. That was the past. She knew exactly where he'd be tonight.

✿✿✿

Bursting with excitement at the thought of getting the elusive Dr. Kenneth Harding back in her bed where he belonged, Kai cruised into the Old City section of Philadelphia and pulled into a parking lot on the corner of Third and Market Streets. Before exiting her Benz, she sat with her thighs squeezed together as she waited for the internal sexual throbbing to subside.

Two Haitian parking attendants smiled widely. "My eyes are having a feast," said one of the men in a voice loud enough for Kai to hear.

Kai interpreted his words, intended to compliment, as disrespectful. The whites of the man's eyes were discolored, rather yellowish, and she was offended that eyes such as his were feasting upon her. Her tight lips spread into a disgusted smirk as she tossed her car keys to him.

"A beautiful woman steps out of such a fine-looking automobile," the man continued, unaware that he had repelled her. "I must be in heaven." Both men chuckled good-naturedly, expecting a smile or some type of acknowledgment from Kai. She wanted to slap the insipid smiles off their primitive faces.

Remembering she had no time for justifiable violence, Kai haughtily flipped her hair from the back of her coat, and strode past the disappointed attendants. The slender heels of her black calfskin shoe boots clicked purposefully across the asphalt parking lot.

"Dinner?" the hostess of the upscale restaurant asked.

"No, I'd like to sit at the bar." Kai walked across the room and perched atop a barstool. Music played softly in the background. She ordered an Apple Martini and impatiently watched the door.

Working Dinner at 8—Cuba Libre Restaurant, Old City was what she had copied from his daily planner. She wondered with whom he had planned to dine? Some pharmaceutical salesperson? His accountant? It didn't matter; Kai was prepared to display her anguish publicly. She'd shed buckets of tears, fall into his arms, cling to him and beg his forgiveness—she'd do whatever was necessary to get Kenneth to forego his dinner plans and leave the restaurant with her. They could pick up something to eat on the way back to her apartment.

And once she had him inside her boudoir, she would dig deeply into her ample bag of sex tricks so that Kenneth would be left with no choice but to forgive and forget. This was an excellent plan, Kai decided, with the element of surprise on her side. It was a brilliant plan, in fact—though it hadn't been her first choice. She would have preferred having an opportunity to appease his anger over the phone, but he hadn't returned any of her calls. Pity. Kenneth detested public scenes and would go to any lengths to avoid drawing adverse attention.

Well, he was about to get a doozie of a scene. As soon as her theatrics commenced, he'd whisk her out of there and then she'd have him in her clutches—in private. Then he'd be nothing more than putty in her hands.

Kai had just turned the glass of the second Apple Martini up to her lips when she heard Kenneth's baritone voice: "Dinner for two." She whirled around so quickly, the green-colored drink splattered down the front of her white chiffon blouse.

"Oh, Kenneth!" Kai shrieked. She leapt from the barstool, knocking her coat onto the floor. As she bent awkwardly to retrieve it, she twisted her ankle, slid into a semi-split and broke the heel of her left boot.

Gazing up helplessly at the handsome, distinguished, blond-haired and blue-eyed Dr. Harding, whose normally pale skin now glowed with a recent healthy tan, she realized that his dining companion was a black woman—a regal statuesque woman with her natural hair in twists. She had flawless dark skin that resembled black satin. Adorned with ethnic attire and jewelry, the woman who was older than Kai, but much younger than Dr. Harding's wife, held his arm possessively.

Kai wondered if her involvement with Kenneth had uncovered some hidden yearning for women of a darker persuasion? Was that how he had perceived her—not as an equal, but as an exotic mulatto—someone to dally with behind closed doors?

Though distracted by the presence of this majestic and mysterious woman who obviously knew Kenneth intimately, Kai refused to change her game plan.

Unceremoniously, Kai picked herself up and dragging the broken heel, advanced with outstretched arms, limping and whimpering his name. A far cry from the dignified young lady who'd entered the restaurant, Kai was now rumpled and unkempt. The hostess looked at her in horror. Dr. Harding's date shrank back in fear and bewilderment, while Dr. Harding appeared frantic as if prepared to bolt for the door.

"I'm so sorry, Kenneth," she sobbed, clutching the lapel of his coat and then resting her head on his chest. Dr. Harding stiffened, shot his date an uneasy smile, and cleared his throat. "Kai, this is not the time or place," he said, removing Kai's resistant hands.

"It's never the right time! You go off on vacation with your wife and now you're back in Philly and you don't even have the decency to return my calls?" Kai reached for him again, expecting to be comforted.

Dr. Harding backed away from her grasping tentacles. "You're creating a scene. Please leave; we can discuss this tomorrow."

"Tomorrow!" Kai screamed.

The buzzing conversations of patrons seated at the nearby bar ceased.

"Perhaps I should leave, Kenneth," his companion suggested. "Can you call me a cab?" she asked the hostess.

"No. We'll leave together." He took his frazzled date's arm and turned her toward the door. Looking back, he apologized to the hostess.

Hot on their heels, Kai exited the restaurant also. "What's the matter, Kenneth? Am I too fair-skinned for you now?" She heckled. Despite the broken heel, she hobbled closely behind the couple determined to keep pace.

"Huh? What's the problem, Dr. Harding? Does she suck your dick better than I do?"

Dr. Harding waved his hand, anxiously beckoning the parking lot attendant to hurry and get his car.

"Let me tell you something, Ms. Nubia," Kai continued, "you're going to have to suck that little pencil for damn near an hour before it comes to life."

The woman gasped, but Kai was relentless. "And after all that sucking, I can guarantee you the little bugger is going to deflate the second it touches your nappy pussy."

Dr. Harding race-walked his appalled companion toward his Jaguar and away from Kai's scorching words.

"Are you prepared for the worst sex of your life?" Kai screamed as she stumbled up to the Jag and banged on the passenger-side window.

Dr. Harding started the ignition; Kai did a hasty shuffle to his side of the car and pulled frantically on the door. It was locked.

The Haitian attendant, who only an half-hour earlier had been snubbed by Kai, pulled her away, using the soothing tone one would use if trying to calm a dangerously insane person. "Miss, please, let go of the door. You're going to hurt yourself." He managed to pry her fingers from the door handle as Dr. Harding screeched away.

"Take your grimy hands off me." Kai yanked away from the attendant, turning her fury on him. "Where's my fucking car? Go get it...and it better not have one scratch on it. Do you hear me? Not one scratch, goddamit."

"Yes, Miss. I'll get your car, but do you think you're able to drive safely?"

"Fuck off; who asked for your concern! Just get my car and mind your damn business."

Kai bent down and ripped the broken heel off her boot. She flung it across the lot, aiming at the head of the retreating attendant.

Chapter Nine

No frantic last-minute arrangements had to be made with her employer, for a stroke of luck had sent Marquise, accompanied by two county marshals, to Terelle's front door on her day off.

She screamed in delight when Marquise stepped inside the apartment. He nodded his head in approval at the sight of her, his full lips spreading into a smile, beautiful white teeth gleaming. Long braids, much longer than when he'd left, hung beneath a black scull cap. He had on a new pair of Timberlands, but he was wearing the same sweat pants and hoodie he'd worn on the day he'd gotten locked up—two years ago. She forced the thought of that awful day from her mind and flashed her gorgeous man a big welcoming smile.

"Pull up your pant leg, man." The taller marshal barked the order. Judging by his expression, he was pleased to break up the exchange of loving smiles. He then slapped on the ankle bracelet that would track Marquise's movements. The shorter of the two men hooked up the black monitor to the phone in the kitchen.

"Did you remove all the features from your phone, ma'am?" the shorter man inquired authoritatively.

Terelle nodded.

"No answering machine, no call-waiting..."

"No, nothing."

"Are you on the Internet, ma'am? If so, you're going to have to disconnect it."

"No, I don't have a computer."

"Okay, well...the red light will flash if you're out of range," the marshal said to Marquise. "And you're out of range if you step outside this apartment. You can't even stick your foot out the door."

"I gotchu, man. I gotchu." Marquise was getting annoyed. Terelle stood next to him rubbing his arm soothingly. "But what about when I have to go see my P.O.?"

"That visit will be documented; however, the red light will be on until you return to this apartment. If you haven't returned in the allotted time frame, a warrant for your arrest will be issued."

Those words made Terelle shudder. Marquise placed his arm around her protectively. She covered the hand that was draped over her shoulder with kisses. The two marshals cast disapproving glances at Terelle's show of affection.

Marquise groped beneath her top. Both marshals sighed loudly before slamming out the door. Marquise and Terelle erupted in laughter.

"Baby girl, baby girl! Look at you," Marquise said,

turning Terelle in a complete circle, checking her out from top to bottom. She had on a velour low-waisted sweat suit that hugged her buttocks. He couldn't keep his hands off that area. Kissing her passionately, he walked her backwards to the futon. They collapsed upon it.

"Wait a minute, Marquise." Terelle gently nudged him.

"What's wrong, baby?"

"I've been dreaming of this day for two years. We gotta do this right. This futon is too small; let's get in the bed." She guided him to the small bedroom and began to unzip her velour jacket.

Marquise sat on the creaking bed and started pulling off his boots. When he looked up, Terelle had removed her clothing and stood naked before him. Her big dark chocolate breasts were pointed in his face. He feasted upon them, moaning her name. Panting, she pulled away and began tugging at the waistband of his sweat pants.

They stayed in the bedroom for three hours straight. The bedroom and the entire apartment reeked of sex. Luckily, Markeeta, away at day care for most of the day, was spared from inhaling the scent of their passion. Terelle couldn't remember ever being as happy as she was on this day.

Her dream had come true: Marquise was home at last. Markeeta had her daddy. She had her man.

He'd grown up in prison—matured. The things he used to do, he was no longer interested in doing. He promised: no more running the streets; no jump-off chicks on the side; no more hustling; no more hugging the block all day and until the wee hours of the morning. The drug game couldn't be won. He realized that now. He was going to work a straight job. Be a family man.

✿✿✿

After two weeks Marquise and Terelle were still behaving like honeymooners. Terelle had expected the physical need she and Marquise had for each other to diminish after a few days of practically nonstop lovemaking. But their desire had grown stronger.

Marquise got up with her every morning to help get Markeeta ready for day care. Having his assistance in the morning was a godsend.

He fixed breakfast, packed Terelle's lunch, and even ironed Terelle's work uniform when necessary. And between these chores, he hugged and kissed Terelle, telling her over and over how much he loved her, all the while begging to make love one more time. Having to tear herself away from him to go to work seemed so unfair. And today was particularly hard; they had overslept and missed their morning quickie. The ache of telling him goodbye was powerful—

almost physical. Markeeta, on the other hand, was none too pleased with the new family member. She was accustomed to having her mother all to herself and showed her displeasure by refusing to accept her father's affection. She wouldn't let Marquise kiss her or even pick her up without screaming and reaching for her mother. Marquise was visibly hurt by his daughter's rejection.

"It's your mustache and beard." Terelle smoothed his beard with her fingers. "I think it scares her; she's not used to you yet."

"She didn't act this way when y'all usta visit me at the joint. Now she sees me every day, but she acts like I'm a stranger."

"Give it some time, Marquise. She'll come around." Terelle stroked Marquise's beard. He bear-hugged her, lifting her off the floor as he nuzzled her neck, tickling her. "Put me down." Terelle giggled. "You wrinkling up my uniform."

Feeling left out, Markeeta reached for Marquise. Holding Terelle with one hand, Marquise scooped up Markeeta with his other. He kissed Terelle on the lips and then turned to his daughter. To her parents' amazement, Markeeta offered puckered lips. Marquise gently lowered Terelle to the floor. The six-foot-five man danced around the living room while holding his tiny daughter in his arms, singing "My Girl" off-key.

From her seat on the futon, Terelle observed the

bonding between the two people she loved most in the world. Tears stung her eyes. She leaned forward with her hands pressed against her chest, an unconscious attempt to keep her heart from bursting with joy.

Chapter Ten

There was nothing like a good workout to relieve the frustration of pent-up sexual tension. Sitting on the edge of the bed, Kai laced her Nikes, keenly aware of a palpable hunger between her legs. She closed her legs tightly hoping the pressure would take the edge off the constant throbbing. It didn't.

She missed Kenneth terribly. Certainly, she had experienced feelings of disappointment when he was occasionally unable to maintain an erection, but he always compensated with oral sex. And when it came to oral sex, Kenneth was a master.

Two weeks had passed since their volatile and acutely embarrassing encounter. And two weeks was too long to go without sexual release. How could he do this to her? Kai had left numerous messages pleading for forgiveness, but he still hadn't called.

He ignored her at work—walked brusquely by her as if she didn't exist. It was humiliating.

She finger-combed her hair, applied lip-gloss, grabbed her Louis Vuitton duffel and was quickly out the door.

Instead of using her membership at the posh gym in her apartment building, or the upscale facility she sometimes frequented, which was also located in Center City, Kai decided to work out at Urban Exercise in West Philly. She'd never been there but was braced for a dismal environment.

Her therapist had suggested that she bond with women of color, and now was as good a time as any to get in touch with her roots. But forming a kinship with her sisters wasn't the only reason for Kai's visit to Urban Exercise.

She had a decidedly ulterior motive for her sojourn to the ghetto. Through some detective work on her part, she learned that Khalila Wallace—Ms. Nubia herself—was the executive director of the establishment. Kai intended to get a closer look at that woman. Perhaps she'd have a word with her nemesis, get a feel of her personality and search for the chinks in her armor that would enable Kai to devise a new and improved plan.

There was no parking provided at Urban Exercise. That figured. Kai cruised up to a meter, but decided against on-street parking. She pulled her Benz into the nearby McDonald's parking lot, defiantly ignoring signs that declared it available for patrons of the fast-food restaurant only. Violators would be towed and charged $75 to reclaim their vehicle. Kai sneered at the warning as she boldly pulled into the middle of two parking spaces, making certain there'd be no scratches on her shiny car when she returned.

The black instructor of the 6 p.m. body sculpting class was overweight and sloppily attired in a faded and shapeless sweat suit. Scruffy sneakers and dingy socks completed the instructor's disheveled appearance.

Kai was disgusted. Was this a joke? She was accustomed to the stylish appearance and taut bodies of the annoyingly perky white women who instructed her Center City fitness classes. Well...there was *one* black instructor whom Kai respected—Stacey Long, a light-skinned, rather cute, freckle-faced kick-boxing instructor. Stacey was well-trained and definitely had it together.

Kai scrutinized the dumpy Urban Exercise instructor. Perhaps there was some muscle hidden beneath the woman's thick, boxy frame, but as far as Kai's eyes could see, no part of the woman's body looked sculpted.

What were the criteria for the position—only butch-looking dykes need apply? She had paid ten dollars for the class and briefly considered getting her money back. She imagined herself storming into Ms. Nubia's office to demand that someone more suitable—someone in shape, replace the misshapen cow leading the body sculpting class?

That reverie provided devilish pleasure, but it wasn't an option. Kai had noticed that the light was out in the lobby office with the cheap nameplate that read:

Executive Director. Ms. Nubia had escaped for the day, but not for long. Kai would return another day—much earlier, and with a more clearly defined plan.

Deciding to make the best of her drive to West Philly, Kai left the body sculpting class in an ostentatious flurry of displeasure and followed the signs pointing to the weight room.

There were no rules that excluded women from this room, but most were intimidated by the sounds of crashing metal, the groans and contorted faces of serious fitness devotees as they lifted tremendously heavy weights. These pumped-up males did not intimidate Kai; she was amused by their exhibition of testosterone in overdrive.

Exuding confidence, she glided to the center of the room, paused to consider the antiquated treadmills, and then moved toward the stair climbers. She pulled her sweatshirt over her head and tossed it on top of her duffel bag.

Bold male eyes watched her. The men were eager to offer assistance with the equipment. Kai didn't need any help. She was quite familiar with this particular manufacturer's equipment, but she'd never encountered a model quite as outdated. She pushed buttons and the machine jerkily engaged.

Kai looked stylish and felt sexy in her workout gear: a pink half-top and snug pink and black flared sweat pants. Many pairs of admiring eyes wandered the length of her body. From head to toe, she was flawless. Well...almost. There was a missing patch of hair—the size of a quarter—above her left ear. Hair she'd pulled out during a highly stressful time. If she left it alone, the hair would grow back in no time. Until then, she carefully arranged her heavy locks, secured with a hairpin to cover the offensive bald spot.

She climbed onto the stair climber, set the timer and began peddling. A few minutes later, a heavyset young woman, with a clip-on curly ponytail, lumbered over. She cast Kai a shy smile before clumsily straddling the seat of the stationary bike next to Kai's stair climber. Kai quickly assessed the woman as urban, unsophisticated, uneducated, and definitely unworthy.

"I was gonna get on the stair climber, but that thing wears me out," the woman said, offering another smile accompanied by a set of deep dimples. The dimples, Kai felt, were a complete waste on that pudgy woman's face. Kai was prepared to ignore her, but remembered she was supposed to make an attempt to form relationships with black women, so...what the hell...she begrudgingly smiled back.

"I was too late to join the body sculpting class, so I'm going to try to ride this thing for ten minutes. Sure hope I don't pass out." The woman gave an annoying giggle at the end of the sentence. Kai stopped stepping and looked around for another stair climber—one that put some distance between her and this chattering numbskull. She was simply unwilling to suffer through foolish dialogue for the sake of appearing to have good manners. The hell with bonding!

"My name's LaVella." The woman, obviously in need of a friend, smiled again.

"Kai," Kai said, stretching her lips into a semblance of a smile. "You need to pedal for at least twelve minutes if you want to burn calories." Kai's tone was deliberately authoritative. For some unknown reason, she was bothered by the woman's laziness.

LaVella looked puzzled. "I didn't know that."

"That's what they say. But everyone's metabolism is different. I have a lot of nervous energy. I'm constantly fidgeting; I burn calories just standing still." Kai gave a gleaming smile.

"I wish I could burn off some of this weight. I get fatter just thinking about food." LaVella laughed heartily.

"You need to restrain yourself and learn to demonstrate some self-control," Kai said sternly, intending to curtail LaVella's irritating laughter. "Plan your meals. Portion-control. You shouldn't just eat whatever is available. And...you can boost your metabolism by merely walking a half-hour a day."

"I can't stick to any kinda exercise program. I try, but something always comes up." LaVella shook her head in defeat.

"Hey, don't look so despondent. You can have a body just like mine if you're willing to do the work.

And, I can help you." Kai wanted to fall out laughing at the light of hope that shone in LaVella's eager eyes. The woman was downright stupid. Pitiable, actually. She had a lot of nerve striking up a conversation with someone like Kai—someone clearly out of her league. Under normal circumstances, Kai wouldn't have given her the time of day. But she had picked up on the woman's vulnerability—probably the result of her weight problem and the stranglehold of an underprivileged existence.

Since she insisted that Kai chat, she should consider herself fair game. Until she figured out what the insufferable fool could do for her, she'd just have to string her along. She'd have to continue to pretend she was an expert in fitness and weight control. She'd also have to pretend to give a damn about LaVella's fat ass.

She'd missed the opportunity to get up close and personal with Ms. Nubia, so why not have some fun with one of her indigent members.

"I'll tell you what...I'm going to make you my special project."

"What kinda project?"

"I'm taking a nutrition class at Temple," Kai said, lying. "I have to write a paper. You can be my case study. My grade-point average will increase and you'll get a new body...free of charge. All you have to do is be willing to work hard and follow the meal plan and exercise program that I develop for you."

LaVella looked impressed. "When can we start?"

"How much do you weigh?" Kai inquired.

"Um…about one-ninety."

Kai sensed she was lying. The disgustingly fat pig had to be at least two hundred and twenty-five pounds. "How tall are you?"

"Five-six."

"Well, I'm five-seven and I only weigh one-eighteen."

"I wouldn't look right being that skinny." There was a defensive note in LaVella's tone.

"Do you think you look good at your current weight?" Kai looked LaVella firmly in the eye.

LaVella shook her head.

"Then, let's do something about it!"

Kai stepped off the stair climber and pulled a pad and Montblanc pen from her duffel bag. She jotted down her home number and handed it to LaVella. "Here you go. Call me tomorrow."

LaVella gazed at Kai's telephone number with the expression of someone just being handed a winning lottery ticket.

"Wait a second; I have an idea," Kai said. LaVella cocked her head curiously.

"Let's go out and celebrate. My treat."

"Really?"

"Sure. I want you to gorge yourself on the foods you enjoy the most because tomorrow you're going to start your diet as well as begin some behavior modification."

Puzzled, LaVella raised a brow.

"We're going to discover the triggers for your eating binges. But in the meantime, let's just go out and have some fun. What do you like? Chinese? Italian?"

"Oh, I'm not picky. I like everything!" LaVella grinned.

"Fine, then let's get some take-out," Kai said, noticing that LaVella's mouth turned down a notch at the mention of take-out. Fatso must have expected to be taken to an expensive restaurant. On second thought, she probably would have loved to feed all night at one of those all-you-can-eat buffet-style eateries. Their steaming trays reminded Kai of troughs—the kind farmers use in pigsties. Yuck!

But Kai didn't have time for that; she had an urgent need. And, until Kenneth came to his senses, LaVella would do just fine.

"You can eat at my place. We'll have a celebratory drink and map out a plan for you." Kai tugged LaVella's arm impatiently. "Come on. My car's parked in the McDonald's lot and I don't want to get towed."

In the parking lot, she practically shoved LaVella into the passenger seat.

"Do you live nearby?" LaVella asked meekly. "I don't know if the bus runs…"

"I live in Center City. But don't worry about the bus, dear. I'll drive you home after you eat. Where do you live?"

"Green Street. Near 40th and Lancaster."

Kai nodded, but couldn't begin to imagine where 40th and Lancaster was located. It could have been on the moon for all she knew or cared. She had no intention of coming back to this part of the city. She'd send this moron home in a cab—if her performance deserved such generosity. "Shame we didn't get a chance to shower after that workout."

Confused by the change in conversation, LaVella sniffed at her armpits. "I'm cool. Girl, stop trippin'. Don't be worryin' 'bout no shower just to please me."

"Okay!" Kai said without hesitation. She displayed a sparkling smile as she started the car. She turned away from LaVella as she reminisced about her former college roommate, Cindy, a hick from Idaho who used to get off by sniffing Kai's crotch after Kai's step aerobics class. Getting sniffed would get Kai worked up and horny—but it was just foreplay—she refused to let Cindy touch her with her tongue. She preferred the feeling of a hard dick and would push Cindy away, shower and get ready for her date with her most recent boyfriend. Cindy's sad expression brightened when Kai promised to let her taste her juices when she returned from her date. On the rare occasions that Kai came back from a date sexually unfulfilled, she'd stomp over to Cindy's bed and kick the metal rail, jolting Cindy awake. Then, she'd plant her shoe on Cindy's pillow, grab Cindy's hair and impatiently guide the half-asleep idiot's slobbering mouth to her point of pleasure. After climaxing, Kai had little tolerance for the now wide-awake, greedy girl who always continued licking and slurping as if she intended to suck Kai dry. Aggravated, Kai would take the heel of her shoe and send Cindy sprawling to the other side of the bed. She laughed at the recollection.

"What's funny?" LaVella asked with an innocent smile.

"Nothing. Just admiring your cute dimples—you're absolutely adorable." Kai failed to mention her attraction to LaVella's large lips. Oh well, all things in time. She'd share that with her new ghetto girlfriend when the time was right. Moist with perverse excitement, Kai revved the engine, reversed out of the lot and sped down 52nd Street.

Chapter Eleven

"All finished." Terelle kissed the top of Marquise's freshly braided head.

Sitting comfortably between her legs on the floor, Marquise watched *Monday Night Football.* "Thanks, babe," he muttered softly without budging.

Terelle shifted her position.

"Don't move. Stay where you are," Marquise whined. He wrapped both arms around her legs, making himself a willing captive cushioned inside her soft thighs.

"Let me up, Quise. I gotta get Keeta's clothes off and put her to bed," she said, glancing at their daughter who was stretched out beside her on the futon, fully clothed and sound asleep.

"Aw," Marquise groaned as he reluctantly released his grip on her legs.

Terelle surveyed the neat rows of her handiwork before rising. Her work looked good but she wished she were talented enough to create intricate designs similar to the styles Allen Iverson wore. Since Marquise worshiped AI., Terelle thought she might take a couple classes at the African hair salon on Woodland Avenue.

She hated to admit it, but life with Marquise restricted to the apartment was so sweet she almost dreaded his being released from house arrest. Knowing his whereabouts around the clock gave her a sense of peace and well-being she had never known before. In ninety days Marquise would be free of the ankle bracelet that kept him confined to their apartment. What would he do with his newfound freedom, she wondered? Before troublesome thoughts could disrupt her peace, she turned her attention to Markeeta and lifted her from the futon.

"I'll put her to bed," Marquise said as he stood up. He gently took Markeeta from Terelle's arms. "I hate to ask you to go out, but..."

"You need cigarettes?"

"Yeah, my pack's gittin' low."

"I don't mind going out for you; I just wish you'd try to cut down."

"Can't. Not right now. I'm locked up in here all day long—I'd go crazy if I didn't have my smokes. I'll think about quittin' when they cut this shit off my leg."

"You promise?"

"Promise," he said, his expression earnest. "Now, gimme some sugar."

Terelle stood on her toes and offered her lips. The feel of his lips weakened her. Getting herself together to go to the store wasn't going to be easy. Leaving Marquise was never easy.

"Hurry up and git back." He patted Terelle's backside suggestively, a gesture he'd made numerous times, yet Terelle blushed as though touched by Marquise's hand for the very first time.

She grabbed her handbag and coat, and pulled on Marquise's new Eagles scull cap. "I'll be right back," she said to his retreating figure as he carried Markeeta to the bedroom. She didn't think she'd ever stop beaming with pride whenever her eyes beheld her man and their child together—at last.

It took less than ten minutes for Terelle to walk to the corner store, purchase the cigarettes and walk back home. As she neared Kingsessing Avenue, she noticed a cab pulling up to the curb. Inexplicably, the sight of the cab did not bode well. Terelle's bouncy footsteps slowed and then came to a complete stop. To her astonishment, her mother emerged from the cab; her movements were jerky—agitated. For the past few months, her mother had been keeping up with her appearance, but tonight she looked haggard. A faded red bandana was tied around her head, no doubt concealing uncombed hair. Was she back on drugs? Terelle shuddered.

Cassandra Chambers glimpsed Terelle and began yelling, "He tried to kill me! That dirty son of a bitch tried to kill me!" she sobbed dramatically into her hands.

Terelle sprinted to the parked cab. "Who tried to kill you? What happened, Mom?"

"Pay the cab, baby," Cassandra cried. "I left my money and all my stuff at the place."

"Who tried to kill you?" Terelle shrieked, her face etched with worry. She pulled her mother's slim hands from her face and emitted a small scream when she realized her mother's right eye was blackened. "Oh my God! Who did this to you?"

"Give the damn driver eight dollars and stop tryin' to put my business all over the streets," she yelled irrationally. "We'll talk about it inside," Cassandra said in high-pitched annoyance.

Terelle hastily produced a ten-dollar bill and handed it to driver. She couldn't imagine who had harmed her mother. She wondered if she'd gotten into a fight with one of the hard-core women she lived with in the group home. Her brows furrowed in concern as she glanced at her mother. Her mother was so thin; it would be easy for any of those burly women to get the best of her.

"Do you want me to call the police?" Terelle asked, determined to sound calmer than she felt.

"Hell no!" Cassandra shouted as they climbed the stairs to the third-floor apartment.

They stood outside the door while Terelle fumbled inside her handbag looking for her keys. "Okay, Mom. Just tell me who did this to you before we go inside."

She was completely bewildered and dreaded Marquise's reaction to her mother's unexpected visit.

"Harry did it."

"Harry? Who's Harry?"

"The guy I've been stayin' with."

"But…you're stayin' at the group home—aren't you?"

"I left. I told you I had to get out of that place. You wouldn't let me stay here with you…I had to do somethin'."

"But Mom…"

"Don't start up with me, Terelle. I did what I had to do. At least I had enough sense to leave. I ain't gonna stick around and let no nigga kick my ass every day."

"He hit you before?"

"No. But once a man gets a taste for putting his hands on you, you can bet he's gonna do it again. And trust me…I ain't the one. I'll kill that muthafucker before I…"

"Calm down, Mom. Come on in so me and Marquise can figure out what we should do."

Marquise opened the door before Terelle was able to turn the key.

"Look what the cat dragged in," Marquise said with a smirk.

"I could say the same thing about you." Cassandra pushed her way inside; her hand covered her injured eye.

Terelle tossed Marquise the pack of cigarettes. She chastised him with a scowl before turning her attention back to her mother. "Let me put some ice on that for you." She pulled an ice tray from the freezer and began wrapping cubes inside a dishtowel. "This should keep it from swelling up too much." She pulled her mother's hand away from her eye.

"Dayum!" Marquise exclaimed as he gawked at Cassandra's eye. "Okay, Frazier," he said, laughing. "Now, you know you gotta get your weight up before you try to mess wit Laila Ali!" He lit a cigarette. "Whatchu weigh now, Miss Cassy? 'Bout a buck ten?" He drew on the cigarette, exhaled, and then chuckled maliciously.

"Quise! This ain't funny." Terelle hadn't expected Marquise to greet her mother with open arms, but she was surprised by his lack of sympathy and his blatant disrespect. "A woman didn't give her this black eye."

"Naw? Who did it, then?"

"Harry," Cassandra said tonelessly.

"Who the hell's Harry?" Marquise inquired. There was a mixture of confusion and annoyance in his voice.

"She left the group home. Harry's some nut she's been staying with," Terelle explained as she applied the ice pack to her mother's eye. "She doesn't want me to call the police, but something sure needs to be done. Can you get some of your friends to go whip Harry's ass?" Terelle nudged her mother before Marquise could respond. "What's Harry's address, Mom?"

"Yo, Babe! Don't be putting me in the middle of this shit. We don't know the whole story..."

Terelle angrily slammed the ice tray on the kitchen table. The remaining ice cubes popped out and slid to the floor. "I know that punk-ass ain't have no business putting his hands in my mother's face." Terelle's lower lip twitched as she screamed the words at Marquise. "If you don't do something about it, then I'll get somebody else to go see about that nigga."

Cassandra's eyes gleamed as they moved from Terelle to Marquise, excitedly waiting for the drama to unfold.

"Babe, calm down." Marquise quickly stamped out the cigarette; he wrapped both arms around Terelle. "Let's find out exactly what happened before we git all caught up in this."

"We're talking about my mother...*I'm already caught up in it!*" Terelle tried to wriggle out of Marquise's tight embrace.

"Okay, babe," he cajoled. "If you're involved, then I'm involved. We're in this shit together, aiight?" He pulled out a kitchen chair, sat down, and lowered Terelle onto his lap and turned to Terelle's mother. "Whassup, Miss Cassy? What happened?" His voice took on a gentle, concerned tone.

"Now that's a stupid-ass question; you can see what happened." Cassandra spat out the words, twisted around in her chair, and looked around the kitchen in disgusted disbelief as if she had an audience of equally appalled spectators.

Moving Terelle quickly off his lap, Marquise stood

up abruptly. The chair toppled over making a loud crashing sound when it hit the floor. "Don't call me stupid." He pointed his finger at Cassandra.

"You better get your damn finger outta my face," Cassandra warned, looking at Terelle for support.

"Whatchu gonna do? Call Harry? I'll whip you and your man's ass."

"Quise!" Terelle's voice cautioned Marquise to get a grip on his emotions. She tugged at his arm as he advanced toward Cassandra.

"Let him go, Terelle. Let him hit me so I can call the cops. They'll haul his black ass back to Graterford prison so fast..."

Terelle gasped. She looked at her mother with horror. After being without Marquise for two years, the very thought of him being locked up again caused her heart to crash against her chest. "Mom, after all I've been through, how can you even talk about getting Marquise locked up again?"

"Well, that's just what's gonna happen if he gets in my face one more time."

Seething and frustrated, Marquise kicked the toppled chair. The loud thump awakened Markeeta; she screamed for her Mommy. "Ain't this some shit! You didn't wanna call the cops on that muthafucker who punched you in your fuckin' face, but you wanna call the cops on me?" Marquise bellowed.

"Mommy," Markeeta yelled again.

"I'll git the baby, Terelle; you deal with your crazy

mother." Marquise glowered at Cassandra, spun around and stomped toward the bedroom.

Breathing heavily, Cassandra slammed the ice pack on the table and stood up abruptly. "Who you calling crazy?" Her chest rose and fell as she waved her hand wildly in the air.

Marquise halted, and then turned to face Cassandra. As he approached her, Terelle watched him struggle for composure. She was prepared to jump between Marquise and her mother if necessary.

"I didn't stutter," he said, finally in a voice that was chilling. "I'm calling *you* crazy," he added. "Why'd you bring your ass over here in the first place? You know I ain't got no pity for you. Me and Terelle both seen you in worse shape than this. That black eye ain't nothin' compared to the shit you been into..."

Cassandra gave Marquise a long dirty look but was silent. He whirled back around; furious steps carried him into the bedroom to attend to his daughter.

Terelle picked up the chair, and repositioned it beneath the kitchen table. She looked around in bewilderment. How had a perfectly tranquil evening turned so quickly into an absolute nightmare? Though she loved her mother dearly, she would not permit her to destroy the peace she'd worked so hard for and had endured so much to attain.

Terelle sighed. "Marquise is right, Mom."

"About what?" Still breathing heavily, Cassandra sat back down and reapplied the ice pack.

"You didn't want me to call the cops on that Harry person...and he punched you in the face...gave you a black eye." Terelle shook her head, trying to rid herself of the image of her mother being beaten. "But you were ready to send Marquise back to jail." Terelle paused. "And Quise didn't even touch you, Mom. I can't believe you'd make that kind of threat. Why would you want to destroy my family?"

"Oh, stop being such a damn drama queen. Did I call the cops? No, I did not," Cassandra said, responding to her own question.

"Mom, you know I'm trying to have a peaceful life... and um..." Terelle shook her head. "It just seems to me like you don't want that for me."

"That's bullshit!" Cassandra yanked the ice pack from her eye in protest.

"Is it? Then why did you come over here with your problems when you know you and Quise don't get along?"

"What was I 'posed to do? Stick around and let Harry whip my ass all night long?"

"First of all, you're supposed to be in an addiction program. You're supposed to be living in the group home—getting treatment. But here you come, barging over here—out of the blue—expecting me to put a roof over your head because you decided to move in with that nut instead of finishing up with your treatment. That's real selfish, Mom."

"Selfish? Oh, now, I'm selfish?" Cassandra sputtered. "Fuck that group home. They wasn't doing nothin' for me. All they wanna do is make you live by a bunch of stupid rules. I'm a grown-ass woman; I make my own rules. I only asked you for a little help. Now, tell me… how in the hell is it selfish for a mother to turn to her daughter for some help?"

"What did you ever do for me? Huh? Have I ever been able to turn to you for help?" Terelle yelled.

"Don't you raise your voice at me. You may be over twenty-one, but I'm still your mother."

Marquise returned carrying Markeeta. "Terelle! This shit is whack. Your mom is trippin'. She got you all upset; she got the baby all worked up…Would you please show her the door so we can git some peace and quiet around here?"

Cassandra glared at Marquise. "Nigga, I ain't even worried about you. How you gonna make my daughter put me out? You payin' rent now?"

"I'm about two seconds from throwing your little scrawny ass outta here," Marquise warned. "Terelle, you better do somethin' wit your mom before she gits her ass hurt."

Feeling panicked, Terelle looked at Marquise pleadingly. She couldn't throw her own mother out into the street. But she knew the situation between her mother and Marquise would only escalate if one of them didn't leave the apartment.

"Mom, you think you can stay over at Gran's if I call you a cab?" she asked weakly.

"Oh! So, you just gonna send me out into the night. Treat me like I'm some stranger off the street."

"Mom, please!" Terelle shouted. Then, as if surprised by her outburst, she lowered her head, and rubbed her temples. "Marquise is on house arrest. You know he can't leave. Now, calm down. I'm gonna call Gran and tell her you're coming, okay?"

"I can't believe my own flesh and blood would put this worthless...," Cassandra started.

"Worthless!" Marquise shoved Markeeta into Terelle's arms, and then edged closer to Cassandra. "Let me tell you 'bout worthless..." His mouth twisted furiously. "I can't even count how many times I had to front your worthless ass when I was hustlin'. You just ran wit that shit, Miss Cassy. You was always up in my face beggin'. I couldn't turn you down 'cause you're my girl's mom. And every time my money came up short, it was because of your beggin' ass. "

"You didn't front me shit," Cassandra began, "so, let's not get it twisted. I have a problem, but I damn sure don't have amnesia." Nodding her head, Cassandra's mouth curved into an ugly smile. "Since you wanna run your mouth, why don't you tell Terelle the *real* story?"

With growing alarm, Terelle whispered, "What? What's she talking about, Quise?"

"Man, she talkin' shit." Marquise shot Cassandra a murderous look.

"Am I? The way I remember it, we came out even. You gave me drugs; I sucked your dick!"

"Oh my God!" Terelle screamed, and then covered her mouth in shock.

"You lyin', stank-ass bitch!" Marquise grabbed Cassandra's arm and roughly pulled her toward the door. "You're outta here," he said, as he turned the doorknob.

"Get your hands offa me." Refusing to be put out, Cassandra gripped the doorframe. "Terelle, help! Tell this muthafucker to let me go," she shouted.

Terelle didn't respond. She couldn't. She paced and whimpered as she rocked Markeeta in her arms. She felt disabled: blind, deaf...mute. Tears blurred her vision; she could barely see the two figures tussling near the now open doorway. Her mother's accusation —*I sucked your dick*—rang loudly in her mind. The sound of those words was so deafening, she was unable to hear the slamming door. She sensed Marquise's presence. Felt him gently touch her shoulder as he turned her around. *Don't touch me*! She wanted to scream, but she could not speak.

"She lyin', babe," he said. "I would never disrespect you or myself like that." His eyes, moist with emotion, attempted to convey sincerity.

She wanted to believe him—needed to believe him because nothing else made sense. But Terelle was tired, beat down.

"I can't deal with this tonight," she said in a choked voice.

"Okay, go get some rest. I'll straighten up the kitchen. Try to get some sleep, okay, babe?"

Teary-eyed and dazed, she nodded, and then stumbled to the bedroom. She put Markeeta in her own small youth bed, stripped out of her clothing and slid into bed.

Sleep did not come easily.

Chapter Twelve

"This is one of my favorite places for outdoor exercising. Isn't it lovely?" Kai asked as she pulled into a parking spot along Kelly Drive that faced the Schylkill River. En route, she'd decided against taking LaVella to her apartment and definitely against feeding her. Kai became nauseous at the thought of LaVella stuffing her face. More importantly, she was certain she didn't want her new "friend" to know where she lived.

"Have you been here before?"

LaVella shook her head and looked around anxiously. "Rode pass…saw all the people riding bikes, jogging and skating, but I never thought about coming here myself. I'd probably feel outta place."

"It's a beautiful place in the spring and summer. I love to watch the boat races. That's the front of Boathouse Row over there," Kai said, pointing. "I'm sure you've seen the back view from the expressway—the rows of tiny houses that are always lit up as if it were Christmastime…"

"Oh yeah." LaVella brightened. "I used to call them Santa's houses when I was a little girl."

Kai groaned inwardly; she couldn't have cared less about LaVella's silly childhood remembrances. However, seeing that LaVella was now a bit more relaxed, Kai cut the motor and spoke in a kind tone. "Do you mind if we sit here for a while and talk? We'll get your food shortly."

"I'm not really that hungry and it's getting late. My mom's watching my kids and…" LaVella's voice trailed off; her worried expression returned.

"Hey, relax. I don't intend to keep you out late, hon." Kai flipped LaVella's ponytail playfully. "I just want to help you. I used to have a weight problem also," she lied.

"For real?" LaVella's eyes widened. "But you're so thin."

"That wasn't always the case. My parents spent a lot of money sending me to camps for fat adolescents."

"Are you rich?"

"My parents are wealthy. I reap the trickle-down effect of their wealth."

LaVella looked appropriately impressed.

"That's why I chose to major in nutrition. My minor is addiction counseling for eating disorders. That's also why I'd like to help you," she went on. "I know you're underprivileged and can't afford the intense therapy that would be required to overcome the grip your food addiction has on you."

"I like to eat, but I'm not addicted; I mean...I can stop myself if I really tried..."

"You're grossly overweight," Kai said crisply.

"Wait a minute, I ain't that bad." LaVella giggled nervously.

"Well, according to the charts I rely upon, a woman of your height and weight is, unfortunately, considered morbidly obese."

"Morbidly obese!" LaVella leaned forward, indignant.

"I'm not saying that I personally believe you to be morbidly obese. I'm just telling you what the charts indicate and how you're viewed by society."

LaVella fell silent and pressed her head against the leather headrest.

"Ease up, girlfriend." Yuck! Kai had never used that colloquial expression, and hoped she'd never have to again. However, she felt speaking in jargon was a necessary tool in forming an intimate relationship. Her therapist would be so proud. Ha! She reached over and caressed the back of LaVella's neck.

"By the time we've finished, you're going to be flaunting your beautiful new body in a two-piece swimsuit." Kai chuckled. When LaVella joined in the lighthearted laughter, Kai cut her off, her tone turned serious. "You have to be honest with me. We're going to be together a great deal during the next three months. We'll be best friends—closer than best friends. We're going to know each other intimately."

Kai stroked LaVella's cheek. LaVella tensed, looked away.

"I'm going to expect you to keep a journal of every morsel that passes your lips. I think I'll start you at fifteen-hundred calories a day and a structured exercise routine, an hour a day, five times a week. But tonight, the sky is the limit!"

"You said something about us knowing each other intimately—what did you mean?"

"You know..." Kai looked off in thought, then turned back to LaVella. "I want to be really close to you during this time of change...metamorphosis. But the wonderful future I envision for you won't come to pass if you're hesitant to share everything with me."

"I wouldn't lie about what I eat 'cause I know the scale is gonna tell the truth." LaVella chuckled nervously and fidgeted in the passenger seat.

"That's true. But in order to effectively treat your disorder, I'll need to know intimate details about you—your thoughts—your behavior." Kai noticed LaVella flinch when she heard the word *disorder*. She had to restrain herself from laughing aloud. She was really good, if she said so herself.

"Listen," Kai continued, "I'm providing you with the same services my parents spent thousands on for me. I think you can honestly say their money was well spent." She gave LaVella a dazzling smile as her hands made a sweeping movement over her body. "Every woman wants to feel beautiful," she informed LaVella. "Can you honestly tell me that you feel beautiful?"

"No." LaVella spoke in a whisper, eyes downcast.

Kai lifted LaVella's chin with her finger. "Look at me, LaVella. Do you think I'm beautiful?" LaVella nodded her head. "Tell me," Kai demanded. She pushed curly tendrils out of her face, allowing LaVella a better look.

"You're real beautiful," LaVella said meekly, then turned her gaze to the shimmering moonlit Schylkill River.

Kai nuzzled LaVella's ear, whispering, "And you too can be as beautiful as I am. You already possess inner beauty..." Kai had to force the smirk from her face. "You have good bone structure...uh, a cute face. You owe it to yourself—to take advantage of this opportunity. Allow me to improve upon your natural gifts. Just put yourself in my hands and trust me. Okay?"

LaVella sat in rigid silence.

"Look," Kai spoke in a gentle tone. "I know that part of your disorder stems from the fact that you trusted in the past and got hurt. Am I right?"

LaVella nodded; tears began to pool. "I know, I know," Kai cooed. "You've been taken advantage of... disappointed...abused. But you've got to start trusting again. Let me help you." Kai's voice was now a whisper. Kai held her breath and bit the inside of her mouth to keep from laughing. "Do you trust me, LaVella?" LaVella nodded and Kai was relieved for her patience was wearing thin. Being deceptive was exhausting. It was time to cut to the chase. She kissed LaVella's cheek; her lips traveled to her neck, then moved back up to her lips. "Kiss me, LaVella," she said breathily.

"But I'm not like *that*," LaVella said in a hoarse voice. "I'm not..."

Kai cut her off. "I'm not like that either. This is something special between us—our secret." Her tongue flicked lightly across LaVella's tightly closed lips. Losing her resolve, LaVella uttered a small whimper, slowly parted her lips and became lost in the kiss.

Kai caressed the side of LaVella's face. With her other hand she stealthily untied the drawstring of her sweatpants and began wriggling out of them. Impatient, she yanked the pink and black fabric down to her thighs, abruptly broke the kiss, and nudged LaVella's head southward.

"No," LaVella uttered in weak protest.

"Taste it," Kai whispered, inching up to meet LaVella's lips.

"No." LaVella tried to turn her head away from the soft musky pubic hair that brushed her face.

"Lick it," Kai commanded, her tone a mixture of passion and hostility as she increased her grip on LaVella's hair and pushed harder.

No...please...no! God help me! LaVella screamed in her mind as she helplessly submitted to Kai's powerful will and tasted the pungent salty juices of this cold-hearted woman who hadn't bothered to bathe after her vigorous workout.

Chapter Thirteen

Piercing the silence, the alarm clock buzzed loudly, and Terelle's eyes popped open. She reached over to the nightstand, hit the snooze button, and then returned to Marquise's cocoon-like embrace. Suddenly remembering her mother's incriminating words, she extricated herself from his arms. When Marquise had gotten into bed last night, Terelle had clung to the edge making sure there was ample space between them. Evidently at some point during the night he had eased up behind her, pulled her close to him and had wrapped both arms and one leg around her.

Irritated, she kicked at his thick imprisoning leg.

"What's the matter, babe?"

"Nothing," she muttered, sounding peeved.

He raised his head and squinted at the clock. "Don't get up yet. You have a few more minutes." He wrapped his leg around her thighs again.

"Quit it, Marquise." She jerked her body away from him, flung off the covers and got out of bed.

"You still mad about last night—about that shit your Mom said?"

"What do you think?"

"I think you should know by now that your Mom don't wanna see us happy. She's a miserable, lying bi..."

"Watch it, Quise," Terelle cautioned, cutting him off.

Marquise reached for Terelle's hand, but she snatched it away before he could grasp it.

"I can't deal with this right now; I gotta get ready for work."

"Call out; we need some time."

"You must be crazy. I'm already on the abuse list at work for calling out, and you of all people know we can't afford for me to lose my job."

Marquise stared at her with wounded eyes, and then quickly glanced away.

Though she had intended for her words to sting, to remind him that she was the breadwinner, she was unprepared for the pained expression that crossed his face.

"I'm sorry, Quise," she said, sighing. "I didn't mean..."

Obviously recovered from the blow, he regarded her with now hardened eyes. "I knew you were gonna throw that shit up in my face sooner or later. It was just a matter of time."

"I said I'm sorry."

"But it's cool, though. I know what I have to do," he said as he lit a cigarette and began rapidly puffing and blowing out smoke. "I knew this shit wasn't gonna work."

"Marquise..." Terelle tried to caress the side of his face, but Marquise pulled away from her touch.

She withdrew her hand and began quietly preparing herself for work. Marquise trudged to the kitchen to start Markeeta's breakfast.

✿✿✿

An uneasy feeling plagued Terelle throughout the workday. She called home every chance she got, but there was no answer. The law forbade Marquise to leave the apartment, so where the hell was he? The possibilities were too scary to ponder, so Terelle concentrated on her work.

At 3:22 Terelle and a throng of coworkers stood by the time clock with their employee ID badges poised and ready to swipe. Melanie from the Laundry Department was the first in line. She looked back at Terelle. "Still honeymooning?"

Terelle confirmed the inquiry with a big smile that did not match her unhappy heart.

"Trouble in paradise? Girl, don't tell me Marquise is acting up already?" Keeping one eye on the clock, Melanie cocked her head and screwed up her lips as if the likelihood of Marquise misbehaving was a personal affront.

At 3:24 Melanie swiped her badge and waited for Terelle. "You need a ride to the subway?"

"Yeah, thanks," Terelle replied.

Terelle knew that nosy Melanie had only offered the ride so she could probe deeper and try to get the latest scoop on her and Marquise. As badly as Terelle wanted to decline the offer, she couldn't. She had to pick up Markeeta and get home as quickly as possible to find out what was going on with Marquise.

The subway stop was only a few minutes away from the nursing home, yet Melanie managed to fire off a million questions in the short time span.

Terelle skillfully maneuvered around every question. Her acceptance of the ride had not been a promise to be forthcoming about her relationship with Marquise.

Successfully keeping her business to herself, Terelle got out at Broad and Girard.

"Thanks, Melanie."

As if she'd been deceived, Melanie sucked her teeth and angrily zoomed off.

By the time Terelle reached her daughter's day care center, she could no longer keep her worry at bay.

Using the center's phone, she called her apartment again. The phone rang and rang. Feeling frantic, she quickly zippered Markeeta into her snowsuit and hurried out to catch the bus.

Running with Markeeta in her arms, Terelle hailed down the 52 bus as the driver attempted to pull off.

Finally home, she hoisted Markeeta on her hip and took the stairs to her apartment two at a time.

"Marquise," she yelled outside the door as she fumbled for her keys.

He opened the door and took a fussing Markeeta

from her arms. "How's Daddy's girl? Where's my sugar?"

Markeeta giggled and kissed him as her father carried her to the living room.

"Why didn't you answer the phone?" Terelle asked as she trailed behind him. "I've been going crazy, worrying all day."

He put Markeeta on the futon and unzipped her snowsuit. "I ain't have no rap for you," he said coolly with his back to Terelle. "I tried to talk this morning, but you gave me your ass to kiss."

"That's not true…I was willing to talk, but you wanted me to take the day off. I couldn't. Besides, I was still confused about everything that happened last night…" Terelle paused. "I mean…my mom really messed my head up when she said…"

Turning around to face her, Marquise didn't allow Terelle to finish the sentence.

"You gotta be crazy to take your lying-ass mom's word over mine? You trippin', but go 'head…think whatchu want."

"Quise," she said, sighing. "Why can't you understand how I felt—how I still feel? My mom accused you of something so shocking, it's a wonder I didn't pass out on the spot."

"What about me? I'm the one she was lyin' on—how the hell do you think I felt? I'll tell you," he said, the veins in his neck bulging. "I felt like puttin' my fist down her lyin' fuckin' throat."

Terelle groaned, then instinctively picked up and patted Markeeta as if to protect her from the foul language that had fallen from her father's lips.

"Miss Cassy was into some wild ass shit when I was on my grind. I ain't say nothin' 'cause I ain't wanna hurt you. But I'll tell you this...she'd do anything for a hit. First of all, she's your mom and I don't get down like that and second...after all the shit I seen and heard about Miss Cassy, ain't no way I would let her put her nasty mouth on my jawn."

Terelle gasped. She had no illusions about her mother's morality, but Cassandra was still her mother and she was therefore extremely sensitive about her and fiercely protective of her. Everyone, including Marquise, knew better than to make malicious comments about her. Marquise had crossed the line, but Terelle couldn't muster the strength to defend her mother—to dispute his damning words. Challenging his honesty had the potential of uncovering far more than her heart could bear.

Marquise was silent for a few seconds, then added in a solemn tone, "And I'm gonna tell you something else—your mom's gittin' high again."

Terelle dropped her head, massaged her temples. "No, she isn't...that's a lie."

"Trust me. I know the signs," he said, nodding. "You saw her. *You* know the signs, too: nervous and fidgety, mad at the world, hair all nappy under that raggedy-ass scarf. Shit, she looked like she been gittin' it in for a coupla days or more. Her and that Harry dude was probably fightin' over the last rock."

"She promised," Terelle said in a faint voice, shaking her head in disbelief. As if in a trance, she carried her drowsy daughter to the bedroom to lay her down.

Marquise followed. "Forget her. She ain't never gonna change. Ain't no rehab in the world stronger than that drug."

"You should know," Terelle said, giving Marquise a mirthless smile.

"Don't blame me 'cause your mom's all messed up again. Damn right, I was out there gittin' mine; I was doin' what I had to do. But, I ain't never put a pipe in nobody's mouth. Now, I did my time and I'm tryin' to move on." Softening his tone, Marquise continued, "Babe, why you tryin' to act like your mom's lookin' out for you when we both know she ain't got no motherly instincts. Think about it; what she ever do for you?"

Terelle flinched.

"She don't care 'bout nothin' but a hit. She's miserable and wants everybody around her to be miserable, too. She wants to ruin our relationship...and she can if you let her." Marquise gently tugged at Terelle's arm. "Use your head, babe. You gotta keep her outta your life. She don't bring nothin' but trouble." He gave a bitter smile. "Don't let her come between us. You think we can move forward together?" he asked in a whispery voice.

Terelle responded by laying her head on his chest. Feeling his heartbeat, she closed her eyes; a warm feeling flowed through her. She'd been desperately waiting for this feeling, this love for so long.

She had faint memories of a time when she could feel her mother's love. But drugs entered their lives like a raging storm, ruining everything. Drugs had destroyed her mother, prevented her from loving or properly caring for Terelle. And although Children and Youth Services had stepped in, no love was shown in the foster care system in which Terelle was placed for three years.

The only kindness ever shown was from her last foster mother, Mrs. Genwright, who had dressed and fed Terelle properly and even offered an occasional hug. Too bad the woman was a religious fanatic—a Holy Roller—who dragged Terelle to church every day of the week and all day on Sundays.

To this day, Terelle had never stepped foot inside another church, and absolutely never prayed. But the Bible passages she'd been force-fed were indelibly etched in her brain. And so was the day one of the church members concluded that Terelle's mother's transgressions had been passed on to the child. Sins of the mother, which had to be stamped out.

"The Lawd done spoke to me and we gotta save the soul of this here innocent chile," said a zealous church member.

The flock of men and women who called themselves Prayer Warriors encircled the frightened child and began praying over her, speaking words they were convinced would ultimately cast out every one of Satan's demons. They worked themselves into a feverish frenzy, and then as if on queue, the Prayer Warriors shrieked simultaneously and broke into a well-choreographed dance that resembled some of the old-time dances that Gran used to do. Screaming, Terelle broke away from the circle, but she was chased and caught just as she reached the big brass handle of the main door—the door that would have led to safety. Terrified, Terelle kicked and screamed. She tried to fight them off, but couldn't. She pleaded for Mrs. Genwright to save her, but her foster mother shook her head sadly and assisted in holding Terelle down. The members prayed passionately, insisting that she was plagued by the demon of drug addiction, the demon of the flesh...the demon of damn near everything. According to the parishioners she'd inherited all her mother's demons and they were hell-bent or perhaps *heaven-bent* to rid the poor child of Satan's power. Terelle quaked with fear when her foster mother began touching the top of her head and praying so passionately her eyes rolled into the back of her head. And when Mrs. Genwright started to speak in a scary-sounding gibberish, Terelle clawed, spit, and sputtered until she peed on herself and passed out from exhaustion.

From that day until the day Aunt Bennie got out of the army and came to reclaim her, she was labeled as the little girl who'd been possessed by demons.

Terelle closed her eyes tight as she squeezed back tears and horribly painful memories.

Her mother had made her choices. And now it was time for Terelle to choose. She lifted her head and gazed first at her sleeping daughter and then at Marquise and decided that the love of these two people was all the love she needed.

There was no room in her life for her mother. Not now, not ever.

Chapter Fourteen

Kai played her messages. There were six from LaVella, each plea sounding more desperate than the one before. She listened to the pathetic babbling and choking sobs, hearing clearly only the plaintive wail at the end of each message: "Come on, Kai. Don't do me like this! I really need to talk to you. So call me, okay? Please!"

Just thinking about LaVella's fleshy face buried in her sweaty, odiferous groin, gave Kai sadistic pleasure mixed with a mild case of the willies. What perverted demon had possessed her to dally with someone as unsophisticated and physically unappealing as LaVella? And she must have totally taken leave of her senses to have given her home number to a potential stalker. After three days of leaving numerous unanswered messages, the average person would stop calling, but LaVella just wouldn't take a hint. What a desperate pest!

Kai promptly pushed the numbers that would block LaVella's future calls.

A stabbing hunger pang reminded Kai that she hadn't

eaten all day. She studied the menu of the take-out Japanese restaurant down the street. What was she in the mood for—tempura, chicken teriyaki or sushi? Her frustration told her that she was in the mood for all three dishes.

There would be a forty-five-minute wait for delivery, so she poured herself a glass of Kirin beer and ran bath water, pouring in a generous amount of an expensive bath oil—a souvenir from her parents' most recent trip to Paris. Recalling her mother's advice to use only a droplet of the rich bath oil at a time, Kai smiled devilishly and shook out a generous amount.

A half-hour later, she emerged from the bathtub shimmering from the expensive bath oil and slightly tipsy. She threw on a hooded cotton sleep shirt. Famished and missing the hell out of Kenneth. She poured herself more of the Japanese beer. With each sip the yearning and emptiness intensified. Without giving it a second thought, she reached for the telephone and pressed the digits to Kenneth's pager.

A few minutes later, the phone rang. Kai grabbed it on the first ring.

Damn! It wasn't Kenneth; it was the delivery person, announcing the arrival of her food.

Moments later, Kai lifted the plastic lids from three entrées which consisted of a delectably exotic combination sushi platter, crisp golden shrimp and vegetable tempura platter, as well as aromatic chicken teriyaki over rice. She studied the colorful arrangement that comprised the feast spread before her and deliberated on which delight to sample first.

Lovingly, she toyed with each entrée and imagined the soothing balm, which would overtake her on the first bite. Deciding that she needed to start off with a bang, Kai used her finger to pile a heaping portion of wasabi atop a piece of yellowtail tuna. Taking a bite, she endured the searing assault to her sinuses as the burning sensation shot to the top of her head. Mmm, such sweet pain.

As she placed a sliver of pickled ginger on her tongue, enjoying the tingling sensation, her mind drifted to Kenneth. He didn't care for raw fish but always indulged her cravings, sitting with her for hours at the sushi bar of her favorite Japanese restaurant.

He used to delight in hand-feeding her each piece—groaning as she licked the wasabi or teriyaki sauce from his fingers—right there in the restaurant—for all eyes to see. The musing was vivid; it aroused her, but being aroused with no available dick left her feeling hollow and agitated.

A shadow fell over Kai's face; more than enough time had passed for Kenneth to respond to her page. Why was he going to such lengths to punish her? He'd never remained angry for such an extended period. What had she done that had been so unpardonable? Was it that silly photo she'd attempted to send his wife? It couldn't be—he'd intercepted it. Or was it the subsequent petty argument on the phone? No, Kenneth wasn't overly sensitive. Besides, he knew she hadn't meant any of the hurtful things she'd said. Perhaps he was still holding a grudge because of their encounter in the restaurant? Maybe his date—Ms. Back-to-Africa was offended by their public display of affection. Yes, that's it, Kai rationalized. She must have severely berated him after having witnessed his and Kai's lover's spat. No one could deny that the passion they had exhibited obviously meant they were deeply, profoundly in love. Of course! And, the conniving Nubian whore probably threatened to withhold sex. Now, Kenneth was punishing her to make that wooly-headed bitch happy. He's trying to prove that he doesn't love me anymore so he can keep fucking that black whore. *But, my darling Kenneth, we both know something she doesn't. You do love me, you will always love me, and there's nothing she or anyone else can do about it. And that is emphatically that!*

Kai smiled wistfully, comforted by the newfound revelation. *Don't you worry, Kenneth; since you can't control your new dick licker you leave me no choice but to take care of the situation for you—for us!*

Pleased with her deductive abilities and relieved to have found a culprit she could blame for Dr. Harding's neglect, Kai relaxed and gradually returned her focus to the massive meal before her. As she glanced around the table, a frown of incomprehension began to form.

She was stunned. Every single morsel had disappeared!

Where the hell is my dinner? she whispered with genuine disbelief. The gradual realization of an aching pain in her distended stomach gave her the only plausible answer to the question. She had eaten three entire platters of food and had no conscious awareness of doing so.

Kai's anger swiftly returned. *Goddamn you, Kenneth; just look what you and your slut made me do! How dare you treat me like yesterday's trash for the sake of that Swahili-speaking slut? The sheer gall of that woman manipulating my Kenneth!*

Needing release from the growing rage inside her, Kai grabbed an empty container. Wishing it were Kenneth's head, she flung it against the wall. The violent act gave her instant, however, momentary gratification. She required a prolonged fix, thus one-by-one she cleared the table: containers, platters, utensils all crashed against the wall and fell to the floor. Kai was filled with glee until she noticed the vile multicolored residue from the containers had splashed against her pristine white walls leaving nasty streaks as the muck slowly made its way to the tiled kitchen floor.

She looked at the mess. Repulsed, she looked away, refusing to lift a finger to clean it. Matilda would have to do it. Matilda, her parents' cleaning woman was on loan to Kai once a week—every Wednesday. But it was Sunday night and looking at that gook for the next two days was entirely out of the question.

Suddenly, a stabbing pain and a wave of nausea overtook her. Kai clamped both hands over her mouth. She bent over and ran like hell for the bathroom.

She'd barely made it into the bathroom before she was projectile vomiting chunks of undigested food all over the Italian marble floor. Falling hard onto her knees in front of the toilet she managed to lift the toilet seat. With her face buried in the bowl, Kai hugged the rim while her body convulsed violently.

After what seemed an eternity, her regurgitation ceased, but she didn't dare rise until the gagging dry heaves had subsided. Kai crawled over to the pedestal sink, then slowly, unsteadily pulled herself to her feet. The acrid taste of bile filled her mouth and burned her throat. Panting and holding onto the sink for balance, she lifted her head to peer at the reflection in the mirror. She was horrified by the ravage that had been done to her face. A vomit-smeared, swollen-faced, bloodshot-eyed, snotty-nosed monster was looking back at her. Shrieking, Kai jumped into the shower fully clothed, turned on the pulsating heads and began to strip as the cleansing water washed over her.

Feeling refreshed and looking—thank God—more like her beautiful self, she snatched the phone from its base and called the front desk of her apartment building.

"This is Kai Montgomery."

"Yes, Ms. Montgomery, what can I do for you?" asked the clerk in a crisp tone.

"Is the maintenance man still on duty?" she asked hopefully, picturing the new Puerto Rican maintenance man she'd seen earlier. He was a buffed cutie and they'd made eye contact in the lobby earlier that evening. She hoped he was packing what she needed. Some men tended to build muscles to compensate for what they were lacking between their legs. But the sexy Puerto Rican had a confidence that told her he was more than capable of easing her tension.

"Is there an emergency, Ms. Montgomery?"

"Yes, would you please send the maintenance man to my apartment immediately?"

"What's the nature of the emergency?"

"I don' believe that's any of your business."

"I have to keep a log of all repairs; I can't just send someone up there without..."

"I see. This is a race issue, isn't it?" Though she didn't consider herself as being African American, she pulled the race card when necessary.

"Of course not, madam." The man sounded genuinely offended. "There's just one person on duty and he's here to maintain the aesthetic appearance of the building. He's not licensed to make repairs, but I can make a note of your request..."

"I pay nineteen hundred dollars a month to live here and I expect to be treated with the same respect you give the white occupants of this supposedly posh building."

Kai paused and sighed heavily. "What's your name?"

"Stewart," he said in a nervous, barely audible voice.

"I don't appreciate this inquisition, Stewart. Do I need to speak with your supervisor?"

"No, I regret the inconvenience, Ms. Montgomery," Stewart sounded sincerely contrite. "I'll send the maintenance man to your apartment immediately and I'll just make a note that there's a clogged drain in your kitchen sink."

"Whatever," Kai sighed, faking exasperation. She was actually quite giddy; the throbbing sensation between her legs would be soothed in a few minutes.

She couldn't wait to get her hands on the cute Latino. There'd be no small talk; she wouldn't even pretend there was a clogged drain in her apartment. Kai was certain that the moment she opened the door, he'd drop his useless plunger and pull out the tool she really needed. She needed something thick and long-lasting to unclog her drain.

Dabbing French perfume (another hand-out from her parents' Parisian vacation) at her pulse points, Kai stared into the mirror and decided to rearrange herself. She changed from the sleep shirt to a very provocative lace slip with spaghetti straps. She fluffed up her hair and loosened one thin strap, allowing it to fall seductively onto her shoulder.

As she practiced striking a progression of inviting poses, there was a soft, timid tapping at her door.

Feeling predatory, Kai moistened her lips with her

tongue and crossed the room to admit the sexy stud.

"Evenin', ma'am, I'm Howard. You got a clogged drain?"

She thought her eyes were deceiving her as she stared mutely at the puffy-faced, middle-aged white man who stood in her doorway holding the tiniest plunger she'd ever seen. He regarded her with disinterested eyes that were red from lack of sleep or too much drink.

"Where's the Latino guy?" she finally inquired, miffed.

"Off. He got off at ten," the man stated with a finality that caused Kai's heart to sink.

Can this night get any worse? No Kenneth, no Latin lover. No dick. Nothing...except a trashed kitchen and a disgustingly befouled bathroom!

Being dealt lemons, she decided to make some lemonade. "Come with me." Kai led the lumbering man to the kitchen.

"What the heck happened in here? I don't do this kind of work...looks like you're gonna need Housekeeping. They'll be in tomorrow morning."

Ignoring his protests, Kai turned and led him toward the bathroom. "Follow me. There's another problem that requires your expertise."

The handyman reluctantly followed looking longingly at the entry door. Kai stood beside the bathroom door waving a hand at the revolting sight. "My toilet overflowed...when you're finished in the kitchen you can clean this up, too."

Howard stood transfixed as he absorbed the horrific sight and what he had been asked to do. "Look, ma'am. I'm a handyman...not the clean-up man. This ain't part of my job description. I can't help you here." Howard turned to leave.

"Look at me, Horace...Huey or whatever the hell your name is. Take a good look at my face and tell me something. Do I look like the type of individual who gives a good goddamn what kind of *man* you think you are or what is or is not your fucking job? Just clean this shit up!"

Howard kept walking.

Incredulous, Kai screamed, "Do you know who I am? I'll have your job, you insolent bastard!"

Never breaking his stride, Howard responded, "Take a good look at my back, ma'am, and tell me if you think I give a shit."

Kai streaked to her bedroom, flung herself across the antique cast-iron bed and screamed into her pillow. Unwilling to endure another moment of such a miserable night, she sat up, reached for the bottle of pills on her nightstand and shook out a blue Xanax—and then another. Nights like tonight required two of those blue boys. She gulped down the pills, propped herself up with two fluffy pillows and enjoyed the palpable sensation of her tense body relaxing.

Tortuous thoughts flitted away and her mood was brightened by an image of Kenneth making passionate love to her in broad daylight on the private beach of some Caribbean island.

Exhibitionist that she was, Kai's reverie wasn't complete without an unwitting audience—the island's hired help would do nicely. She imagined the staff being a prim and proper married couple who attempted to discreetly perform their duty of providing fresh towels and exotic drinks. Flush-faced, the imaginary couple tiptoed around Kai and Kenneth's writhing sweat-glistened bodies.

Stimulated by her own erotic thoughts, Kai pressed her middle finger against her clit and began to rub in a circular motion. Straining to reach an orgasm, her mind raced for a totally decadent scene.

On her mental screen, Kai and Kenneth switched positions: Kenneth on the bottom, Kai on top. Aroused and curious, the married couple stared openly. Kai crooked her finger, beckoning the wife. Shy and hesitant, the wife looked to her husband for approval. He nodded and nudged her forward as he unzipped his pants. The husband stroked himself as Kai dismounted Kenneth and invited the wife to lift her skirt and slide onto Kenneth's pole that was slippery from Kai's hot juices.

Somehow her annoyance with Kenneth crept into the scene. She angrily directed the aroused husband to come forward—hard dick in hand. Stroking himself wildly, the husband was further instructed to shoot his ample load into Kenneth's despicable, cheating face.

At that moment Kai came. The intensity of her orgasm caused her to shriek.

Minutes later she fell into a deep, blissful sleep.

Chapter Fifteen

Look at the camera. Smile, Keeta." Click. Click. Click. Terelle grinned and aimed the disposable camera again.

"Hold up, babe. She's tired of posin'," Marquise intervened. "Let her run around and play wit her toys."

"But I have seven shots left."

"Save 'em for later."

"Nope. I'm gonna get this film developed on my way to work. I want to see these flicks as soon as possible."

"Why they got you workin' on Christmas? That should be against the law. You should call out."

"Can't. I had Thanksgiving off. It's cool, though, because I need the overtime to pay for your shit," she said, laughing, nodding toward the pile of brightly wrapped and bowed presents that lay unopened under the tiny artificial tree.

"Are you gonna open your gifts or should I let Keeta come over and tear them up for you?"

Marquise grinned and looked around like he didn't know where to begin. For a moment he looked like the seven-year-old she had fallen in love with in the second grade. Back then they were both the pampered only children of working single mothers who dressed them to the nines and made sure they had the best of everything. Terelle could barely remember Marquise's mom. She recalled her being tall, deep-dark chocolate and beautiful, just like Marquise. A jealous boyfriend's bullet ended her life, and although Marquise never got mixed up in the foster care system, he was shuffled to a myriad of don't-give-a-damn relatives who cared more about the social security and kinship care checks than they cared about him.

She took a deep breath, swallowed and shot a glance at Marquise. He was playing with Markeeta, blissfully unaware that Terelle had been taking an unpleasant stroll down memory lane.

The hell with those sad memories, she decided. This was the happiest day of her life. She didn't have to clock in until three in the afternoon and she was determined to enjoy every moment of her family's first Christmas together.

"Quise!" Terelle shouted.

Marquise sat on the floor helping Markeeta push the buttons to a Fisher Price toy that made animal sounds. He looked up, scowled quizzically.

"You plannin' on opening your gifts before I go to work?"

"Here, baby," he said to Markeeta, putting her finger

on the bright yellow button. "Push it all the way down, Keeta," he instructed as he stood up.

"I don't feel right havin' all these presents when I didn't get you nothin'," he said unhappily.

"Baby, you're my present," she said, embracing Marquise who had slumped sadly down onto the futon. Terelle didn't want Marquise to feel inadequate. "Look at us! You, me, and Keeta, finally together on Christmas..." Overcome by emotion, Terelle paused.

"Quise, you know this is the best Christmas of my life. So stop messin' up my day."

"Why'd you git me so much stuff?" Marquise asked, shaking his head in embarrassment.

"Because I love you. Now stop pissing me off and start unwrapping." Terelle glided to the mountain of gifts and picked up the largest box. "Here, I'll make it easy for you. Open this one first—and don't shake it—it's fragile."

"I ain't opening shit 'til you rip into this!" Grinning, he pulled out a small gold wrapped box that was tucked under the futon cushion.

"Quise!" she squealed. "Oh my God, Quise, what is it? I can't believe you got me something. How?"

"Don't worry about how. Yo, I got friends and associates. Just because I'm on house arrest don't mean I can't make major moves. A lotta niggas still owe me from before I got popped, so a coupla my dawgs handled my business—collected some of that cheddar out there that belongs to me." Looking proud of his accomplishments, Marquise nodded and nibbled at his bottom lip.

Terelle didn't know how to feel about Marquise dabbling in his old life—collecting debts. Troubling thoughts were pushed to the back of her mind.

"I'm waitin'," he said.

Blushing, she shook the square box. It was heavy—probably a watch. Terelle ripped off the wrapping and tore into the box. There was another small box inside; it obviously contained a ring. Had Marquise managed to replace the emerald birthstone ring he'd given her on her eighteenth birthday? The precious ring she had to twist off her finger and hand over to the man in the pawnshop when Marquise was arrested? The ring that had been sold by the time she had acquired the money to get it back? She refused to get her hopes up. There was absolutely no way Marquise could have come up with enough cash to buy another emerald ring.

"Open it, babe," he implored.

Terelle's hand shook as she raised the lid of the velvet box. She stared incomprehensibly at the gleaming rock that blurred her vision. She lifted her gaze and stared at Marquise, confused.

"Gotta git engaged before we can git married, babe," he explained.

Moved to tears, she cried out, "Oh Marquise… Marquise!" She cried as she clung to his shirt and buried her head into his chest. His arms quickly enfolded her.

"Whatchu crying for? This is a happy occasion, right?"

"Yes," she said, sniffling. "I just can't believe..."

"Man, if you don't let me put this ice on your finger and kill that noise. I thought this would make my baby smile."

Terelle forced a smile, but the tears continued to stream down her cheeks.

Marquise took the box from Terelle who was now limp, leaning against him for support and still weeping. He put the ring on her finger. "It's a carat and a half," he informed her with pride.

Terelle held up her hand to admire her ring and shook her head in disbelief. "We're really engaged, Quise?"

"Uh-huh. We'll set the weddin' date as soon as they cut this bracelet off my ankle."

There was too much happening. Terelle was beginning to feel dizzy. Markeeta had mastered the mechanics of pushing the buttons of her new toy. A cow mooed, a dog barked, a cat meowed, and apparently particularly fond of the pig sound, Markeeta pushed that button over and over.

Overly stimulated and feeling lightheaded, Terelle eased down onto the futon and stared at her ring.

"Guess it's time to open up my presents," Marquise stated.

Terelle nodded but was uninterested. She continued to gawk at her ring. *Married! They were finally going to get married!* Her lips slowly spread into a smile as she envisioned them at the altar, Marquise lifting her veil to kiss her.

Marquise crept over and snapped her picture. The flash of light broke into Terelle's reverie, brought her back to the present.

"Whatever was going on in your head gave you a glow. I had to get a flick with you looking so peaceful…so beautiful."

His compliments made her uncomfortable. "You like your gift?" she asked, taking the spotlight off herself.

"Yo, I needed this Xbox," Marquise shouted. "I get tired of watchin' TV all day." He tore open another box. "Oh shit, you even got the extra controller, the memory card…the remote…everything!"

"And three games," Terelle added, finally tearing herself away from her mental wedding plans. She got up and handed him a present wrapped in paper with tiny Christmas trees.

Marquise tore open the wrapping of two sports games and one game that required killing everybody in sight. "Okay, aiight," he said, gnawing on his bottom lip and nodding happily. "You know what your man likes. Thanks, babe." He gave her a quick peck on the cheek and began plugging in the Xbox.

"Hold up. Open the rest of your presents," Terelle demanded.

Eager to play the Xbox, Marquise seemed disinterested in the remaining pile of gifts, but began opening boxes to pacify Terelle. There were several pairs of Miskeen jeans, Dickie sets in various colors, a tan-colored Diesel watch, Sean John sweats, two pairs of Rocawear jeans and hoodies, a leather belt with the Rocawear logo on the buckle, buff-colored high-top Timberland boots and a pair of white Nikes.

"Damn, babe," Marquise exclaimed. "How you afford all this fly shit?"

"Christmas club," she replied, lying. "Been saving all year." Actually Saleema had provided the cash. Saleema couldn't stand Marquise but she made sure her best friend was able to feel the joy of giving her man the best Christmas ever.

✿✿✿

Terelle walked to the bus stop holding her hand in front of her face. Then, worried that some desperado would knock her upside her head to relieve her of the cherished diamond, she quickly stuffed her hand inside her pocket.

She picked up speed; she couldn't wait to get to work to show off her ring. Coworkers who were engaged or married all wore rings with tiny stones. Terelle laughed to herself because she would have been satisfied with just a diamond chip, but Marquise had gone all out and had shown his love by adorning her finger with some bling-bling that would not go unnoticed.

For those who had talked behind her back, calling her a fool for her devotion to Marquise...she'd simply flash her left hand and keep on steppin'.

Chapter Sixteen

Kai's father, Dr. Philip Montgomery, was on the board of directors and made healthy contributions to the nursing home where she worked, thus Kai was given the preferential treatment she felt she deserved.

Doctors, department heads, board members, and visiting VIPs were given reserved parking in a secluded area close to the entrance and far away from the peons who scrambled for parking in the limited spaces provided in the employee parking lot. Since Dr. Montgomery hardly ever visited the nursing home, Kai was permitted to use his parking space.

Getting dumped by Dr. Kenneth Harding was not a situation Kai took lightly. And so, as luck would have it on this cold and windy day, Kai had the good fortune of finding a parking space two cars away from Dr. Harding's British Racing green Jaguar. Eyeing the rear of his prized possession, Kai rolled her eyes at the nauseating vanity plate. *DRLOVE.* How could a mature, seemingly sophisticated, prominent member of society display such a lack of good taste and still maintain his status in the community?

Sacrificing her delicate Italian knit hat, that was more for show than for the warmth the gusty January weather required, Kai placed her finger under its tight band, shook her head and permitted the hat to slip off her head and set sail. It landed on the hood of the Jag. Prying eyes from nearby windows would realize she had to recover her wind-blown hat. With a handy set of keys in her hand, Kai retrieved the hat and engraved angry jagged lines into the hood of the car. There was no time to admire her craftsmanship as she dragged the key from the headlight past the passenger door and all the way to the taillight. Feeling creative, she walked to the other side of the car and etched looping circles into the door of the driver's side.

Securing her hat on her head, she threw her head high with satisfaction and pranced to the employee's entrance. Inside the elevator with her jangling keys still in hand, Kai stroked the special key—the one used as a weapon. Running her fingers across the ridges, she flicked off bits of green paint. She'd give anything to witness *Dr. Love's* expression when he viewed her artwork.

"Good morning," Kai chirped as she breezed past the nurses' station.

Taken aback by Kai's sudden acknowledgment of their presence, the nurses and nursing assistants were too shocked to utter a return greeting.

In the hours after her exhilarating morning activity, Kai became alert each time the receptionist made an announcement on the intercom. Expecting to hear something pertaining to the vandalism of Dr. Harding's car, she was surprised there was no mention of it.

By two that afternoon Kai had attended a Care Conference meeting, a two-hour-long meeting held for each resident every ninety days and comprised of a clinical team. Every blue moon, family members showed up to hear about their loved one's progress. Whenever this happened, the meeting would go on endlessly. On this occasion, the wife of Mr. Randolph joined the team around the table. She had lots of questions and complaints about her husband's care. Kai could have killed her, but since that wasn't an option, Kai had sat twirling her hair, not even pretending to be mildly interested throughout the coma-inducing session.

"I'd like to update you on your husband's current diagnosis," the registered nurse who was conducting the meeting said with a gracious smile. "Mr. Randolph has a history of a CVA, dysphasia, hemi paresis on the left side, dementia of the Alzheimer's type, hypertension, and diabetes. He had a recent fall when he tried to transfer himself from his wheelchair to the toilet, but sustained no injuries. For his safety, we've placed an alarm on his chair that will sound if he topples forward."

The nurse continued to drone on, but Kai tuned her out. Having to listen to the long list of ailments that plagued the hopeless man was making Kai grumpy. *Oh, why doesn't someone just put the man out of his misery?*

Next, the nurse listed about a thousand medications the resident was given each day. She disclosed that he was incontinent and wore adult diapers and was being trained to use a urinal at night.

Oh yuck! Kai fidgeted in her seat.

Then, the physical therapist discussed the resident's inability to self-propel his wheelchair with his hands due to having a contracted hand brought on by the stroke. Thus, he scooted about using his feet. However, if his cognition improved, the physical therapist promised, he'd be put on the waiting list for a motorized wheelchair.

Oh, that makes a lot of sense. The man's missing half his marbles, but if there's some improvement, they're going to provide him with a motorized vehicle so he can zip about the facility like a speed demon, running recklessly over the feet of anyone in his path.

The physical therapist continued talking about exercises...active and passive range of motion exercises and the resident's ability to transfer in and out of bed.

Boring, boring, boring!

The dietitian muttered something about the resident consuming 75 percent of his meals. Sensing that she was expected to say more, the woman launched into a spiel about Mr. Randolph being on a special puree diet (food that was ground in a blender until it had the consistency of baby food) and drinking honey-thickened juice. The dietitian smiled broadly as she spoke as if the poor geezer's meal plan was appealing and appetizing.

Oh, I'm gagging. Yuck, yuck, yuck!

For Kai, having to listen to all that medical gobbledygook was absolutely unendurable. Thus when it was her turn to speak, she simply stated that there had been no significant changes in the resident's mood and behavior since the last review.

After Kai's unenthused report, the monotonous meeting should have been over. However, the nurse coordinator turned to the recreation therapist and inquired about the resident's activity involvement. *As if anyone cared.*

On queue, the recreation therapist became instantly animated and began rattling off a long list of activities that sounded therapeutic, sophisticated and fun. The dippy recreation therapist gushed on and on about all the activities that were offered: Sensory Stimulation, Armchair Travel, Culinary Arts, Golden Games, Morning Stretch, Scenic Variation Hour, Pleasure Bus Rides, Field Trips. *Lies, lies, lies.* Kai was ready to pull out a machete. Bloodletting was definitely in order if she didn't get out of that bullshit meeting so she could attend to the important matter of locating Dr. Hardy. Surely, everyone seated at the table knew the County Nursing Home residents didn't do all those grand activities. They all lived only to play BINGO. Morning, noon, and night...that's all they wanted to do and when not engaged in a game of fucking Bingo they cluttered the corridors, causing traffic jams. They hung around the nurses' station, or rampaged each others' rooms, stealing anything from horded sugar packets to packs of generic-brand cigarettes.

As the recreation therapist continued bullshitting the family member and the team, Kai covered her ears and looked down at her lap and gasped in surprise. At some point during the insufferable two-hour meeting, she had managed to pull out enough hair to knit a pair of baby booties. The evidence—a, clump of hair the size of a tennis ball lay on her lap.

Back in her office at last, she immediately checked her messages. None from Kenneth. *Damn!* She hated to admit it, but what she'd done was a crime of passion. She'd keyed his car so that he would have to pay her some attention. Even negative attention was preferable to none. Had he come storming into her office as she expected, she would have pled her innocence and then cajoled him back into her life. Hell, she would have stripped right there for him. Fucked him on top of her desk or sucked him off while seated in her swivel chair. Whatever it took.

✿✿✿

Awakened by the office telephone while taking a power nap at her desk, Kai clumsily reached for the receiver. "Hello," she said, sounding annoyed and sleepy.

"I hope you enjoyed your little stunt this morning."

It was Kenneth. Not having her wits about her, Kai was momentarily speechless. "What stunt?" she asked a few seconds later.

"You know damn well what I'm referring to."

"I haven't spoken to you in weeks. You refuse to return my calls and now you call me—out of the blue—accusing me of something…and I have no idea what you're talking about."

"Cut the crap, Kai. I know you. I know what you're capable of…"

"Kenneth!" she cried. "Please stop it. Why are you tormenting me? This is cruel and sadistic. Is this your idea of a joke?" To authenticate her role of the falsely accused, Kai's mind quickly raced to retrieve a memory sad enough to produce tears.

She thought about the sixth-grade Valentine's Day party. Her mother had told her she'd be the prettiest girl there, but she didn't feel very pretty when none of the white boys asked for a dance. *"I'm not dancing with that chocolate drop,"* she overheard one of the boys saying. *"Yeah, a chocolate drop who thinks she's a Vanilla Wafer,"* another boy said, laughing.

Their words had sent Kai running to the restroom in tears. Locked in a stall and crying hysterically, she refused to return to the dance. Her parents had to be called.

Wearing embarrassed faces, they ushered their inconsolable daughter out of the restroom and past the gawking pale-faced children and teachers who all considered Kai high-strung and oversensitive.

Caught up in that painful memory, Kai burst into tears. "We haven't spoken for months and you finally call. Why? To torment me?" she asked, sobbing.

"Your theatrics don't move me," Kenneth said with a mirthless chuckle.

"I miss you, Kenneth." Her voice cracked. "I'd do anything to start all over again. I'm so sorry about the picture…the threats. I was acting childish, but I…"

"You're sorry about everything…including my car?"

"Your car!" she screeched. "What about your car?"

"You disappoint me, Kai. You're a poor actress."

"What the hell are you talking about?"

"Listen, little girl, get yourself some help—get to the root of your problems before you get hurt."

Her tears were useless; she wiped her eyes. Flooded with anger and indignation, she cleared her throat and asked, "Are you threatening me, Kenneth?"

"As a matter of fact, I am."

"Well, I don't take threats lightly. I'm going to report this call…"

"Report whatever you'd like. However, if you come near my car or me ever again, I won't waste time getting a restraining order or anything else the legal system has to offer. Your face…your beautiful face is going to look far worse than my Jag. Am I making myself clear?"

"Fuck you, Kenneth," Kai shouted.

"I did." Dr. Harding gave a low chuckle and clicked off the line.

Fuming, Kai gathered her purse, hat and coat. There was no way she was sitting in that closet of an office a second longer. She needed air and she needed some dick. Yes, she needed a good hard fuck. The mere thought started her juices flowing. And somebody, somewhere was going to give her what she needed.

✿✿✿

Kai strode into the lobby of her apartment building. The daytime desk clerk, a pretty dark-skinned woman who reminded Kai of a younger version of Ms. Nubia, greeted Kai with a smile. "Good afternoon," the attractive mocha-colored woman said.

"Has anyone unclogged the drain in 2605?" Kai demanded to know.

Furrowing her brows, the young lady searched through a large ledger, then smiled slightly when she came across the information.

"That request was cancelled a few weeks ago."

"By whom?" Kai asked.

"It doesn't say."

"I'm spending a small fortune to live in this dump. Now, I've been patient up to this point, but no more. I want my drain unclogged—immediately! Understand?"

The young woman bristled in indignation, but managed to keep a civil tongue. "I'm not sure if there's anyone available right now, but…"

"I'm not waiting a moment longer—find someone."

"I can try to get..."

"Do the job you're paid to do before I make a complaint to your superiors," Kai said, dismissing her. Strolling to the elevator, Kai looked back to make sure the woman was sufficiently rattled by the encounter. She observed the clerk picking up the phone and rapidly pushing numbers. Satisfied, Kai stepped into the elevator and hummed merrily as she rode to the twenty-sixth floor.

Inside her apartment, she flung off her hat and began to shed her remaining winter gear. Before she could strip out of her sweater and slacks there was a light tap at the door.

It didn't matter who was on the other side of the door as long as he had a functional dick.

Kai opened the door and locked eyes with the maintenance man. Ortiz was the name embroidered on his uniform. She didn't know if it was his first or last name. Nor did she care. She was concerned only with the size of his assets and trying to make a determination, she stared openly at his crotch.

"You got a clogged drain, Miss?" he asked with a Spanish accent, which Kai found sexy.

"It's in the bedroom," she said in a sultry voice. "Follow me...Oh, and leave that plunger by the door. You won't be needing it."

His teasing grin and the glint in his eyes told Kai that

Ortiz was open to whatever she had in mind. Without a word, he got rid of the miniature plunger and eagerly followed her into the bedroom.

Kai sat on the bed looking Ortiz up and down and licked her lips as he sauntered over. Perhaps her eyes were deceiving her but she could have sworn his hips were swiveling as he slowly unbuttoned his shirt. Kai sure wished she had some stripper music on hand. He was a cutie with his curly dark hair. He was medium height—about 5'10"—not as tall as she liked her men, but she wasn't proposing marriage, so what did she care?

Ortiz made a big production of flinging his shirt on the floor and then snatching off his undershirt. Kai nodded in approval as he revealed his broad, hairy chest and well-defined arms.

She pulled off her sweater and tossed it on top of her vanity table. Ortiz kicked off his shoes and helped Kai pull off her boots. Kai unzipped her slacks and allowed Ortiz to ease them off. By the time he had taken off his pants, he was fully erect and she was moist. There was no need for kissing or fondling. All Kai wanted was some rock-hard dick.

She wiggled out of her panties, then tugged at the waistband of his boxers; he obeyed, quickly shedding them. Kai's eyes zoomed in on his genitals and she liked what she saw. His cock was mid-sized in length and was as thick as hell in width. Not bothering to remove her bra, Kai laid back. She smiled and spread her legs.

"Damn," Ortiz exclaimed. "You're a sexy little bitch."

She parted her vagina lips to reveal the sticky moisture produced by lust, then guided him to the center of her desire.

Kai moaned as he covered her body with his and pushed inside her. Hungry hands pulled him in deeper as she wrapped her legs around his waist, locking her ankles together as if to trap him inside forever.

"Let's do this my way, honey," Ortiz suggested, stopping the momentum and unlocking Kai's ankles. As he pulled out, Kai let out a whimper of protest. Ortiz moved to the edge of the bed and sat up. He motioned Kai to straddle him. Easing herself onto his slick thickness, Kai gyrated slowly. But Ortiz held her still with his strong hands.

"I got this," he said sternly. As Kai sat atop him, he gripped her waist with both hands and moved her slim body in a circular motion.

Being rotated around a dick was a new sensation. Her breath caught as she wrapped her arms tightly around his neck and groaned in ecstasy each time she felt the friction created when her clit rubbed against the base of his dick.

"Oh my God," she cried out. "Damn! Oh my God!"

"You like this, honey?" he asked, speeding up the pace.

"Love it," she responded in a breathy whisper.

Ortiz suddenly changed the rhythm. He clutched Kai's ass so tightly, she winced. He bounced her up and down the length of his pole, and then began alternating between the bouncing and rotating movement. Ortiz had total control and Kai didn't mind at all. She threw her head back, grimaced in exquisite pain, and bit her lip to contain the building passion that threatened to explode.

"Hold on, honey; wait for me."

"I can't," she wailed as her pussy muscles began to clench and unclench uncontrollably.

Ortiz waited for her spasms to subside, then pushed her off roughly and arranged her on all fours. Mounting her from behind, he grabbed a handful of hair and yanked her head back and forth repeatedly. "You like it when I pull your hair, honey?" he asked and smacked her ass hard before she could whimper the word, *"yes!"* Ortiz was a fabulous fuck; she could fuck him all night long. He thrust inside her quickly and deeply and until he, too, was satisfied. Afterwards, he collapsed in a panting heap at the bottom of the bed with his back to Kai.

Needing to be close to the man who had just given her exactly what she needed, Kai scooted down and caressed the back of his neck and then worked her hand up to his head. As her fingers glided through his curls, Ortiz shifted his position, moving away from her touch.

Before Kai could process the meaning of his body language, Ortiz sat upright and streaked off to the bathroom.

The sound of the toilet flushing after he urinated was followed immediately by the sound of running water and vigorous scrubbing.

Kai scratched her head in bewilderment, then decided Ortiz had a hell of a nerve rushing to her bathroom to wash away all evidence of her. What was his problem? she wondered and then chided herself for not using a condom. Shaking her head, she prayed she hadn't been infected with anything.

Back in the bedroom, Ortiz dressed hastily. "One good turn deserves another, right?" he asked in his accent that now bugged the hell out of Kai.

"What are you talking about?"

"You know..." He grinned sheepishly.

"No I don't," she insisted, but began to slowly get the picture and definitely didn't like what she saw. "Are you hinting for some type of payment?"

"I figured that was understood. Ain't nothing free in this world...you know that. Right, honey?"

Kai's breathing quickened; rage coursed through her. Unaware that she had bent down and picked up her boot, Kai looked surprised as she watched the boot zing toward Ortiz' head.

He ducked.

"Get your slimy ass out of my apartment before I pick up the phone and scream rape."

Ortiz walked to the door. With his hand on the knob, he said, "You played me, honey, but that's okay.

You made me think there was something in this for me, but..."

"Get out, you low-life scumbag," she screamed. "How dare you...," she began, but was silenced by the slamming door.

All she wanted was a good fuck. He should have been honored, yet he felt he had done her a service worthy of monetary compensation. Was he out of his fucking mind—or was she?

In dire need of a visit with her therapist, Kai picked up the phone to make an emergency appointment.

Using her shoulder to keep the receiver pressed against her ear, Kai twirled her hair nervously with one hand and with the other, she reached inside the nightstand drawer and groped around for the bottle of quickly dwindling blue pills.

"This is Kai Montgomery," she whimpered to the receptionist. "I'm having a crisis and I need an appointment as soon as possible."

Her migraine began the moment the piece of hair she'd been twirling separated from her scalp.

Chapter Seventeen

"Phone call, Terelle," said the distorted voice over the intercom.

"I'll be back in a few minutes, Miss Sally," she said to the elderly woman whose hair she was combing. She didn't expect a coherent response. The woman, blissfully unaware of the world around her, continued to mumble nonsensically.

Expecting a call from Marquise, Terelle dashed to the pay phone down the hall.

"Hello."

"Good news, babe," Marquise said.

A tremor of anticipation went through Terelle's body. "What?"

"I told my P.O. I had a job lined up, so he's gonna pull some strings to git this shit cut off my ankle in a coupla days."

"A couple of days? For real, Marquise?"

"Would I lie about my freedom?"

"Well, don't you have to show some type of proof of employment?"

"Look, I'll deal with that when the time comes. Right now I'm focused on gittin' lit."

"You're kidding? I know you're not about to smoke weed!"

"They won't be checkin' my piss no time soon. Dante is on his way over now—he's gonna front me a half-pound 'til I git back on my feet."

Terelle was speechless. Her head was spinning—she felt faint. Was she hearing Marquise correctly? Did he say he was planning to not only smoke weed, but also sell it?

"A half-pound?" she asked when she finally found her voice. "Marquise, have you lost your mind? What do plan on doing with that much weed? Please don't tell me you're thinking about hustlin' again?"

"Yo!" he cut in. "We shouldn't be discussin' this over the phone. I'll see you when you git home."

Marquise hung up. Terelle listened to the dial tone for a few seconds and then moved uncertainly back to Miss Sally's room.

The rest of the day was a blur. When she got into the elevator to go home, she was so deep in thought, she didn't notice Mr. Hicks, the head of the Housekeeping Department.

"How are you, Terelle," he said warmly. He was always nice to Terelle. She suspected he had a crush, but he'd never said anything out of the way.

"Hi, Mr. Hicks. I'm okay. How are you?"

Mr. Hicks shook his head. "You know how it is around here. People say they need a job, and then after we hire them, they start calling out. We have to write them up, suspend them...and inevitably, we have to fire irresponsible employees. I heard the Health Department is coming in tomorrow and I just don't have enough staff to get all the work done around here," Mr. Hicks said, wearily pressing his wrist upon his brow.

"There's an opening in Housekeeping?" she asked coolly, trying to downplay her interest.

"Two openings," he said, shaking his head woefully.

"Mr. Hicks, my fiancé really needs a job..."

"Isn't your boyfriend in..." His voice trailed off. He knitted his brows in thought.

"My fiancé," she said, correcting him. "Yes, Marquise was in jail."

Terelle dropped her gaze, then forced herself to look up.

"But he's done his time. He's on house arrest and his probation officer says he can get released early if he has a job lined up..."

"Listen, I might be able to help you. The City is in the final stages of implementing a program to train and hire former inmates. Plant Operations and Housekeeping plan to design a pilot program. I can't say how long this will take. But, why don't you stop by to see me tomorrow; I'll make some calls to see where things stand."

Terelle thanked Mr. Hicks and actually gave him a hug, which caused the man to blush.

"Don't thank me yet. I don't know how this is going to turn out," Mr. Hicks said.

"I'm just happy you're willing to help us," Terelle said as she stepped off the elevator.

She breezed over to the time clock, swiped her ID badge with visions of an extra paycheck brought into the home by her hardworking, and gainfully employed man.

As far as she was concerned, Marquise was already hired!

Chapter Eighteen

The experience with Ortiz had been jolting. A reminder that despite her beauty, class and family wealth, someone would always see through her—see the flawed and tarnished reality of who she really was. The kids at school knew: *Why does Kai look different? Shh! Her real parents didn't want her, and so Dr. & Mrs. Montgomery were kind enough to adopt her.* Kenneth found out: *You're so beautifully packaged, who would have guessed you're psychotic?* And now Ortiz! A fucking Hispanic janitor had the audacity to expect her to pay for sex.

Kai needed time out. Time to lick her wounds. Her therapist advised her to check herself into Spring Haven, a pricey mental health facility.

Her father would have to concoct an acceptable lie for her employer. Kai had to move out of her residence because the memory of her encounter with Ortiz was entirely too painful. Therefore, her father would also have to handle the unpleasant task of breaking her lease and make arrangements for her to move. Hopefully daddy dear would see fit to place his loving daughter in a more expensive building—one that overlooked calming water as well as a sweeping view of the city's skyline.

✿✿✿

Aside from providing nurses who dispensed pills that made her forget there was no reason for her existence, Spring Haven was a joke. She saw the house psychiatrist every few days and his only interest was in finding out if she wanted him to switch her Xanax to Klonopin, stating that Klonopin had longer-lasting effects. No thanks; Kai loved her 10 mg. Xanies.

The social worker visited Kai's room to discuss the outpatient care Kai would receive after she left the facility. At their first meeting, one glance at the woman's cheap shoes with run-down heels informed Kai that this social worker was in no position to help her. Kai promised to have the woman fired if she ever bothered her again.

There were no real therapy sessions. The groups were ran by mental health technicians—total imbeciles who possibly didn't even possess a GED, so Kai stayed in her room munching on the granola bars she kept hidden in a secret compartment inside her purse (she didn't dare eat the food they served crazy people) and waiting for the next medication pass.

When her mind was clear, she cheered herself up by

thinking about her college years. That had been a glorious time. On campus, far away from her lily-white, privileged community, she was viewed as beautiful—exotic. Not an oddball whose appearance had to be explained. Hungry for attention, she had taken advantage of her new identity and status, allowing both men and women to share her bed. It was fun, the power she had over those blithering fools. They had no idea that despite her father's wealth and social status, she was perceived in her hometown as someone to be pitied—a poor little black girl who was given a handout by the kind and liberal Montgomerys. No one knew and her father would never admit that Kai was his own flesh and blood. And if she was as crazy as her parents thought her to be, they had only themselves to blame.

Most nights she drifted off to sleep in the midst of her favorite fantasy. A fantasy so dark she'd never shared it with anyone, not even her therapist. She loved to imagine herself hunting down and capturing her birth mother—the person she believed was most responsible for her fucked-up life. Kai was emotionally scarred, and those scars were the result of a lifetime of emotional torture. Thus, she'd torture her mother—physically. She'd burn her nipples with lit matches, use a razor blade to play tic-tac-toe on the woman's fat Negroid ass, pull out her fingernails with pliers, and stick a hot-ass curling iron up her putrid pussy hole. Then she'd laugh at the black whore as she made one lame and desperate excuse after another for abandoning her child and leaving her with a white man who was too ashamed of her to even claim her as his own.

An eye for an eye.

It gave Kai shivers of delicious pleasure to imagine herself finally putting the bitch out of her misery. After hearing enough of her lies, she'd carefully aim a gun, then gleefully pull the trigger and watch the blood spurt right between her mother's eyes.

On that note, the pills having taken effect, Kai drifted off into a peaceful sleep.

Chapter Nineteen

The bedroom door was closed but the unmistakable scent of marijuana filled the air. Terelle sighed, opened the door and looked disgustedly at the large marijuana buds that filled the lid of a Timberland box. Marquise sat on the rumpled bed puffing on a blunt. He set it in an ashtray and began to break up the buds, carefully taking out the twigs and throwing them inside a wastebasket beside the bed. Inside the Timberland box were more buds, small plastic bags and two unopened blunts. Marquise didn't utter a sound; he didn't even turn his head in Terelle's direction. He was in a zone, his face as serious as a surgeon performing a risky operation, as he diligently continued to bag up weed. His defiant silence spoke volumes: *I told you what was up, so just kill whatever noise you're about to make.*

Feeling helpless to stop Marquise from this downward spiral that was certain to send him back to jail, Terelle shut the door and went into the living room. She came out of her coat, flung it on the futon and flopped down beside it. Perhaps sitting still would provide inspiration. She needed to come up with the right words to make

Marquise realize he was jeopardizing his freedom—their future together. She tried to calm down, but kept hearing Saleema say, "*Girl, all that shit Marquise is talkin' ain't nothin' but jailhouse promises.*"

Marquise had broken their agreement. Painfully aware that Saleema was right, Terelle wept softly; her hands covered her face.

A moment later, Marquise crept up behind her. She felt his hand on her shoulder. The gentleness of his touch caused Terelle to sob. Shoulder-shaking, wracking sobs. She wondered how someone so gentle and caring could also be so reckless and irresponsible?

"Terelle?" He stroked her hair. "It's gonna be aiight." Marquise sat down, removed her hands from her tear-stained face and entwined her fingers in his.

"I know you're disappointed. You think I'm about to fuck up again. But you're wrong. I got this...I know what I'm doin'."

He lifted her chin with his thumb. She turned away from him, lowered her gaze and stared unseeingly at the floor.

Terelle took a deep breath, and looked up at Marquise. "I gotta go pick up Keeta from day care. I don't want her to smell weed or be around your drug paraphernalia. Think you'll be finished when we get back?"

"Damn, you act like I'm sellin' crack or somethin'. Ain't nothin' wrong with weed. It don't destroy nobody's life. Doctors prescribe this shit to heal people."

"Justify it anyway you want, Marquise," she said, glaring at him. "It's illegal and you can do time over it and doin' time is something you said you'd never do again." Terelle wiped her moist eyes. "I can't believe you're actually smokin' a blunt when you know you're gonna have to take a urine test when you visit your P.O."

"Yo, Terelle, tighten up. Cut this shit out," he said with a grimace and an angry tone. "First of all, I was just testin' the product, had to see what it was hittin' for. It'll be outta my system by the time I see my P.O. I promise...I won't be gittin' high no more."

Terelle stood up. "Why should I believe your promises when you break every promise you've ever made?"

Marquise nervously bit his lip. "I know my track record is fucked up, but babe...You gotta understand. I gotta do somethin' to put some money in my pocket. I can't sit around here day after day askin' you to give me money for cigarettes and every other little thing I need. How you think I feel when I have to ask you for money all the time? "

"I know you don't like it, but that's the way it is for now," Terelle said apologetically.

"Don't *like* it? I hate it! I'm used to havin' my own. I feel like shit havin' to ask you to buy me a pack of cigarettes."

"That's not my fault, Marquise. I'm doing the best I can. I give you everything I can. I do without—I don't buy shit for myself, just so I can keep us afloat. I have to pay Keeta's day care bill, pay that high-ass cable bill with all them premium channels so you won't get bored at home all day. I spend a fortune on junk food—pizzas, cheese steaks, Chinese food...whatever you're in the mood for. And I do it with a smile. Never have I made you feel like you were getting on my nerves. Because you're not. I'm so happy to have you home, I'd do anything to keep you happy."

She paused in thought, then continued, "Damn, Quise...do you realize that as bad as we could use the money, I don't even accept overtime anymore because I know you'll be home by yourself...bored and lonely."

"If I was doin' what I'm supposed to be doin', there wouldn't be no need for you to work no damn overtime," Marquise replied.

He started breathing hard, walking back and forth... making Terelle nervous. Then he went to the kitchen, poured some juice, but instead of drinking it, he threw the plastic tumbler followed by the container of orange juice against the wall.

It sounded like an explosion; Terelle jumped and jerked her head toward the kitchen.

Orange juice splattered the walls, the counter tops, and the floor. Marquise was working himself up into a rage—trying to go to that place where neither she nor anyone else could reach him.

"Quise!" she yelled. "Calm down."

"Calm down?" he asked, storming into the living

room, his tee shirt stained with orange juice. "How the fuck can I calm down when I'm tired of spongin' off you...taking food outta my baby girl's mouth?"

Terelle could see the bulging veins in his neck.

"I ain't tryin' to make no major moves. I just wanna be able to help out so I can feel like a man again," he roared. "Damn, this shit is so fucked up!" He punched the wall, making a fist-sized dent.

But Terelle refused to be intimidated. She'd hear him out, but she was not going to compromise her principles.

"You know what kinda man I am," he said, continuing his tirade. "How long do you think I can just sit still and watch you go to work to take care of me? And on the real...I can't stand thinkin' 'bout you cleanin' and wipin' them old people's asses. Fuck that, Terelle. The only person you supposed to be takin' care of like that is our daughter." Woefully, he cupped his head with both hands.

"I don't have the trainin' to do anything else. But now that you're home, I plan on taking some classes," Terelle said, speaking softly and hoping she sounded reasonable. "It only takes eighteen months to become a licensed practical nurse. The job will pay the tuition, but the classes are full-time. I can't go to school if there's no paycheck coming through."

"That's what I'm sayin'. If you wanna go to school, you should be able to. If I was handlin' my business the way I'm supposed to, you could just sit home...relax and do...you know, whatever. You been carryin' my weight long enough."

Terelle's face crumpled in confusion. "Why would you risk getting back into that life when you'll be off house arrest in a couple days? Don't you think you should be thinking about working a real job?"

"Who's gonna hire me? Nobody."

"I spoke to the Housekeeping supervisor—Mr. Hicks and he might have an opening for you. And that department gets lots of overtime," she said brightly. "With both us bringing home a regular paycheck... before you know it we'll have a car, a house, a little somethin' in the bank...and we'll ride off into the sunset," she said with a chuckle she didn't feel. She hoped Marquise would listen to the voice of reason.

"Get serious. Like I said, ain't nobody gonna hire my black ass. And if the best offer is to clean up that stinkin' nursing home, you can forget it. I ain't tryin' to disrespect myself like that."

Terelle was growing weary of this "poor Marquise" routine; she could feel herself becoming angry. "Do you think it's honorable to be out there huggin' the block again? You wanna be out there 'til the wee hours—again—getting stuck up, dodging the police, having your money come up short? Do you want me goin' off over the phone numbers I'm surely gonna find in your pockets—in the cell phone you're bound to acquire as soon as you get back out there? I'm a lot wiser than I was before, Marquise, and you won't be able to convince me that every female name attached to a phone number is just a customer."

"Here you go," he said, laughing and shaking his head. "What did I put on your finger? What else I gotta do—tattoo your name on my forehead?" Terelle laughed despite herself. "Can't nobody come between us."

"Sounds good right now, but once you're out there… anything goes. And another thing, why do you wanna disrespect our people by selling drugs and whatnot all out in front of their homes—in front of their children?"

Marquise smiled and shook his head condescendingly. "You don't understand, Terelle. I'm not goin' back out there like that. I'm twenty-three years old. Too old for that shit. I ain't standin' around outside like a sucker. Not no more."

"So what are you talking about?" She felt relief wash over her.

"I plan to deal with weight—and I'm only selling weed. I refuse to fuck wit nics and dimes."

"So, why are you bagging up those dime bags?" she asked, deflated.

"Babe, I'm on house arrest. This is the best I can do right now. My young buck Nazeer is gonna move this shit for me. I only have to give Nazeer a dub off every hundred he sells. And check it, Dante is only chargin' me three seventy-five for that half-pound," Marquise said, beaming at Terelle.

"So, once you deduct the three seventy-five from the money you make after paying Nazeer, you're not gonna have very much for yourself." Terelle sucked her teeth. "It doesn't seem worth it to me."

"That's just to git started," he explained. "Somethin' to put some change in my pocket for now. But once I'm out there...Shit, once I'm back out there, the shit is on! I got a connection with this Jamaican brotha—he's gonna set me up. He gotta little grocery store, a take-out restaurant and all kinds of shit..."

"Good for him," she said sarcastically. "You better believe he's selling more than weed 'cause weed money don't come fast, Marquise," Terelle said forcibly. "You know that. You're gonna get frustrated and it's only a matter of time before you start handlin' coke again."

"Naw, babe. I learnt my lesson; I ain't sellin' no coke; I promise."

"Yo, check this!" he added. "The Jamaican dude got a sweet hook-up. He don't even talk to mufuckas on the phone. You call his cell, leave a message...If you want an ounce, you tell 'em you wanna git a onion... he got codes for everything. He'll fill your order but he has to meet you at a different location every time. He calls his setup, The Delivery Company," Marquise said, looking hopeful that he had swayed Terelle to his way of thinking.

In fact, he looked so hopeful, Terelle thought it safe to bring him back to reality. "You should see yourself," she said, laughing, depending on her laughter to take him off guard. "You're all hyped...just itchin' to get back into the game, aren't you?"

"True dat," he admitted. "But it won't be the same. It'll be different this time."

"Listen, Marquise. Things will never be different. You and nobody else is ever gonna win the game."

Marquise looked stunned. He'd obviously thought he'd persuaded Terelle to trust his judgment.

Terelle continued to hit him with her words. "As much as I love you, Marquise...and you know I'd kill for you. But after all I've been through, I can't sit back and let you take us all down with this stupid small-time hustling."

"How you figure I'm gonna take us down," he asked, his voice sounding both peeved and curious.

"You made a promise to me and you're gonna stick to it." She twisted her engagement ring for effect. "This ring means the world to me," Terelle said softly. "But I'll give it back," she announced in a serious tone and wearing a serious expression. "It's me and Keeta... or drugs. You make the choice."

Terelle grabbed her coat and handbag. "I'm going to get our daughter." She nodded to the kitchen phone. "Call Dante and tell him to come get his shit. For the sake of our family, I hope you get rid of it before I get back."

Terelle left, closing the door softly behind her. She

meant every word she'd just spoken and Marquise knew it. She'd risk losing the only man she had ever, could ever love before she'd go back to living the hellish existence she'd lived before.

✿✿✿

Night had fallen when Terelle returned home with Markeeta. The darkened apartment did not bode well. Also troubling to Terelle was the silence. Had Marquise packed up his drugs and fled? With a sense of dread, and scarcely able to breathe, she clicked on the kitchen light and was surprised to find the room was spotless—no traces of orange juice anywhere.

The steady green light of the house arrest monitor reassured her that Marquise was in range—he was home.

"Daddy," Markeeta called, breaking the silence as she toddled away from her mother.

Terelle followed her daughter to the bedroom. The door was open. The light from the kitchen illuminated the room and cast an angelic glow upon Marquise. The temper he'd displayed earlier followed by the thorough cleaning he'd done in the kitchen must have taken an enormous toll for Marquise appeared comatose. He was in a state of slumber so deep, he didn't respond to Markeeta's calls.

"Daddy," Markeeta said again, this time in a softer voice.

"Shh, Keeta. Daddy's asleep; be quiet," Terelle whispered as she stood in the doorframe, holding her daughter's hand.

"Daddy go night-night," Markeeta informed her mother, whispering also.

Terelle did a quick scan of the bedroom and was relieved when she spotted the Timberland box—empty.

Their agreement that he'd leave the drug game alone had been non-negotiable, yet he'd expected Terelle to accept his irrational reasoning and cave in. She'd stood her ground. Giving Marquise an ultimatum was not her nature, but he'd left her little choice.

Terelle gazed at her man—gave a faint smile and closed the door.

Chapter Twenty

Kai hated leaving the seclusion of her room, but a sudden and powerful hunger pang drove her out into the corridor. Wearing a silk brocade robe and satin slippers, she set out to find a nurse or anyone who could point her in the direction of food.

A female patient who was a ghastly pale and wore a hideous brown flannel robe looked lost and fretful as she wandered the hallway. Kai was revolted by the sight of her. She looked around hoping to solicit the information she needed from someone sane, but there was no one else around.

"Is breakfast served on the floor?" Kai asked curtly.

"No, we eat in the cafeteria," the pale woman replied eagerly. "It's on the ground floor."

"Oh," Kai said. And without so much as a thank-you, she turned away from the woman and glided toward the elevator.

"You can't go alone," the woman called out.

Kai swirled around. "Why not?"

"You have to wait for Reece."

"Who's Reece?"

"He's the morning coordinator," she said, twisting her hands nervously and Kai found herself moving away from the obvious lunatic.

"My name's Elana," she added quickly.

"Nice name," Kai muttered without giving her own name. She wasn't revealing anything about herself to this nut. "Well, where the hell is Reece?"

"He already took a group down. You'll have to wait until he comes for the next group."

"Oh really? Well, I don't think so. I'm famished... and I don't need an escort to get something to eat."

"He should be back soon." Elana looked at the clock. "We could go down together." She gnawed on a fingernail awaiting Kai's response.

Kai groaned and stepped into the elevator.

"We're not allowed to go anywhere alone," Elana said, looking frantic and sounding seriously alarmed. "We have to follow the rules."

Kai waved her hand dismissively. As the elevator doors slowly closed, she could see Elana's woebegone expression. The woman looked like she expected the authorities to suddenly appear and haul her and Kai off to jail.

A mixture of wonderful aromas wafted out when Kai opened the cafeteria door. She happily picked up a tray, consulted the posted menu, and got in line. To her dismay, she discovered she was standing behind a noisy pack of psychos. These people had glinting, demented eyes that roamed everywhere. Some mumbled nonsensically and others laughed aloud for no apparent reason. They looked and acted more insane than the patients on her own floor did. Disgusted, she wanted to turn right around and leave, but hunger held her there.

From her peripheral vision, she could see the familiar faces of the loonies from her mental unit. They were seated together at a table, waving and trying to catch her attention. Squinting up at the menu, pretending to be in deep concentration, she ignored them.

She sensed someone approaching and figuring it to be one of the nut cases, Kai bristled and prepared to be extremely impolite.

"Hello. You're Kai, right?" said a masculine voice.

With her face set in a scowl, Kai jerked around. Her expression softened when she discovered the voice belonged to a young man with exceptional good looks. His hair was styled in a platinum crew cut; he had a strong chin, tanned skin despite the season, sensual full lips, and green eyes that sparkled in devilish amusement. He looked to be around Kai's age and he most definitely was not a patient.

Kai tossed her hair and smiled radiantly.

"I'm Reece." He smiled confidently and extended his hand.

Adrenaline pumped as she offered her hand and continued to look him over. A silver hoop, which dangled from his right ear, suggested an adventurous spirit. Broad-shouldered with a V-shaped waist, his shirt was loosely tucked inside baggy pleated pants. Reece was one hot white boy! He looked like he should have been traveling with a rock band instead of schlepping around with a group of mental patients.

"Hello, Reece." Kai's voice was soft and inviting as she schemed on getting Reece into her bed—today.

"Would you care to join us after you get your food?" He nodded toward the table. "You really shouldn't travel alone."

She made a big show of looking around, her eyes shifting from the group at the table to the patients in line in front of her.

"I guess you're right about that," she said, turning toward Reece. "I'm here for rest and relaxation. I had no idea this place would be overrun with the criminally insane."

"I wouldn't go that far," Reece replied with a chuckle.

"No? Well, that's how it appears." She glanced at the line of waiting patients once more, then shivered dramatically. "Look, forget these lunatics. I'd like to be alone with you," Kai said brazenly. She paused to look him up and down. "Is that allowed?" There was no time to be coy. She wanted him to know exactly what she wanted.

A hint of mischief danced in his green eyes, then he laughed as if Kai had cracked a hilarious joke. And that laughter, as noncommittal as it sounded, told Kai that Reece was interested, but he was buying time—trying to figure out a way to accept her offer without appearing too eager.

"Hmm," she said, focusing on the menu again. "What did you have?" she asked Reece.

"Oh, I didn't eat. It's not my lunch hour; I'm on the clock," he said cheerfully, then studied the menu himself. "The western omelet looks good."

"Okay, that's what I'll have for breakfast. For lunch... Hmm, I think I'll skip what's on the menu. I'd rather spend that time tasting you," she said with an innocent expression while knowing full well the shock value of her words.

When Reece, startled by her shameless proposal, choked and bent over in a coughing bout, Kai knew she had him. Men! Their dicks would be the death of them.

"I'll have the omelet and orange juice," Kai said to the server.

"You okay?" she asked, turning her attention back to Reece.

He nodded, wiping his eyes with the back of his hand.

"So...are we on for lunch?" Kai wanted to know.

"Sure...why not?" he said casually.

But his nonchalant expression and tone didn't fool Kai. Reece was excited and nervous at once. And his discomfort emboldened her.

"What time is your lunch break?"

"Noon. But I can't...uh...just walk into your room, you know. Um...maybe we could meet somewhere private?"

"Certainly. Where do you suggest?"

As Reece wrinkled his brow in thought, the server handed Kai the omelet on a large plate along with a glass of orange juice. She moved down the roped-in aisle, and Reece hurried behind her as she picked up a plastic fork and knife and a few napkins. She carefully arranged the items on her tray.

"I'm going to eat in my room. Is that okay with you?"

"Not a problem. But if anyone asks, you didn't get permission from me." He winked flirtatiously.

She was glad his confidence had returned for he was surely going to need every bit of it.

"I'll see you upstairs. Maybe I'll even attend your little therapy session," she said teasingly. Then Kai turned and walked toward the door.

"Wait a minute," Reece called out.

Kai stopped; she smiled inside. The promise of pussy had Reece completely unglued. And his eagerness to participate was all the therapy she needed. She'd be checking out of Spring Haven tomorrow if Reece turned out to be as good a fuck as she hoped he'd be.

"Yes?" she asked, tilting her head to one side.

"I have an idea."

"I'm all ears."

"My group ends at eleven-thirty. There's uh, a closet...

I mean the utility room at the end of the hall on your floor—near the windows. You can pretend like you're looking out the window, then..."

"You want to fuck me in a closet?"

Reece look troubled. "No, it's not a closet…it's like a storage room. I can get the key from the cleaning guy."

"I'm glad you know people in high places," she said with a deadpan expression.

"I'm sorry. But off the top of my head, I just can't think of…"

"I'm kidding," she said with a convincing smile. "A closet is fine. Kinky, actually. I'll be there!" She swirled and left the cafeteria.

✿✿✿

She could see Reece's reflection in the window; she could hear him whistling as he approached. He looked around, then stealthily slipped inside the closet. Kai waited a full five minutes before making her move, then she too eased open the closet door.

The room was dark and smelled of cleaning agents. Kai immediately heard Reece locking the door behind her and before her eyes could adjust to the darkness, he was all over her. He kissed her passionately, sliding his tongue into her mouth, biting her neck—licking and moaning into her ear while dry humping her like a sex-starved adolescent.

"Are we in a rush?" she whispered.

"Yeah...I mean no," Reece said, breathing hard.

"Then slow down."

"Sorry," he murmured as he began to unbutton her robe. His fingers trembled and she found herself losing respect for him.

Annoyed, Kai pushed his fingers away and calmly unbuttoned the robe. Beneath it, she wore a black lacy thong. No bra. She came out of the robe and flung it into the darkness, unaware and uncaring that it had landed inside an uncovered trash container.

Looking momentarily confused and not knowing where to begin, Reece groped her bare tits, kissed them sloppily, then his hungry hands darted to the elastic band of her thong, pulling—trying to rip the delicate material away from her body.

Kai frowned. She wasn't having fun. Reece was not arousing her; he was not the skillful lover she'd anticipated.

"Lick my pussy," she demanded in a breathy voice. Cunnilingus was a surefire way to get her juices flowing.

He hesitated, then dropped to his knees. The thong was hanging by a thread; she pulled it to the side, smoothing his hair as she guided his head to her crotch. And with a tenderness he'd not demonstrated earlier, he parted her labial lips; his tongue slowly snaked its way inside her.

Kai's body went limp. Reece was good—too good.

She had to steady herself by gripping the sink behind her. Feeling her passion building, but not wanting to cum just yet, she pushed his forehead, stopping him suddenly.

Reece looked up, confused.

"Put me on the sink." She yanked the torn thong and tossed it on the floor.

Without a question, he lifted her easily onto the edge of the sink.

"Now fuck me," she commanded as her legs spread wide.

Reece stood up. "I don't have a condom," he said mournfully.

"The hell with a condom," she hissed.

In an instant, he unzipped his fly.

Kai scooted forward holding onto his shoulders. "Hurry up," she moaned. "Put it in."

Reece was panting as he pushed his stiffness into her dripping wetness, thrusting deeply. *Oh shit*, she thought to herself, *I can't believe this fucking bastard is hitting my G-spot!*" Involuntarily, she tightened her vaginal muscles around his dick and at that moment Reece exploded. Body spasms, guttural groaning, facial contortions…the whole nine.

"No, you didn't!" Kai spat in disgust. "I can't believe you came already."

Reece wore a helpless puppy-dog expression as he clung to her, his body still convulsing as he deposited the last drop of semen.

"How could you?" She poked him in the shoulder, angrily. "I wasn't ready, you asshole. Do you think I fucking came into this godforsaken closet just so you could get your shit off? Huh?" She poked him again—harder. When she opened her mouth to chastise him further, she was startled into silence by the sound of movement outside the closet door. Someone fitted a key into the lock and turned it. The door creaked open, filling the room with light.

Kai screeched.

Panicked, Reece swiftly pulled out. Losing his footing, he stumbled into Kai and knocked her off the sink.

Using the palm of her hand, Kai instinctively tried to break her fall. She could feel and hear the sickening crunch of breaking bones as her outstretched hand crashed into the concrete floor. Before she could even feel the searing pain, her face hit the floor; she was plummeted into instant unconsciousness.

The electrician had come to check the wiring in the room. He clicked on the light and stared in disbelief at the scene before him: Kai was face down on the floor, butt naked. Her expensive robe was in the trash; her thong ripped and discarded lay inches from her body.

And Reece, caught with his pants down, started yelling, "It was consensual! I swear to God, it's not what it looks like!"

Pandemonium followed. The electrician called for help as Reece, protesting loudly and hysterically, pulled up his pants.

A stampede of pounding footsteps could be heard. Stunned staff members as well as patients rushed into the utility room.

The electrician pointed to Kai. There were gasps and gaping mouths as they all gawked at a naked and seemingly badly beaten Kai.

Heads now turned toward the culprit—Reece! He was crying and denying everything despite the damning evidence.

The charge nurse turned Kai over. Blood covered her face. "Call 911," she shouted to no one in particular. "And call security." A cleaning lady ran to make the calls.

"Get a blanket, hurry!" the nurse barked at a befuddled intern.

Kai awakened to the bedlam, but lay very still beneath the blanket, pretending she was still knocked out. In her confused state, she had no idea what was going on. Stabbing pain jolted her into awareness, and she was able to establish what the commotion was all about as the confusion of panicking voices finally began to make sense.

According to the buzz that swirled around her, an employee had brutally raped and beat a patient in a mental hospital—her! Now that was some damn good fucking luck. The hell with waiting for her inheritance; Reece and Spring Haven were going to pay dearly for her pain and suffering.

"Help...somebody please help me," she whimpered.

"Kai! Can you hear me, Kai?" asked the charge nurse.

Kai responded with a groan. The pain in her wrist was severe.

"What happened, Miss Montgomery?" The nurse leaned close to Kai's mouth.

"He raped me," she said, her voice barely audible.

"Who did?"

"Reece raped me. I...I think he broke my wrist."

"You lying bitch." Reece rushed toward Kai but was tackled and held down by the beefy security guard who'd arrived at that precise moment.

Chapter Twenty-One

"I hope you don't think I'm gonna be making deliveries every time you decide to make something fancy for your man," Saleema said playfully as she tossed the Acme bag containing a pound of Italian sausage.

"My fiancé," Terelle corrected and flashed her ring.

"My bad." Saleema lifted the lid of the biggest pot on the stove. "Mmm, it smells delicious. What's it called again?"

"Shrimp Jambalaya."

"So why do you need the sausages?"

"Hell if I know. The recipe called for it and I didn't want to leave anything out."

"Can I taste it?"

"It's spicy, but go ahead…help yourself."

Saleema scooped up a heaping tablespoon of jambalaya. "Damn, girl. You ain't playin'; this grub is bangin'! I see you're seriously tryin' to speed up the wedding date. They say food is the way to a man's heart."

"I already have Marquise's heart. I'm just trying to show my baby some love because this is his first day on a real job. Ever."

"Uh-huh." Saleema studied her French manicured nails. "Marquise needs to be showin' me some love since I'm the one who fucked the brains outta his new boss."

Terelle looked around apprehensively, as if the walls had ears. "Please don't ever let Marquise hear you say that; he'd be so hurt if he found out how he got hired so fast."

"I know whassup; you ain't gotta tell me." Saleema looked offended.

"I know you do. I just don't wanna take any chances because I let Quise believe Mr. Hicks was really impressed..."

"Drop it, Terelle. I *said* I know whassup."

"So why you complainin'—Mr. Hicks paid you, didn't he?"

"I ain't complainin', just reminding you that I'm not pressed for customers and I damn sure didn't need that little bit of dough Mr. Hicks paid me. That cheap bastard only wanted to give me a bean." Saleema snorted. "Now, what's a hundred dollars gonna do for me? I told 'em two hundred is my lowest rate. Had to threaten to leave his naked ass in the hotel room before he gave up the rest of my cheddar." Saleema paused, shaking her head at the memory of the event. "And I put myself through all that aggravation just for you. I fucked Mr. Hicks so you could stop worrying about Marquise going back to jail—now tell me if I ain't the best fuckin' friend in the whole wide world?"

"You da bomb and you know it," Terelle said teasingly while feeling like a hypocrite for asking Saleema to turn a trick on her behalf. "I wouldn't have even asked you to do that if I wasn't desperate," she explained. "Mr. Hicks promised to give Marquise the job, but the paperwork for the ex-inmate-training program was takin' too long."

"I know! You told me a thousand times. I just want to set the record straight because I could have been out with one of my white clients makin' ten times what that cheap dickhead paid me."

Saleema was exaggerating the amount she earned from her other clients, but Terelle let it slide. No point in debating the amount Saleema could have made. The fact that her friend had done her a major favor was the only important matter.

"I owe you big time," Terelle stated, bending over to hug her friend.

"So start paying up. Hurry up and do something with those sausages. Fix me a real plate—I'm starving."

Terelle began slicing the sausage and placing the bite-sized pieces in a pan of sizzling oil. She stood at the stove, her back to Saleema. "There's something I have to tell you."

"What?"

Terelle turned to face Saleema. "My mom popped over here and started a bunch of shit right after Quise got out of jail."

"Get out! You never told me that."

"I know. It was a mess. I couldn't talk about it."

"What happened?"

"Long story short...she left that rehab place and wanted to stay here..."

"That's messed up. Miss Cassy oughtta know that ain't cool."

"But that ain't the worse part of the story."

Saleema cocked her head and stared at Terelle with great interest.

"When she couldn't get her way, when I refused to let her stay here..." Terelle smiled sadly. "My mother accused Quise of something so rank; I can't even get the words out."

Saleema lifted a brow. Terelle studied the floor, grimacing as she relived the horrible experience.

"Girl, what happened? What did your mother say?"

Terelle took a deep breath. "My mother said Quise made her go down on him in exchange for a hit when he was hustlin'."

Saleema was silent.

"Say something!" Terelle demanded.

"What the hell do you want me to say?"

"Something—anything. What's your opinion?"

"You don't want my opinion," Saleema snapped. "Now whassup with the grub?"

Terelle's eyes pooled with tears. "Quise wouldn't do no shit like that," she said sobbing. "Not with my mother. I can't understand why my own mother would try to hurt me like that?"

Saleema stood up and embraced Terelle. "I want to say something to make you feel better. But I honestly don't know what to say. When it comes to sex, I don't put nothin' past men. I think they're all perverted sleaze bags."

"Okay," Terelle said, pulling away from Saleema and wiping her eyes. "I know Marquise hasn't always been faithful. And with that lifestyle he was into…the temptation was always there. But he wouldn't…Not with *my* mother!" Terelle shook her head emphatically. "No way."

"You're probably right. Is your mom smokin' again?"

"I don't know. I couldn't tell because she was looking really bad. She'd had a fight with some dude she was stayin' with. He punched her in the face—gave her a black eye."

Saleema shook her head.

Terelle shook her head, too. "Marquise thinks she's getting high again. And she probably is because I haven't heard from her since that night."

"Well…there's your explanation."

Terelle looked hopeful.

"You know how them crack addicts act when they start schitzin'…they'll say and do anything. Miss Cassy is famous for causing a commotion when she's tryin' to get high."

"That's so true," Terelle sadly agreed. "I don't know why I even let her in here."

"You let her in because she's your mother."

"Yeah, but she brings too much drama. I can't deal

with her bullshit anymore." Terelle prepared Saleema's plate and placed it on the table.

"Damn, girl. Where's the camera? This looks pretty enough to be in a gourmet magazine."

Terelle beamed proudly and watched Saleema dig in. "How's it taste?"

"Mmm, it's bangin'. You get high chef points for this meal."

Terelle checked the clock. Marquise would be home with Markeeta in another hour. She had scented candles, a congratulatory card, and some new lingerie to celebrate his first day on the job.

After Saleema finished eating, Terelle hustled her to the door. "Hate to rush you, girl. But I gotta jump in the shower and get myself together before Quise gets home."

"Ain't no thing...it's all gravy...I was leaving anyway," Saleema said. She sounded slightly hurt and that bothered Terelle.

Oh well, she'd figure out a way to make it up to her friend later.

Chapter Twenty-Two

Curled lazily on the big cushy sofa in her spacious sunlit living room of her new waterfront condo, Kai gazed happily at the million-dollar cast that covered her hand, wrist and part of her arm. Well…not quite a million. But, thanks to her escapade with Reece, she was no longer at the mercy of her miserly, controlling parents; she was now an independently wealthy woman.

Reece had been slapped with a five-year sentence for assault and rape. Kai snickered, naughtily amused by the thought of that pretty boy getting reamed in prison. Sure, she'd lied on Reece, but it served him right for being such an abominably bad fuck!

In a few days, the cast would be removed, then she'd be able to easily reach inside her purse to start spending some of the money she'd been awarded in her negligence lawsuit against Spring Haven.

According to the attorney who'd represented her, Spring Haven had made a promise upon admission that Kai would receive professional care and respite. Instead, he declared, she'd been left in care of a brutal, sex-crazed rapist. Out for blood, Kai's attorney demanded and was certain he could get five million dollars—perhaps more. He cautioned that the litigation could drag on for years, but advised Kai to allow the case to go to trial.

Wanting to settle quickly and quietly, Spring Haven offered close to a million dollars and against the advice of her attorney, Kai eagerly accepted. The hell with waiting to go to trial; she needed the money NOW!

With the security of a healthy bank account, she should have been able to quit her stupid job and relax while she waited for her inheritance, but unfortunately her racist paternal grandmother had prevented that luxury. Fearing Kai had the propensity to become a slacker due to the black blood running through her veins, the grandmother, who died when Kai was a toddler, had stipulated in her will that Kai remain gainfully employed in a meaningful profession until her twenty-fifth birthday. How ridiculous!

There was a bright side, however. Keeping tabs on Kenneth required close proximity, but she refused to toil for the pittance the nursing home paid her. She'd show up for work, but her focus would be on Kenneth—not the residents who bothered her constantly for trivial matter such as ordering their clothing, placing phone calls for those who could verbalize their desires, listening to their constant whining at the Resident's Council Meetings she was forced to facilitate, dispensing cigarettes, and passing out their fucking mail for crying out loud! No more. The administration could complain to her father until they turned blue; it simply didn't matter. She'd do as she pleased and that was emphatically that!

Kenneth still loved her, she was certain. His marriage was a joke and his new relationship with that Kente cloth-clad woman was absurd.

Sending the photo to his wife was insensitive, Kai admitted to herself, but she was hurt and offended—he should have understood that. Besides, it was time his wife found out about him and Kai. He should have been grateful for her assistance in trying to rid him of the worthless woman.

But, his male ego demanded that he handle his marital situation himself, Kai decided with a wan smile. In the future...once she and Kenneth were man and wife, she'd have to remind herself to allow him to believe he was running the show.

Buoyed by the notion of being married to Kenneth, Kai sprung up and meandered toward the window. With her good hand, she pulled back the drapes. The view of the river was spectacular; Kenneth was going to love it!

She had eight hours a day to work on him—to convince him that they belonged together. She felt confident that she could persuade him.

All she had to do was get him in bed. Once she worked

her magic on him in the bedroom, he'd have no choice but to acquiesce.

Standing at the window, feeling deliriously happy, she hugged herself as she imagined the enveloping warmth of having Kenneth's arms wrapped around her.

Feeling magnanimous, Kai decided she and Kenneth would allow his ex-wife to keep the house in Chestnut Hill. Kai preferred living in the city, but a beachfront residence would make an awesome second home.

She opened her laptop and pecked with one finger: *Kai Montgomery Harding*.

Her future name had such a nice ring.

Chapter Twenty-Three

Unable to sleep without Marquise in bed beside her, Terelle sat up and began clicking cable channels. Her gaze shifted from the TV to the clock on the bedside table.

She stared in dismay: 2:30 a.m. Late. But, then again it was early when compared to the hours he'd kept in his former life when he was out on his grind until the wee hours of the morning. Back then, it was normal for him to come home at the crack of dawn. It was a typical day in the 'hood for someone to tell her Quise had been seen in the company of another woman—on the creep—and the woman in question was usually someone whom Terelle considered a friend. There were times, like just before he got locked up, when days would pass without a word from him. Those were terrible times. Times she didn't even want to think about.

But that was back then. Before they were parents, before they'd begun to plan a life together. Things were different now.

Today was payday, Marquise's first. And with almost forty hours of overtime reflected in his paycheck, Marquise was in a celebratory mood and wanted to hang out with his friends for a few hours.

Or so he'd said.

A few hours had turned into eight. Where was he?

A pang went through her as she felt a stirring of suspicion. Was he out creepin'? Of course not, she answered herself, twisting her engagement ring reassuringly.

Something on TV caught her attention, briefly taking her troubled mind off Marquise. But unable to focus on the TV program for long, she shot another uneasy glance at the clock. Fifteen minutes had passed.

Now she was really worried. Had something happened to him? Gripped by fear, Terelle sat on the edge of the bed, unconsciously rocking back and forth as she massaged her temples.

The sudden sound of jangling keys caused her heart to leap for joy. Marquise was home! But instead of vaulting out of bed and running to the front door as her heart desired, Terelle grabbed the remote and pushed the off button, clicked off the light from the lamp bedside the bed, and dove under the covers.

"You sleep, babe?" Marquise whispered. Terelle didn't answer. He crept around the bedroom, opening and closing drawers quietly. He quickly peeled off his clothes and quietly padded to the bathroom.

The sound of running water in the bathtub prompted Terelle to sit upright. Marquise had taken a shower before he'd gone out, she recalled, so why was he taking another?

In an instant, it became painfully clear. Terelle's stomach knotted tightly. Marquise was washing away the scent of some slutty woman.

Was it someone he'd met that evening? Or one of the flirtatious heifers he and Terelle encountered in the mornings on their bus ride to work—or God forbid… was it someone from the job?

The moment he returned to the bedroom, Terelle clicked on the light. His expression of surprise would have seemed comical had Terelle not been so angry.

"Did you make sure you washed away all the evidence?"

There was silence as the accusation hung between them momentarily.

He tightened the towel around his waist. "What?" he asked finally. He had a dark brooding look.

"You heard me," she said in an icy tone.

The dark look transformed into a smile. "Yeah, I heard you, but I can't believe you trippin' like this." He laughed, but there was a nervous edge to the laughter.

"Is something funny?" Terelle could feel her left leg beginning to shake with rage.

Marquise bent over laughing. His laughter sounded so fake. "Look at you twitchin' and carryin' on. Damn, babe. You lettin' your imagination run wild."

"I asked you if you think this shit is funny?" She

sprang out of bed and pushed Marquise, knocking him off balance.

"Yo, stop playin' all the time," he said, and laughed again after the shock of having lost his footing wore off.

"*You* better stop playing with me," she exclaimed.

"Yo, sit your little ass down and chill." He let out a taunting laugh and before Terelle knew it she had thrown up her fists. As if possessed by the spirit of Joe Louis or some deceased heavyweight boxer, Terelle started throwing combinations: right-left, right-left, right-left to Marquise's arms, chest, and gut. She even got in a couple of kidney shots, which made him grimace and grunt in pain.

Restraining her in a bear-hug, he shoved Terelle onto the bed. Unconcerned that the towel had slipped off and fallen to the floor, Marquise straddled her, gripped her shoulders and shook her hard. "What's wrong witchu, Terelle? You gotta be crazy, puttin' your hands on me like that."

"Get off me, Marquise!" Terelle said through clenched teeth. She wriggled and bucked, trying to topple him over. But she couldn't budge the 230-pound man.

"You think you can put your hands on me any time you get ready? Huh? You think it's sweet like that?" His face, twisted in fury, was lowered so close to hers she could practically taste the toothpaste he'd just used to brush his teeth.

"Stop, Quise," she pleaded as she continued to squirm

and struggle beneath him. "You're gonna wake up Keeta."

Snapped back to reality by the reminder that his daughter was asleep in her little youth bed on the other side of the room, Marquise froze. He shot a concerned glance in his daughter's direction. Undisturbed by her parents' sharp voices, Markeeta appeared to sleep soundly.

He eased his body off Terelle. She raced across the room, wrapped Markeeta in her *Elmo* blanket, and carried her into the living room and made her comfortable on the futon.

"Why'd you leave Keeta out there by herself?" Marquise barked when Terelle reentered the bedroom.

Terelle gave him a long narrow-eyed look. "You may not care how you act around your daughter, but I don't want Keeta to see her daddy acting like a park ape."

As if Terelle's words made him suddenly aware that he was naked, Marquise picked up the fallen towel, readjusted it around his waist. Blowing out frustrated air, he went to the bureau, pulled out the bottom drawer and grabbed a pair of boxers and a white tee shirt. He dressed quickly, then flopped down onto the bed beside Terelle.

Hunched over in resignation, his elbows pressed into his thighs, Marquise rubbed his forehead. This gesture usually prompted Terelle to dispense affection immediately.

But tonight she ignored him. And realizing that neither

a kiss of forgiveness nor a reassuring pat was coming his way, Marquise sat up. Renewed anger glinted in his dark eyes. "Damn, babe, why you come at my neck like that?" His words had a challenging tone.

"Don't try to flip the script, Marquise. I didn't drag my ass in here at two-thirty in the morning—you did!"

"That ain't the issue, Terelle. You all hyped because I took a goddamn shower."

"Why shouldn't I be upset? I mean…damn…you took a shower before you went out tonight, right? So why wouldn't I be suspicious when you jump in the shower again—as soon as you get home?"

"Whatchu suspicious about?"

"Don't play dumb," she hissed. "It seems like you're trying to hide the fact that you had sex with someone tonight."

"Aw, shit!" he bellowed, then stood up and paced. "You need to check yourself 'cause this jealous shit ain't gon' git it. Damn, what happened? You used to be so cool, but it seems like you lettin' that ice I put on your finger go to your head."

Wearily, Terelle pushed back a wisp of hair that had fallen into her face. "Look, Marquise…something ain't right. I can feel it and our engagement ain't got shit to do with it. Just because I'm not willing to sit back and let you run all over me like you used to, don't mean I'm the crazy bitch you're tryin' to make me out to be."

"I didn't call you a bitch," he said in his defense.

"Whatever," she replied. Then, eyeing him curiously, she raised a brow. "Why'd you knock me around like that? That's suspicious, too."

Marquise frowned. "Damn, Terelle. Stop blowin' everything up! I didn't hurt you, did I? You came at me swingin'—tryin' to fight me like a man...Whatchu expect me to do?"

"I expect you to act like a man...not some punk-ass pussy who beats on women."

Marquise's face crumbled into a frown. He leaned to the side expressively. "Oh, now you tryin' to say I beat your ass?" Marquise sighed heavily. "Tighten up, Terelle. you blowin' this shit way outta proportion. I held you down—restrained you. That's all."

"You held me down and shook me like I was some crack head who owed you money," she corrected.

Marquise sat down beside her; his expression softened. "You right, babe. I'm sorry. I was kinda rough with you, but you made me mad. You know I don't like nobody to be puttin' they hands on me. I snapped and I apologize." Marquise stroked Terelle's arm, then caressed the fine hair on the sides of her face. "I'm really sorry. You accept my apology?"

It would have been easy to accept his apology and leave it at that. But the knot of suspicion was still balled at the pit of her stomach, prompting Terelle to press further.

"I wish I could let this go, Quise. But I can't. I have

to know..." She paused, allowing her painful gaze to meet his eyes. "Were you sexually involved with someone tonight?"

This time Marquise didn't make light of her inquiry. Wearing an angelic-looking expression, he shook his head. "No," he said without so much as a blink. "The club was packed tight—niggas was up in there wall-to-wall. I danced a coupla times...It was hot as hell and you know how bad I sweat..."

Terelle instantly conjured a mental picture and swiftly shook it away. She didn't like the idea of Marquise dancing delightedly and having a good time with some nasty-ass skank.

"I couldn't get in bed with you smelling all funky and whatnot...so I took a shower."

Terelle's heart lightened. "Damn, Quise, why didn't you say that when I first asked?

He shrugged. "You ain't give me a chance. Before I could open my mouth, your little ass had balled up your fists and started flarin' on me. If I ain't know no better, I woulda thought I was in the ring with Tyson." They both fell out laughing. The air was cleared and Marquise knew it was safe to joke.

"I didn't hurt you, did I?" Terelle asked, blushing.

"You got skills, girl," he said, softening her further with a handsome grin that he knew she couldn't resist. "Yo, if I didn't know how to bob and weave, you woulda straight up knocked me out!" He demonstrated by leaning from side to side.

Marquise used humor to diffuse tense situations. It was a trait she'd always appreciated. His humor, however, was tinged with mockery, yet Terelle could not contain her laughter.

Marquise checked the bedside clock: 3:10 a.m. "Come on, babe," he said, climbing into his side of the bed. "Let's get some sleep."

Happily, she got into bed. Facing him, she smoothed out his thick dark eyebrows, then ran her fingertip along his nose, outlined his lips. Marquise gave a low moan of appreciation. "I'm sorry, Quise," Terelle whispered.

"Me, too," he said. "Now, give me some sugar." He scrunched up his lips; they kissed. But it was more a friendly smooch than the romantic kiss Terelle wanted.

"Night, babe," Marquise said as he turned away from Terelle, pulling the comforter up to his neck.

She cuddled up behind him and wrapped her arm around his waist. A sexual encounter wasn't her primary objective; it was, however, the quickest route to the intimacy she desired.

Afraid he'd drift off to sleep, Terelle urgently rubbed his hip—his thigh. But Marquise didn't stir. Boldly, she slipped her hand into the opening of his boxers in search of his loin. She fondled the flaccid flesh with the expectation that it would soon become rigid in her grasp.

Marquise inhaled and exhaled audibly; his breathing pattern soon changed to the sound of snoring. Terelle released his member, and slowly—reluctantly, withdrew her hand.

Lying on her back, she waited for the peace of slumber. Finally, sleep claimed her, but it did not bring her peace. In her tortured dream, she observed Marquise engaged in a seductive dance of betrayal. When the music finished playing, Marquise turned to leave the dance floor, but his partner, a nameless, faceless and relentless temptress, kept pulling him back onto the dance floor.

Chapter Twenty-Four

One month later. As the 52 bus approached Girard Avenue, Terelle and Marquise stood up. Before dismounting the bus, Terelle, feeling too irritated to ignore the disrespect made it a point to grit on the freckle-faced woman who'd been flagrantly flirting with Marquise throughout the entire ride.

Every morning without fail, the moment Marquise and Terelle boarded the bus, some slimy female made it her business to send a flirtatious smile in Marquise's direction. Terelle might as well have been invisible because her presence—the fact that she was sitting right next to him and wearing his ring—did nothing to deter this behavior. It was disgraceful the way they flaunted themselves, using provocative body language, seductive glances, shameless lip licking—anything to get Marquise's attention.

And it irked Terelle to no end that Marquise didn't put them in their places. He just sat there trying to play it off as if nothing foul were going on.

Every female in Philly, it seemed, wanted to get with her man. She was so irritated, she could hardly appreciate the extra paycheck that his hard work and overtime for the past six weeks had brought into their household.

When he was broke and on house arrest, she'd had him all to herself. She was ashamed to admit it, but she missed those days when she had his ass on lock.

Terelle and Marquise crossed the street and walked toward the next bus stop on their journey to work.

Quietly seething, Terelle walked in silence, while Marquise made cheerful comments about Markeeta—how she no longer cried when they dropped her off at the day care center.

"You're suddenly quite talkative, Marquise." Terelle's tone was sarcastic and confrontational. "You didn't have too much rap while we were sitting on the bus. And since you never talk to me while we're ridin' the bus, it's no wonder those tramps start their shit every morning. I mean…damn…how do you expect me to feel?"

"Huh?" Marquise attempted a puzzled expression, but Terelle wasn't fooled.

"Don't play dumb, Quise. I said how do you expect me to feel when I gotta put up with a bunch of bitches hittin' on you so hard, I wouldn't be surprised if they started throwing their panties at you right there on the bus." Terelle was talking fast and breathing hard. "I saw you and that freckle-faced jawn grinnin' at each other—flirting right in my damn face!"

Marquise lit a cigarette and inhaled deeply. "You didn't see me flirtin' wit nobody. I can't help it if those smuts be tryin' to crack on me. I ain't even look at that broad, so chill out." His final words came out with a thick stream of smoke.

"Don't be acting like you're totally innocent?" Terelle gave a bitter laugh. "You could put a stop to all that bullshit if you didn't try to act like you single."

"How the hell did I act like I'm single?" Marquise's face twisted into a disgusted grimace. "Yo, it's too early in the morning for you to be startin' your shit," he said harshly.

"My shit?" Terelle asked, her eyes enlarged with disbelief. They stopped walking and stood at the next bus stop, which was directly in front of a deli that sold more malt liquor than cold cuts.

"Dig, I don't know whatchu talkin' about, so tighten up. Aiight?" Marquise smiled condescendingly.

"You know exactly what I'm talking about. Every damn morning I gotta put up with the same crap—a bunch of slimy women skinnin' and grinnin'—all up in your face like my ass is invisible. I wouldn't be surprised if they've been slippin' you phone numbers while my back is turned."

"Chill! Damn! Ain't nobody tryin' to hear this shit all early in the mornin'," Marquise said with much animosity.

"Oh, I'm talkin' shit....you think I'm crazy? Okay, I'll tell you what...let another bitch disrespect me this morning and I'm gonna show you crazy."

Marquise responded with a loud, exasperated sigh, then stepped off the curb to look for the bus. "Where's the fuckin' bus?" he muttered as he angrily flicked his cigarette into the middle of Girard Avenue.

"Why do you let them bitches disrespect me like that?" Terelle asked quietly; pain lined her face.

"Please let that shit go. You gonna drive yourself crazy." He shook his head, then spoke in a gentle tone, "Who's wearing my ring—you or that jawn on the bus?"

Terelle didn't have a quick comeback, but refusing to allow Marquise to diffuse her anger with his brand of logic, she emitted a loud disgusted sigh.

"Why you actin' like it's my fault shorty was all up in my grille? See, that's why I gotta hurry up and get my own ride. Ridin' the bus and listenin' to you bitch every morning ain't gittin' it."

"Oh! So, now...*you're* gonna buy a car? When you were locked up, *we* were gonna buy a car." She hated the sound of her own voice; she sounded insecure and unreasonable, but she was too angry to stop ranting.

"Where's the fuckin' bus?" Marquise bellowed, refusing to respond to Terelle's accusing comment.

"Now, you're gonna ignore me?" she asked with an uplifted brow.

Marquise nodded his head defiantly. "Do you know how crazy you sound? At first you was bitchin' 'bout shorty on the bus; now I make a simple statement about our car..."

"*Our* car! I didn't get it twisted; you were talkin' about *your* car."

"What the fuck is your problem?" he asked in a booming voice that everyone at the bus stop could hear.

"All right, calm down, Marquise," Terelle said in a whisper. "Don't make a scene in front of all these people."

"Don't tell me to calm the fuck down—you started this shit," he said, shouting even louder, while furiously pointing at Terelle.

There was an empty forty-ounce bottle of malt liquor leaning against the base of a stop sign. Furious, Marquise kicked the bottle; it set sail, then smacked the asphalt, and shattered into crude, jagged pieces. The crowd of onlookers gasped in shock, then quickly looked away when Marquise jerked around and glared at them.

"Man, you makin' me mad," he said, poking out his lips. "Don't nothin' satisfy your ass. You expected me to fuck up while I was on house arrest, but I didn't. And as bad as I needed some dough, I stayed outta the game. Are you satisfied? Hell no! Now, I'm tryin' to play my position; I'm workin' on that funky-ass job—workin' doubles damn near every day and I still gotta hear your mouth." Marquise was working himself up; he was so angry, the veins in his neck stood out. Terelle knew she had to calm him down.

"Quise, lower your voice or let's talk about this later." She spoke in a hushed tone.

"Fuck no! I ain't lowerin' a mothafuckin' thing." His voice grew louder. "You got the raps all early in the fuckin' morning, so let's rap."

Terelle shot a mortified glance at the crowd, and then looked at the ground in silence.

"For your information, females be tryin' to hollah at me all the time. Yeah, it's like dat," he responded to Terelle's shocked expression. "They be tryin' to throw pussy at me all day long…on the bus—at work—everywhere I go. But I don't give 'em no play 'cause I know how to handle myself." Marquise started pacing and breathing hard.

Work! Did he just say the bitches on the job were sweatin' him? Terelle was stunned. There were no secrets at The County Nursing Home; her co-workers knew she and Marquise were engaged. So, who the fuck was hittin' on Marquise at work? Melanie would know; she knew all the gossip and she'd be more than happy to share that juicy information with Terelle. But there was going to be hell to pay the second Terelle found out which triflin' ho had the audacity to try to fuck up her relationship.

"You need to start playin' your part, Terelle," Marquise advised, breaking into her thoughts. "Think about it—who do I come home to every day? Who do I go to bed wit every night? And who's wearin' my ring?"

She wanted so badly to feel reassured that their relationship had a solid foundation, but knowing that women were coming at him from every direction, she found little comfort in his words. Her mind had traveled to the nursing home, roaming every floor, trying to figure out which back-stabbing bitches required a Southwest Philly-style ass-whoopin'.

"You gotta stop lettin' these lonely-ass smut-jawns drive you the fuck crazy. Now, I'm through wit this subject." The moment Marquise fired up another cigarette, the 15 bus pulled up.

All the seats on the bus were taken; Marquise stood behind Terelle. He held onto the back of a nearby seat with one hand and placed the other hand lovingly across Terelle's shoulder, keeping her anchored as the bus rumbled along Girard Avenue.

Soothed by his touch and enjoying his public display of affection, Terelle leaned comfortably against Marquise and closed her eyes. Sensing suddenly that something was amiss, her eyes popped open. She instantly noticed a young woman sitting in the seat that faced the aisle. Long sandy-colored hair hung over her face, which was buried in a book. The alarmingly attractive young woman wore a short skirt that indecently exposed long, perfectly shaped legs. She was causing a commotion on the bus. All the male passengers were craning their necks to ogle her. Marquise was facing the woman, and Terelle figured he was also sweatin' the hussy.

It was irrational, she knew, but she was furious with the sexily attired woman.

The woman looked up. But her eyes went past Terelle's hateful gaze. She looked up—way up—in Marquise's direction. And then her eyes sparkled—danced in delight. She blushed and looked back down. Fidgeting flirtatiously, she crossed her legs and looked up again. This time she smiled and moistened her lips provocatively.

Terelle wanted to fight! She swung around and gave Marquise an accusing scowl. He gave her a blank stare. The young woman, looking ever so innocent, uncrossed her legs, lowered her head and resumed reading.

Was it her imagination or were Marquise and the woman openly flirting? Constantly plagued by jealousy, Terelle was at her wit's end. Somebody was going to get hurt if Marquise didn't figure out a way to ensure Terelle's peace of mind.

The woman closed the book, tugged at her skirt. She stood up at 29th Street.

Terelle peeped the title: *All That Drama* by Tina Brooks McKinney. Terelle sucked her teeth. Let that bitch flutter her eyelashes up at Marquise one more time and she'd give her more drama than she could handle!

The behavior that Marquise regarded as harmless flirtation, Terelle considered blatant disrespect. And she had endured more than enough for one morning. Gritting on the woman, Terelle silently informed the heifer that if she made one false move, if she even cracked a hint of another smile in Marquise's direction, she should prepare to get her ass kicked up and down the aisle. And neither Marquise nor any other well-meaning passenger would be able to pry Terelle's hands from the bitch's neck.

Taking Terelle's unspoken advice, the woman shot to the front of the bus, pulling nervously on the hem of her too-damn-short skirt.

Feeling victorious, Terelle watched the hussy hastily depart the bus.

Chapter Twenty-Five

Braving the elements in style, Kai returned to work on a snowy Monday morning draped in dark blue braided chinchilla. She looked stunning, clearly out of place in the nursing home. Her mission, however, required her to look sensational.

Her sense of self-importance was boosted by her large bank account. Kai did not bother to confer with her supervisor in the Social Services department; she would deal with her later. Right now, she had to attend to more pressing business. Taking the stairs to the second floor, Kai swished down the carpeted hall that led to Kenneth's office.

She tingled with excitement as she quickly ran her fingers through her curls, then breezed into his office.

Realizing the unsettling effect her beauty and obvious prosperity had on the have-nots who worked like slaves for their meager pay, Kai greeted Kenneth's secretary with a humble smile that she manufactured to put the woman (whom she needed on her side) at ease.

"Hello. I'm Kai Montgomery. Would you please tell

Dr. Harding I'm here?" Kai's words dripped with saccharin.

Startled by Kai's unexpected appearance, the secretary knocked over a container of paper clips. The way the woman gaped, one would have thought J.Lo had taken time from her busy schedule to grace the facility with her presence. Amused by the woman's discomfort, Kai chuckled to herself.

"I'm sorry. Dr. Harding's not available; he's on vacation," the secretary finally said, shaking her head regretfully.

"Vacation!" Kai blurted, forgetting her humble role. "Again?"

"Yes, he takes several trips a year," she explained. "Was he expecting you?" The woman's eyes squinted with concern.

Kai shook her head. Her impulse was to smack the silly secretary for relaying such disturbing news. Restraining herself, she took a deep breath and exhaled; her lips formed into a polite smile. "When will he be back?" She managed to keep her voice calm.

"Next week—Wednesday."

"Thank you," Kai mumbled as she exited the office.

Feeling forlorn and off kilter, she rode the elevator to the fourth floor. The heavy heels of her boots rapped the tiled floor as she hurried past the nurses' station to her office.

The underlings gathered near the nurses' station cast admiring glances at her coat.

"Her coat is sharp," muttered a woman pushing a cleaning cart. "What kind of fur is that?" a nursing assistant murmured inquisitively. Slighting her co-workers by ignoring their presence, Kai whisked past wordlessly.

Walking toward her office, she approached two cleaning men engaged in the massive task of carbonizing one of the rooms. Complete opposites, one was young, extremely tall and muscularly lean; the other—middle-aged, short and squat. The tall man pulled heavy furniture out of the room, while the short man went behind him sweeping debris out into the hall.

Not wanting even a speck of dust to land on her shiny blue boots, Kai stopped suddenly.

"Do you mind watching where you fling that dust," she said disgustedly to the undersized man.

"I see you, baby," he said in a raspy voice. "I ain't gonna mess up those pretty shoes."

Kai thought for a moment, then *tsked* and moved on. The runt, with broom-in-hand, was not worthy of her response. However, when he uttered a suggestive guttural sound, Kai stopped walking, whirled around in indignation and advanced toward the man.

"Excuse me...Is this a work environment or did I mistakenly wander onto some street corner in the 'hood?"

"Naw, baby, this ain't no street corner. I apologize," the man said with uneasy laughter.

"Don't refer to me as baby!" she snapped. "It's offensive and considered sexual harassment, you know."

"What?" The man looked around in disbelief. "I ain't sexually harass you. I ain't say nothing about sex...I called you *baby*...just tryin' to be polite!"

"Well, I heard those vulgar sounds you made...and I don't appreciate being called baby by the likes of *you*." She looked him up and down, turning up her nose the way she did when she unwittingly traversed the corridor while the nursing assistants changed the diapers of residents who were incontinent of their bowels.

"I ain't mean nothin' by that. I was just playin' with you."

"Oh please," she said disgustedly. "What's your name?" She stooped slightly to read the name on his employee ID badge. "Spencer Blake...Hmm. I think you'd better make a call to your union representative, Mr. Blake, because I'm definitely going to file a sexual harassment complaint."

"What!" Spencer Blake recoiled visibly. "I can't believe this shit. Yo, big man," he said, turning his attention to the tall worker. "Wasn't I just playin' with her?"

"Man, I'm not in this. I'm still on probation; I don't want no trouble."

"But this is bullshit."

Aware of the friction, which was taking place in the corridor, the nursing assistants and other support staff, their faces creased with curiosity, started slowly progressing toward Kai and the two men.

"You makin' it worse, man. Stop arguing wit her. Don't say nothin' else; just call your union rep," the tall man counseled, shook his head and went back inside the room to resume working.

"Good advice," Kai agreed. Then she pointed a finger at Spencer. "If you're not out of here by tomorrow, the administration will be hearing from my attorney, and I don't think they're going to enjoy hearing what he has to say."

There was a chorus of gasps from the nursing staff. Their eyes glimmered with excitement. "You gonna sue this place?" asked one of the women.

Kai ignored the question. "See you later, Spencer," she said, then whisked down the hall to her office.

It was hot and stuffy inside her small office. She ripped off the chinchilla and carelessly slung it across the back of an empty chair. Sighing, she collapsed in her swivel chair.

Whom she should call first, she wondered: her supervisor or the director of Human Resources to report Spencer Blake. Better yet, perhaps she would call Kenneth's Bala Cynwyd office and attempt to connive the dippy secretary at that office into disclosing his whereabouts. An unexpected visit to his vacation hideaway was an option she hadn't considered. The thought brought a wicked smile to her face.

She reached for the phone, but withdrew her hand when someone knocked on the door. It was probably the runt, she surmised. He had to be nuts if he thought he could convince her to change her mind. There wasn't a chance in hell she'd reconsider filing the sexual harassment complaint. Kenneth was somewhere in the Caribbean, carousing no doubt with his black whore. Someone was going to pay dearly for Kenneth's transgressions and it may as well be the runt, Kai reasoned.

She swung the door open and was momentarily taken aback to find the tall man standing there. She hadn't realized how good-looking he was. Her anger at the runt had blurred her vision. His looks, however, didn't matter, she told herself. He was just a cleaning man and a black one at that.

"If you came to plead your friend's case, forget it. I don't have anything to say. My attorney will speak on my behalf," Kai said huffily.

"Naw, naw. It ain't like that. I don't even know dude that well. I'm tryin' to make sure you ain't plannin' on gittin' me all caught up in this mess." The tall man's even white teeth grazed against his lower lip. "Check it...I just started workin' here and I make sure to mind my own business. I don't need my supervisor comin' at me all crazy with no questions 'bout sexual harassment. Like I said, I'm on probation...I got a little daughter and I'm 'bout to git married. I'm just tryin' to maintain... ya know what I'm sayin'?"

The man used gestures with practically every word. For some strange reason, Kai enjoyed watching his long body dip and bob as he spoke. It was an interesting sight. Sexy.

She'd disapproved of people who spoke in jargon; it sounded like a foreign language and listening to it was painful. Yet, listening to this young thug speak did not invoke revulsion. She was intrigued, actually. The man had a powerful presence. He was rough around the edges, but handsome and possessed an animal magnetism that she found oddly appealing. Sexually stimulating.

Yes, despite the glaring cultural differences, she felt drawn to him. Aroused by him. Without a doubt, she wanted to fuck him. Damn! She'd just been hit by a severe case of *Jungle fever!* The thought caused a hint of a smile to play at the corners of her lips. It didn't matter that she was part black. She didn't feel black, didn't know anything about being black, and had never been sexually involved with a black man. She wondered if there was any merit in that saying: once you go black, you never go back. Hmm. She had a sneaking suspicion she would soon find out.

"What's your name?" she inquired, eyeing his employee ID badge, straining to read his name. The badge, however, was clipped backwards to his shirt pocket—concealing his image and name.

The tall man frowned. "Why you wanna know my name? I told you I ain't tryin' to get all caught up in this shit!"

She shrugged. "I just wanted to attach a name to your face. Is that a problem?"

"Oh, aiight," he said, obviously relieved. His dazzling smile lit up her gloomy office. Kai was deliciously enthralled.

"My name's Marquise...Marquise Whitsett," he offered as he turned the badge around for Kai to inspect.

"Kai Montgomery," she said, offering her hand.

Marquise took her hand, squeezed it lightly and released it quickly. "Well, nice meeting you...uh, Miss Kai..."

"Hey, you don't have to be that formal. Call me Kai. Please."

"My bad. Okay. So...we're straight, right?" Marquise asked, biting on the corner of his bottom lip.

"Sure. And you can tell your little friend that I'm going to give him another chance. But in the future, he'd better watch how he speaks to me. I won't tolerate his disrespect."

Marquise nodded. "Now that's whassup. My man was just actin' stupid; he ain't mean no harm."

"We could debate his intentions all day," she said, laughing. It felt good to be in the company of a real man. Had she known thugs were so desirable, she'd have dabbled long ago.

She suddenly remembered that Marquise had mentioned something about getting married. Hmm. Oh well, it didn't matter. Pending nuptials would not deter her.

Marquise looked at his watch. "Yo, I gotta get back to work before my supervisor starts lookin' for me."

Kai felt let down; she didn't want him to leave.

"I'll hollah at you later." He disappeared before Kai could think of a response.

There were unlimited possibilities with that beautiful Mandingo warrior, Kai mused, but she would need a crash course in Ebonics if she expected to converse with her new thugged-out lust interest!

Chapter Twenty-Six

It was lunchtime, but food was the last thing on Terelle's mind when she entered the cafeteria. She surveyed the room, spotted Melanie eating alone. Taking advantage of the opportunity to speak to Melanie privately, Terelle walked briskly toward Melanie's table.

"Hey," Terelle said, pulling out the chair next to Melanie. Melanie's plate was piled high with double portions of fried wing dings and onion rings.

"Whassup?" Melanie greeted her with a smile, which Terelle interpreted as an invitation to get straight to the point.

"I've heard that a female in your department's been crackin' on Marquise. Know anything about it?" In all honesty, Terelle hadn't heard anything concrete, just the vague information that Marquise had allowed to slip out. He hadn't identified the woman and he most definitely had not indicated that she worked in the Laundry Department.

Melanie shook hot sauce on her food. Her eyes sparkled with excitement. "Somebody in the Laundry Department? You lyin'? Who?"

"I don't know. I figured you must have heard something."

"Girl, I ain't heard a thing about nobody in my department—but I did hear somethin' 'bout some girl who works in the kitchen."

"Oh yeah, what's her name?" Terelle stood up, prepared to storm into the kitchen to confront her enemy.

"She's not on the day shift," Melanie said.

Disappointed, Terelle sat down.

"She works three-to-eleven."

"Okay, I'll pay her a visit before I clock out today at three-thirty. What's her name?" she asked again.

"Heather...But, girl, don't be puttin' my name all up the middle of this shit. I'm just goin' by what I heard. And from what I'm hearin'...she ain't the only female in this place that's pushin' up on Marquise."

"Who else?" Terelle's brows furrowed with worry.

"Too many to name..." Melanie paused, screwed up her lips. "Girl, the females 'round here been disrespectin' you real bad."

Terelle's entire body felt inflamed. "Don't they know me and Marquise...?" Her mouth went dry. "Don't they know we're engaged?"

"Don't matter. That makes it more excitin'. You know how these hoes play...I just can't understand why you would bring your fiancé around all these haters." Melanie shook her head disgustedly and then went on. "I wouldn't dream of bringin' my man up in this whorehouse." Her tone was tinged with accusation, as if she blamed Terelle for their co-workers' lack of scruples.

Her man! Melanie didn't even have a man. She must have been referring to some phantom-lover because Terelle had never known her to be in a long-term relationship. And listen to the pot calling the kettle black! It was rumored that Melanie had slept around with so many men at the nursing home, there wasn't a soul on the premises who would go anywhere near her worn-out coochie.

"So, are you going to name names or keep me in suspense?"

"I ain't trying to get all caught up in the middle of this mess." Melanie poked out her lips and tore open a packet of ketchup. "By the way—where was Marquise last Friday night?" she asked as she squeezed ketchup on the onion rings.

Sensing that Melanie was about to drop a bomb, Terelle repositioned herself in the chair, cleared her throat. "He...um...he was out with his friends."

"At Chrome—on Delaware Avenue?"

Terelle shrugged. "I don't keep tabs on Quise."

"Maybe you should start," Melanie said. "Word has it, Marquise was out with some big ballers at the club. They was treating all the women to Hypnotic and Remy Martin. Now I don't have the whole story, but I heard that a certain nursing assistant from the second floor was all over Marquise—actin' like he was her man."

Terelle's stomach did a double flip. She couldn't bear to hear another word. Abruptly, she pushed back her chair and stood up. She had to find Marquise and hear what he had to say about Friday night.

"I'll talk to you later, Melanie." Terelle fled the cafeteria.

✿✿✿

Running up the stairs, Terelle made it to the fifth floor without feeling even slightly winded. Her search for Marquise didn't take long. She found him sitting on the bench in front of the elevators. He was kicked back, his long legs sprawled out—relaxed—with an arm outstretched across the back of the bench. Beside him sat a nursing assistant named Danita, a big-breasted heifer who worked on the second floor and who was notorious for dressing provocatively. She bought uniforms several sizes too small and pranced around the facility flaunting her body in skintight scrubs.

In the throes of laughter, Danita's head bobbed and fell back, resting on the back of the bench near Marquise's outstretched arm. She was deliberately giving the impression of intimacy, making it appear as if Marquise had his arm draped around her shoulder. Jolted by the sight of her fiancé and another woman interacting with such familiarity, Terelle stopped dead in her tracks. She silently absorbed and tried to make sense of the scene before her. When Danita, emphasizing a point, brushed Marquise's kneecap with the tips of her fingers, a chill went up Terelle's spine. She gasped in horror. A sledgehammer began pounding inside her chest as the shocking realization washed over her: Danita was the woman who had been up in Marquise's face at Chrome. Making matters worse, Danita and Marquise had the audacity to continue carrying on—at work—completely out in the open for all eyes to see.

Seconds later, with her lips pressed together tightly and a confrontational hand positioned on her hip, Terelle approached Marquise and Danita. Her eyes, blazed in anger, burned holes through the faces of the two cheaters.

Briefly perplexed, Marquise looked up. His lips spread into a slight, uncomfortable smile. "Whassup?" he asked. There was annoyance in his tone and his expression quickly changed from discomfort to agitation.

Danita, apparently intending to resume her conversation with Marquise, didn't budge from her position. "Hey, Terelle," she said, regarding Terelle with curiosity, as if she expected Terelle to state her business and quickly move on.

"*Whassup?*" Terelle asked indignantly. "I should be asking you two that question! What's all this?" She nodded at Marquise's arm, which remained casually outstretched across the bench, a defiant testament that he'd done nothing wrong.

"What's what?" Marquise chewed his lower lip and scowled.

"Excuse me, Danita. I'd like to speak to my fiancé in private." Contempt dripped from every word.

"Excuse *you!*" Danita exploded. "I ain't goin' nowhere. Hmph! I was sitting here first; he sat down and started talkin' to me."

The hand on Terelle's hip instantly balled into a fist. "Bitch!" was all she had managed to say before Marquise sprang up and grabbed her. Knowing Terelle was a second away from putting her fist in Danita's mouth, Marquise pulled Terelle away from Danita and backed her out the door leading to the stairwell.

"What's your problem? Why you startin' your jealous shit on the job?" he fumed through clenched teeth. "You tryin' to git us both fired?"

Breathing hard, heart hammering, Terelle jerked away from Marquise's grip. "You're disrespecting me on my job, and you have the nerve to ask me, *what's my fuckin' problem?*"

"Ain't nothin' goin' on between me and Danita; she's just a co-worker," he said in a tone that was low and deliberately calm as if he were talking to a crazy woman with a tendency toward extreme violence.

"Just a co-worker my ass," Terelle fired at him. "Was she just a co-worker Friday night at Chrome?"

The question caught him off guard. As he struggled to come up with words to pacify Terelle, Marquise bought time by making a big show of looking shocked—looking falsely accused.

"Your night out with the boys...," she reminded him.

"I *was* out with the boys. Danita just happened to be at one of the spots we was at."

"What a coincidence."

"Whatchu tryin' to say? You think I took her out Friday night?"

"I'm trying to say that there're ain't no secrets in this nursing home, Quise. Everybody knows you hooked up with Danita at the club."

"I ain't hook up with no damn Danita...I bought her a few drinks; that's it."

"Is that right?" Terelle said sarcastically. "So, when you came home Friday night, you just forgot to mention that you spent time and money on someone we both work with?"

"Yo, Terelle. I ain't got time for this bullshit. I gotta git back to work and so do you. We'll talk about this when we git home, aiight?"

"No, it's not all right. You know how people talk, and you didn't even have the decency to prepare me for the gossip circulating around here. People are talking about you—about us—on every floor of this damn nursing home."

"Fuck 'em; I don't give a fuck what they think."

"And obviously you don't care what I think either. If you did, you would have had some consideration for my feelings before you struck up a conversation with the woman you're accused of fuckin' with." Terelle's voice raised several octaves.

Marquise covered his face with both hands and shook his head in exasperation. He removed his hands. "Oh, so now I'm fuckin' Danita?" He chuckled as if Terelle had lost her mind.

"Since we both know you were too worn out to fuck *me* Friday night, why don't you tell me who you're fuckin'?" Terelle angrily poked him in the shoulder.

Marquise shot her a look of fury and then took a menacing step toward her. He towered over her, but Terelle didn't feel threatened. In fact, she welcomed the release of a physical altercation, she took a defensive stance, reached up and poked him in the shoulder again.

His eyes told her he wanted to hit her, but he punched the wall instead. He stared at his bruised knuckles, opened his mouth to speak but abruptly closed it when a male employee from the Respiratory Department bounded the stairs lugging a green oxygen canister.

"How ya doing?" the man said, looking surprised to find the couple huddled in the stairwell. Terelle mumbled, "Hello," and then lowered her head, taking a sudden interest in the concrete floor. Marquise nodded a greeting and even managed a low, "Whassup, man?"

After the man had passed from view, Marquise held Terelle in a fiery gaze.

"I'm through wit this conversation. And I'm gittin' fed the fuck up with your insecure bullshit."

"Then make me feel secure," she yelled.

"You need to check yourself. I don't know how much more of this I can take." Marquise pushed the door open and attempted to pass through, but Terelle, having a lot more to say, grabbed his shirtsleeve. He yanked away from her grasp, slipped through the door and slammed it closed.

She started after him, but suddenly stopped. Staring at the door, she was struck by the realization that Marquise had not only closed the door, but had closed his heart as well. Feeling abandoned and betrayed she burst into tears. The family life she'd worked so hard to create was swiftly deteriorating and she was helpless to stop it.

It was as if Marquise were doing everything in his power to keep the relationship from going to the next level. He'd put a ring on her finger and seemed content to remain in the engagement mode forever. His fear of commitment was why he'd been behaving so recklessly, she decided as she blotted her tears.

Well, she damn sure wasn't going to just sit back and allow a bunch of bitches to disrespect her. But she wasn't going to play herself by getting physical with any of them, either. She'd provide her girl Saleema with the name of each and every smut she even thought was crackin' on Marquise. She knew Saleema wouldn't get her own hands dirty, but she'd put together a squad of tough young girls who feared nothing. They'd be on the case without hesitation.

And Danita's name would be the first on the list.

Marquise, she decided with a smile, was going to make good on all his promises. She'd have to devise a new plan of action—come at him from a totally different angle. No more actions motivated by jealousy. No more admissions of insecurity. No more signs of weakness. No more living to please him.

Starting today, she'd shift her focus from Marquise and concentrate on herself and Markeeta. It was time to reinvent herself. She'd begin the transformation by buying new clothes, get her hair styled, learn how to wear makeup, and start going out and having fun with Saleema. She'd show Marquise that it wasn't all about him. And in time, motivated by the fear of losing her, Marquise would come around, see things her way and finally agree to set a wedding date.

Rejuvenated by visions of a September wedding day, Terelle happily bounded the stairs.

Chapter Twenty-Seven

Heathens and barbarians! I just can't escape them. I'm surrounded by them all day and have to run the gauntlet through them just to get the hell home.

Suddenly Kai was disgusted by her surroundings as she made her way home through the streets of North Philadelphia. Kai possessed no love for her black brothers and sisters. In fact, she deeply resented the black blood running through her veins and was prone to lash out in hatred at what she perceived as negative reminders of her true heritage.

They're all degenerate laggards and absolutely good for nothing. However, her mental tirade abruptly shifted gears when she spotted Marquise...*they're good for nothing except...mmm...a good fuck!*

She immediately assumed her more natural state of predator—instead of victim—when she caught sight of this potential sex toy. *Oh goody, prey!* He was just what the doctor ordered to hold her thoughts of persecution at bay and fill her empty evening with a decadent fix.

Reeling this one in should be child's play. Kai pulled over at the corner of Broad of Girard and lowered the passenger window. "Need a ride?"

About to descend the subway stairs, Marquise stopped and looked in her direction. His surprised expression was quickly followed by a hearty smile of recognition. With a swagger, he strolled toward the car, nodding approvingly at her CL500 Mercedes-Benz.

Her eyes swept his long body, zooming in at in his crotch. His swagger and the bulge in his pants told her he was packing major meat. She took a deep breath and let it out.

"Hey, whassup?" he asked as he approached the car.

"I just want to make amends for my bad behavior the other day. I overreacted," she said, feigning remorse. "I'm sure your friend meant no harm…Hop in; I'll take you wherever you're going." She twirled her hair coquettishly as she awaited his response.

Marquise shook his head. "Naw, I'm straight. The train should be here in a minute. And you don't owe me no apology 'cause like I said before…Spencer's aiight and everything, but we ain't like that. He was just trainin' me for the day."

His body language told Kai he was as comfortable in his grimy work boots and uniform as he'd be wearing the current urban garb or whatever thugs wore. Marquise was totally in touch with his sensuality, she observed excitedly as she squeezed her thighs together and rocked back and forth in an attempt to relieve the pressure building between her legs.

A loud rumble announced the arrival of the subway train.

"Let me buy you dinner," she offered, feeling desperate and attempting to take his attention away from the train's arrival.

"Yo, Mommy, this ain't exactly my dinner gear," he said, laughing.

Mommy! She'd never been called that before. Should she be offended? No, she decided. It sounded delicious coming from his lips which had become slightly moist from gentle gnaws and licks—reminiscent of LL Cool J. Hmmm. Conquering the prey was going to be more difficult than she expected. Kai surreptitiously began to pull her knees apart, causing her skirt to hike up a bit to show more of her creamy well-toned thighs.

"A drink?" she asked, pouting, her head leaning to one side.

"You gonna have to give me a rain check, Shorty; I gotta catch this train."

Shorty? Yuck! She liked "Mommy" better, but there was no time to quibble over ghetto monikers. "One little drink," she whined, holding up an index finger and holding her breath in anticipation. Kai loved the chase and this one was giving it to her good.

Marquise paused in thought, turned and cast a fleeting look at the subway stairs.

"What's this about? Why you wanna take me out for a drink?"

"We got off to an unfortunate start. I'm just trying

to make amends," she said with an innocent shrug. "You're a co-worker and I'd like to get to know you better." Her voice took on a low, throaty tone despite her efforts to cloak her mounting arousal.

There was a loud whooshing sound as the train pulled off. "Damn," Marquise muttered.

"Get in." She nodded toward the passenger door. "I'll take you home."

"You tryin' to hollah?" His eyes danced with amused devilment.

"Wait a second while I attempt to translate that," Kai said, grinning. "Are you asking if I'm flirting with you?"

"Somethin' like that." he responded, amused.

"Yes, I'm flirting," she admitted. "Now, let me ask you something?" Kai leaned in his direction.

"You got it…whassup?"

"Are you afraid?"

He threw his head back and laughed heartily. "Afraid? Of what…you?"

Kai shook her head. "Yes. Me! Look, I promise…I won't bite."

"Naw, Mommy. I ain't skert." He laughed uproariously, then turned serious. "I fear nothing and no one."

"Actually, I'm the one who should be afraid—picking up a man that I hardly know—so stop making excuses and come with me."

"Yo, check this out though…I told you, I'm in a relationship. I'm engaged." He held her in his gaze;

his eyes were sincere. "Me and my girl...we goin' through a little somethin' right now, but we gon' git it together in a minute. So, what I'm sayin' is...I'm not tryin' to git into nothin' too serious."

She gave him a "don't flatter yourself" look.

"I'm just tryin' to keep it real," he responded with a shrug.

Kai shook her head. "Just a drink." There was patience in her tone as she slowly spoke each word. "I'm not trying to stop the wedding," she added with laughter.

Marquise opened the door and slid in. "Nice ride," he said as he adjusted the passenger seat to accommodate his height and then reclined the seat until the headrest practically touched the backseat.

"Thanks." She pulled off and stopped at the light. "Where to?"

"It's your world, Mommy; you tell me? I'm down wit whatever."

Does this man ever speak plain English? She wondered as she made a right on Broad Street. "I'm not in the mood for a crowd, so why don't we have a drink at my place?"

"Now that's whassup," he said with a nod.

Kai felt relief for she had no intention of being seen in public with a common laborer—and a black one at that. No, that was absolutely out of the question.

"What do you drink?"

"Thug Passion."

"Thug what?" she exclaimed, amused.

"Hennessy and Alize," Marquise explained.

"I see. We'll have to make a stop at the liquor store."

"Aiight."

She stopped in front of a parking meter near the corner of 18th and Chestnut Streets. "I don't have any quarters for the meter. Do you?"

Marquise searched his pockets. "Just dimes and nickels—no quarters," he said, examining the change in his hand.

"Do you mind waiting in the car? I may need you to drive around the block if the stupid meter maid comes around." Kai used an apologetic tone as if his driving her beautiful Benz would cause him undue hardship.

"No problem," he said without expression.

She wanted to erupt into laughter at the way Marquise managed to keep a straight face when she knew he was restraining himself from turning cartwheels at the mere possibility of getting behind the wheel.

Kai exited the liquor store carrying a large bag. She wasn't surprised to find an empty space where she'd parked. A few moments later, Marquise cruised up, and despite his work attire he looked damn good sitting in the driver's seat.

Indulging him, Kai walked around to the passenger's side and got in

"This ride is phat!" he exclaimed, no longer able to contain his excitement. "Where to?"

"I live on Columbus Boulevard. Near Penn's Landing."

"Bang a left?" he asked at the traffic light.

"Uh…yes…turn left." *Damn. The language barrier alone is going to give me a migraine before the night ends. He had better be worth this aggravation. I deserve a superior fuck and he'd damn well better deliver the goods.*

Her eyes darted to his crotch again and she wished she had X-ray vision. Unable to make an adequate appraisal, she took the liberty of lightly placing her hand on his inner thigh. Marquise bit his lower lip and uttered a low growl. The soft bulge quickly sprang to life, transforming into a beast that was thick… long…hot and actually seemed to pulsate. This was no ordinary dick—it was Shaka Zulu dick. Exactly what she needed to tame her savage libido.

"I can't drive like this," he said, nodding his head toward her hand.

She gave a sigh and reluctantly withdrew her hand.

"Don't worry," he reassured her. "I gotchu, Mommy," he said with a wink that promised to give her exactly what she was yearning for.

Chapter Twenty-Eight

The liquor bottles remained inside the bag atop the kitchen counter, unopened, untouched.

It was not a romantic rendezvous. There were no preliminaries. No small talk. No foreplay. Kai had ushered Marquise straight into the bedroom and shed her clothes. Following her lead, he did the same.

Now, almost two hours later, lying on her stomach with her face buried in a pillow, Kai gripped the sides of the 500-count Egyptian cotton sheets while Marquise thrust deeply inside her. Changing the position, she turned over and wrapped her legs around his waist. This allowed him even deeper penetration, which caused her to shudder convulsively. Feeling uninhibited, she licked, then bit his salty shoulder, and inhaled his thick masculine scent.

Marquise stopped moving.

"What's wrong?" she asked, troubled.

"You gonna make me cum." His words were a breathy whisper spoken directly into her ear—tickling it, and arousing her further, causing her vaginal muscles to contract involuntarily.

Unlocking her ankles, she released him.

Rolling away from her, Marquise sat on the side of the bed.

Kai moved in his direction. "Come here," she whispered.

"I need a minute," he said firmly, without turning around.

Kai suspected he was thinking about his girlfriend. Refusing to acknowledge his sudden attack of guilt, she slithered over to his side of the bed and eased down to the floor. Facing him on her knees, she parted his legs. "You'll feel better when I lick that pussy juice off you."

Marquise groaned and fell back, allowing Kai to have her way with him.

She licked the length of his rock-hard shaft and then concentrated on the smooth head, slowing rolling her tongue around it. "Mmm," she moaned.

He grabbed a handful of her hair and pulled it. Kai moaned. Having someone pull her hair was a new and erotic sensation. She finally cried out, "I can't wait—put it in," she whimpered as she came up for air and straddled him. With a trembling hand, she directed him inside her slippery opening. He thrust upward, she pushed down—they moved together frantically, moaning like savages until Marquise exploded.

"Oh no," she whimpered as he lay panting.

"What's the deal?" he asked when he finally caught his breath.

"Are you finished?" she asked in a tiny voice.

Marquise propped himself up on an elbow and looked at her. "Yeah, I'm finished. Ain't you?"

She shook her head mournfully.

"We been at it for damn near two hours—maybe longer," he said crossly. "Who you think you dealin' wit? I ain't the damn Energizer Bunny, and I don't keep no battery pack in my back."

Kai sighed and then fell onto the pillows, sulking.

"Yo, cut that shit. I need a break. Gimme a minute; you'll git yours."

"When?" She threw a pillow at him playfully.

He cut his eyes at his watch. "Tomorrow."

"Tomorrow," Kai yelped. "I can't wait until tomorrow."

"Yo, I'm hungry...I'm tired...and I gotta git home." He spoke slowly and deliberately.

Kai's mind raced for a quick solution. "I can order something to eat. What are you in the mood for—Chinese...Japanese...Italian...what?"

"American," he said, laughing. "Chicken, steak, seafood—whatever."

Butt naked, Kai sprinted into the kitchen and returned with a large, fancy-looking menu. "This place has the best steak in the world—and they deliver," she said in an upbeat tone. "Do you want to order?"

She noticed him frowning down at his watch. "The filet mignon is so tender, you can cut it with a fork," she said brightly, urging him to place an order—

yearning for him to stay—to finish what he'd started.

"Aiight," he finally said. "Go 'head and place the order."

She twirled her hair with one hand and held the phone pressed against her ear with the other—pacing while she ordered dinner.

"Mind if I take a shower?" Marquise asked.

"Go right ahead. You can use the bathroom down the hall."

Marquise slipped on his boxers and padded toward the bathroom.

Kai finished ordering, hung up the phone and rummaged through the kitchen drawers for her little red book, *The Bartender's Guide*. She located the book, thumbed through it, but couldn't find any mention of Thug Passion. She shrugged and decided to mix equal portions of Hennessy and Alize.

Wanting to be fresh for round two, Kai showered quickly in the second bathroom. When she was finished, she threw on an expensive, thick terrycloth robe.

She found Marquise, who had finished showering also, standing in the living room, wearing a white towel, which was tucked tightly around his waist as he browsed through her DVD collection. On the coffee table, there was a half-filled glass of the Hennessy and Alize concoction she'd mixed for him. Something about the way the white towel contrasted with his black skin made Kai's nipples hard and her pussy moist. He looked edible—like a giant piece of Godiva chocolate.

She had to restrain herself from wrapping her arms around him and biting into his skin.

"Find anything you'd like to watch?"

Startled, he jerked around. "Yo, don't be sneaking up on me like that. You lucky I ain't got my gun on me," he said teasingly. "I usually blast niggas and ask questions later when niggas creep up on me like that." Marquise erupted into laughter. Kai laughed along with him, but there was a nervous edge to her laughter. *Does he really have a gun?* She had never met anyone like Marquise. She was both appalled and intrigued at the same time.

His mood was obviously elevated. Perhaps he was relaxed from the shower—or maybe the Thug Passion he'd guzzled had removed the edginess that was apparent earlier.

Grimacing, Marquise read the back of a DVD. "Man, your DVD collection is whack. Why you like these weird-ass movies?"

"They're not weird. There's a combination of both foreign and independent films. Oh, and there's a sprinkling of commercial movies. But don't knock my taste in films until you've tried them."

"I like action flicks. Murder, mayhem, car chases, gunshots...lots of bloodshed."

Kai shook her head. "I've got a few action movies in my collection. You just didn't recognize the titles."

"Yo, do your action flicks have words runnin' all

across the screen? 'Cause I ain't got no patience for those typa jawns."

"Some have subtitles; some don't," she said with an indulgent smile. But, instead of thinking him an idiot, as was her nature, she found his rough edges and inexperience endearing. Unlike that hopeless LaVella, Marquise had potential. She'd have him polished and presentable in no time.

The food arrived and Marquise was appropriately impressed with the filet mignon. His, well done and Kai's prepared rare.

Holding a fork close to his lips, Kai offered Marquise a taste of her steak. She was relaxed with Marquise and felt comfortable in the intimate act of offering him food from her plate. He, however, wrinkled his nose and recoiled from the juicy rare meat.

After dinner, they shared a slice of cherry cheesecake—the best in the city, Kai informed him.

Finally, Marquise muttered something about the time...that it was getting late.

Pretending to not hear him, Kai took their empty plates into the kitchen and began pressing the buttons on the microwave. She returned carrying a small bowl.

"Close your eyes. I have a surprise for you," she announced.

He spun around to face her. Kai put the bowl behind her back.

An aggravated look flashed across his face. "I don't like surprises—what's in the bowl?"

"You'll find out when you close your eyes," she said in a singsong voice.

"Seriously, stop playin' all the time." There was a threatening note in his voice, which Kai chose to ignore.

"Okay, you don't have to close your eyes...just turn around."

Turning slowly, Marquise sighed. "Hurry up with this little game 'cause I gotta go—I gotta git up early."

Ignoring his grumbling, Kai crept behind him and unfastened the towel. It fell to the floor. She kissed his back, stooped and kissed his buttocks, tickling the crack with her tongue. Marquise, suddenly quiet, except for a low groan, stood naked and trembling in the middle of her living-room floor. From the bowl, Kai scooped a small portion of melted Godiva chocolate, reached around and spread it all over his dick.

Taking his hand, she led him to the sofa, nudging him until he sat down. On her knees before him, Kai licked and sucked the chocolate from his member, and then spread the gooey mixture to his scrotum. "Mmm. You taste delicious," she whispered against his balls. "I love this deep, dark...double chocolate treat. Tell me, Marquise..."

"What?" he asked in a raspy groan.

"Are you going to stay here and fuck me all night?"

"Yeah, Mommy...I'm stayin'. I ain't goin' nowhere. I'm gonna wax that red ass all night long."

Chapter Twenty-Nine

Frantic with worry, Terelle picked up the phone.

"Marquise is missing and I don't know what to do," she blurted when Saleema answered the phone.

"Damn, girl. Calm down. It's only nine o'clock; you sound like he's been missing for days."

"Quise got off work at three-thirty. Something's wrong, Saleema."

"You're stressing for nothing and you need to stop. He's probably hanging out with his friends. Can't a brotha go out and have a drink after work?"

"Not without changing out of his work uniform."

"Hmm." Saleema pondered aloud. "Y'all have an argument or somethin'?"

Terelle was silent. She wondered if she should divulge that type of personal information.

"You there?" Saleema asked.

"Yeah."

"Yeah what?"

"Yeah, I'm still here and yes, we've been arguing." There was a defensive tone to her voice that she couldn't help.

Terelle took a deep breath and then told Saleema about the trouble she'd been having with Marquise: the women on the bus, the night he came home late and fell asleep while she was attempting to initiate sex…and the recent suspicion that he was creepin' with someone on their job.

Saleema listened without comment.

"Say something, Saleema. You know I hate it when you do that."

"Here we go again." Saleema sighed heavily.

"What?"

"You don't really want my opinion. You want me to say something—anything to make you feel better and I just don't fuckin' feel like it tonight," Saleema yelled.

"Why are you screaming at me like I did something wrong?"

"Because…it don't make no sense the way you let that nigga get over on you."

Terelle cringed at the word *nigga*, but didn't feel like correcting Saleema.

"Damn, Terelle…wake the fuck up. Marquise ain't shit, ain't never been shit. You need to fire his ass and move the hell on."

"Break up with Marquise?" Terelle's voice faltered. "That's your advice for me?"

"Yeah. He ain't gonna change. Marquise is a ho and you know it. Just because he got a job…and just because he ain't hangin' on the corner sellin' drugs don't mean he ain't a ho…"

"Look who's talking," Terelle said, cutting Saleema off.

"That's right. But at least I'm a well-paid ho. How much money does Quise get?"

Terelle was silent. She held the phone to her ear and gazed into space.

"He ain't getting nothin' but STDs," Saleema continued. "I hope he has enough respect for you to cover his Jimmie up."

"Uh...that's my other line, Saleema. It might be Quise. I gotta go," Terelle said, lying.

"You got your call waitin' put back on?"

"Uh-huh. I changed it back when Quise got off house arrest. Look, I gotta go," she said impatiently.

As she hung up, she could hear Saleema shouting for her to make sure she called her back. Perhaps she would call her in a week or so...after she and Marquise straightened things out. With Marquise missing and with the current uncertainty that surrounded their relationship, she was in no shape for a verbal battle with Saleema. And with her emotions so close to the surface, she was liable to say something that would ruin the relationship with the best friend she'd ever had.

She heard a noise in the bedroom and rushed to check on Markeeta. Markeeta slept peacefully, but the baby doll she slept with had fallen on the floor. Terelle picked up the doll and tucked it under her daughter's chubby arm. Warmth flowed through her as she gazed at Markeeta and marveled at her beauty. Bending down, she smoothed the edges of her daughter's hair and kissed her face. With her hair styled in cornrows, Markeeta was the spitting image of Marquise.

Marquise! Struck by the painful reminder that Marquise had not come home, Terelle rubbed her chest in a circular motion and plodded back to the kitchen. Her instinct told her he was alive—he was well—but something else was terribly wrong. Her face twisted in agony when the disturbing image of Marquise and Danita appeared in her mind.

Sitting at the kitchen table, waiting to hear from Marquise, her eyes roved desperately from the clock to the soundless telephone. After all she'd done for him, after all he'd put her through—how could he do this to her?

Anger replaced fear and uncertainty. Marquise was not going to trample over her heart and get away with it. She jumped up from the table, yanked open the cabinet beneath the kitchen sink, pulled out a green plastic bag. Marquise had to go!

Let that bitch Danita put a roof over your head! Terelle stormed back to the bedroom, began snatching his clothes from hangers, and stuffed them into the bags.

Chapter Thirty

Six-thirty in the morning. Kai should have still been asleep. But she found herself weaving through traffic instead. Marquise sat beside her in the passenger seat. Giving him a ride to work was inconvenient and had disrupted badly needed sleep. However, after the two strong orgasms he'd given her, it seemed cruel to cast him out in the early morning cold in a neighborhood where public transportation was limited at best. Besides, it would not behoove her to make an enemy of him—at least not yet. Who knew when she'd require his services again?

She turned on the radio and hummed along with a tune by Metallica.

"Why you listenin' to that white-ass music?" Marquise asked, an annoyed frown on his face. "Turn on *The Dream Team?*"

"Who?"

"Golden Girl and Q-Deezy. Power 99."

"Never heard of them," Kai said nonchalantly and continued humming the song.

"Man, this corny-ass music is givin' me a headache."

"You're truly adverse to new experiences, aren't you?" Kai said sarcastically.

"I ain't tryin' to listen to no heavy metal," he shot back. "Fuck it," he continued, his face twisted in a grimace. "Do what you wanna do...just hurry up and git me the fuck to work." He reclined his seat even further than it had been and stared out the window.

Was this a tantrum? She wondered, perplexed. *What nerve!* He'd complained about her film collection—her musical taste was not up to par. He'd neither voiced nor demonstrated anything remotely resembling gratitude for her getting out of bed to give him a ride to work. Well, fuck him and his big dick, too, she concluded, pulling the Benz to a screeching stop two blocks away from the County Nursing Home.

"What's the deal?" he asked, suspiciously.

"This is the end of the line. I called out sick today... I don't want to be spotted near the job." Kai spoke without looking at him; she stared straight ahead, drumming her fingers rapidly to the frenetic beat, which poured from the radio.

"Ain't this some shit!" he said, blowing out furious air. "Yeah, aiight, it's cool, though; it's all gravy, baby." And as if expecting Kai to have a change of heart, he exited the car slowly. Then, realizing that she was serious, he slammed the door shut with a bang that could have shattered the window.

"See you later," she yelled in a taunting tone. Marquise did not respond and didn't turn around. Kai shrugged, and turned up the volume when a new song by the rock group Coldplay came on. Blasting music and singing badly, she drove away, casting lustful glances at the construction workers who drilled and hammered along Broad Street.

✿✿✿

Terelle arrived at work at 6:55 a.m. to find Marquise standing by the time clock. He looked at her with tired, repentant eyes. Part of her was relieved he was alive—unharmed. That part also wanted to embrace him. But she didn't. She rolled her eyes, swiped her time card and tried to get past him.

He grabbed her left arm, and stared in amazement at her bare ring finger. "Where's your ring?"

"That's all you have to say?" she asked saucily, oblivious to their gawking co-workers who'd gathered near the time clock.

"I know you mad, babe," he said in an offhand manner as if his staying out all night was of little consequence. "We'll talk about that later…at home, aiight?"

"You're going to talk to me at home?" Terelle gave a contemptuous chuckle. "Well, check this out, Marquise…You don't have a home. And for your information, the ring is in the trash with your clothes." As intended, the impact of her words landed like a left hook that Marquise didn't see coming.

The throng of employees murmured excitedly.

Looking around embarrassed, he asked in a lowered voice, "Why you puttin' our business out there like that?"

"You put our business out there when you fucked around with a bitch that works right here on our job," Terelle yelled, not caring that she and Marquise were creating a scene.

"I'll talk to you later," Marquise said testily. Moving swiftly, he disappeared from view and descended the stairs to the ground floor to check in with his supervisor.

Terelle sucked her teeth. "Whatever," she muttered for the benefit of the onlookers.

The encounter with Marquise felt anticlimactic. Now, thoroughly pissed off and needing a target for her rage, Terelle rode the elevator to the second floor in search of Danita. Cursing Danita out, Terelle decided, might provide some satisfaction. Whether or not it became a physical altercation depended entirely upon Danita because Terelle would not hesitate to slap the shit out of that slut if she so much as looked at her wrong.

She wondered where Marquise and Danita had spent the night. Danita, she'd heard, lived in the projects. Danita's mom, her three kids, her sister, her sister's kids and a host of other relatives were all packed in tightly together. Hmph! Marquise didn't even have enough sense to cheat on her with someone with adequate living space for him to rest his head.

As she stepped off the elevator, Terelle took in the sight of staff members huddled near the water fountain, absorbed in gossip. She wasn't the least bit surprised. Word traveled quickly in the nursing home. A soon-to-be-married man who fucked around with a co-worker was a hot topic—getting busted by your future wife was an even hotter topic.

Nona, a woman who worked in the Laundry Department, was so engrossed in the gossip, she didn't even notice a male resident with severe dementia ransacking the laundry cart she'd left unattended in the corridor.

There were nudges and sheepish grins as Terelle approached. "Seen Danita?" Terelle directed the question to no one in particular.

Their faces instantly took on expressions of innocence, as if they'd been merely shooting the breeze or discussing the weather.

"Who?" asked Nona, her brows knitted in feigned confusion.

"I didn't stutter, but since you wanna play dumb, I'll ask the question again... Have you seen Danita?" With her eyes narrowed murderously, Terelle spoke slowly and clearly.

Nona shrank back in fear. She finally noticed that the laundry she should have been sorting and distributing now littered the corridor. And worse, a woman's extra-large brassiere sat atop the head of a confused male resident. The cups of the brassiere covered the sides of his head like earmuffs. Nona scurried away to pick up the scattered laundry.

"I haven't seen Danita," offered Lydell, a giant of a man who worked in Plant Operations. "I don't think she came in today." Seeking confirmation, he turned to his co-workers. They murmured in agreement—Danita wasn't there.

Terelle took a deep, frustrated breath and walked away. Then, coming to a sudden standstill, she looked over her shoulder and called out, "If any of y'all talk to Danita…let her know I'm lookin' for her. And make sure she knows that when I catch up with her—it won't be a social call." A buzz of excitement emanated from the crowd.

By the end of the workday, Terelle had a change of heart. Her chest tightened at the thought of another night without Marquise lying beside her. Marquise was her life—had been her life since childhood. She had no real proof that he was fucking around with Danita. For all she knew, Danita could have set the whole thing up. How, Terelle wondered, did the whole damn job know about Marquise buying drinks in the club? They knew because Danita had quickly spread the word, knowing it would get back to Terelle and cause major problems in her relationship with Marquise.

Well, Danita's little plan wasn't going to work. Terelle wasn't about to just hand over her baby's daddy to that nasty, trifling ho.

Chapter Thirty-One

Waxed to the max, Kai's pubis was as smooth as a baby's behind. She glided toward the parking garage at 19th Street and Rittenhouse Square, wondering why it had taken so long to find the courage to get a Brazilian Bikini Wax. A small amount of hair left on her mound was cut into the shape of an upside-down triangle with the tip pointing to her labia. So sexy!

Throughout the procedure, the female technician's face was only inches away from Kai's genitalia. The experience had been a real turn-on, and it required enormous restraint for Kai not to lock her legs around the woman's head and force the technician to use her long, pointed nose to penetrate Kai's wet pussy. And when the technician parted Kai's vaginal lips to determine if there were any hidden stray hairs that needed to be plucked, Kai thought she'd cum all over herself.

The recollection of the technician trying to get a firm grip on her slippery wet labia caused Kai to burst out in wicked laughter. The sound echoed throughout the cavernous parking garage.

The Brazilian Bikini Wax had cost a king's ransom and for all the money she'd paid the salon, Kai figured a complimentary pussy lick should have been included with the service. After all, Kai reasoned, only a pussy-licking dyke would engage in a profession that required her to get up close and personal with a zillion strange cunts every day.

Kai eased into her Benz, rocking in the seat as she imagined the technician tonguing her, making her purr like a kitty cat—licking and sucking until she roared with pleasure.

Feeling too aroused to drive, she sat in the darkened parking lot, rocking and squeezing her thighs together.

Her eyes landed on the phallic-looking gearshift. Giving herself more leg room, she pushed a button that slid the seat back, then swung a leg over the gearshift—straddling it. She rotated her hips to achieve just the right angle—aligning the tip of gearshift with her clit.

As she humped the gearshift, Kai was startled by a glimpse of herself in the rearview mirror. Her face was red and contorted; the veins in her forehead bulged as she strained to reach an orgasm. It was an unattractive sight. And feeling closer to having an aneurysm than reaching an orgasm, she abruptly stopped all movement and dismounted the gearshift.

To get her freak on, she needed a red-blooded person—not an inanimate object. She revved the motor, and ripped out of the garage.

✿✿✿

Kai sauntered into a trendy new restaurant located on 12th & Pine Streets, an area purported to be heavily populated by gays. The food was good, she'd heard. Food, however, was not on her mind. Getting into something freaky with a lesbian might provide the quick fix she needed.

Taking a seat, she graciously accepted a menu from a rather cute, though butch-looking waitress.

"Hi, my name's Tory," said the waitress who was dressed entirely in black, and was pierced in numerous places: her nose, both brows, the left corner of her bottom lip. But it was the silver ball that pierced the middle of Tory's tongue that had Kai mesmerized. Shifting her attention, she gazed at the menu.

"Today's special is Blackened Red Snapper," Tory recited.

I've got your red snapper! Kai thought, amused.

As if she'd been won over by the special, Kai lifted her gaze and beamed. Her mind was spinning, trying to think of a way to get that silver ball twirling between her legs.

"I'll have the special," she said, smiling. Then, her expression became pained. "Did it hurt?" Kai asked.

Tory looked baffled.

"The tongue ring," Kai explained. "I was thinking about having my tongue pierced, but I'm afraid of the pain." She fluttered her eyelashes.

"Oh no, it doesn't hurt much. Just a quick sting. But, let me warn you...," Tory said, shaking her head. "Until you get used to it—it's really hard to talk."

"Yes, I suppose it would be hard to talk...but I'm sure it's great for other... uh...more intimate things," Kai said with a suggestive wink.

Offended, Tory frowned. "What are you having to drink?" There was an edge to her voice.

Kai couldn't imagine why the dumb dyke was ticked off. "Draft beer." Then, to spite the waitress, she added haughtily, "I'm rather parched, so would you please hurry."

Beet red with anger, the waitress scrawled on her pad, then hurried away.

Kai turned to survey the patrons seated nearby. She looked around hopefully, but discovered they were all unattractive. Dogs. None worthy of even a weak smile.

Furious, Kai considered canceling her order, but as requested, the waitress returned quickly with a mug of beer. Kai guzzled it quickly, beckoned her waitress and ordered another. After a few swigs from the second mug, she felt the urge to relieve herself.

There were two stalls in the restroom. A pair of scuffed black boots was visible beneath the first stall. Kai turned her nose up at the dreadful boots and dashed inside the second stall.

Having to urinate badly, she could only briefly admire her newly buffed muff. She squatted and aimed, and enjoyed the deliciousness brought on by relieving her bladder. Thinking she heard a squeaking sound emanating from the stall next to her, she contracted her vaginal muscles, instantly cutting off her stream.

"Do you mind if I wipe?" asked a squeaky voice.

Kai was shocked. She'd heard about freaky men who hung out in public bathrooms, but she'd never heard of women indulging in anonymous restroom sex.

Not wanting to waste time pondering which gender is more depraved, Kai quickly responded, "Be my guest!"

Leaning forward, she gleefully unlatched the door.

A homely redhead entered Kai's stall. Wearing an unattractive ankle-length velvet skirt and a velvet vest with a cotton turtleneck beneath—and of course, the accursed black boots, the woman was a fashion disaster! And worse, her complexion was blotched, red and dry. A fistful of tissues was balled in the redhead's hand. Her hands, Kai noticed with disgust, were covered with dry flaky patches.

She had penetrating emerald green eyes that were perhaps pretty, but until she paid a visit to her dermatologist, the focus would always be on her skin. Kai looked away quickly when she noticed the woman's gnawed nails and ragged cuticles.

"Hi. I'm Morgan."

Frowning, Kai nodded an acknowledgment of the woman's name, but didn't offer her own. Kai's eyes traveled toward the ceiling as she debated whether or not she should allow this scaly, nail-gnawing woman to go down on her.

"I saw you sitting out there and I noticed how pretty you are. Are you Puerto Rican?" Morgan asked brightly. "Or just part black?"

Just part black! The insulting words caused Kai to abruptly stand and pull up her thong.

"What're you doing? I thought you said I could wipe." She sounded panic-stricken.

Kai wanted to slap the woman senseless for calling her black, but restrained herself. Too horny to bypass a freakish thrill, slowly and with much resentment, she lowered her thong.

"Oh, it's beautiful," the woman gushed, referring to Kai's bikini wax. "What's it called?"

Kai told her the name of her wax job and then put one leg up on the toilet seat. "Wipe," Kai said impatiently.

Using the tissue, the woman dabbed Kai's pussy. "I'll do more if you promise to do me, too."

"But of course; I'm not selfish. Giving pleasure is my pleasure."

The redhead gave a satisfied smile and carefully kneeled before Kai. She nibbled at Kai's crotch. Her technique was creepy—more irritating than stimulating.

Kai pushed her head away. "Are you going to eat my pussy or not?"

"That was foreplay." Morgan sounded hurt.

"This is a public bathroom," Kai informed her. "Save the foreplay for later. I just want to get off and I assume you want the same."

Without hesitation, the young woman dove in—slurping and licking, but not touching the spot Kai needed touched.

"Let's change positions." With a nudge, Kai urged Morgan to turn around. She bent her backwards over the toilet, the back of her head rested on the edge of the toilet seat. Straddling her, Kai lowered herself over the redhead's face, and then locked the woman's head between her strong thighs. Fast and furiously, she rode Morgan's face.

Behaving and sounding as if she were suffocating, Morgan twisted and made gurgling sounds.

Kai, unconcerned about her lack of tenderness, refused to release her vise-like clamp until she shuddered from the final wave of orgasmic pleasure.

"Why'd you have to be so rough?" Morgan complained, rubbing her slightly bruised face.

When Morgan removed her hand, Kai reached back and slapped her with all her might. "Don't ever call me black." Kai's voice was low and deadly.

"What's your problem?" Morgan asked, inching away, fear in her eyes.

Kai adjusted her clothing, slipped her Hermès bag off the hook on the bathroom door and left the stall. She glanced in the mirror, applied lip-gloss, shook out her curls and turned to leave.

"What about me?" Morgan stepped forward, blocking Kai's path. Kai's vaginal juices brought a sheen to Morgan's dry lips, Kai noticed with revulsion.

"Aren't you going to do me?" Morgan asked meekly.

Kai stopped and peered at Morgan. "Some other time; I'm famished," she said as she observed with interest the pinkish handprint she'd left on Morgan's unattractive face. "I'll get a migraine if I don't eat, so please get out of my way, you ugly bitch!"

Morgan gasped. Her body went limp.

Kai pushed the stunned woman aside and left the restroom.

Ignoring the covered platter that had been left at the table, Kai grabbed her coat from the back of the chair.

"Is something wrong with the food?" the waitress asked as she rushed to Kai's table.

"I can't eat here," Kai exclaimed, clutching her chest. "There's a disgusting pervert loitering in the bathroom." Kai spoke urgently and shot an anxious glance toward the restroom. "She's asking to do unspeakably sordid things," she said in a hushed tone. Then raising her voice, she said, "If you don't do something about her, I'm going to alert the authorities and have this place shut down." Kai shouted the last two words before throwing on her coat and bristling away.

Every eye in the restaurant fell on Morgan as she slipped from the restroom, and attempted to casually return to her table.

✿✿✿

An hour later, at home—showered and in bed, Kai caressed her hairless mons pubis as well as the smooth upside-down, triangle-shaped pubic hair.

It felt wonderful.

What a pity her pretty pussy hadn't been seen by anyone who mattered. The thought of that nasty woman in the restroom made Kai want to puke. Damn, she hated having to resort to pussy when she really needed dick.

Wracked with self-pity, Kai jerked her hand away from her mons pubis and turned on her side. Now facing the bedside table, her eyes landed on an unfamiliar, cheesy watch.

Sudden recognition curved her lips into a smile. The watch belonged to Marquise! Now, *he* was a good fuck. What had gotten into her? How could she have alienated the best dick she'd ever had?

Infused with enlightenment, Kai bolted upright. She'd return the piece of junk tomorrow. In the meantime, she'd come up with a plausible explanation for her dreadful behavior—she'd concoct a story about being on medication—temporarily, of course—medication that had turned her mood inexplicably sour. Yes, that sounded convincing.

She picked up the watch, stared at the brand name. Diesel. She'd never heard of it. It looked cheap, like something bought from a vendor's stand. How utterly tacky! She'd buy him another watch—an authentic Gucci or something else classic and expensive. Something that would get him back in her good graces and back into her bed.

Chapter Thirty-Two

Anger and confusion had clouded Terelle's reasoning. She hadn't even considered what a breakup with Marquise would do to Markeeta. Now, feeling composed and having her wits about her, she realized it was out of the question for her to even think about becoming a struggling single parent while Marquise ran off, free as a bird with a slut like Danita.

Danita had a pack of rug rats—three or four, Terelle had heard, and there wasn't a father in sight. A tramp like Danita would never have a man of her own.

As hard as it had been for Terelle to get Marquise's life in order—to get him to work a regular job—to become a responsible family man, she'd be damned if she'd simply hand him over to some undeserving chicken head like Danita.

Marquise was innocent, Terelle convinced herself. He was a victim of a conniving skeezer, desperate to snag a man. But, Terelle wasn't having it.

For the sake of their child, Terelle was prepared to hear Marquise's side of the story, kiss and make up and move forward. She'd been through too much for too long to end up struggling to raise Markeeta alone.

These thoughts filled her mind as she replaced the engagement ring on her finger. Next, she carefully returned Marquise's clothes to the bedroom closet.

She took a deep breath and sat on the side of the bed contemplating how she should respond when he came home to beg her forgiveness. Should she make him suffer? No, she decided. Why play games? Marquise had her wide open—she knew it and he damn sure knew it. A few moments later, she heard the sound of the turning lock. Her heart pumped in excitement.

Marquise plodded slowly to the bedroom. His sluggish movements suggested remorse and Terelle was prepared to forgive him.

"I'm sorry," he said in an unsteady voice. "I wanna explain how that shit went down today." Eager to hear him out, Terelle nodded. Marquise inhaled deeply. "I was on the second floor hiding out from Mr. Hicks," he began. "That muthafucker act like he tryin' to work me to death. He got me doin' all kinds of dumb shit just 'cause I'm the new man on the job."

"Get to the point, Quise," Terelle said firmly, wielding her power while she still had it.

"Aiight. So, check it…I was takin' a break, sittin' on the bench—chillin'. Danita came up on the floor…she saw me sittin' there and the next thing I know, she sittin' there chillin' wit me. That shit wasn't 'bout nothin'.

We was just sittin' there bustin' it up—havin' a friendly conversation. But I fucked up by lettin' her sit all up under me like that. I wasn't even thinkin' 'bout how that shit looked...I didn't realize how close she was up on me 'til you popped up." He shook his head regretfully. "I froze, man. I ain't know what to do. I mean...I think it woulda looked more fucked up if I jumped up like I was doin' somethin' wrong. I didn't budge 'cause I was innocent, babe." His eyes were glazed and filled with remorse. "When you walked up on us—I felt like I was busted, like I was caught cheatin' or something..." He nipped nervously at his bottom lip. "But I wasn't. It just looked that way." His pain-filled eyes beseeched Terelle to believe him.

"But Quise...you should have your guard up with those treacherous women we work with." Terelle's voice rose sharply. "Do you know how I felt—seeing you two sitting all close like that?"

"I never touched that girl. I swear."

"Well, tell me this...why did you get so mad at me, Quise? Why did you act like you were ready to take my head off because I caught you sittin' too close for comfort with another woman?"

"It's the way you came at me, babe. You know I can't stand nobody hollerin' and cussin' at me. I'm sorry." Marquise looked at Terelle. "I just lost it; I'm sorry."

"Under the same circumstances, how would you have acted if you walked up on me and some nigga?"

"Ain't no tellin', babe. I probably woulda turned into

a madman. I'd be in jail right now for a double homicide," he said with a sorrowful chuckle. "Look, the bottom line is this...I was really mad at myself. I played myself by lettin' that jawn who don't mean shit to me git my baby all upset." He shook his head sorrowfully, and entwined his fingers. Clearly aggrieved, he looked down at the floor.

It saddened Terelle to see him looking so beaten and haggard. He'd been in the same work uniform for two days. She tugged at his shirt, inviting him to sit down on the bed beside her.

He sat down and enclosed her in his arms. He squeezed her so tight, she had to shift her position to breathe properly.

With her head pressed against his broad chest and buried securely in his strong embrace, Terelle felt loved and protected. She knew she'd made the right decision.

"I know whatchu talkin' 'bout now."

Terelle looked confused.

"I see how those jawns be playin'. They be prowlin' around lookin' for trouble. From now on I'm gonna play my part and make sure nobody disrespects my baby ever again."

He took her hand in his, grasped her ring finger and bobbed his head up and down happily when he discovered she was wearing her engagement ring. "Now, that's whassup," he said, grinning. "When I peeped your hand today and saw you wasn't wearin' your ring..."

Overcome with emotion, his voice broke. Too choked to speak, Marquise looked down at his shoes and shook his head. He looked up finally. "It felt like I was takin' body blows." He stood up and jabbed at the air demonstratively. "Body blows," he repeated. "All of 'em was landin' on my heart." He touched his heart with the palm of his hand.

Warmed by his confession, Terelle stood up and gave him a lingering kiss, an apology for causing him such distress.

Breaking their embrace, Marquise's eyes darted to the closet. A wide grin spread across his face. "I swear to God, if I had come home and found my side of the closet empty; probably woulda just passed the fuck out!" Marquise let his long legs wobble comically. Terelle burst out laughing.

Laughter felt good. It felt so much better than feeling angry and suspicious. She had her man back and that was all that mattered.

"I never cheated on you, babe," he began, his eyes sincere. "Never," he insisted, taking her hand, squeezing it. "And you ain't gotta worry about no jawns gittin' all up in my grille ever again. If one of 'em starts rappin', I'm gonna say, 'scuse me, I ain't tryin' to be rude or nothin', but I gotta go hollah at my fiancée real quick."

Terelle beamed with pride.

"I feel stupid 'cause that shit them dumb-ass broads be rappin' 'bout ain't even about nothin'; it ain't worth listenin' to. I can't believe I let that smut bring trouble to my household." His eyes became dark and brooding. "I fucked up; I'm so sorry. I swear it won't happen again." There was gentleness in his tone; his eyes were moist. Terelle's heart went out to him.

With her home life intact, and wanting it to remain that way, Terelle decided that the next person who came at her with one word of hearsay about Marquise was going to get cussed the fuck out. Especially that meddlesome, gossiping Melanie!

It had conveniently slipped her mind that she'd approached Melanie for the damning information involving Marquise.

"Oh shit, what time is it? I gotta go get Keeta." Terelle shot a look at the bedside clock.

Marquise looked down at his bare wrist. "Damn!"

"What?"

"I think I left my watch at work—in my locker."

"It's locked up, right?"

"Uh-huh."

"Then what's the problem?"

"I love that watch because you gave it to me; I feel naked without it."

"Aw, that's so sweet, Marquise." Terelle kissed him on the cheek.

"Speakin' of naked, why don't you get out of them clothes, relax, go take a hot shower? I'll go pick up Keeta. And don't worry about dinner. I'll bring something home. You in the mood for seafood?" Marquise asked.

Terelle nodded enthusiastically.

"Call and order two Snow Crab platters from Bottom of the Sea. Oh yeah, and order me a side order of mussels. I'll catch a cab and pick it up on the way home."

"Bottom of the Sea! Oh, all right," Terelle said grinning. "It ain't even pay week and you're gonna spend that kind of money on dinner and a cab ride?"

"That's a small thing. To see my baby smiling again—man, that's worth way more than two seafood platters." He looked upon her with adoration, then added, "When you get out of the shower...put on something sexy for me—aiight?"

"All right," Terelle said, blushing. "Should I put on the red lace or the black silk set?"

Marquise was silent for a moment, his silky brow furrowed as he considered the two options. "The red one," he said huskily. "That jawn fucks me up."

And with a wink, he was out the door.

other hectic. You're in the mood for [illegible] Marquise [illegible]

Jerome nodded [illegible].

"Call and order two [illegible] from [illegible] on the [illegible] I'd catch a cab and pick it up on the way home."

[illegible] Tarille said [illegible] we [illegible] work [illegible]

[illegible]

"[illegible]," Tarille said [illegible]

[illegible]

[illegible]

Chapter Thirty-Three

At two in the afternoon, Kai breezed onto the fourth floor gaily swinging a brocade Prada shoulder bag. Inside the bag was a watch, purchased from Macy's in the Cherry Hill Mall during her lunch break. While trying to select a watch, she'd decided against paying the exorbitant price for an authentic Gucci. Marquise didn't deserve that—not yet.

Not knowing what to buy, Kai had picked up a Vibe magazine to find out what the young urban males were wearing and found a colorful full-page advertisement for Aqua Master watches.

Unwilling to spend a fortune on tentative dick, she selected the cheapest style in the store, an Aqua Master diamond-crusted men's sport watch with a textured black-leather band on sale for a little under five-hundred dollars. Though, it was a bit gaudy for Kai's taste, it was trendy and the price was right. Not too expensive, but it cost much more than the piece of junk he'd left in her apartment. She was certain Marquise would love it.

Kai had taken the watch, which was contained in an

oddly shaped case to the gift-wrap department. Unimpressed by the displayed wrapping paper, she pulled out five crisp twenty-dollar bills and firmly requested the befuddled Macy's associate to gift-wrap the watch with the currency. She further instructed the woman to top it off with a green bow.

Filled with the joyful expectation of presenting the cleverly packaged gift to Marquise, she smiled brightly at the crowd of peons converged at the nurses' station.

They were all gushing over baby pictures—no doubt, photos of some unfortunate, illegitimate child.

"Hey, Kai. Wanna see some pictures of Sionnee's baby?" exclaimed a woman wearing a blue uniform and pushing a cleaning cart. The cleaning woman excitedly waved a pack of photographs. Mistakenly, she had perceived Kai's smile as an agreement to join the gathered staff members.

Kai slowed her stride. "No thank you. I detest looking at newborns; they're all so ugly," she explained with a grimace and an apologetic shrug.

The dizzying number of women who worked at the nursing home and who turned up pregnant unceasingly amazed Kai. These women waltzed around the facility proudly flaunting their swollen bellies without so much as a hint of the name of the man who had committed the crime of fathering the child. Often, early in the pregnancy, citing some made-up malady, the pregnant women would stop working, and get on public assistance. But instead of staying home convalescing, the young women made repeated visits to the nursing home throughout the entire pregnancy. Then, after giving birth, with child in arms, they'd strut proud as peacocks from floor to floor showing off the baby and waving around photographs of the poor little bastard expecting kudos and pats on the back for a job well done. It was oh so very ghetto!

"I know that bitch ain't just called my baby ugly," Sionnee blurted, pulling off her earrings. "I'll snap that bitch's head off." She handed her baby to one of the nursing assistants and started after Kai.

The charge nurse grabbed Sionnee's arm. "Let it go. I know you don't want to lose your job before you come back from maternity leave."

"Fuck this job; let me go," Sionnee shouted, breaking free from the charge nurse's grasp. "Don't nobody call my daughter ugly. I should whoop that ass right now!" She started after Kai again.

The baby began to cry. The residents seated nearby in wheelchairs began to murmur discontentedly.

A female employee from the Dietary Department holding a tray filled with snacks for the residents slammed the metal tray down at the nurses' station, and quickly grabbed Sionnee. "Don't mess with her here," the woman advised. "Handle your business after work. She gotta leave sometime. You can catch her in the parking lot."

"Okay, everybody break it up; go back to work," demanded the charge nurse. "Sionnee...you're causing an uproar on my unit; if you don't pull yourself together and calm down, I'm going to have to ask security to escort you off the premises."

"Ain't that some shit," Sionnee exclaimed, gaping at her co-workers, astonished. "Ain't nobody gotta escort me nowhere. Hand me my baby...I'm leaving. But that yella bitch better watch her back!" Sionnee threw a large diaper bag over her shoulder, took her fretting baby, rocked her and stormed away.

"Sionnee!" the charge nurse called sharply. "Why would you make a threat like that? If your words get back to the Director of Nursing or anyone in administration, you could lose your job. And I could lose *my job* for not reporting you. You know this place has zero tolerance for that kind of behavior. Don't you know that social worker has some kind of clout with the board members? I think her father is on the board—so please don't make any trouble on my unit. Just take your baby and go!"

Murmuring profanity, Sionnee stormed away.

Kai was at the far end of the corridor. Wondering what the commotion was about, she turned around curiously, shrugged and picked up her stride.

Inside her office, she picked up the phone and punched the extension to the Housekeeping Department.

"Good afternoon," she said to the secretary. "This is Kai Montgomery. Where is Marquise Whitsett working today?"

"Is this business or personal?" the secretary wanted to know.

Kai wound a lock of hair around her finger. "What difference does it make? It's actually none of your damn business."

"Don't use that language with me, Miss whatever you said your name is. You're going to have to page his supervisor because I can't give out that information." The secretary gave a satisfied snort after putting Kai in her place.

"I'm not paging anyone. *You* page his supervisor. I believe you work in the Cleaning Department—that's what you're paid to do."

"I beg your pardon; I'm the administrative assistant for Plant Operations," the woman said with great pride.

"Whatever. Plant Operations...Cleaning Department....They're all the same to me. And while we're on the subject of pay, I'm going to assume you look forward to receiving your meager paycheck. Am I right, Ms. Administrative Assistant?"

"My name's Lynette Cleveland," the secretary said, attempting to keep a touch of arrogance in her tone, though her confidence was fading.

"Ms. Cleveland, I have connections in this nursing home—you should know that. I prefer not to complain to my father about this ridiculous mistreatment."

"Your father! Why on earth would a grown woman..."

"My father—Dr. Philip Montgomery—I'll have you know, is on the board here. He donates large sums of money to the nursing home annually. He's a wealthy man who has a soft heart for the disadvantaged. Now, I don't believe your superiors would want me reporting unhappy news to my father." Kai paused, allowing the meaning behind her words to sink in. "Therefore," she continued, "I'm instructing you to page Marquise's supervisor."

Kai spoke in a taunting singsong voice. "Or...," she said, switching to a gruff tone, "you can get a hold of him on that annoying walkie-talkie thing you cleaning people have attached to your hip. I don't give a damn how you make it happen—just have Marquise Whitsett in my office ASAP!"

Chapter Thirty-Four

Anticipating a very close encounter with Marquise, Kai smoothed on lip-gloss, misted her neck and wrists with Estée Lauder's Beyond Paradise, and gazed into the full-length mirror kept in a corner of her office.

She looked alluring in a camel and ivory snake-print silk top with a revealing keyhole opening at the top. A five hundred-dollar, French-pleated mini skirt that she'd gotten on sale for three-hundred dollars was worn over sheer brown tights. Long chocolate boots that laced up the sides completed the classy, yet incredibly sexy look.

She shook out her gleaming frosted curls, checked her nails. Deciding her appearance was impeccable, she placed the gift in her top desk drawer and sat behind the desk to wait for Marquise to tap on her door.

Kai checked her watch. Ten minutes had passed. She swiveled impatiently in her chair, then grabbed the phone and redialed Lynette Cleveland.

"Where's Marquise?" she hissed into the receiver.

"I contacted his supervisor…I told him it was an

emergency. He should be there any minute." Lynette Cleveland sounded frazzled.

Twirling her hair and swiveling in her chair with a fury, Kai demanded the name of Marquise's supervisor. The secretary quickly provided the information.

"This place is run by a bunch of incompetents," Kai went on, "and I will not be subjected to..."

Three heavy raps at the door abruptly halted her tirade.

"Come in," she sang. She gently placed the phone in the cradle and sat poised behind the desk.

And there he stood! Tall, black, and despite the scowl that indicated he was none too pleased about being summoned to her office, he looked delicious. Sexy as hell! Had Kai known black could look so damn good, she would have dabbled years ago.

The doo-rag he always wore and which seemed permanently attached to his head was sticking out of his shirt pocket. She admired his intricately styled cornrows. Thick, long braids nearly touched his shoulders. He looked regal. Kai supposed his supervisor had finally informed him that doo-rags were not appropriate for work.

With his broad shoulders slouched defiantly against the doorframe, he refused to step inside the office completely. The petulant scowl he wore enhanced his masculine appeal. Kai shivered and felt her nipples harden.

Instead of wearing the standard blue uniform, Marquise

added a black sweatshirt with a hood, which he wore beneath the short-sleeved blue shirt. It was an act of rebellion. She liked it. Looking him over, she felt an explosion of passion ripping through her.

"Whassup?" He spoke in a disinterested monotone.

"Have a seat." She motioned toward a tan-colored chair.

"I'm cool," he mumbled, refusing to sit.

"Still angry?" She swiveled around and crossed her legs.

"Should I be?"

"Depends."

"On what?"

"Depends on your level of maturity." She raised a brow.

"Yeah, and I guess that dumb-ass shit you pulled was real mature?"

"What did I do?" She held up both hands in a gesture of helplessness.

"You threw me out your ride just because I didn't like that whack music you was forcin' me to listen to."

"Oh! I was premenstrual," she explained with an innocent smile. "I felt too crazy to even come to work that day. You can't hold me accountable for behavior that's caused by a hormonal imbalance."

"Yo, I don't know what that shit is," he said, shifting his position and slightly straightening his stance. "Sounds like some female shit—but what I'm saying is—ain't no excuse for disrespectin' me the way you did. I don't know who you used to dealin' wit, but I ain't that dude."

"Okay, now that I've been thoroughly chastised, can we move forward?"

"Aiight. What's the deal?"

"You left your watch at my place."

"Damn!" He smacked his forehead dramatically. "I was wonderin' what happened to that jawn. You got it witchu?"

"No. I tossed it." Kai delivered the news with a straight face.

"You did what?"

"I threw it out," she said, her tone matter of fact. "It was cluttering my boudoir."

"What the fuck's your problem? How you gonna just throw my shit out? You know what—fuck it. You got issues, Shorty; I'm out!" He spun around and stalked toward the open door.

Kai placed a small shiny black gift bag on her desktop. White tissue paper jutted out; a small tag hung on the side. "Mar-qu-ise..." she sang his name, making it three syllables.

Marquise stopped, regarded Kai with a scowl. "Now what?" As he noticed the bag, his expression softened.

"This is for you." She dangled the bag before him.

Instead of leaving, he made awkward steps toward her. An embarrassed smile played at the corner of his lips.

This little trick would have never worked with Dr. Harding, she admitted to herself. He would have laughed in her face.

But Marquise, she noted, was greedy. A cheap fuck!

He could have as many gaudy watches and as much ghetto garbage as his silly heart desired—as long as the dick remained good—and on call! Yes, a few cheap trinkets were worth having a dick-in-a-glass—to be broken in case of a sexual emergency.

Momentarily forgetting the thug's code of conduct, Marquise blushed like a schoolchild. His legs, Kai noted, appeared to wobble slightly when he pulled out the money-wrapped gift.

His eyes widened as he inspected the twenty-dollar bills. "Is this real money? Real dubs?"

"Of course. Does it look like Monopoly money?"

"Dayum!" he exclaimed as he tried to peel off the tape. "It's wrapped all delicate and shit—I'm scared I might rip these jawns." Then, concentrating, Marquise carefully peeled the tape from the twenty-dollar bills. "Now, that's whassup," he exclaimed as he separated the money.

"Is that a fact? You didn't even look inside the box and you're as pleased as punch already. Boy, it doesn't take much," she muttered sarcastically.

"How many bills is this?" he wondered.

"Five," she answered impatiently. "Hurry up! Stop worrying about tearing the money; you can spend torn bills."

Smiling and gnawing on his lip, Marquise continued to peel carefully. He laid each twenty on the desk and then gawked at the Aqua Master case. "Damn, baby. How'd you know I gotta thing for watches."

"I didn't. Now open it, dammit."

Grinning, Marquise took out the watch and put it on his wrist. "Dayum! Check out the bling-bling. How much was it? A gee?" He turned his wrist admiring the sparkling diamonds that surrounded the stainless steel face of the watch.

"It's tacky to inquire about the price, Marquise. Believe me, it wasn't cheap. Now can I get a hug?" Kai asked, cutting him off. She raised up from the swivel chair and came around to the other side of the desk.

Marquise enveloped her in his arms while cutting his eyes at his new watch.

Kai lifted her head and kissed him. His full lips felt particularly good—better than she recalled. She parted her lips, inviting his tongue to touch hers. As his tongue explored her tongue, her gums, her teeth, his big hands squeezed her shoulders. Kai moaned, broke the kiss and threw her head back in surrender. On cue, Marquise kissed and nuzzled her neck. Holding onto Marquise, Kai began to take steps backwards. With her back pressed against the office door, she reached behind, turned the lock, and then brushed her hand against his stiffening manhood.

Marquise groaned.

"I've missed you, Marquise," she whispered as she pulled her top over her head and flung it across the room. In one swift motion, she lifted up her bra, exposing her breasts.

In an instant, Kai's nipples grazed Marquise's face and lips.

Marquise grabbed both breasts, pressed them together and greedily alternated between flicking his tongue against and sucking each nipple. Aroused to the point of pain, Kai cried out.

Marquise moved a few steps backwards and fell into the tan chair. He tried to pull Kai onto his lap, but Kai turned around, facing him. She hitched up her skirt and straddled him—with the barrier of clothing between them, she gyrated against his dick. She looked into his eyes, cupped her bare breasts and offered them.

"Damn, Mommy...you fuckin' my head up," he murmured. Obligingly, he lowered his head and hungrily suckled each breast.

His long, firm dick seemed about to burst through the fabric of his pants. It felt like a dagger trying to cut its way inside her aching hole.

Willing to be sliced and slaughtered by this big dick, which had the dual capability of causing pleasure as well as pain, Kai spread her legs and rocked on his thickness. Losing control of the part of her that was civilized—sane, she yelped softly, bit into his shoulder to control the screams pressing against her throat, and began pulling violently at the ends of his braids.

"Slow down. Slow down." He pried her fingers from his hair. "Calm down, Shorty." His voice was a concerned whisper. "Shh! You gotta be quiet before somebody hears us."

"You have to fuck me—this is torture," she whimpered pitifully. "I can't take anymore. My kitty cat is purring for you, Marquise." Kai grabbed his hand and shoved it between her legs. The crotch of the tights was sticky and wet. "It needs you," she murmured as she urgently tugged on her tights, trying to get them down. Her boots, however, were in the way. Breathing hard, she muttered curses as she struggled to use the heel of one boot to wedge off the other. It didn't work; the boots were laced too tightly.

With her eyes riveted to his, she silently pleaded for help.

Seeming to understand these feelings drawn from deep reserves of passion, Marquise eased Kai off his lap and into the chair to help pull off the confining tights.

She couldn't control herself; she wanted him to have instant access. "Get the scissors from my drawer and cut these fucking tights off!" she pleaded desperately.

"Naw, we ain't gotta do all that. I gotchu," he said as he kneeled to unlace her boots.

She wanted the boots off her feet NOW! Breathing hard and now pulling on her own hair in frenzied frustration, some unfamiliar feeling took hold of her—or perhaps it was just the need to do something with her hands—whatever the case, Kai found herself rubbing the side of Marquise's face. Then, uncharacteristically affectionate, she used her finger to feel along the complex parts that separated the cornrows. But even that wasn't enough. Feeling primitive—uninhibited, she ran her tongue along this unfamiliar territory, aroused by the smell and the taste of his scalp.

"Damn, Mommy. Whatchu doin' to me?" His voice was shaking as he removed her boots; they fell heavily to the floor.

Marquise gave the tights a hard yank, causing Kai to slide out of the chair and onto the floor.

"My bad. But damn, you got me all worked up." He looked down, indicating the huge bulge in his pants, and then placed her hand upon the swelling. Feeling the monstrous-sized member, Kai moaned loudly. Marquise scooped her up from the floor, carried her across the room and placed her on the desktop. The tights dangled around her ankles. She was wearing a thong.

She groped around her desk, felt for the top drawer and pulled out a pair of scissors and shoved them into his hands.

There was no need for verbal communication. Marquise clipped the elastic band and snatched the thong away from her body. "Oh shit," he exclaimed as his eyes landed on her waxed and upside-down, triangle-designed pubis.

Kai closed her eyes and listened to the metallic sounds as he unsnapped and unzipped his pants. She opened her eyes briefly and witnessed Marquise releasing the beast that would set her free. His eyes were glazed over, mouth slightly parted, bottom lip slack. It was a sensual sight—the sight of a man who was no longer concerned about risk taking. A man who didn't care that he was about to copulate in an office during regular business hours at his place of employment. A man who had completely forgotten about the family he claimed to love. A man who was willing to jeopardize everything to get inside her pussy.

Kai scratched the desktop, gripped the pages of a desk calendar and cried out in utter ecstasy as Marquise aimed and slid his dick inside her. Guttural, animal-like sounds escaped his lips as he spread her legs apart, the backs of her knees cradled by the crook of his arms. He pulled her closer. Then lifted her and with his penis still inserted, he pulled her off the desk and fucked her as he walked in frenzied circles around the small office. Overcome, or perhaps just exhausted, he stopped pacing, pressed Kai's back into a wall and plunged into her again and again until she screamed his name into his shoulder. Biting into the fabric of his shirt, her vaginal muscles contracted rapidly. Still holding her—still connected to her, Marquise collapsed into the chair.

"Are you tired?" she asked.

"Gotta cramp."

"Relax," she whispered. It was his turn to cum. She slid off his lap, and turned around with her ass facing his crotch, she squatted onto his slippery dick. She placed his hands over her breasts. "Squeeze them." He obeyed. Bouncing up and down at a fast pace and declaring the goodness of his dick in the most graphic and guttural terms, Kai brought Marquise to orgasm.

It took a few moments for Marquise to catch his breath. "Damn, girl. I don't know…you might be too much for me." He smiled and shook his head, awed by the intense sexual encounter. He hugged her briefly, then glanced at his watch. "Yo, you better get dressed; I gotta get back to my floor."

Naked, Kai walked to her desk as if she were in her own bedroom. She tore off a yellow post-it and wrote down her phone number. "Call me tonight; we have to make arrangements to see each other again."

Marquise nodded thoughtfully, adjusted his work clothes, folded the piece of paper and placed it in the pocket of his shirt.

"Don't forget this." Kai pushed the five twenties toward him.

"No, I'm straight." His eyes shot to the floor in embarrassment. Kai knew he wanted to take the money.

"Take it," she insisted. "It's part of the gift."

"Thanks," he said as he stuffed the bills in his pocket. He gave Kai a quick peck on the lips. "I'll try to give you a call tonight. Stay sweet, gorgeous." He hurried out of the office.

Naked as a jaybird, Kai sat behind her desk, satisfied.

Feeling the afterglow. A dark piece of fabric lying on the desk caught her eye. It was Marquise's doo-rag. It must have fallen from his pocket while they were marking their territory on top of the desk.

She picked it up—sniffed it. Mmm! It smelled just like him. She inhaled again…and again, and then made herself stop before she OD'd on his scent. Folding it carefully, she put the doo-rag inside her Prada bag, happy to have a part of him until their next encounter.

Chapter Thirty-Five

Terelle ran smack into Marquise as she got off the elevator on the fourth floor.

"Keeta's sick," she said worriedly. Perspiration plastered loose strands of hair to sides of her face. "The day care center called; Keeta's been throwing up all morning. I have to leave."

"She was aiight this mornin'. You think she got the flu or somethin'?" Worry interlaced Marquise's thick brows.

"I don't know, Quise. It probably is the flu—you know it's going around." Terelle smoothed back her hair anxiously. "Where were you?" she asked as an afterthought. "Weren't you supposed to be working on the third floor today?"

"Yeah, but Mr. Hicks told me to come up here and clean that office back there." He nodded toward the long corridor that led to Kai's office.

"Hmph. Where's Spencer? Isn't this his floor? It's not fair for you to have to clean up his mess." Terelle was disgusted.

"Don't get me to lyin'; I don't know whassup around here. But I think they moved Spencer to another floor." Marquise's eyes shifted down to his boots. "Look, I don't want no trouble outta these people; I just do what they tell me to do." He tried to sound resigned to the ill treatment of his superiors.

"I'll be glad when they stop making you float from floor to floor. I called the secretary in your department, but that evil-ass heifer wouldn't give up any information. When there's an emergency like this, I shouldn't have to run all over this building looking for you."

Marquise stuffed his hands in his pockets uncomfortably. "You want me to go with you—in case we gotta take Keeta to the hospital?"

"No, you're still on probation; we don't need any static from the assholes that write our paychecks. I just wanted to let you know I was leaving. Me and Keeta should be home in about an hour." Terelle looked at her watch. "Call home at around two o'clock. If we have to go to the hospital, I'll call the switchboard and ask the operator to overhead page you."

"Naw, fuck that. My baby girl's sick; I know I ain't gonna be able to work or even think straight." Marquise gazed at his new watch.

"That's not your watch. Where'd you get that?"

"Oh, this?" He looked down at it as if he were seeing it for the first time. "The watch you got me wasn't in my locker; I don't know how I lost it." Marquise sucked his teeth. "But it's cool though. I won this one and it cost a lot more than my Diesel jawn." He proudly held the new watch up for inspection.

Terelle felt stung, but she kept an impassive expression. "You won it? How?"

"Shooting craps in the locker room." He smirked guiltily.

"Quise, you know they got cameras all over this place. Why you gotta be doing dumb shit like that on the job?"

He shot her a look that told her to watch her tone. "Chill—aiight? Your boy ain't stupid. I checked and there ain't no cameras in the locker room. Can we focus on our daughter, please?" he asked, perturbed.

Terelle nodded absently; her mind, temporarily off Markeeta, was filled with concern about Marquise gambling on the job.

"Wait right here—I gotta tell Mr. Hicks I'm leaving."

Marquise ran down the stairs before Terelle could protest. It wouldn't have done any good anyway. Nobody could tell Marquise shit. She shook her head. He'd just said he didn't want any trouble out of his boss and two seconds later, he was ready to abandon his job. She massaged her temple and hoped Marquise would find Mr. Hicks because she knew if he didn't locate his supervisor, he'd punch out anyway—without permission—and face the consequences later. He'd be written up for job abandonment and possibly face a three-day suspension or even termination being that he was still on probation. Lord, that man never gave her a moment of peace.

Angry now, she directed her feelings toward the day care center. There was probably nothing really wrong with Markeeta that they couldn't handle; they were just trying to get out of doing their job. They sent kids home over dumb shit like a runny nose or the sniffles—she doubted if Markeeta was seriously ill.

Prepared to wait at least five or ten minutes, Terelle sat down on the bench in front of the elevators. Heavy heels clicking against the tiled floor caught her attention. She glanced up and looked back down instantly. That snippy half-white social worker was prancing down the hall, taking long important strides as if she owned the nursing home.

There were two offices at the end of the corridor: the Recreation Therapist's office and the Social Worker's office. Terelle wondered fearfully if Marquise had been cleaning the social worker's office. She hoped not. She'd heard that the social worker had accused Spencer of sexual harassment and had almost gotten him fired. The last thing she and Marquise needed was a sexual harassment charge. She'd have to warn Marquise to steer clear of that trouble-making woman.

Curiously, Terelle peeked up and observed Kai's attire as she swung open the door of the women's rest room. Kai had on a short wool skirt and a pretty satin blouse—her fly-ass boots had laces and shit hanging all off the sides. Damn! Terelle had to give the woman her props—the bitch could dress.

Oh well, Terelle's day was coming. Once she and Marquise were married she could start nursing school. After she graduated and started bringing home some real money, her wardrobe would start looking a hell of a lot better.

Marquise returned to the floor breathless. "Come on, babe. Let's roll." Terelle got up and walked to the elevator.

"Let's take the stairs," he said impatiently.

Terelle didn't feel like taking the stairs. She responded with a headshake and grimace and pushed the down button. "Did Mr. Hicks say you could leave?"

"Yo, babe. I'm a grown man; I didn't ask for no damn permission. I told 'em my baby girl was sick—told 'em I was out and I'd see 'em tomorrow."

At that moment Kai came out of the bathroom surrounded by a cloud of expensive-smelling perfume. She glanced over at Marquise and Terelle and momentarily froze. She opened her mouth to say something—but apparently changed her mind. Stunned, she looked Terelle up and down, stumbled slightly, turned around and stared at them again, then resumed walking. Kai threw her head up high, moved down the corridor swinging her arms and swaying her small hips with the vigor and pomposity of a runway model.

Terelle felt offended and took it personal.

"Goddamn! I know she thinks she's grand and all that, but damn…the way she walked away was kinda whack. Did you see the way she was grittin' on me? Looking me up and down? That was crazy. You think she was in the bathroom getting high?"

Marquise scowled in thought and then walked over and jabbed the down button twice. "I wasn't even paying her no mind; I don't know whassup with Shorty. I mind my own business."

"Sis got issues," Terelle said. "Marquise, make sure you stay out of her way. I heard she be trying to get niggas fired left and right around here."

The elevator arrived, but Terelle still had Kai on the brain. "Were you cleaning *her* office or the Recreation office?" Terelle asked.

"Recreation," he responded without hesitation and stepped into the elevator.

✿✿✿

Markeeta had a low-grade temperature. Nothing serious. Terelle had to force a spoonful of Children's Tylenol into her mouth and down her throat. A half-hour later, Markeeta was fast asleep.

Marquise was aiming the remote when Terelle noticed the watch again. Walked over and examined it.

"That's a nice watch; looks brand-new."

"It is. White dude that runs the kitchen had just bought it."

"Get out! Cliff hangs out in the locker room shooting craps with y'all?"

Grinning, Marquise dug into his pockets and pulled out two of the five twenties Kai had given him. "He lost more than his watch today." He handed Terelle one of the bills. "Here's some lunch money," he said, laughing.

Smiling while shaking her head in resignation, Terelle took the twenty. "Seriously, be careful, Quise. You never know who's a snitch on the job. If you keep winning from Cliff, the next thing you know, your black ass will be terminated."

"Damn, Terelle. Why you always worrying about everything? Cliff's aiight—he's down."

"Keep on believing that. Didn't I tell you about the time they had this undercover dude in there acting like he was in the Housekeeping Department? He got a whole lotta people fired. He even got some people locked up."

"You lyin!" Marquise blurted, laughing.

"I ain't lyin'. Ask anybody on the job about it. A couple of the young adult residents and about three or four staff members was led off the premises in handcuffs."

Marquise let out a loud guffaw of disbelief.

"I'm serious—they did a drug bust right there on the job. Took the two employees out in handcuffs and I swear—my hand to God—the cops took the young adult residents outta there handcuffed to their wheelchairs. I don't know how they kept that shit out of the news. That should have been the top story of the day..."

"You got jokes," he said, laughing hard.

"I ain't lyin', Quise. You were locked up at the time and I didn't tell you 'cause I probably didn't wanna waste our precious minutes talking about my damn job. But seriously, that shit really happened. The undercover dude used to hang out in the locker room chillin' with everybody. That's how he found out who was selling weed and cain and shit."

"Selling weed and cain to who?"

"Niggas on the job be sellin' to the residents and to each other." Terelle was thoughtful for a moment. "Check this out! We usta have this old-ass resident who could make wine out of the juice that comes up on the trays."

"How?" Marquise sucked his teeth.

"He used juice and pieces of bread and some other shit to make wine. He'd wheel around snatching juice off of other residents' trays and then he'd hoard the shit in his room in a big old nasty container. I think he used to mix it up in his urinal."

Looking sickened, Marquise asked, "Urinal? What's that? You talkin' 'bout them nasty-lookin' plastic piss jars wit the hook?"

"Yup."

"Aiight, Terelle that's enough—you makin' my stomach hurt. Let's change the subject 'cause I ain't feelin' none of this shit you talkin'. Them old dudes and even some of the young ones be turnin' my stomach the way they ride around in their wheelchairs wit their piss jar strapped to the side of the chair. Ain't no shame in their game—they be ridin' around actin' like carryin' a piss jar is as normal as carryin' a forty-ounce bottle of Hurricane."

"Hold up—hold up," Terelle said through her laughter. "Dude had one of them electric wheelchairs and he'd get so drunk, he'd be wheelin' around the facility real fast, runnin' over the old people's feet..."

Marquise let out a loud guffaw. "Stop playin'. How come I ain't seen no drunk old people?"

"Give it time. You will. You haven't been there long enough to peep all the behind-the-scenes shit that goes on. I'm just trying to let you know that we don't work at no innocent rest home. A lot of our residents are old ass ex-cons, too sick to be kept in prison, so they ship 'em to the County Nursing Home to spend their last days. And most of the younger residents got messed up from either doing or selling drugs. Some of 'em caught AIDS from contagious needles..."

"They got people with AIDS up in there?"

"Uh-huh. There's an HIV wing on the third floor."

"Damn, that's the floor I was working on." Marquise looked troubled.

"You can't catch nothing from cleaning the floors."

Still looking troubled, Marquise asked, "Do you be cleaning those AIDS people?"

"Uh-huh. Sometimes...when I'm pulled to that floor."

"Babe, that don't seem safe."

"It's cool. I'm careful when I have to give them care. Besides, I'm not having sex with any of 'em. The people you gotta look out for are the people like *Danita!* Tramps like her be carrying diseases but don't nobody know about it."

"Aw, shit. Here we go again. I ain't fucking Danita or nobody else."

"Anyway, " Terelle continued, "like I was saying... some of them young residents had strokes from hitting the pipe—or they got shot in the back—or hit upside the head with metal pipes for fucking up somebody's money while they was out there hustlin'. In other words, we take care of drug addicts, criminals, ex-playas...the same types you were locked up with and that's why the administration be having undercover cops all up in the joint. So be careful with that gambling, Quise. Please!"

"Aiight...I feel you." Marquise pulled Terelle onto his lap. "You so cute when you be making up shit—trying to scare me straight, huh?"

"I'm serious, Quise. Ask Spencer. He knows about the drug bust. Shit...everybody knows about it."

Marquise kissed the back of her neck. "Check this, babe...why don't you take off that nursing uniform and let me hollah at you real quick."

"Oh, you tryin' to hollah?" Terelle asked sexily.

Nodding, Marquise grazed his lower lip and started pulling up Terelle's top.

"Wait. I'm all sweaty...and you ain't smelling too sweet yourself. Let's take a shower together—then you can scream at me all night long if you're up to it."

Holding Marquise's hand, Terelle led him into the shower.

Chapter Thirty-Six

Kai had been prepared to lash into Marquise for not telling her his girl worked at the nursing home, but when she heard his low sexy voice on the phone requesting to get together on Friday night, she decided to let it go—for the moment.

She surprised him with a trip to Borgata, the largest and newest casino in Atlantic City and gave him five crisp one hundred-dollar bills to play with. His eyes lit up like she'd given him five thousand. Amazingly, he'd never even been inside a casino before. What a hood rat!

Later, pretending to be too tired to drive home, she convinced him to stay over. She secretly reserved a plush room with a panoramic ocean view and other amenities. He was so impressed, they stayed the entire weekend. Heating up the sheets and steaming the windows, Kai and Marquise tried practically every position in the Kama Sutra. Kai had intended to check out the spa and fitness center, but whenever she and Marquise came up for air from their sexual marathon, they'd order room service and soak together in the luxurious oversized sunken tub, and start all over again.

"Now, this is whassup!" he said, referring to the sunken tub. "I ain't sat inside a bathtub since I was a little kid. It's too uncomfortable. My legs are too long for a regular-sized bathtub," he said, reminiscing.

"Aw, poor baby," Kai said before dunking her head underwater to give him an aquatic blowjob. After their bath, she rubbed him down with the oversized complementary cotton bath sheet, and Marquise's eyes rolled into the back of his head as if she were still giving him head.

Despite the expensive good treatment and all the good sex she was giving him, ever so often, she'd catch him whispering into the phone—no doubt, talking to his girlfriend—concocting some story for his absence. Ha!

Kai didn't mention the clandestine calls. She refused to insult herself by questioning him about a woman who scooped poop for a living. That girlfriend of his was tacky beyond belief. She had hairy legs and hair on the side of her face—sideburns for Chrissakes! She seriously needed some electrolysis. Kai shuddered to think what her furry muff must have looked like.

The poop-scooping wanna-be nurse would find out soon enough that she was no competition for Kai.

Marquise was where he wanted to be—with her in Atlantic City and he wasn't going back to his dreary abode any time soon. Apparently, little nursey had no power whatsoever. Kai would send Marquise back when she was good and ready, and judging by the way that he continually hit her spot with his long-lasting big dick, only God knew when she'd relinquish him—perhaps she'd keep him for an additional week, Kai thought maliciously. No one had ever made her cum like he did. She paused and gave that admission some thought and agreed with herself: nope, not a soul. Marquise had the dick of life.

That Ms. Nubia bitch may have gotten away with stealing Kenneth, but Kai would be damned if she'd let another black bitch take a man from her.

✿✿✿

The mood was tense when they checked out of the hotel on Sunday afternoon. After such a great weekend, Kai was surprised by Marquise's gloomy disposition. On their way to the elevators that would take them to the parking garage, Kai chattered gaily, but Marquise, in a pensive mood, barely uttered a word. Kai assumed he was worrying about that hairy hussy he'd left at home; he was most likely trying to contrive a plausible explanation for his three-day disappearing act. *Well, he's shit out of luck if he expects me to rush back to Philly just to appease his girlfriend. I'll take him home when I'm good and damn ready.*

After experiencing the luxurious Borgata, why in God's name would he wish to hurry to some uninhabitable hole in the wall to be with a snot-nosed child and a disgruntled ghetto girl? And where the hell was home? He'd vaguely mentioned living somewhere in Southwest Philly, but was extremely secretive about the precise location. Kai wanted his exact address, but his morose mood discouraged her from pressing the issue. She'd bide her time and find out everything she needed to know about Marquise Whitsett and that girlfriend of his.

"Want some lunch?" she asked cheerfully as they walked toward an Italian restaurant inside the casino.

"Naw, I'm tryin' to get back to Philly. I got some business to take care of."

Kai wanted to laugh. *Business my ass!* "Oh yeah? What kind of business are you involved in?"

"Personal business. Whassup with the third degree?" Marquise said contemptuously. An uneasy silence hung in the air.

Feeling offended by his tone, Kai left Marquise standing alone as she crossed to the other side of the crowded shopping area. Looking through the window of a jewelry shop, she leisurely browsed. She'd be damned if she would allow Marquise to hurry her along. He had to be crazy if he thought she was going to zip through traffic so he could rush home to his little urchin and his so-called fiancée. The hell with him and his fucked-up little family.

Relying on Kai for a ride home, Marquise had no choice but to follow her, but refusing to stand next to her and gawk through the glitzy window, he stood with his back turned.

"Look, Marquise. Do you like that ring?"

He turned around reluctantly, then seeing that it was a man's ring, he nodded, but with minimal enthusiasm. She pointed at a variety of interesting pieces of jewelry and then suggested they go inside. His ugly mood switched to jovial the instant they crossed the threshold of the jewelry shop.

For over an hour, Kai insisted he try on a number of rings, but his eyes kept resting on the wristwatches behind the glass case. Then, she remembered his penchant for watches and asked the salesman to open the glass case that displayed men's watches.

They chose a classy Cartier watch. It cost twenty two-hundred dollars. The dick-on-demand was getting expensive!

After a pleasant lunch in a posh restaurant that provided Marquise with a jacket and tie, they jumped on the Expressway and headed for Philly. Marquise popped a five-dollar bootleg CD into the player. Risking a migraine, Kai endured listening to the endless ranting by the various rap artists featured on the CD.

They rode over the Benjamin Franklin Bridge and instead of intersecting onto I-76, a route that would lead to the University City exit, which was somewhere near the vicinity of his home, Kai detoured to Penn's

Landing. She decided that having to listen to nonstop insanity for over an hour entitled her to another shot of dick.

Marquise, focused on the enclosed booklet that came with his new Cartier watch, did not notice that they were en route to Kai's condominium.

Chapter Thirty-Seven

Terelle brought her leg up high as she climbed inside Saleema's SUV, Jezebel. "I can't believe I'm letting you drag me out on a Sunday night to go hang out with the old heads at Club Beyond. I'm really not feelin' no damn oldies tonight," Terelle grumbled.

"Stop complaining. We're just gonna fall back, have a few drinks and kick it with the old heads. I might make a new connect and your dumb ass won't be sittin' around the house lookin' depressed waitin' around for Marquise."

Changing the subject, Terelle said, "Club Beyond has a black clientele."

"So!"

"I thought you didn't mess with black men."

"I don't—not usually. But I'm doing this for you. You wouldn't want to go where I usually hang."

"And where's that?"

"Various hotel bars. Yeah, girl, I be gittin' it in with the rich white tourists at the Ritz-Carlton, the Four Seasons...but I know that ain't your type of party, so we gonna hang with our own peeps tonight."

"I ain't tryin' to sit around in no oldies dip; why can't we hang at Chrome or somewhere that's poppin'?"

"Because them young bucks ain't tryin' to part with their cash—you can't even get a damn drink outta their tight asses. Them old heads might not be rich, but they sittin' on somethin'—they been on their jobs for years and most of 'em have phat bank accounts and a decent amount of credit cards."

"It just don't feel right to be goin' out when I know I'm not gonna have a good time," Terelle whined.

Saleema gave Terelle a long disgusted look. "How long has Quise been MIA? Three damn days...right?"

"He called a few times. This isn't like him—I'm worried. Something probably happened..."

"As your best friend, I refuse to allow you to sit home stressin' over Marquise. He's been lying and telling you he's on his way home ever since seven o'clock Friday night. What I gotta do...smack you upside your head or somethin' to make you see the light? Any nigga that's been gone that long has to be layin' up with some chick—somewhere."

Terelle flinched and grimaced like she'd been sucker punched dead in the face.

"If you plan on being with Marquise, you gonna have to change *you* 'cause he ain't nevah gonna change. If you wanna straighten his ass out, you gotta start treatin' him exactly the way he's been treatin' you—like shit."

Terelle shifted in her seat. Treating Marquise badly was not an option; she might as well have been asked to jump off a cliff.

"I wish I could be a fly on the wall and see Quise's face when he comes home to that empty-ass apartment." Saleema giggled maliciously. "And since your Aunt Bennie is watching Keeta overnight, you should really give him your ass to kiss by spending the night at my crib." Saleema cut her eyes at Terelle, trying to gauge her friend's response.

Wearing a troubled look, Terelle massaged her temples. "I don't know, Saleema..."

"Why not? Give me one good reason? Why don't you turn the tables and let him try to track your ass down for a change."

"I can't sleep right if I'm not..."

"Up under Marquise!" Saleema said, finishing the sentence for Terelle. "Do you know how dumb you sound? You ain't slept with him for the past couple of nights and you ain't guaranteed he's coming home tonight, so stop looking for excuses to take more of his shit." Saleema backed up, pulled out of the parking spot and whipped Jezebel onto Woodland Avenue.

There was a crowd hanging around outside Gorman's Bar. "Slow down," Terelle ordered, thinking one of the loiterers might know of Marquise's whereabouts.

Saleema pulled to the curb. "Y'all seen Marquise?" Saleema yelled out the window.

"Naw," said a grinning young buck named Pookie. Pookie was on his grind outside the bar. He approached Jezebel—ogling the SUV as if Marquise's absence was an invitation for him to hop in and take a ride with the two women.

"'Sup, Saleema? How ya doing, Terelle? What y'all gittin' into tonight?" His eyes gleamed with expectation as he leaned on the passenger door.

"None of your business, Pookie," Saleema said. "You said you ain't seen Marquise, right?"

"Damn. Why you gotta come at me like that?" Pookie said. He looked hurt.

"My bad, playa. Feel better? Now...have you seen Marquise?"

"Naw, I ain't seen that nigga for a minute."

"All right. Thanks. Now back the fuck off my ride." Saleema pulled off, causing Pookie to lose his balance and stumble backwards.

"That was mean," Terelle said, shaking her head.

"The hell with Pookie. He knows I don't fuck with no broke-ass bitches. Did you see those cruddy-ass boots he had on? That nigga be outside huggin' the block all day and all night. Now, you would think with all those hours he's puttin' in, he'd be able to at least buy hisself a new pair of Tims."

"They don't wear their fly gear while they on their grind," Terelle said. "Them young bucks know whassup—the cops would be all over them if they was out there flaunting their shit the way niggas used to do," Terelle explained.

"Whatever. I don't give a fuck what they wear. All I know is fools like Pookie be gittin' locked up—doing three...four years for selling little dumb-ass nics and dimes. They barely make enough loot to buy a new Dickie set yet they're willing to risk gittin' popped and having to give up years of their life for a little bit of chump change. Now that's downright pathetic and I ain't got no rap for no dumb-ass, broke-ass niggas."

"All right, Saleema. You're feeling yourself right now 'cause you're doin' good, but who knows...you might need Pookie one day," Terelle cautioned.

"Shit, if I ever have to depend on the likes of Pookie, we both know I'm gonna be up shit's creek." Saleema and Terelle both fell out laughing.

Then turning serious, Terelle said, "Maybe Quise is chillin' over his cousin's house. Make a left on Conestoga Street. I wanna check that out before we go to the club."

Saleema sighed in disgust, but complied. When she turned onto Conestoga Street there was a blue and silver truck parked in the middle of the narrow street. Saleema leaned on her horn. The driver of the truck was apparently inside one the houses on the street. "Why niggas can't park their shit instead of leaving it running in the middle of the damn street," Saleema complained.

A door opened and a woman came running toward the truck.

"Here I come; I'm sorry," she called out cheerfully.

"That's Miss Norma!" Terelle exclaimed.

"Hey, Miss Norma," both young women yelled happily.

Norma Towns walked over to the driver's side. "Hi, girls!" she squealed. "Look at my girls all grown up and beautiful."

Saleema and Terelle blushed like teenagers. Norma Towns, a pretty, brown-skinned woman in her early forties, was the manager at the neighborhood KFC. She'd given Terelle and Saleema their first jobs and had acted as a mother figure to the young girls, counseling and providing guidance during their turbulent teens. They hadn't forgotten her kindness and always gave her the utmost respect.

"We were out here tellin' you off, Miss Norma. We didn't know that was your truck," Saleema admitted with laughter.

"That's Rocky's truck; he just bought it," Norma explained.

"Are you and Mr. Rocky still together?" Terelle wanted to know.

"Uh-huh. We've been together since we were twelve years old. I guess you could say we're soul mates." Norma paused in thought. "How's Marquise? I heard he was out. You two still together?"

"Uh-huh. We're gonna be just like you and Mr. Rocky—together forever," Terelle said proudly.

"I know that's right. Well, let me get home before Rocky starts blowing up my cell phone. You girls take care." Norma got in the truck and drove away.

"Why'd you lie to Miss Norma?" Saleema asked.

"You know Miss Norma don't like hearing no bad news."

"That's true," Saleema agreed. She slowly cruised Conestoga Street and stopped in front of Marquise's cousin's house. "You gonna ring the bell?"

"No, he's not there; I can feel it. And I'm not tryin' to let his nosy aunt and cousin be all up in my business."

Without hesitation, Saleema pressed on the gas pedal.

They parked in an outdoor lot near Club Beyond. Saleema scoped out the expensive cars in the lot and nodded with approval.

"Damn! Niggas is out thick," Saleema observed inside the club as she and Terelle squeezed through the crowd. "That's Butterball," Saleema informed Terelle, pointing to the DJ hosting the club for the evening.

Terelle did a double take. "Damn, I didn't know Butter was white. I've been hearing that voice on WDAS all my life and I never had a clue he was white."

"Yup, he's Italian. I heard he's married to a black woman. And I also heard he's loaded. Practically owns the radio station." Saleema was pensive. "I wonder if Butter gets his trick on? Shit, fuck these waiting-for-a-paycheck niggas. I should go hollah at Butter," Saleema said, laughing.

✿✿✿

As it turned out, Butter wasn't interested, but Saleema was able to make a connection with one of his friends.

Twisting and turning, unable to sleep in Saleema's spare bedroom, Terelle grabbed the phone and called home. Marquise picked up on the first ring. Feeling a mixture of anger and relief, she hung up without saying a word. As much as she would have loved to be home in her own bed with her own man, Terelle knew Saleema was right. *She* had to change if she expected Marquise to treat her as she deserved.

Judging by the theatrical moans and groans emanating from Saleema's bedroom, the girl was doing her best to coochie-whip Butter's affluent friend into becoming a regular customer. In a futile attempt to muffle the torturous sounds, Terelle covered her head with a pillow. Miserable, she flopped from one side of the bed to the other until sweet sleep finally claimed her.

Chapter Thirty-Eight

On Monday morning Terelle called out sick. Angry and confused, there was no way she could concentrate on her responsibilities at work. Marquise had the day off and she needed to get home to attend to her business. She tried to awaken Saleema to get a ride, but Saleema, worn out from her Oscar-worthy performance, slept like the dead. As was her habit, she'd probably sleep until noon or later.

Terelle groaned at the thought of having to go out into the early morning cold to wait for the bus, but she wasn't about to sit around and wait for Saleema to come back to life. Thank God she didn't have to pick up Markeeta. Aunt Bennie had volunteered to drop her off at the day care center.

An hour later, Terelle bounded the stairs to her apartment. Marquise was sitting in the living room watching TV. He sprang up when Terelle entered the apartment.

"I know what you thinkin', but I can explain," Marquise said in a broken, pained voice as if he were the one who'd been wronged.

Although her eyes projected rage, feeling drained of energy, Terelle plodded to the closet and hung up her coat. "How are you going to explain staying out for three damn nights?" she asked wearily. "I can't understand why you even bothered to come back. You want Danita? Go ahead…pack your shit and go live with her and her kids." Terelle nodded to the bedroom. "Want me to help you pack?"

"You talkin' crazy. I told you…I ain't fuckin' wit Danita."

"Well, you're fuckin' with somebody. Now pack your shit and go back to the tramp you been layin' up with all weekend. I'm through, Marquise. Me and Keeta will be just fine without you."

A grave expression covered his face. He lit a cigarette, puffed deeply, but didn't utter a sound.

"That's right," Terelle continued, irate. "While you were in jail," she sneered, "I took care of Keeta by myself and I did it from the day she was born." She gestured angrily, her movements a quick succession of furious finger pointing and heated hand waving. "Now, after all I've been through…" She paused, her rapid movements slowing down as she began to brush wisps of hair from her face. "You gotta be crazy if you think I'm gonna let you and that smut disrespect me and my child."

Marquise folded his hands in his lap, looked down and studied them. Then, raising his gaze, he said sadly,

"You think I fucked up, but it ain't the way it looks."

"It looks pretty damn bad, Marquise."

"I know, I know. But I been makin' major moves all weekend..."

"I bet," she said sarcastically.

"Naw, on the real...I hooked up with these Jamaican boys; I been tied up with the Jakes all weekend, making major moves like I said."

"Even if I was stupid enough to believe you, I still ain't tryin' to be with nobody stupid enough to keep getting back into the game." She sucked her teeth. "You're fuckin' hopeless, Marquise!"

"This ain't about drugs," he said in hot denial. "Babe, you already told me how you feel about that, and I told you...I'm through hustlin'. The shit I'm about to git into is totally legit."

Terelle gave a frustrated sigh.

"Seriously, the Jakes got plans to open up some clubs in Atlantic City—in the black neighborhoods. They want me to run one of their spots." Marquise beamed proudly. "My old head Jocko knew me back when I was a young buck—back when I first started hustlin'. He peeped the way I handle myself; he recognizes a thoroughbred when he sees one..."

"Hmph!" Terelle muttered in disgust. She hated it when Marquise tried to pump up his hustlin' skills. He knew as well as she did that while he was in the game, he took one *L* after another and could never rise above the common street hustlin' level. The hard grindin', the late hours he'd kept were always the result of his having to play catch-up after getting stuck up or trusting some triflin' nigga who inevitably messed up his money.

"Stop lying, Quise!" Terelle sounded flustered.

There was a painful silence, then Marquise crossed to the other side of the room; he took a box off the windowsill and handed it to Terelle. She opened it.

"That's the good faith gift Jocko and his boys gave me. Look at the price tag—that watch cost over two G's."

With obvious relief, Terelle examined the price tag and then the watch. "It's beautiful, Quise. But, I wouldn't trust them Jakes. Who knows what they're really into? You think Donald Trump gonna let some damn Jamaicans get a slice of that Atlantic City pie? I think it's a scam. If they are opening up a spot, you know damn well it's just a front for drugs. They're cutting you in so you can be the one to take the fall when the shit goes down. Damn, Quise—why do you have to get involved in shit that's bound to have us living on the edge? You promised me a normal life...and if these Jakes could get you so tied up that you couldn't even get your ass home, how much worse will it get when you start running the spot?" Terelle rubbed the sides of her head. "I refuse to live like that," Terelle said, shaking her head.

"Just give me a chance to prove I can be the man

you deserve. I can't do nothin' for you if I'm workin' in that stank-ass nursin' home. All the overtime in the world ain't gonna git me no real cheddar. Cleaning toilets and scrubbing floors is killin' me. That ain't me, Terelle—that's not who I am." Marquise's eyes became clouded and moist. "I'm only workin' on that nut-ass job to prove how much I love you."

Terelle felt vulnerable; she could feel herself weakening.

"I know life gotta have somethin' better than what I been gittin'. It's my time, babe. I can feel it; please don't make me miss out on this chance."

Terelle felt a lump in her throat. She rubbed Marquise's hand, silently telling him that she understood; she'd give him her support.

"The spot don't open for another month." The words flew from his lips so quickly it was as if he'd known all along that Terelle would cave in. All signs of the inner turmoil he'd previous exhibited had quickly vanished. "In the meantime," he enthusiastically added, "I might have to attend a meeting—once a week, but that's it. And I promise...look at me, babe." He lifted her chin with his finger and looked into her eyes. "All this stayin' out all night and makin' you worry is over. I know whatchu expect outta me. I'm through wit the dumb shit; it's a wrap. Aiight, babe?"

Wanting—needing to believe him, Terelle nodded sadly and rested her head on his chest.

Marquise put his arms around Terelle. "I love you, babe. I know I been messin' up, but all that's behind us now. You ready to set a date?"

"For what?"

"Our weddin'," he whispered.

Hearing the words put a tingle up her spine. She cleared her throat, tried to speak but couldn't. *Had he actually asked to marry her?*

"When? Spring...summer...fall?"

"Fall," she managed to utter in a raspy voice. Clearing her throat again, she said, "We're gonna have to cut back and start saving for the wedding. I could get some overtime..."

"Fuck that! I should be rollin' in a couple of months. Babe, I'm gonna have so much loot, we gonna need a money-countin' machine to keep track of it," he said, laughing. "But we can get married in September if you want to. Go 'head, set the date."

Terelle went to the kitchen to check the wall calendar. "September 20th?" she said in a small voice.

"Sounds good to me. Now come here with your pretty ass, sexy self and give your future husband some sugar." Embarrassed by the compliment, Terelle made timid steps toward him. Marquise picked her up and swung her around.

"Put me down, Quise. You're gonna drop me!" Terelle squealed happily.

"Yo, be quiet. I gotchu—you ain't goin' nowhere,"

he said as he covered her face with kisses. “Damn, I missed you, girl,” he said, then paused to kiss her lips. He parted her lips with his tongue, then pulled away abruptly, and looked into her eyes. “I’m in for the long ride, babe…it’s you and me…ridin’ this thang ’til the wheels fall off. Feel me?”

She nodded and stared deep into his eyes, sending him a message of undying, eternal love.

Chapter Thirty-Nine

Lounging in pajamas and slippers and browsing through a ton of bridal magazines while Markeeta watched her favorite cartoons, Terelle was enjoying a tranquil Saturday afternoon. The ring of the telephone disrupted her peace. She wanted to ignore it, but had to pick up just in case Marquise was checking in. Damn, Marquise had been off house arrest for months now and yet she kept forgetting to get the Caller ID feature put back on the telephone.

The meetings Marquise had with the Jamaicans required his being out every Saturday—all day until late at night. To keep Terelle from worrying, he called several times throughout the day and evening via his new cell phone (another gift from the Jamaicans). Assuming the call was from Marquise, she trotted to the kitchen to pick up.

Terelle was shocked to hear Aunt Bennie's voice; her aunt's voice was unusually high-pitched; her words were jumbled—incoherent. The only words Terelle could make out were *hospital* and *mother*. And for a horrifying moment, afraid that something awful had happened to her mother, Terelle trembled with fear.

"What's wrong; what happened to her?" Terelle asked, nearly hysterical.

"She had a stroke," Aunt Bennie cried.

"A stroke! How? She's not even forty years old. How'd she have a stroke?"

"I'm not talking about Cassy. I'm talking about *my* mother—Gran had a stroke," Aunt Bennie explained through sniffles.

A pang of guilt accompanied the relief that flooded through her. Thank God her own mother was all right. Terelle hadn't talked to her mother since the fateful night that she'd allowed Marquise to kick her out. She'd never forgive herself if something happened to her. This was a wake-up call; she had to make peace with her mother.

"Is Gran gonna be all right? Where are you?"

"It doesn't look good, Terelle. I can't find Cassy. I haven't heard from her in weeks. She's back out there, you know." *Back out there* meant Terelle's mother had succumbed to drugs again.

"You're going to have to get to the Crozier-Chester Medical Center as soon as you can."

"Where's that?"

"In Chester."

"Why'd you take Gran to a hospital so far away?"

"We were on our way to Dover, Delaware. Gran was

tired of Atlantic City; she wanted to try her luck on the slot machines in Dover. I was driving down I-95 and she started breathing funny, then she started having some type of seizure. I pulled off at the first exit—Edgemont Avenue in Chester, Pennsylvania." Aunt Bennie gasped as she recalled the ordeal and began sobbing again.

"Terelle, I gotta get back to check on my mother. I don't know if she's going to make it. You have to get here as soon as possible, okay?"

"Okay, stay calm, Aunt Bennie. I'm gonna call SEPTA travel information to find out how to get there. I'll be there as soon as I can," Terelle assured her aunt.

Aunt Bennie let out a small whimper before hanging up. Stunned by the news, Terelle stared at the phone in her hand. She pressed the numbers to Marquise's cell phone and got his recorded message. Irritated, she quickly redialed. The phone that was intended to be the link for her to reach him whenever she needed him was turned off. She slammed down the receiver, picked it up and pushed redial once more and again she got his voice mail. Beyond pissed, she stubbornly jabbed each digit again. The phone was still off! She wasn't trying to hear one damn word about him being tied up in a meeting. Her Gran was at death's door and she couldn't reach him? This was inexcusable.

Terelle scooped up Markeeta and began to dress her, bundling her in extra layers in preparation for the long journey they were about to embark upon in the freezing cold. Oddly, instead of thinking about Gran, Terelle's thoughts were focused on Marquise—where the hell was he?

Needing to justify her limited concern for her grandmother, Terelle thought about the two years she'd spent in foster care. Aunt Bennie would have taken care of her, but she was in the army—overseas somewhere. Her grandmother, on the other hand, had been right there in Philly—running her speakeasy. "I ain't got no time to be raising nobody's damn kids," Gran had told the social worker when asked if she were willing to allow Terelle to live with her.

Terelle found herself tearing up at the memory. She vividly recalled the day when she was introduced to her new foster-family fear. She remembered the fear—the feeling of abandonment. She forced the memory from her mind and skipped ahead to the day Aunt Bennie came and rescued her. Aunt Bennie lived with Gran, and that's where she took Terelle, promising a discontented Gran that she would assume full responsibility for her niece. Gran responded by grumbling under her breath. The words *nuisanc*e and *burden* came out loud and clear. Terelle had no memory of Gran ever uttering a kind word to her.

Still, Gran was blood and Terelle was obligated to show some support. Besides, Aunt Bennie sounded like she was falling apart. Terelle had to get to the hospital to help keep Aunt Bennie straight.

Ten minutes later, the phone rang. "Yizzo! What's crackin'?" Marquise asked cheerfully.

"My grandmother had a stroke and I needed to get in touch with you. Why the hell was your phone off?" She fumed.

"I'm sorry, babe. I must have pressed the off button by accident. Is she gonna be aiight?"

"I don't know. She's in a hospital—somewhere in Chester. I've been busy getting Keeta ready; I haven't even had a chance to call SEPTA to find out which buses ride out there."

Terelle paused. "I just remembered...there's a commuter train to Chester that leaves from 30th Street Station. Can you meet me and Keeta there in about a half-hour?" Terelle asked breathlessly.

"Sit tight. I'm gonna tell my man Jocko what happened and see if he'll let me hold his wheel. I'll call you right back."

Terelle's downturned lips formed into a slight smile as her anger slowly melted away. Marquise—her knight in shining armor was on the case; she could relax. Feeling relieved and proud, she waited for Marquise to call back.

A few minutes later Marquise called to tell Terelle he had access to his business associate's car and would be there shortly.

Terelle quickly changed into a pair of jeans, a heavy sweater and boots.

A half-hour later, Marquise arrived. He escorted

Terelle to the car and strapped Markeeta into the backseat. Terelle was surprised that the borrowed car was a beautiful Mercedes-Benz.

"Jocko has a nice ride," she said as she adjusted the seat belt and arranged herself in the front seat. "Someone at work drives a car just like this. I've seen it parked on the lot..." She paused in thought. "I think it belongs to one of the doctors." She turned around to check on Markeeta—to make sure Marquise had strapped her in properly. "Saleema swears her truck Jezebel is the shit," Terelle continued, chuckling. "She'd kill for a car like this."

"I told you...Jocko and his boys ain't playin'. Them Jake niggas is all about money." Marquise glided down Woodland Avenue and turned onto Grey's Ferry Avenue.

"I know that's right," Terelle agreed. Marquise looked extremely handsome as he wheeled the Benz. Terelle wished they could afford a new car, but there was no point in even dreaming about a car that cost more than most houses in their neighborhood. "I'll be glad when we can get our own car, Quise. We don't need anything as expensive as this—I'll be grateful for anything with wheels and a motor," she said, laughing.

"I saw the new F150—that jawn is the shit! It's fuckin' wit the new Cadillac truck, so you know that jawn is hot?" Marquise spoke excitedly as he merged into eastbound traffic on I-76. "If things work out with Jocko, I'm damn sure gonna git *that* truck."

"You expect to be makin' that kind of money, Quise?"

"Damn right," Marquise said with conviction. "Shit, we gon' need a money-counting machine *and* a safe if things work out accordin' to plan."

"But for now...wouldn't it make more sense to get something we can afford...and then move up to an expensive truck?"

Marquise stuck in a CD and started blasting Biggie's classic, "Juicy." "I'm not tryin' to think small," he yelled over the music. "I'm goin' after what I really want and I want a fly-ass truck with some bangin' twenty-inch spinnin' rims. That's right, I'm gon' put some dubs on my truck!" Moving his neck and shoulders rhythmically to the beat, Marquise rapped along with Biggie while he drove.

Terelle didn't know what to say. The Jamaicans seemed to be changing the way Marquise looked at life; the jury, however, was still deliberating on whether the change was for the better.

✿✿✿

A shocking gasp escaped her lips when Terelle was finally admitted to Gran's room. The helpless-looking woman lying in the bed surrounded by wires, tubes, and monitors hardly resembled her feisty grandmother.

"Gran?" she whispered as she worked her way around the pole that held the feeding tube. "Can you hear me, Gran?"

"I don't think so," Aunt Bennie replied solemnly. "She's still sedated. God, I hope my mother pulls through this. I had to sign all kinds of papers and it was so hard making those kinds of decisions."

"What kind of decisions?"

"My mother didn't have a living will and I had to give permission for them to keep her alive with a feeding tube and to put that thing—that trachea tube or whatever it's calllled—in her throat to help with her breathing or something. I really don't know what I was signing. I signed whatever they said she needed to stay alive. I could have used Cassy's support, though. It's not fair the way Cassy never has to be accountable for anything..." Aunt Bennie burst into tears.

"I'm so sorry, Aunt Bennie," Terelle said, consoling her aunt with a tight hug. "I'm here now...I can stay with Gran. Do you want to go home and get some rest?"

Aunt Bennie shook her head vigorously. "I have to be here when my mother wakes up." Aunt Bennie wiped her tear-streaked cheeks.

Marquise was in the waiting area with Markeeta, and Terelle was glad he didn't have to witness this sad scene in Gran's room. He would have just stood around fidgeting, not knowing what to do or say.

"I want to stay here with you, but they won't let Keeta in the room, so I'm gonna tell Quise to take her home. I'll be right back. Okay?"

Sniffling, Aunt Bennie nodded. There was appreciation in her bloodshot eyes.

Marquise looked up expectantly when Terelle entered the waiting area. "How's your grandmother doin'?"

Terelle shook her head regretfully. "Not too good. I'm gonna have to stay here with Aunt Bennie...I know you have to take the car back to your friend..."

Marquise nodded. "Yeah, I told him I'd only be gone an hour or so. You gonna be all right here with Keeta?"

"That's the problem...Keeta isn't allowed in the room, so...you'll have to take her with you. Think your friend would mind dropping you and Keeta off at home?"

Marquise gripped his chin thoughtfully. "I'm not sure...you think Saleema or one of your other friends can watch Keeta? Um...I have to get back 'cause we were in the middle of some important business when you called."

"Marquise! What's your problem? I don't know if Gran is going to make it through the night and you're talkin' this shit about finishing up some important business." Terelle's eyes blazed in indignation.

"Calm down, babe." He grasped her hand. "I'm sorry. Look, don't worry about Keeta; I got that covered. You stay here and look out for your grandmother. Can you get a ride with your aunt?"

"Yeah, she'll take me home," Terelle said with a sigh.

"Aiight. Hit me up later." Marquise kissed Terelle and left carrying Markeeta.

When Terelle returned to her grandmother's room, she found Aunt Bennie hovering over Gran's bed; she looked completely wiped out. She gazed at her grandmother and quickly looked away, telling herself she was there only to support her aunt because her grandmother had never been there for her. Terelle cast another look at Gran and winced. Gran had always seemed larger than life, but now she appeared so pitifully small and fragile. When had that happened? Gran had been a large woman, a threatening being with a loud booming voice who had terrorized her own two daughters throughout their childhood and even after they'd become adults. Terelle had been raised to fear and respect her grandmother. Though she no longer feared her, to this day, not once had she ever raised her voice to Gran. That respect was motivated by love—a feeling Terelle had been unaware of until that moment. Seized suddenly by the fear of losing her grandmother, Terelle burst into tears. Her sobs shook her shoulders.

"Don't leave us, Gran," she cried. "Please, Gran…I love you…Don't die."

Aunt Bennie gathered Terelle in her arms. Though tears fell from her eyes, Aunt Bennie tried to comfort Terelle. "Don't cry, baby," she said. "Everything is going to be all right. Your grandmother is a fighter; she's gonna pull through this." Aunt Bennie released Terelle and looked her in the eye. "But when she gets herself together and starts cussing out the doctors and nurses, we're gonna miss the peace we're having right now. So let's enjoy it!" Aunt Bennie laughed as she wiped tears from her eyes.

And through her tears, Terelle smiled, then laughed aloud. Aunt Bennie was right. Mean ol' cantankerous Gran was gonna wake up and commence to cussing out everybody—from the doctor on down to the cleaning crew. Terelle shook her head. The hospital staff had no idea of what they were in for.

Chapter Forty

Marquise was missing. He had promised Kai he'd be gone for only an hour, but six hours had passed and he hadn't so much as picked up the phone to let Kai know he was all right. But, the hell with him, she decided suddenly as she switched mental gears; she needed to know her car was safe, that he hadn't wrecked it. Why in the world did she trust an unlicensed driver with her most prized possession?

There were consequences for getting caught driving without a license in the City of Philadelphia. She couldn't shake the distressing image of Marquise getting pulled over for running a stop sign, a red light or committing some type of traffic violation. When the police discovered he'd been driving without a license, her car would be impounded. The notion of her car being impounded made Kai grimace. Oh, the thought of the scratches, scrapes, and dents her Benz would incur during the brutal towing was pure agony. She'd have to sit through the shameful ordeal of traffic court, and then pay exorbitant fines to retrieve her car from the impoundment lot.

Kai considered calling the police to report her car missing, but thought better of the idea. Marquise had mentioned something about his recent release from prison.

Adding a car theft charge to a convicted felon's record could mean a prison sentence. Moreover, did she really want her good dick locked up? Hell no!

Still...good dick or not, she was getting frustrated to the point of rage. She called his cell phone again and listened impatiently to his recorded message: *Yo, I peeped your digits and I ain't got no rap...you know what to do...Hollah!*

Ugh! He thought he sounded cool, but to Kai, he sounded immature, ignorant, and insulting. How dare he turn off the phone she'd so generously provided for the express purpose of instant communication whenever she felt the need? The sheer gall of that man!

The moment she parted her lips and inhaled in preparation of leaving Marquise a scathing message, her doorbell rang.

"I'm sorry I took so long," Marquise said with a guilty smirk as he entered her condo.

"Where's my car?" Kai demanded. "I was two seconds away from reporting it stolen."

"You was gonna git me locked up?" He scowled in disbelief.

"You told me you'd be gone for an hour. Keeping my car without so much as a phone call is criminal behavior and criminals deserve to be in jail," Kai said, unable to conceal her contempt.

"Damn, Shorty. That's kinda harsh, don't you think?"

"Fuck you, Marquise, and stop calling me Shorty! Give me my keys." She shook curls from her face as she held out her hand and patted her foot in impatient agitation.

Marquise stared at her as if wanting her keys back was an unreasonable request. Reluctantly, he dug into his pockets and pulled out the key ring.

In a flash of temper, Kai snatched it from his grasp. "Why in the hell did it take so long for you to get back? You knew your phone was off and I couldn't call you…so why didn't you have the decency to call me?" She screamed at him. "Do you think I bought you that fucking cell phone to listen to your stupid voice mail every time I call? I bought it so I can stay in touch with you—particularly when you're gallivanting around in my car."

"Yo, I said I'm sorry. Why you makin' a big deal outta nothin'." He sighed. "Now, kill this shit!" he advised testily.

Kai ignored him. "And in case you didn't know, allow me to inform you that I didn't give you the keys to a fucking hooptie. No! I trusted you with an expensive foreign automobile that most people will never even get the opportunity to sit inside—let alone drive! I'm absolutely appalled that you'd mistake my kindness for weakness. I won't tolerate this kind of treatment... it's appalling...and totally unacceptable," she said, backing away. She opened her mouth to tell him to leave, but before she could speak, Marquise was upon her, his lips pressed against her lips.

She felt herself melting in his arms and helplessly parted her lips.

Marquise broke the kiss. "I can't even begin to tell you all the shit that went down while I was out..."

"Did something happen to my car?" she asked, alarmed.

"Naw, the ride is cool. I got a little carried away and lost track of the time."

"But I thought you said you needed to borrow the car because your grandmother was sick."

"Yeah, she was...but when I got there she decided not to go to the hospital. She talked to her doctor and he called in a prescription and I went and picked it up for her. Then, on my way back here...I ran into my man, Jocko. He's a Jamaican brother who's gonna put me down wit a side gig. Anyway, he wanted to slide through this new dip...a club that just opened down the way."

"Down the way?"

"Yeah, Southwest—on Chester Avenue. So anyway, we went to the club and niggas we knew was up in that dip twenty-deep, so we hung out for a minute, you know...bustin' it up with the fellas...and like I said, I lost all track of time."

"That was completely irresponsible of you."

"I know, baby. I fucked up and I'm so sorry. It won't happen again." He gave her a lingering look that went from her face to her red polished toenails.

Kai felt her anger dissipating. She focused on the bulge in his crotch. "Young man," she said, faking a stern tone. "I hope you realize you've lost your driving privileges."

Marquise dropped his head, pretending to be distraught. He raised his head and looked at her through narrowed eyes. "What will good behavior git me?" His top teeth scraped against his bottom lip seductively.

"Let's find out." Kai smiled sexily and unzipped his pants.

Chapter Forty-One

Monday morning was far from being the blue Monday Kai typically experienced. She awakened feeling euphoric. She sang as she showered and washed her hair. With a huge grin plastered on her face, she got dressed for work. The only thing missing from her merry Monday morning was Marquise lying in bed beside her. But that would change soon enough.

She was in love and she wanted Marquise to know it—she wanted the whole world to know it. She snickered as she thought of how her parents would react when they were introduced to Marquise. Her mother would probably clutch her pearls the moment she caught sight of that doo-rag thing that seemed permanently attached to Marquise's head. Her father would turn red as a beet when Kai revealed that the love of her life toiled as a janitor in the very nursing home he had insisted she work. Ha! The embarrassment would serve her father right for forcing her to work in that hellhole. Her punishment, she supposed, for being half-black. Having Kai work in the County Nursing Home was a slap in the face and another carefully devised method of dispelling any notion that she was his natural daughter. For surely, her father, the prominent doctor and respected citizen he was perceived to be, would never dream of placing his natural daughter in such a horrid and thoroughly degrading situation.

After meeting Marquise, her parents would voice concern that the class distinction between she and Marquise was bound to cause future problems. She'd have to bite her tongue to keep from reminding her father that he was apparently unconcerned about the class distinction between himself and her black biological mother. Whom did they expect her to bring home? A doctor? Well, she'd tried to live up to their expectations, but Dr. Harding had rejected her. And fuck him, too! It was his loss—the stupid fuck. She didn't need his money or prestige. She'd serve her penitence at the fucking nursing home and emerge independently wealthy in two years.

Kai grabbed her briefcase and dashed to her car; she couldn't wait to get to work to see the new love of her life: Marquise. She couldn't even begin to imagine how he would respond when she shared with him her desire to get married. Kai wouldn't have been the least bit surprised if Marquise decided to break the news to his little girlfriend that very day—right there on the job. Hopefully, the unfortunate girl would bow out gracefully, seek employment elsewhere, and never force Kai to lay eyes upon her again.

Humming a love song, she swung open the door of her car, then remembering that she hadn't driven since Marquise borrowed it; she decided to check for damages. She gave the inside of the Benz a cursory glance, closed the door and inspected the outside of the car. There wasn't a scratch. Oh, how she loved her man! Completely satisfied, she tossed her briefcase on the floor of the back seat and drove to work.

Still humming happily, Kai turned into the parking lot of the nursing home, pulled into the spot designated for her father and cheerfully exited the car. Walking fast, she quickly reached the entrance to the building, and then suddenly remembered she'd left her briefcase inside the car. Instead of cursing the injustice of having to trek all the way back to the parking lot, she giggled uncharacteristically and jokingly chided herself for being so forgetful. Ah, the wonder of sweet love!

She trotted to the car. When she retrieved the briefcase, she noticed something pink lying beneath the floor mat. She squinted at the object in bewilderment, picked it up and gawked. It was a tiny pink barrette shaped like a butterfly as she held it between her thumb and index fingers. A child's barrette. Now, how could such a thing find its way into the back seat of her car?

Clarity hit her like a ton of bricks: Marquise's daughter had been in her car! And that meant his so-called fiancée had been in her car as well.

As if her fingers had been scorched, Kai dropped the barrette.

That bastard had used her car to take his funky family for a cruise through the ghetto! She could just imagine the three of them behaving as if they were the First Family of the 'hood, grinning and waving at their fellow hood rats and claiming her beautiful vehicle as their own.

She hated having to pick up the revolting and vile barrette, but she needed it for evidence. Kai looked at the inanimate butterfly and grimaced as if she were holding a dead mouse or…feces. Frowning, she tossed it inside her blue Italian leather Fendi bag.

In a rage, she stomped up the walkway leading to the entrance of the building, and then stormed into the lobby. Preoccupied with thoughts of murder, she didn't bother to respond to the receptionist's cheery "good morning." She marched to the elevator and stepped in front of a slow-wheeling male resident who was trying to maneuver himself inside the elevator before the doors could close in his face. As the resident continued struggling to scoot his wheelchair into the elevator, Kai stepped forward and pushed the button marked *closed* and rolled her eyes at the man as she watched the doors shut in his defeated face.

With mounting fury, she swept past the nurses' station. Walking briskly down the corridor, Kai nearly collided with a nursing assistant who was coming out of a resident's room. The coffee-colored woman wore her thick long hair pulled back in a ponytail. There was an abundance of curly hair at her temples. Though her looks were downplayed—no makeup, not even a touch of lip-gloss on her thin lips, she was quite pretty. She had large luminous dark eyes with silky long lashes. The young woman was curiously familiar.

"Excuse me," said the nursing assistant.

Kai said nothing, but managed to look offended as her eyes quickly darted to the woman's name badge: Terelle Chambers, Certified Nursing Assistant. She glanced at the woman's legs. Terelle's nursing uniform, a green top and paler green skirt, revealed thick, shapely legs that were covered with hair. Kai bristled. This woman was Marquise's so-called fiancée! Furthermore, she still hadn't shaved those awful hairy legs. Yuck! Kai glared at her in passing, but Terelle didn't seem to notice as she resumed walking in the opposite direction of the corridor.

After hanging up her coat in her office, Kai paced back and forth vigorously as she debated whether she should call the Housekeeping Department and summon Marquise to her office. His girlfriend's presence on the floor posed a problem, however. The fourth floor was apparently short of nursing staff and Terelle had been pulled from her own unit to Kai's floor. Kai surmised that Terelle's hovering presence would alarm Marquise and prevent him from speaking candidly.

Kai called his cell phone. Expecting to get his voice

mail, she was prepared to leave a scathing message. Amazingly, Marquise picked up.

"I need to see you," Kai said in a frosty tone.

"What's wrong? You aiight?"

"No, I'm not all right."

"Whassup?"

"Where are you? I need to speak to you face-to-face."

"Home."

"You're at home! Why aren't you here—at work?"

"Whatchu wanna know for? You interrogating me like you the cops or somebody," he said, laughing.

Kai sighed in disgust.

"Damn, Mommy, where's your sense of humor. Aiight, check this—I'm off probation at work, so it's cool to call out sick. I'm home chillin'. You gotta problem wit dat, um...Detective Montgomery." Marquise chuckled.

Marquise's jolly mood heightened Kai's anger. Desiring to slap the smile out of his voice, she asked in a calm tone, "Who was in my car Saturday?"

There was silence on the other end of the line. Clearing his throat before he spoke, Marquise finally responded. "Wasn't nobody in your car; just me." He paused. "Oh, yeah...I forgot...my man, Jocko, was wit me Saturday. Don't you remember? I told you we hung out for a minute."

"Did this Jocko person bring his child along?"

"What?"

"You heard me...did Jocko bring his daughter along?"

A deafening silence followed Kai's question.

"Marquise?"

"Yeah?"

"Say something."

"I'm trying...but you're fuckin' wit' my head. I'm tryin' to figure out where you comin' from."

"Well, let me assist you in figuring this thing out. This morning—the very morning I planned to propose to you..." Kai paused, allowing the significance of her words to sink in.

"Propose?" he asked, sounding troubled.

"Yes, I was planning to bring up the subject. I think we should get married."

Marquise listened, but was dead silent.

"We're good together and I can offer you a better lifestyle than you're currently leading. As you've probably assumed, I'm wealthy. My paternal grandmother left me an inheritance that's been put in a trust fund. I can't touch that money until I'm twenty-five years old. I have to remain gainfully employed if I expect to collect the full amount, which is in the millions." She heard Marquise gulp at the word *millions*. She chuckled as she imagined him sweating bullets wondering where this conversation was leading and how it could benefit him—the greedy bastard!

"I was recently rewarded a large sum from a lawsuit. I live off that money as well as the money my parents provide. My lifestyle, as you've gathered, is quite comfortable and will improve drastically. In two years, I'll be a multimillionaire… Now, if there's to be even a modicum of trust between us, I need to know who was in my car."

"Slow your roll, Shorty. I never said I was tryin' to get married to you. I told you I'm already engaged."

"Who was in my car, dammit?"

"My man," Marquise said, his voice filled with defiance.

"Does your *man* wear pink barrettes?"

"Yo, whatchu tryin' to say?"

"I found a pink barrette on the floor in my car. So I'm asking again…who the hell was in my car?"

The expected silence followed Kai's question.

"Oh!" Marquise finally blurted. "My little cousin was in the car. I gave my little cousin a ride to the store just before I picked up Jocko. She must have lost one of her barrettes."

"So you took it upon yourself to provide the entire ghetto community with a joyride at my expense?"

"Naw, it wasn't like that. Why you comin' at me like this? Tighten up, Kai."

"You're such a liar. You know what I think? I think you were running family errands in my car. I think the dire emergency you had to attend to had nothing to do with your grandmother. You've never mentioned a grandmother and I doubt if you even have one. You had the audacity to use my car to benefit your fucking family?"

"Yo, I don't know whatchu talking 'bout but I'm gonna have to call you back. My battery's dyin'." Marquise abruptly hung up.

With her mouth wide open, Kai stared at the phone she held in her hand. How dare he hang up on her? She replaced the receiver, vowing to make Marquise's life a living hell.

Kai promptly called Verizon Wireless and terminated Marquise's account. Ha! She would give anything to see his expression when he tried to make calls on a dead cell phone.

Did he actually believe she'd invest her precious time and money into him and then allow him to go traipsing off to that hairy whore at home? Oh, hell no!

It was a good thing she'd taken that photo of him on Saturday night. After hours of hot sex, he'd collapsed into a deep sleep and Kai couldn't resist snapping a nude shot of him as he slept like a baby.

And after rummaging through his pockets, she'd found his Pennsylvania State ID, which listed his current home address. Thank God she'd had the foresight to copy it. His address, printed on a small piece of paper, was tucked in a secret compartment inside her wallet.

Kai gave a wicked chortle and thought, *Let the games begin, you bastard!*

Chapter Forty-Two

A few days after having the stroke, Gran had another and was now on a ventilator. With Gran out of commission, Aunt Bennie had brazenly stepped out of the closet. She brought her female lover to Gran's hospital room. The woman's name was Sheila. She was attractive with long reddish locks. Though she was taller than Aunt Bennie, Terelle surmised that Sheila was the *woman* in the relationship.

Aunt Bennie's lesbian relationship was too much for Terelle to absorb; she thought she would pass the hell out when Aunt Bennie kissed Sheila on the lips right next to Gran's bed. She didn't want to be judgmental, but damn, anyway you looked at it—that shit just wasn't cool! Couldn't Aunt Bennie have at least prepared her for such a shocking revelation? Couldn't she have pulled her to the side and confessed that she liked chicks before bringing Sheila to Gran's room? It seemed like an inappropriate time to finally admit she was gay. Terelle would have appreciated a little time to marinate on the subject.

It was a wonder the spectacle of all that lesbian kissing and hugging didn't cause Gran to snap right out of her coma. Terelle kept her eyes fixed on Gran because she expected her grandmother at any moment to rise up in a fury and start pulling out the trachea and all the other tubes and wires that kept her alive so she could cuss Aunt Bennie out. If Gran had caught sight of her daughter with her lips pressed against the mouth of another woman, she would have somehow gathered the strength from somewhere to give Aunt Bennie a beat down like no other.

But Gran had remained silent and still—she remained in a vegetative state and Terelle knew her grandmother wouldn't be with them much longer. Aunt Bennie also knew, and apparently had accepted the fact, which is why she risked flaunting her lesbianism. Oh well…live and let live. That had always been Terelle's motto.

A few hours later, Terelle left the hospital dealing with the sad realization that she had lost her own mother a long time ago and would soon lose her grandmother as well.

In that melancholy state, she'd stopped to pick up the mail from the mailbox in the vestibule of her apartment building. Standing out among the bills and junk mail was a large manila envelope addressed to Terelle Chambers, Nursing Assistant. Terelle's pretty face crinkled in confusion.

Too curious to wait until she was inside her apartment, she'd ripped the envelope open as she climbed the flight of stairs.

She gaped at the nine and a half by twelve-inch photograph she pulled from the envelope. Turning it upside-down, she viewed it from different angles as she tried to make sense of what she was seeing. She desperately needed her eyes to focus—to stop playing tricks on her. She squeezed her eyes shut, then opened them again, but there was no denying what she saw. With a sinking feeling, she had to admit that what she held between trembling fingers was a photograph of Marquise. Naked. Lying on his back with his legs spread open—dick hanging to the side—in someone else's bed! He was obviously sound asleep for in a waking state he would have never allowed himself to be photographed butt-ass naked.

Danita! The name exploded in Terelle's mind. With rage building, she examined the photo closer and wondered how Danita could afford such a richly furnished bedroom. Project dwellers, she thought angrily, paid little to no rent and minimal utilities and apparently could afford to hook up their cribs with the best of everything.

Terelle grabbed the phone feeling so shaken, she kept pushing the wrong numbers as she tried to call Marquise on his cell.

With unsteady hands, she tried again—slowly and deliberately this time. But she got a recorded message—

Marquise's cell was no longer in service. Unbelievable! This was an emergency—a dire emergency—and his phone had been cut the fuck off! What the hell was going on? It seemed every aspect of the world she thought she knew was crumbling before her eyes.

She tried to calm down. Perhaps it was just a joke. Someone had sent her a photo of a Marquise look-alike. Heart pounding, she chanced another peek at the picture and winced. Without question, it was Marquise. Moreover, it was his unmistakable dick. For even in a limp state, his dick was thick, long, and slightly curved. She cried out in anguish and flung the photo across the room. Her head began to throb. She massaged her temples and walked back and forth whimpering and murmuring that Marquise was a no-good...slimy...dirty...whore...bastard. And she hated his fucking guts.

Terelle felt lightheaded. If she didn't talk to Marquise soon she was going to go ballistic and start breaking up every damn thing in the apartment—starting with his shit.

She called his cell again. Listened to the recording again.

In a stooped position, she yanked open the doors to the cabinet under the kitchen sink, rummaged around until she found a hammer. Then, with hammer in hand and walking like a zombie, she proceeded to the bedroom. Terelle gripped up Marquise's precious Cartier watch, placed it on the nightstand and smashed it into smithereeens.

✿✿✿

The apartment was pitch black. Terelle sat in the dark and listened to Marquise's hard footsteps as he climbed the steps that led to their apartment. Smirking, she waited with wicked anticipation while Marquise fiddled around with his keys, trying to locate the one that would open the door. She enjoyed hearing the rattle of the chain that prevented his entering the apartment.

"Terelle," he yelled through the cracked open door. "Open the door—why you got the door locked up with the chain?" Annoyance coated his words.

She calmly walked to the door and slid the photo through the opening.

"What the fuck is this?"

"Take a good look," she said tonelessly.

Marquise quietly studied the picture, then laughed. "You mad about this? Babe, this is a joke Jocko and his boys played on me. If you don't believe me, you can call him right now…"

"Fuck you, Marquise. If that's true, then this situation is worse than I thought. Because if Jocko took this picture then I have to accept that being in jail for two years has turned you into a fuckin' faggot. So whatchu sayin'—you one of those homo thugs? Huh? You on the down low?" The venomous words came through lips that were twisted in rage. Marquise flinched, then quickly recovered, his eyes ablaze in self-righteous indignation.

Feeling safe behind the chained door, Terelle took pleasure in watching his mounting rage. He gnawed on his lip furiously, his mind raced, his eyes darted wildly as he tried to figure out a way to break through the door to wring Terelle's neck.

"That's bullshit and you know it," he finally said. His voice was ice.

"Whatever. But check this shit out...you're creating a disturbance. Keeta's asleep and I was trying to get some sleep. So take your cheatin', whorin' ass back to the bitch or faggot you been fuckin' around with."

Marquise flinched again at the word, *faggot*, but forced himself to speak in a soothing tone. "Babe," he said, "I swear to God, I'm not lyin'. Why don't you calm down and let me explain?"

"No."

"Well, can I at least come in and get my things?" he pleaded.

"Hell no! The lease to this apartment is in my name. That means all the contents—everything in here belong to me. Now if you don't hurry up and get the fuck away from my door I'm gonna call the police."

"You gonna call the cops on me after I worked all day?" He exploded. "I'm tired as hell and all I got is the grimy work uniform on my back. You gonna do me like that?"

"Damn right. That's exactly how I'm gonna do you. And that's a small thing compared to how you been doin' me!"

"Yo, this ain't the time to be feedin' into this bullshit. I told you some muthafucker is playing games. Babe, after all we been through, do you think I would fuck up this relationship?" He spoke humbly—desperately. "Open the door and give me a chance to explain?"

"What you've done to me is a crime, Marquise. You've been fuckin' everything that moves ever since we were teenagers...and I've been taking your shit for all these years. The way you treat me is a fuckin' crime and I want justice. The way I see it...your whorin' ass deserves to be behind bars, and I can make it happen with one phone call. Feel me?" Terelle asked sarcastically. "So...stop pushing your luck and get the fuck away from my door."

A dispirited figure, Marquise smiled bitterly, turned and walked away.

Chapter Forty-Three

The elevator was crowded. Noisy support staff conversed loudly, made inane jokes and laughed uproariously about absolutely nothing. It was too early in the morning for such merrymaking. Kai despised them all with a passion.

"Hey, Terelle. Where you been, girl?" someone yelled.

Kai's ears perked up when she heard Terelle's name.

"Hi, Melanie. I took some time off; my grandmother had a stroke," Terelle responded softly.

"Oh. That explains why Marquise has been walking around lookin' so sad," Melanie said.

Curious, Kai craned her neck to witness the look on Terelle's face. She wanted to see the effect her package had on Marquise's fiancée.

Without expression, Terelle gave Melanie a shrug. There was no visible indication that her world had been shattered. She looked at peace—serene.

Irked, Kai sucked her teeth and exited the elevator when it reached the fourth floor. As she passed the residents' dining room, she thought her heart would stop.

Marquise was in the dining room, mopping the floor.

She stepped inside and gasped in shock. He looked absolutely horrible! He needed a shave and his uniform looked as if he'd slept in it. His haggard appearance hurt her eyes. To see him looking so disheveled and forlorn was startling. Her first instinct was to flee the gloom-filled room, but she didn't. She had to make up for what she did. It was time to put him out of his misery and welcome him back into her life. After all, she'd wanted to teach Marquise a lesson, not destroy his life. She loved him and it was time to let him know.

"Marquise." She whispered his name.

He looked up, gave her a vacant stare and resumed mopping.

"Marquise, can we talk—privately?"

He stopped mopping and regarded her with hooded evil eyes, which shocked her. She'd expected him to flash one of his sexy smiles.

"What's there to talk about? I lost my girl—my daughter. Everything I own."

"I want to talk about us. I didn't mean to..."

"You didn't mean to what? Send my girl that fucked-up picture?"

"I was angry. You lied to me. I was just trying to get even."

"Okay, well you got even. You won; it's over. Now, roll out—I'm busy." He pushed the mop across an area he'd already cleaned.

Kai didn't budge from where she stood. "I miss you. I miss what we had."

He spat out the words, "We ain't have shit!"

"You're upset. You couldn't mean what you're saying. Call me later so we can try to sort through this mess. Let me make up for what I did...I can help you." She moved toward him.

Marquise drew back. "No thanks. Now, excuse me...I 'm tryin' to git my work done." Marquise pushed the industrial mop bucket past Kai. Leaving Kai alone in the dining room, he went into the utility room down the hall and slammed the door.

Unprepared for his rejection, Kai felt disoriented. Getting Marquise back wasn't going to be as easy as she'd thought.

✿✿✿

At the end of the shift Kai waited for Marquise in the parking lot. Prepared to offer him a ride home, she was stumped when he slid into the passenger seat of a black Camry driven by one of his male co-workers. Quickly gathering her wits about her, she decided to follow the car to find out what Marquise was up to.

Weaving through rush-hour traffic, Kai tailed the Camry.

After cruising Girard Avenue for about twenty blocks, the car slowed and made a right turn onto Merion Avenue in West Philly. Kai turned right also. The Camry came to a complete stop in front of a dilapidated wood-framed row home that screamed for a new coat of paint and had crumbling concrete steps leading to the front door. The majority of the houses on the narrow, desolate street were uninhabited shells with boards at the windows and doors. The houses that were still occupied were in desperate need of repair.

Kai brazenly maneuvered the Benz beside the Camry and gave Marquise a big smile.

Marquise rolled down the car window. "You stalkin' me or somethin'?"

"Are you ready to talk?" Kai asked sweetly.

"I told you...I ain't got no rap for you." Marquise turned to the driver. "Thanks for the ride. I'll see you tomorrow."

The driver, recognizing Kai from the nursing home, turned to Marquise and shrugged in bewilderment. His expression implied he would appreciate being enlightened as to why the sophisticated social worker from the job had followed him and Marquise to the 'hood.

"Yo, I'll talk to you tomorrow, man." Marquise got out of the car without providing an explanation. With an open palm, he tapped the hood of the Camry, indicating the driver should move along and give him some privacy to handle his business.

Reluctantly, the driver pulled off. Marquise sauntered over to Kai's car.

"Dig this...whatever we had is over..."

"Is this your current abode?" she asked, interrupting him.

Incomprehension furrowed his brow.

"In other words, is this where you're staying now?" Crinkling her nose in disgust, Kai nudged her head toward the shabby house.

"Don't worry 'bout where I'm stayin'," he snapped. "Look..." He took a deep breath. "Just leave me alone... please." He waited for Kai to pull off.

"I'm not going anywhere until you give me an explanation for your drastic change of heart. Everything was going so well until you lied..."

"Listen. I ain't got to explain a muthafuckin' thing, but if you insist..." Looking thoughtful, he chose his words with care. "Yo, dig this...I think you crazy and I fucked up by messin' wit a nut like you." He made a snorting sound, then turned and walked away.

Though his unkind words caused her enormous discomfort, Kai kept a straight face. She refused to believe for a second that Marquise had actually stopped caring for her. He was furious with her, but he'd get over it once they were alone and made the sexual connection that was the glue in their relationship.

Refusing to drive away, she stubbornly sat in front of the house and peered at Marquise through her tinted window. She watched as he rang the doorbell and was admitted by a shadowy female figure.

Enraged that he could so easily dispose of someone as refined and well bred as she to run into the arms of yet another impoverished and ignorant ghetto-girl,

Kai hastily parked the Benz. Ignoring the doorbell, she pounded on the door with her fist.

"Who the hell is bangin' on the door like that?" Kai heard the woman ask.

"Let me handle this, Ayanna," Marquise said as he yanked open the door.

"Yo, what the fuck is your problem?"

"You'd better ask yourself that question because if you don't return the watch you stole from me, you're going to have a huge problem."

"You lyin' bitch; you know I didn't steal no watch from you!"

"What's goin' on, Marquise?" With a baby on her hip and a young toddler tugging at the hem of her tight denim skirt, Ayanna squeezed past Marquise to get a look at the woman causing the ruckus at her front door. Thrown off by the fact that the troublemaker was meticulously coifed, well dressed and was most definitely not from the 'hood, Ayanna squinted in confusion.

"Excuse me, Miss," Kai said calmly. "I truly apologize for causing a disturbance in your home, but the man you're involved with is a thief. "

"Stop lyin'! You gave me that watch," Marquise bellowed.

"I ain't involved with Marquise," Ayanna protested. "Jalil is my man. Marquise is Jalil's best friend. He's just chillin' with us 'til he can straighten out his situation at home."

"You don't have to explain nothin' to her," Marquise angrily informed Ayanna.

Kai dismissed Marquise with a look and directed her conversation to Ayanna.

"You should know that he stole a very expensive watch from me and I believe he's hiding it in your home..."

Ayanna's mouth fell open as she shot Marquise a look of stunned disbelief.

"I really hate to involve you," Kai continued, "but you're harboring a criminal and I'm going to have to alert the authorities." Kai flipped open her cell phone and pushed the first digit of 9-1-1.

There was a hint of fear in Ayanna's eyes. She pulled Marquise to the side and whispered, "I don't know what's going on, but I'm not tryin' to get caught all up in the middle of no bullshit. If she sends the cops here and they start diggin' in my business, they'll find out that both you and Jalil are staying here. If they report me... I could lose my Section 8. Where would me and my kids stay if that happens?"

Marquise didn't have an answer.

"I hate to do this, Marquise. I'm really sorry, but you're gonna have to go," she said loud enough for Kai to hear.

Satisfied, Kai smiled.

"Do you want me to call Terelle and ask her if you can come back home?" Ayanna offered.

Marquise shook his head. "When Jalil gets home... just tell 'em I said I'll hollah when I git myself situated."

Ayanna nodded sadly as Marquise made his slow and solemn exit. Kai trailed him. Once outside, he hurried past Kai and headed for the bus stop around the corner.

Kai got in her car and began to follow Marquise. "Where are you going, Marquise? Are you going to try to reconcile with Terelle?" she taunted.

He stopped walking. "Stop followin' me, you crazy bitch! Just leave me the fuck alone." He balled his fists as he approached the car. "I should smash you in your fuckin' grille for causin' all this trouble in my life."

"Is that a threat?" She twirled her hair; her eyes gleamed with excitement. "I don't take threats lightly and neither do the police. Look, I know Terelle's address and I believe my watch is hidden somewhere in her squalid apartment. She lives on the corner of 55th and Kingsessing Avenue—right?" Kai snapped open the clasp of her Fendi bag and pulled out a Palm Pilot.

Marquise blinked rapidly. "Leave Terelle outta this."

Kai pushed buttons. "Should I recite the address?"

Frustrated, he shook his head. "Naw, that ain't necessary."

"Consider yourself forewarned because I'll be at her front door with the police in a few minutes. So...if that's where you're headed, perhaps you should reconsider."

Marquise placed his palm on his forehead and shook his head in frustration. "I can prove you bought that watch for me. All I have to do is go back to that jewelry store in the casino and talk to the dude who works there. He'll remember me."

"You accompanied me to the store, but I paid for the watch and had it insured. I've already reported it stolen and the insurance company won't pay until there's an investigation."

Marquise looked down in disgust. "Whatchu want from me?"

"I want you! I miss you and I want you back in my life," she said softly.

"You talkin' crazy. You never had me—we was just fuckin' around. I was honest at the door—I told you I was engaged."

"That's in the past. You're not in a relationship now, so can we please move forward? It's cold out here… you're homeless and without clothing. Why won't you let me help you? Just come home with me—please?" Kai clicked a button to unlock the car doors.

"You must be out of your muthafuckin' mind; I'm not goin' nowhere wit your crazy ass."

"Nor are you going anywhere without me. You want to run back to your trashy little ghetto girl as if *I'm* the second-class citizen? You should be honored to be in my presence."

"*Honored!*" Marquise said indignantly. "Yo, you be tryin' to put it out there like you all high class and shit, but you ain't nothin' but a smut. I don't give a fuck what you drive, what kinda clothes you wear or how much cheddar you got in your bank account—you still a skeezer." Marquise was silent for a moment, then muttered to himself, "I can't believe I played myself like this." He bit down on his lip and let out a mirthless laugh. "I shoulda seen the signs from jump—the way you was ridin' my jock...followin' me around... throwin' presents and dough at me... Man, that shit ain't normal—that's that fatal attraction shit." He shook his head in self-disgust. "Yo, Mommy...ain't no honor in none of this. I'm gonna feel *honored* when I can make things right wit my baby—Terelle."

"Nice speech," Kai said, clapping her hands together. "I'm touched by your, uh...soliloquy." Smirking, she placed her hand over heart theatrically. "I'm truly touched, but let me make this abundantly clear...if you don't come home with me—if you try to go back to your tacky girlfriend, you can kiss your freedom goodbye." Kai paused, then continued in a frosty voice. "And your little girlfriend can kiss her freedom goodbye as well."

Confused, Marquise frowned. "Terelle ain't got nothin' to do with none of this."

"If you humiliate me by leaving me for that crude ghetto trash, I won't feel vindicated until you're both handcuffed and carted off to jail."

Marquise looked as if he'd just eaten something extremely distasteful.

Delighted by his obvious discomfort, Kai continued. "That's right, ex-convict," she taunted. "I know my watch is at your girlfriend's apartment. And believe me, I won't hesitate to have you and the mother of your child locked up for receiving stolen property!"

Marquise's eyes widened in disbelief.

"I'm very serious. So, go ahead...walk away. But be willing to suffer the wrath of Kai." Finding her words hilarious, she cackled like a witch.

With his shoulders stooped by the weight of his problems, Marquise moved mechanically to the passenger side of the car. He leaned against the door in defeat before opening it.

Infused with renewed hope, Kai pressed down on the gas pedal the moment Marquise got in the car and closed the door. Eager to get out of the slums and back to a more civilized environment she zoomed down Merion Avenue, turned onto 52nd Street, made a quick left on Lancaster Avenue and after a few blocks, she turned left again on Girard Avenue.

Looking dejected, Marquise sat slumped in the passenger seat as Kai zipped onto the Center City ramp leading to the expressway. Kai smiled to herself. The silly boy didn't realize how fortunate he was—but he'd soon find out. The moment she had him back in her condo and back in her bed, he'd realize how very much the gods had smiled upon him.

—

Chapter Forty-Four

"Marquise called out again; he said he was sick," Mr. Hicks informed Terelle as she came out of a resident's room wearing surgical gloves and carrying an armload of soiled bed linen and foul-smelling disposable briefs. With his arms folded across his chest and wearing an expression of displeasure, he stood in Terelle's path waiting for an acceptable explanation for Marquise's absence. Terelle dumped the smelly bundle in the soiled linen cart. Buying time before she responded to Mr. Hicks' announcement, she removed the gloves, tossed them and thoroughly washed her hands at a nearby sink.

She had promised that Marquise would be an exemplary employee, but to her chagrin, she had no excuse for his absence and was completely mystified as to why he hadn't shown up for work.

"He's off probation, Mr. Hicks...why can't he call out sick?" she asked, hoping to cover her confusion.

"He called out last week, Terelle. He's going to get himself in trouble if he starts taking too many sick days. I stuck my neck out for him and I expect him to behave responsibly."

Not knowing what to say, and unwilling to admit to Mr. Hicks that she and Marquise were no longer together, Terelle nodded. "I'll speak to him," she murmured and rushed away to finish her chores.

By eight that morning Terelle had already gotten the seven residents who were under her care out of bed, washed, and dressed. With time to kill until the breakfast trays arrived, she plopped down in a chair near the pay phone mounted on the wall outside the residents' dining room. Although the phone was intended for the residents' use, they hardly ever used it. The pay phone served as a link to the outside world for support staff; they were prohibited from using the phone at the nurses' station.

Prior to being employed by the nursing home, Marquise had called Terelle several times a day on the pay phone. She missed Marquise terribly and wondered where he could be. Forcing herself to be strong, she reminded herself that his whereabouts were no longer her concern.

The first night of sleeping without Marquise had been easy, but the second night was hard—she'd cried herself to sleep. Had it not been for Saleema, who'd come to Terelle's rescue with a Valium in hand, the third night would have been a replay of the night before. Terelle braced herself for tonight—the fourth night of sleeping alone.

She told herself that withdrawal symptoms were normal. After a lifetime of loving him, it would take a while to get Marquise completely out of her system.

"Mr. Bevel has a dental appointment. Would you take him downstairs to the dentist?" asked the charge nurse.

Wanting to keep busy so she wouldn't have time to focus on Marquise, Terelle nodded and went to get the resident who was in his room. "How are you doing, Mr. Bevel?" Terelle patted the elderly man's arm before gripping the handles of his wheelchair. "You have an appointment with the dentist. But don't worry," she said with a teasing grin. "You're not getting your teeth pulled; you're just gonna have a routine check-up."

Uncomprehending, but responding to her pleasant disposition, the disoriented old man chuckled as Terelle pushed him out of his room and down the hall toward the elevator.

Terelle pushed the down button, but the elevator had a mind of its own and switched directions, going up instead of down. It stopped on the sixth floor. The doors opened and of all people, Danita, stepped inside. Terelle glared at her and Danita shifted her gaze. Panicked, Danita pushed the *open door* button, but the door refused to open. The elevator descended.

Terelle fixed a look of pure hatred on Danita's downcast head.

Feeling Terelle's hateful gaze, Danita looked up. "Why you grittin' on me? You gotta problem—whassup?" Nervousness caused Danita's voice to waver.

"Yeah, bitch. I got a big problem with you." Terelle slammed the *stop* button, causing the elevator to stop between floors.

Unwilling to be stuck in the elevator with Terelle, Danita reached for the *run* button, but Terelle grabbed her hand.

"Oh hell no, bitch. It's just you and me now." She moved closer to Danita. "I got your little present and I didn't like that shit one bit."

"What?" Danita's eyes bulged.

Terelle had considered Danita a nice-looking woman—slutty—but still nice-looking. However, this Danita, who was scared out of her wits, looked a hot mess!

"You fucked my fiancé and sent me the evidence. Now you wanna play dumb," Terelle said, pointing a finger in Danita's face as she backed her into a corner.

"Get your finger out of my face," Danita demanded. Indignation replaced her fear. "Me and Marquise ain't nothin' but friends. You need to stop trippin', you insecure bitch!"

Insecure bitch! The words echoed in Terelle's head. Time seemed distorted, unreal. There was no conscious decision to physically lash out, and Terelle was as shocked as Danita when her fist smashed into the woman's mouth. Blood gushed from Danita's split lower lip, motivating her to fight back. Scratching, clawing—tearing at each other's uniforms, swinging punches, and pulling hair, the two women tussled inside the elevator, falling on top of Mr. Bevel and toppling over his wheelchair.

Coming to her senses, Terelle instantly went to help Mr. Bevel. She pulled his wheelchair upright and gasped when she noticed a bluish-colored lump developing on the side of his face.

While Terelle tended to the resident, Danita quickly pushed the *run* button. When the elevator reached the first floor the two women were met by security.

For a stunned moment, the security guards were silent as they gaped at the carnage that had taken place in the elevator: Danita's bloodied lip and scratched face, Terelle's ripped uniform and the rapidly growing hickey on the resident's head.

"What were y'all doing in there?" asked one of the security guards, his tone a mixture of shock and disgust.

"She attacked me!" Danita blurted.

"Oh my God, look at that poor man's head," yelled the other guard. "Call a code red," he yelled to the receptionist at the front desk.

Mortified, Terelle listened in horror to the receptionist's magnified voice over the intercom. "Code red, Code red. All licensed nurses please come to the first-floor lobby."

Running as if he had been murdered, nurses instantly swarmed around Mr. Bevel. They inspected the wound and took his vital signs, clicking their tongues and cutting narrow-eyed glances at the two culprits.

Security escorted Terelle and Danita to the nursing supervisor's office where the two women would face disciplinary action.

✿✿✿

As she mechanically piled chicken nuggets, broccoli, macaroni and cheese on Markeeta's plate, Terelle wondered how her life had so swiftly gone from sheer bliss to such a horror story. She'd been suspended from her job without pay pending further investigation. Marquise had proven to be a cheating whore whose whereabouts were unknown. Her grandmother lay dying in a hospital room in Chester, Pennsylvania. Her aunt had chosen the worst time in the world to announce her homosexuality. And her mother, after all these years and despite the most convincing promises to get clean and stay clean, was still nothing but a crack head.

Looking down at her daughter, Terelle gave a wan smile and affectionately smoothed Markeeta's hair. Markeeta was the one and only bright light in her life.

The peal of the telephone interrupted her thoughts. "Hello."

"Hey, Terelle, this is Ayanna."

"Hey, whassup?" Terelle said without emotion.

"I just called to check on Marquise. Is he back home?"

Terelle took a deep breath. "No. I thought he was staying with you and Jalil."

"He was. But yesterday this chick came by to see Marquise and..."

"Who?" Terelle felt her face grow hot; her heart banged inside her chest.

"Girl, don't get me to lyin'. I didn't ask that ho her name. She was light-skinned and slim with curly light-brown hair. She was dressed real fly and...oh yeah, she was driving a phat-ass Benz."

"A Benz!" Warning bells sounded in Terelle's head. Ayanna had to be talking about the same car Marquise had borrowed to drive her to Chester. It had to be the car he'd told her belonged to his business associate, Jocko. Marquise was such a fucking liar! "What color was the Benz?" Terelle asked suspiciously.

"Black."

Ayanna's response confirmed Terelle's suspicions.

"Anyway, Sis came to my house and pounded on my fuckin' door like she was the damn police. She demanded to talk to Marquise and when he came to the door, Sis started raisin' all kinds of hell. She was screaming at him and accusing him of stealing her watch."

Oh Lord, what's going on? Terelle wondered. Was it a coincidence or was Ayanna referring to Marquise's Cartier watch—the gift from his so-called business associates and the very watch she'd destroyed in anger?

"To hear Sis tell it," Ayanna went on, "the damn watch was so expensive she had to insure it. She thought he had it stashed inside my house so she started threatening to send the cops to my crib." Ayanna took a deep breath, then continued. "Now, girl you know I don't need that kinda drama in my life. Me and my kids could end up out on the streets if those Section 8 people found out Jalil's stayin' with me. Shit, they'd probably try to lock my ass up if they knew I had Jalil *and* Marquise living here. So, I really didn't have no choice...I had to ask Marquise to leave. But I told him he should call you to see if you'd let him come back home." Ayanna paused, waiting for Terelle's response.

"He didn't call me, Ayanna. Do you think Jalil knows where he's staying?"

"Nope. Jalil ain't heard from him either. But check this...after they left, I peeked through the blinds and saw Marquise standing outside arguing with the chick. He looked real mad and walked away, but that hooker started following behind him in the car. I couldn't see them after they got way down the street. That's why I called—I just wanted to make sure he made it home okay 'cause I don't know what was up with Sis. She seemed slightly scattered; you know what I mean? She had this crazy-ass look in her eyes...something about her just wasn't right. Yeah, Sis was definitely scattered."

Who in the hell is this light-skinned woman? Call it female intuition or just plain common sense, but whatever it was, Terelle was suddenly certain that the mystery woman and not Danita had sent the nude photo of Marquise. And Marquise had been spending his weekends with that woman and not with the Jamaicans as he'd claimed.

What a sucker she'd been. Had Marquise been within her reach, Terelle knew she'd slap the shit out of him and then throw her hands up and fight like a man.

Needing a moment to seethe in private, Terelle thanked Ayanna for her concern and rushed her off the phone.

Anger as hot as fire consumed her. Disjointed thoughts and a million unanswered questions flitted through her mind. Terelle rubbed her temples and paced.

Markeeta threw a broccoli spear on the floor and gave her mother an impish grin. Now pacing in high gear, Terelle paid no attention to her daughter. Markeeta tossed a chicken nugget on the floor and studied her mother's face. Still no response. She added a handful of macaroni to the smorgasbord on the floor, but her mother was too distracted to notice. Perplexed, Markeeta bit her bottom lip.

Terelle slipped on the mushy mixture and grabbed the countertop to prevent hitting the floor. She shot a glance at her daughter who sat in her high chair nibbling on her bottom lip, and to her dismay Terelle noticed that Markeeta was not only the spitting image of her daddy, but had also inherited his habit of biting his bottom lip.

Terelle gazed at her daughter, painfully aware that it didn't matter if she kicked Marquise out…tore up his possessions…refused to wear his ring. None of those actions would change anything.

Of one thing she was certain; she was doomed to love Marquise until the day she died.

Chapter Forty-Five

To no avail, Kai tried to placate Marquise. How long did he expect her to tolerate his brooding? For two nights in a row, he'd deliberately withheld sex.

On their first night together, she'd expected hot sex into the wee hours of the morning, but Marquise had fallen asleep the moment his head hit the pillow, forcing her to subdue the urges of her body with a vibrator. She'd hoped the loud whirring sound of the battery-operated apparatus would awaken him, but he sank into an even deeper sleep. He'd been a displaced person. Homeless. Going from pillar to post—sleeping on couches or other makeshift beds his friends from the slums offered had to be exhausting—thus Kai tried to forgive his rude behavior.

But his mistreatment of her tonight was inexcusable. How dare he lie in her bed with his back turned and with the covers tucked beneath him as if contact with her was akin to touching a leper or some other undesirable? After treating him to a steak dinner, Kai had expected a show of appreciation. Granted, the Outback Steakhouse wasn't a five-star restaurant, but Marquise had made the selection. And in light of the fact that he'd been wearing the same scruffy work uniform for almost a week, the low-class eatery had been a damn good choice. Had he been wearing more appropriate attire, Kai would have insisted upon going somewhere tasteful like Ruth's Chris Steakhouse.

She'd offered to buy him a new wardrobe, but he'd stubbornly declined, stating that he had a closet filled with clothes at home.

Whether he liked it or not, it would've behooved him to accept that his new *home* was with Kai.

Feeling horny to the point of considering rape, she determinedly placed an arm around him, snaked her hand beneath the comforter and began to caress his bulging deltoid.

Marquise awakened. Annoyed, he shook her hand off his shoulder.

Kai yanked the comforter from his body. "Let's talk," she said curtly.

Marquise bolted up and snatched the comforter from her grasp. He pulled it up to his shoulders, and angering her further, he pulled the comforter over his head.

"How long are you going to sulk?" she asked the form beneath the comforter. "Your attitude really sucks, you know."

Marquise didn't utter a sound.

"Why don't you stop acting so childish?" She pulled the comforter off his head.

"I guess holding me hostage is real grown-up," he retorted in a sleepy voice.

"I'm not holding you hostage. You're free to leave whenever you want. I just thought you were ready to embrace a better lifestyle. I guess I was wrong. Go ahead...leave! Go back to that hellhole you have the audacity to refer to as *home!*"

Looking ready to sprint, Marquise threw off the comforter and sat up.

Kai hadn't expected him to call her bluff. Her mind raced to come up with a different approach. "Are you content with your current mode of transportation?" she asked as she desperately grabbed the sleeve of his undershirt.

"What are you talking about?" Marquise asked, suddenly interested.

"I would die if I had to stand on corners waiting for buses, but if that makes you happy..." Her voice trailed off.

Marquise silently waited for Kai to continue.

"Are you ready to be upgraded to a more sophisticated mode of travel? If so, let me assure you..." Kai paused for effect. "I can make that happen."

"Yo, speak English. Whatchu tryin' to say?"

Kai chuckled. "What's your pleasure? A new truck—a sports car?"

She suppressed a smug smile when she heard his audible intake of breath. She had the greedy bastard in the palm of her hands now!

Inching up close, Kai ran her fingernails lightly against his back. She whispered in his ear, "You'll look good driving an F-150. I've seen the way you stare at the billboard advertising the new model."

Marquise grunted a reply and propped himself up on an elbow.

"Do you want one, baby?" she cooed and began to place kisses up and down his arm, his neck, and his earlobe.

Marquise didn't answer her question, but his lack of resistance informed Kai that he was ready to submit and give up some dick. Skillfully, she worked her fingers inside his boxers and instantly located her heart's desire. A little friendly persuasion was all it had taken. The tough-guy act was just a façade. Marquise was putty in her hands.

Climbing over him, Kai disappeared beneath the covers and scooted downward. Lying on her side, facing him, she took his growing stiffness into her mouth and sucked softly—slowly. He responded with a low moan, which prompted her to quicken the pace. Like a baby starving for a bottle, she sucked hungrily.

"Stop!" Marquise groaned. He attempted to pull out, but Kai had a pit-bull hold on him and would not let go.

"Please, baby. Stop!" His voice was choked. "You gon' make me cum."

Kai stopped. She wiped her mouth, came up for air and looked him in the eye. "I don't want you to cum—not yet. That would be tragic. My kitty cat is soaking wet. She misses you."

He looked helpless and even emitted a slight whimper as she straddled him. Her eyes radiated triumph. She'd waited a long time for the rough ride that only her wild stallion could give.

✿✿✿

"Now let me get this straight," Saleema said, waving a colorfully manicured finger. "You fucked up the wrong bitch and lost your job over it?"

"No, I didn't lose my job—not yet. The situation is under investigation. I'm on suspension without pay. I made a mistake; Marquise wasn't fuckin' with Danita."

"You gonna apologize?"

"Hell no!" Terelle exclaimed vehemently. "That smut wanted to fuck Marquise! You should have seen the way she was riding his jock—throwing herself at him every chance she got. She deserved a beat down for disrespecting me like that."

"Okay, so who sent this picture?" Saleema scrutinized the nude photo of Marquise. "Damn! Quise is sound asleep and his jawn is still lookin' kinda husky. He must be hung like a horse when he's wide-awake. No wonder he's got all y'all goin' the hell crazy!" Saleema said, laughing.

Terelle snatched the photo out of Saleema's hands. "Stop playing—this is serious."

"Sorry." Sitting in a chair at Terelle's kitchen table, Saleema assumed an upright position and mimicked a serious expression.

"I don't know who sent the damn thing," Terelle said solemnly. "Ayanna described her…said she was tall and skinny…a yella bitch with light-brown curly hair." Terelle paused in thought. "Oh yeah, and she drives a black Benz. I've seen the car, but I don't know who she is. But I know one thing: when I find out…that slut is gonna seriously regret causing all this confusion in my life." There was steel in Terelle's voice.

Briefly pensive, Saleema cleared her throat. "I think you're mad at the wrong person. That chick…whoever she is…don't owe you a damn thing. But, Marquise… Now, that muthafucker owes you the world."

"I'm not saying that Marquise is innocent, but according to Ayanna… Marquise didn't even want to deal with that crazy bitch. Ayanna said the chick was a real nut case—making threats like she had something on him."

Saleema gave Terelle an inquiring gaze, which urged her to continue.

"She's blackmailing him," Terelle said. "I know it. There's no way Marquise would let all these days go by without calling to check on Keeta."

"Get real. Look at his track record. Marquise ain't gotta be blackmailed into sticking his dick into some new coochie?"

Terelle stared off thoughtfully. "Think what you want. You don't understand."

"Make me understand," Saleema insisted. "As your

friend, I have to tell you…you sound like a fuckin' nut talkin' this blackmail shit. Why are you making excuses for him? Why are you allowing Marquise to treat you like you ain't shit?"

Terelle flinched as if she'd been smacked upside the head. She instantly began massaging both temples.

"Look at you! You're not gonna be satisfied until you rub out all the hair around your temples."

Unaware that she'd been massaging her temples, Terelle looked perplexed and then yanked her hands away from her head.

"That's just what's gonna happen if don't stop worrying about Marquise." Saleema wagged a warning finger. "Another thing…" she continued, "You been kickin' ass over Marquise since middle school and now you wanna fight the latest skeezer as if that's gonna put a stop to his cheating. It's not. An ass whoopin' might make the chick rethink the situation, but Quise will be already plotting on the next jawn."

"Marquise belongs here with Markeeta and me and that's all I'm gonna say," Terelle said emphatically.

"So, why'd you ask me to come over? I could have stayed at my gig and worked another shift. Pandora's Box was jumpin'. And every trick that walked through the door wanted to see *me!* I was holding it down on the morning shift and I was getting ready to take over the next one," Saleema bragged.

"I had to talk to you face-to-face. I wanted to tell

you what was going on; I needed to know if you're down? Are you?"

"You know I don't get down like that any more!" Saleema sounded offended. "I'm not trying to break my nails and get my face all scratched the fuck up."

"Come on, Saleema. Talk that shit to somebody who doesn't know you."

"For real. I don't fight anymore. I let my hammer handle things!" Saleema lovingly patted her purse, which was bulged by a silver 22. "Let a nigga or a bitch come at me all crazy...see how they act when I put some of this hot shit up in their ass."

"I'm not asking you to *shoot* anybody. I just need to borrow your ride so I can track that slut down."

"How are you gonna borrow Jezebel when you can't even drive!" Saleema's voice was loud and shrill.

"I want *you* to drive; I'll do the rest."

"Look, we're not young bucks anymore; we're grown-ass women and we don't need to get involved in this dumb shit," Saleema said, shaking her head. "I told you about my young girl squad, didn't I? All I have to do is give the word, and they'll whip that ass in a heartbeat."

"This is personal; I don't want your squad to handle it. That bitch's ass is mine!"

There was a long silence. "Forget it, all right?" Terelle looked and sounded peeved.

Saleema dropped her head in thought as she considered the options.

During the interval, Terelle waited patiently for Saleema's decision knowing that Saleema would not let her best friend go out like that.

Raising her head, Saleema spoke in a deadly tone, "If a bitch fucks with you; she done fucked with me. You know I'm not gonna let you go out like that. Damn right, I'm down. I got your back, girl...don't even worry about it."

Chapter Forty-Six

Thumping head-splitting racket poured from the living room jolting Kai into a state of confused wakefulness. It sounded like someone had set off a series of explosives; her bed seemed to quake. Next, she heard a rough urban voice, hollering at the top of his lungs. She was able to make out a few words: *nigga… muthafuckers…pistol… murder…ain't scared to die.*

"Marquise," she screamed over the pandemonium. Wearing boxer shorts, Marquise appeared in the bedroom within seconds.

"What's wrong?" His voice cracked with concern.

"What the hell is going on out there?" she demanded though she'd figured out that the unrelenting noise that emanated from her living room was that vulgar rap music Marquise listened to. "It's six o'clock in the morning. Why are you blasting that heathen music at this hour?" Kai brushed past Marquise, and headed determinedly toward the stereo system.

"Heathen music? Why you all bent outta shape? I always listen to my sounds when I git ready for work.

What's wrong wit that?" he asked calmly as he trailed her into the living room. There was no hostility in his tone. Kai figured he was controlling his temper and being a good boy because he wanted that new truck.

"The volume's turned sky-high. Damn! Are you trying to give me a migraine before my day gets started?" Kai asked irritably.

Marquise was quiet; he was unusually passive, which emboldened Kai even further. Using an index finger, she stabbed the power button and instantly silenced the rap moron who was ranting about splitting some nigga's head. *Jeeze!*

"Yo, how you gonna come out here and just cut my shit off like that?" Marquise frowned, but made an effort to keep the bass out of his voice.

Noticing Marquise's work uniform draped over the ironing board, which he had taken the liberty to set up in the living room, Kai scowled. She turned the power back on, hit the button to slide open the door, took out the obviously bootlegged CD and handed it to Marquise. "I can cut off your shit because you're playing it on *my* shit." She shut off the power again.

A look of rage covered Marquise's face as he swiftly and threateningly made a step toward Kai.

Instantly regretting mouthing off, Kai wondered if she should run.

He approached and stooped to come down to her height. His face was unnecessarily close to Kai's face.

"Yo, I don't need you or nothin' you got," Marquise said through clenched teeth. It was frightening the way the veins in his neck stood out. Kai shrank back "I got my own shit at my crib," he continued. "You wanted me here—well, I'm here, but that don't mean I'm gonna let you talk to me all greasy like that. What, you think I'm sweet or somethin'?"

He swung around and paced over to the ironing board. He snatched the pants off the ironing board and stepped into them. Grumbling to himself, he began to iron his shirt vigorously. "You think I'm sweet?" he asked, looking up with blazing eyes fixed on Kai's face.

Kai was speechless. Marquise was practically foaming at the mouth. He looked dangerous—like a rabid beast and she wanted him out of her home—this instant!

She swallowed and mentally searched for words that would gently but firmly express her urgent need for him to get the hell out!

"Marquise," she said, now trailing him as he stomped to the bedroom. She cleared her throat and carefully chose her words. "Our cultural differences are more glaring than we both realized and…um...perhaps we should reconsider our decision…uh…maybe it wasn't such a good idea for you to move in." There! She'd said it. Now if she could click her heels and make that sonofabitch disappear forever, her world would be complete.

"Get out?" he bellowed as he advanced, his big hand outstretched. "You took everything from me... my home, my girl, my daughter...everything. Now you tellin' me to git the fuck out? You think I'm gonna let you chump me like that." Marquise's eyes scared her. He looked insane, like someone beyond reasoning. Looking possessed, he gripped her by the chin and pushed her head backward. "I should bash your fuckin' head through the wall." Then, apparently having a better idea, his hand slipped to her thin neck. She felt herself being lifted from the floor, her legs dangled and then kicked comically. Embarrassment replaced fear as it occurred to her that she'd never imagined her life ending in such a humiliating and ridiculous manner.

With one abnormally large hand, Marquise threw her on top of the bed and pounced upon her. In the brief moment before the choking resumed, she managed to sputter an apology. "I'm sorry. Please, Marquise. I didn't mean it. Please don't do this."

"Fuckin' bitch!" he spat as he straddled her and clamped both hands around her neck. "You think I'm a joke? Who the fuck you think you playin' wit?" Pure hatred shone in his eyes.

She twisted and squirmed helplessly. Marquise was too heavy to overthrow. "I'm sorry. Please stop," she pleaded as she gasped for breath, her face contorted into a mask of fear. Suddenly the tiny muscles in her face began to relax; she struggled to control a smile that played at the corners of her mouth for she realized that her squirming and writhing against his crotch had inadvertently stimulated him. His dick was hard!

He looked down at her. Although his face was etched in fury, his lust-filled eyes assured her safety. She peeled away each finger and removed his hands from her neck. She kissed his right hand—flicked her tongue against his palm and between his fingers. Feeling him weakening, she grew bolder and slipped a hand beneath his tee shirt and lightly encircled his nipples with the tip of her finger.

Aroused, Marquise pulled Kai up on her knees and mounted her from behind. He emitted the growl of a tortured beast before plunging inside her and once again submitting to her will.

Chapter Forty-Seven

"Girl, when you gonna get off suspension?" Melanie asked over the phone.

"I'm not sure; I have a meeting with my union rep next week," Terelle said.

"You need to be here 'cause the nursing home is buzzin' today. Everybody's talking about Marquise and that light-skinned social worker," Melanie excitedly informed Terelle.

Filled with a sense of dread, Terelle asked hoarsely, "The social worker on the fourth floor?"

"Uh-huh. That's the one. Kai Montgomery. I heard she got a lotta cheddar and she's been buying Marquise all kinds of shit."

The room began to whirl. Feeling hot, flushed, and lightheaded all at once, Terelle reached for a glass of water on the nightstand.

"Dig this," Melanie continued with an upbeat tone that would have been appropriate had she been giving Terelle good news. "Didn't nobody even know you and Marquise had broke up 'til this morning when somebody peeped him getting outta her Benz. She must have some kinda pull at the nursing home 'cause she wheeled into one of those parking spaces reserved for doctors only."

Terelle was rendered speechless. Melanie, however, paying no attention to Terelle's stunned silence, continued the verbal assault. "Chile, the way she be tryin' to act like she all that, you'd think she'd try to hide the fact that she messin' wit a nigga who works in Housekeepin'. Word is..." Melanie paused and made an annoying smacking sound—a prelude to revealing the juiciest part of the story. "Chile...I heard that conceited hussy leaned over and kissed Marquise—gave the nigga tongue all down his throat before they got outta the car this morning. Now ain't that some shit? They wasn't even tryin' to keep it on the low—they was wide open for all eyes to see."

Melanie's words had the impact of a rain of gunfire aimed at Terelle's heart. Before the bearer of such life-changing, earth-shattering, god-awful bad news could fire off another round, Terelle interrupted. "I gotta go. I'll talk to you later." She clicked the off button before Melanie could utter another word. *Kill the messenger* was truly in order. If Terelle had a weapon and if Melanie were within shooting range, the bitch would be dead.

As if struck by a venomous creature apt to strike again, Terelle flung the phone across the room. Trembling hands covered her mouth as a low moan of agony escaped her lips. *"Oh my God, oh my God...what am I going to do?"* she whimpered.

The thought of Marquise kissing that social worker was beyond her imagination. He didn't even like skinny women and he definitely didn't like high-yella bitches! Or, so he'd always said.

Terelle had an instant flashback to Kai's stricken expression when she'd spotted Terelle and Marquise together on the fourth floor. She recalled asking Marquise what was up with the chick. He'd pretended not to know.

It all made sense now: the Benz, the expensive watch, and that butt-ass naked picture. *They played me!* Terelle admitted mournfully. *Marquise and that skinny, half-white lookin' bitch played me!*

It was more than Terelle could bear. Marquise was supposed to protect her—shelter her from the cold—be her strength when she felt weak—her safe haven when the world was unkind. He'd promised all that and so much more in his letters from jail. But the promises had been empty—meaningless. *Jailhouse promises*, just as Saleema had said.

She couldn't compete with someone as pretty, polished, and prosperous as Kai. Tears stung her eyes and for one terrible moment, she thought about dying. *Death has to be better than this*, she thought as she sank to her knees in despair.

But mercifully, a sudden cold fury replaced the agony of Marquise's betrayal. She wouldn't just roll over and accept the foul deed that had been done to her. She needed some sort of satisfaction—she needed to retaliate. Ah! She was filled with a visceral satisfaction at the thought of revenge.

Terelle got to her feet, wiped her tears and smiled. Kai Montgomery was a rich bitch who thought she could have anything she wanted. Well, Terelle would be damned if she was going to let that high-class smut get away with stealing her man. Kai Montgomery was going to pay dearly for her crime.

With a wry smile, she imagined taking a knife to Kai's face. The best plastic surgeon in the world would be in a quandary as to how to piece together that bitch's mutilated mug after Terelle got through with her.

Chapter Forty-Eight

In battle mode and dressed appropriately, Terelle wore scruffy sweats and sneakers. Saleema, casually chic in a bronze Italian-knit sweater, a dark-chocolate leather fur-lined vest with a Gucci scarf draped around her neck, hardly looked ready to assist in the ass whoopin' Terelle intended to inflict upon Kai.

Hidden from view on a tiny street behind Girard College, they'd been sitting in Saleema's truck for what seemed like an eternity as they waited for Kai and Marquise to leave the nursing home.

"Who's watching Keeta?" Saleema asked idly.

"Aunt Bennie and her friend."

"Damn, Terelle. Why you leave my godbaby with those dykes? Ain't no tellin' what they might do..."

"Why are you so negative? Aunt Bennie loves Keeta; she wouldn't hurt her." Terelle rolled her eyes at Saleema.

"I'm just sayin'...you said you can't stand to see them kissin' and carryin' on. You said it seems disrespectful. So...if they do that shit right in front of you, whatchu think they'll do in front of Keeta? She can't *tell* you what they're doing around her, but she can damn sure *show* you. When she start stickin' her face between her doll baby's legs, you're gonna be sorry you left her with those dykes. I ain't tryin' to be smart or nothin' but I ain't tryin' to be the godmother to a little bulldyke."

Though it had bothered Terelle that Aunt Bennie and her friend were so touchy-feely in public, she had other pressing issues on her mind.

"Is that the car?" Saleema turned around and pointed to a black Benz pulling out of the nursing home parking lot. It stopped for a red light at Girard and Corinthian Avenue. Saleema revved the engine and quickly caught up with the Benz when it turned onto Broad Street.

Rush hour on Broad Street was crazy. Wheeling Jezebel, Saleema darted from lane to lane as she determinedly kept up with the speeding Benz.

Terelle leaned forward anxiously in the passenger seat. Her radar-like eyes frantically tracked the movement of the Benz. She rocked back and forth as if that movement would help Jezebel to pick up speed.

"Step on it, Saleema; why are you driving like somebody's grandmother?"

"Chill! I got this," Saleema snapped. "You're lucky I got driving skills 'cause this ain't as easy as it looks on TV."

"Hurry up!" Terelle shrieked when she saw the Benz

speed through a yellow light. Before Saleema could catch up, a blue Ford Taurus darted in front of her and zipped through the yellow light. The light turned red; Saleema slammed on the brakes.

Grim-faced, Terelle watched as the Benz whizzed in and out of lanes and then disappeared from view. "Damn, we lost 'em. Why didn't you broady that little Ford and take the light?" Distraught, Terelle slumped in her seat.

"I wasn't letting Jezzie get all banged up by that raggedy-ass Ford. Calm down, Terelle! I'm not gonna let you drive me crazy. Your no-driving ass should be concentratin' on how you're gonna deal with that bitch instead of tryin' to play co-pilot," Saleema said with laughter, trying to lessen the tension inside the SUV.

Instead of offering a reciprocal smile, Terelle maintained a fretful expression and massaged her temples anxiously.

"Lighten up, girl. Jezebel's on the case." Saleema patted the steering wheel affectionately. "I got this!" Despite Saleema's reassuring words, Terelle, unable to relax, leaned forward again; her eyes worriedly searched for a glimpse of the Benz.

"We gotta stay in the cut; we can't be all up on them."

"I think we lost 'em," Terelle said, doubling over as if in pain; her head nearly touched her lap.

"There they go," Saleema shouted, pointing. "They're turning on Vine Street." Saleema swerved into the left lane.

Terelle jerked upright; sparks of excitement glinted in her eyes. "Stay on 'em," she commanded.

They rode in silence as Saleema, wearing an intense expression, trailed Marquise and Kai down Vine Street.

The Benz switched lanes. "Where the hell are they going?" Saleema wondered aloud.

"Looks like they're heading for Penn's Landing."

The bumper-to-bumper traffic on Columbus Boulevard slowed the Benz; the traffic came to a complete standstill. Saleema relaxed and turned to Terelle. "Okay, so what's the plan? Are we gonna roll on that skank when she gets outta the ride or what?"

"No, I wanna ask her and Marquise some questions first."

"Hello!" Saleema said sarcastically. "Am I hearing you right?" Saleema stared at Terelle. "You wanna ask some questions? Let me find out we done sat outside that old people's home for hours…actin' like we 5-0 doin' surveillance just so you can ask some damn questions!"

"No, it's not like that. Trust me…I got something for that high-class ho."

"Aw, that shit you talkin' is weak." Totally irritated, Saleema sucked her teeth. "I didn't come out here and risk getting Jezebel all scratched and scraped so you could play detective. The evidence is right before your eyes, what else you need to know? Let me find out you got me zoomin' all over Philly, chasing those two assholes for nothing. The minute we catch up with that bitch, you better go up in her mouth. Ask questions later."

Terelle exhaled. "Like I said, it ain't like that." Terelle unconsciously rubbed the area of her finger where her engagement ring should have been. "I just want to know if she knew..." Terelle's voice cracked; moisture filled her eyes. She thought about all the suffering and sacrificing she had done to create the nest she, Marquise and Markeeta called home. She thought about all the pulling, tugging, and encouragement it took to get Marquise to finally straighten up and become a family man. "What kind of woman would destroy a family... I mean...do you think she knew we were gonna get married?"

Saleema's head snapped in Terelle's direction. "Damn right, she knew you were getting married. Why do you think she sent you that picture? Sis made sure she put the brakes on your wedding plans."

The simmering flame inside Terelle quickly blazed into a raging fire. "That snotty social worker ain't stoppin' shit!" Terelle said with a sneer. She dug inside her coat pocket and pulled out a ten-inch blade. "I got Quise's shank and I'm trying to decide whether I should gut that bitch or carve my initials all over her face." Terelle's eyes took on a deadliness that made Saleema recoil.

"Look!" Saleema exclaimed suddenly. "They're turnin' into the garage at Dave & Buster's. Should I follow 'em?"

Terelle narrowed her eyes in thought, but didn't answer.

"Hurry up! Whatchu want me to do?"

"Wait a minute; I'm trying to think." Trying to make a quick decision, Terelle frantically rubbed her temples. Finally, she cleared her throat and said, "Okay, get in the turning lane and park over there—across the street—in the cut." She pointed, indicating a narrow street off Columbus Boulevard. "I don't want them to see your truck," she explained. "We're gonna have to try and sneak inside the garage on foot."

A few minutes later, the two women ran across the busy boulevard and slipped past the female parking attendant who had come outside her booth to shoot the breeze with a maintenance man holding an industrial-sized push broom.

Terelle gripped the smooth handle of the knife as her blazing eyes searched for Kai's car.

Though the underground garage was not sufficiently illuminated, she quickly spotted the Benz. "Damn! We missed 'em," Terelle moaned as they approached the empty black car. Her heart sank as she peered inside and viewed the familiar interior. As she'd suspected, it was the same car Marquise claimed to have borrowed from his anonymous Jamaican business partner. She now knew with certainty that Marquise had been creeping with Kai—right under her nose. All those weekends he said he'd spent with the Jamaicans were actually spent with Kai.

Terelle shook her head sadly. What a fool she'd been. The drastic change in his routine should have been the first warning sign.

"What should we do?" Saleema asked, breaking into Terelle's thoughts.

Terelle gave a heavy sigh. "I guess we'll have to wait it out."

"You must be crazy! I'm not waitin' out shit. You expect me to freeze my ass off like a nut while Quise and that bitch are all warm and toasty playing video games inside Dave & Buster's?" Saleema gathered her fur-lined leather vest tightly around herself. "Come on, Terelle. We're out—you're gonna have to deal with this some other time."

If Terelle had it her way, she and Saleema would stake out the garage until the next day if necessary. However, weary from the chase and all the drama leading to this anticlimactic showdown, Terelle didn't have the strength it would take to convince Saleema to stay.

"All right; come on, let's go," Terelle said, looking miserable and sounding as if she were about to cry. She buttoned her coat, turned up her collar and cast a pained gaze at the black Benz.

[illegible] The [illegible] charge in his rooms, [illegible] would be here [illegible] the first examination.

[illegible] asked [illegible]

[illegible]

[illegible]

[illegible]

[illegible]

Chapter Forty-Nine

Before Terelle and Saleema had taken one step toward leaving, they heard muffled voices. A light of hope shone in Terelle's eyes. The door that patrons of Dave & Buster's used to enter the garage was pushed open from the inside. They could now hear the voices more clearly, a feminine tone and Marquise's unmistakable deep rumbling voice.

"Duck!" Terelle pulled Saleema down to a squat as they concealed themselves behind a dark-colored Durango that looked like it hadn't been washed since the last snowstorm. It was parked several rows away from the Benz but was close enough for them to spy on the couple. Crouched against the filthy SUV, one knee touching the grimy oil-stained concrete, Terelle tightly gripped the handle of the knife.

Terelle could hear Kai's heels clicking against the asphalt. She inched up and stretched her neck to see, but instantly wished she had not. The sight of Marquise with his arm placed protectively around Kai was like a kick in the stomach. Kai, elegantly attired from her earrings down to her boots, was swinging a handbag adorned with beautiful beads, shimmering shells and gleaming precious gems. The handbag alone looked as if it cost more than all the gear in Terelle's closet.

Terelle frowned down at her Value City-purchased sweats. Never had she felt so flawed. A feeling of hopelessness washed over her. How could she compete with that rich bitch?

"I'm sorry, but I'm famished. I can't even think about playing those silly games until I've been fed. Are you gonna feed me?" Kai asked in child-like playful tone. She looked up at Marquise with adoration. Marquise brushed her curls from her face. The intimacy between them spoke of a relationship that had developed over time—a period when Terelle no doubt had been inexcusably neglected. Betrayed.

It took tremendous effort for Terelle not to just break down and cry.

"We coulda ate in there and I coulda got my game on," Marquise said, laughing. Nothing about his demeanor or tone indicated that he was with Kai against his will.

Listening to her fiancé bantering with another woman was causing Terelle to lose her grip on reality. She was liable at any moment to spring up and confront the illicit lovers, wielding wildly Marquise's knife.

"Why should I eat that game room garbage when Hibachi, which is one of my favorite restaurants, is right next door? You can play as many games as you want after we have a civilized meal. Okay, Sweetie?"

Sweetie! Terelle was ready to slaughter the social worker, but had to restrain herself. Timing was everything. If she expected to successfully scar Kai for life, she'd have to choose the right moment.

"She talks like a white girl," Saleema whispered and wrinkled her face in disgust.

"Shh!" Terelle held a silencing finger to her lips; she didn't want to miss even a snippet of Kai and Marquise's conversation.

"I ain't down wit no ching-chong food," Marquise said.

Apparently looking for the car key, Kai stopped walking and began to fiddle inside her Miu Miu handbag. "For your information, Hibachi serves Japanese food—not Chinese. There's a difference, you know! It's a shame we have to move the car and drive somewhere else when we could walk right over there and enjoy some sushi or tempura. You should try to expand your horizons. Damn, you're such a meat and potatoes type... but don't worry, I love you anyway." Kai puckered up, stood on her toes and waited for a kiss.

Marquise obliged with a quick peck, then said, "You think eatin' raw fish is better than ching-chong food? Yo, them chinks be addin' dead cats in the mix—pretending it's chicken... and the Japs be servin' up food that ain't even cooked." He smiled and shook his head. "But, I ain't gonna lie—I fucks wit Chinese every now and then, but I ain't nevah gonna eat no raw damn fish!"

"Is that so?" Kai sounded coy as she fingered her curls

coquettishly. "Well, how do you explain last night? You seemed to enjoy eating this fish raw." She nudged her chin down toward her crotch.

"Oh, aiight. You win that round." Marquise's laughter echoed throughout the parking lot. He eyed Kai's crotch hungrily as if he were ready to bury his head between her legs on the spot.

"Did you hear that?" Saleema asked, astounded. "That nigga's talkin' 'bout eatin' that bitch's pussy! I can't take much more of this. If you don't get off your knees and put your foot up that bitch's ass, I'm gonna fuck *you* up. I'm not playin', Terelle. Go handle your business." Saleema pushed Terelle's shoulder.

The situation was beyond fucked up. Terelle was crushed. Her eyes glistened with tears as she recalled Marquise's unwillingness to participate in oral sex. Oh, it was okay for her to go down on him, but eating pussy, he'd said was for suckers who had to compensate for their little dicks. Inexplicably, she felt responsible for Marquise going astray. She felt ashamed of herself for lacking the qualities that would keep him faithful. She felt ashamed that Marquise had tasted the juices of a stranger and had never gone down on her. But that shame quickly switched to anger...and then rage.

With knife in hand, Terelle raised up from her haunches.

"Slow your roll," Saleema cautioned in a whispery voice as she pressed Terelle's shoulder, forcing her friend back into a squat. "Marquise ain't gonna just stand there and let you slice Sis up."

"Make up your fuckin' mind, Saleema! You don't know what you want me to do." Terelle's face was twisted in fury and confusion.

"I'm just sayin'...if you wanna do some real damage without worrying about Quise interfering, then you're gonna have to blast that bitch." Saleema produced a silver .22. Her eyes implored Terelle to take the gun.

"I can't," Terelle cried, shuddering as she shrank away from the gleaming revolver.

"I'm not telling you to slump the bitch, but if she'd done that slimy shit to me, I'd blast that bitch in the head." Saleema closed her eyes and shook her head. "Girl, that hooker would have to take a dirt nap; they'd be chalkin' her body right the hell now. But that's me." Saleema shrugged. "You gotta do it your way—do whatchu gotta do. Pop her in the arm...leg...or somewhere. But, you gotta let Sis know that you ain't the one to be fucked with. You dig?"

Terelle nodded. She extended an open palm. In truth, she no longer feared the gun; she now feared the repercussions that firing a weapon and injuring someone could bring. She feared doing time in prison while Markeeta was left in the hands of Children and Youth Services, an agency that had failed Terelle as a child and continued to fail the children it promised to protect.

No, she thought emphatically. She could not rely on anyone in her fucked-up family to take care of her daughter and she would never put her innocent child through the horror of the foster care system.

"Fuck it! Let's go," she said suddenly. "I'm not gonna play myself like this; let Marquise have that yella bitch. It's time for me to move on." She laid the gun on Saleema's lap and began to stand. Trying to regain some dignity, she stood straight and proud. She turned to take one last look at the man who'd been the love of her life and what she saw made the blood drain from her face. Terelle blinked rapidly for her eyes seemed unfocused. With a trembling hand, she covered her gaping mouth to muffle the scream building in her throat.

"What the fuck is goin' on?" Saleema asked as she sprang up from behind the Durango. With widened eyes, she uttered in shock, "Oh my God!"

The scene before them seemed surreal. Kai was bent over the hood of her car, her skirt hitched up around her waist, her bare ass tooted up in the air while Marquise penetrated from behind.

The man humping Kai was not the Marquise Terelle knew and loved. This man seemed primitive in his execution of this age-old ritual. His tongue hung over his slackened lower lip while he grunted like a depraved sub-human. He was definitely not himself; he was entranced. Marquise, Terelle told herself, would never disgrace himself by copulating outside like an animal. That bitch had some kind of power over him and that power was about to end!

Terelle jerked around toward Saleema and stuck out her hand. "Give me the gun!" Her eyes were cold, her face was tight with rage.

Saleema handed her the gun. "Wait," Saleema warned. "You can't get a clear shot; Quise is in the way."

Terelle ignored Saleema. She had to reclaim her man. Fuck shooting her in the shoulder and fuck shooting the bitch's legs, Terelle concentrated and focused her aim on Kai's head.

With her face pressed into the hood, Kai's curls wiggled like snakes as Marquise rode her.

Terelle pulled the trigger. And in one swift horrible moment, Marquise repositioned himself as he bent to grip Kai's shoulders.

Terelle screamed, "Marquise!"

"Oh shit! You shot Quise!" Saleema grabbed the gun from Terelle. She quickly wiped it with her Gucci scarf and tossed it. The gun made a deafening clatter as it hit the asphalt and slid toward Kai who was screaming hysterically as she tried to shake Marquise's heavy body off her.

Having heard the gunshot and fearing for her own safety, the parking attendant ran screaming from her post.

Terelle stood trancelike, staring at Marquise's fallen body.

"Come on." Saleema yanked Terelle's arm. Dragging a sobbing and resistant Terelle by the wrist, Saleema tugged and yanked until she and Terelle were safely past the attendant's empty booth and out of the garage.

"Come on; we gotta get outta here!" Saleema spoke authoritatively as she held Terelle's wrist in a death grip.

Dragging her feet, Terelle cried for Marquise. She tried to pull away. "Let me go. I gotta go back; I gotta help Quise. Let me go, Saleema," she pleaded.

There was no way of determining Marquise's physical status, but needing to flee the scene immediately, Saleema blurted, "Quise is all right. I saw him stand up. The bullet probably just grazed him. Now, come on. We gotta get outa here before we both get locked up."

Unwilling to listen to reason, Terelle tried to jerk away again.

"Do you want to lose Keeta?" Saleema asked desperately.

"*Markeeta.*" Terelle whispered her daughter's name as if just remembering her existence. "You know I don't wanna lose Markeeta."

"Well, that's what's gonna happen if you don't get your ass moving."

Terelle started moving.

"Walk fast—don't run. We don't want to look suspicious," Saleema cautioned.

Terelle complied and dutifully followed Saleema to the narrow street where the SUV was parked.

They hopped inside Jezebel. Saleema shot out of the parking spot and merged inconspicuously into the traffic on Columbus Boulevard.

Startled by the sudden sound of a siren, the two friends gasped in unison.

"Oh fuck!" Saleema yelled. She turned the steering wheel to pull over.

Burying her face in her hands, Terelle began a litany of prayers. "Please God, I know I haven't talked to you in a long time and I'm sorry. Please let Quise be all right. Oh Lord, I'm so sorry. I didn't mean to abandon you and I didn't mean to hurt Marquise…I'd die before I'd hurt Marquise."

When she took her hands away from her face, streaks of dirt and oil picked up from the floor of the garage covered her face.

Saleema cut her eye at Terelle and raised a brow. Terelle's ponytail had come undone during the fracas; it was a tangled mess. There was black grease all over her face giving her the look of a deranged performer in a minstrel show. In addition, since Terelle did not believe in prayer, Saleema could only conclude that her girl was losing it.

Incredibly, the siren did not emanate from a police car as Saleema had assumed. An ambulance with flickering lights and an unrelenting wail whizzed past and turned into Dave & Buster's garage.

Terelle shot a look at Saleema with fearful eyes.

Determined to put as much distance as possible between the SUV and the garage, Saleema pushed the accelerator to the floor and roared away from the scene of the crime.

Chapter Fifty

Someone was trying to kill her! There was that frightening popping sound and a split second later, she'd heard a woman scream. Then Marquise collapsed on top of her. The dangling buckle of his belt dug into her back—hurting her. His body seemed to weigh a ton and she couldn't shake him off.

"Marquise?" she whispered. The silence was deafening. From her helpless position, frantic with fear and perspiring heavily, she looked around trying to make some sense of this absurd situation.

Is this really happening? Kai wondered as she finally mustered the strength to throw Marquise's seemingly lifeless body off her. He hit the concrete hard. Kai gawked at him unbelievingly, but her sense of survival outweighed a desire to investigate his condition. While swiftly adjusted her rumpled clothing, something shiny caught her eye. Amazingly, a small silver gun glimmered before her. Figuring the shooter had dropped it and perhaps had another larger and more lethal weapon of destruction handy, Kai picked up the gun.

Determined to protect herself from whoever was out there trying to kill her, she fully intended to shoot now and ask questions later. She spun around and pointed the gun at anything that appeared to move.

Desperate thoughts flooded her mind. Who were her enemies—whom had she hurt? *Reece!* The convicted rapist instantly sprang to mind. *But...no* his imprisonment ruled him out.

Kenneth? He'd certainly threatened her. But no, he'd never become this unhinged over a scratched car.

LaVella! Hell no! That pathetic cow didn't have the heart for this.

And then it struck her: *Terelle*! A feeling of dread coursed through her. Damn! Had she known the love-crazed ghetto girl was unstable, she would have never sent the incriminating photo.

"Leave me alone; don't come any closer," she yelled. With one trembling hand she dug into her handbag and pushed 9-1-1 while pivoting and jerkily pointing the gun with the other. Uncertainly, she aimed at the shadows cast by parked cars, pillars, and even headlights from outside the garage. Everything was suspect.

"Is there an emergency?" asked a discarnate voice inside Kai's handbag. She jumped at the sound, then realizing that help was soon on the way, she gathered her wits about her and took the phone out and placed it on her ear.

"Yes, someone's hurt. He's been shot," Kai whimpered. "Send the police…hurry. Someone's trying to kill me!"

"Who, ma'am? Who's trying to kill you?" asked the emergency dispatcher.

"How the fuck do I know? Send the police. NOW!" she screamed.

"Calm down, ma'am. You mentioned someone was shot…is the person still breathing?"

"I don't know," Kai stated impatiently. She wanted to check on Marquise, who was ominously silent, but she dared not avert her gaze. Crazy-ass Terelle was possibly still hidden inside the garage.

"Check on him, ma'am. Find out if there's a pulse," the voice instructed.

Without taking her focus off the shadows, Kai stretched out a leg and jabbed Marquise in the side with the toe of her boot. She glanced down briefly. There was blood on her boot.

"He's dead! He's dead!" she screeched. "What the fuck are you waiting for, you bitch? I need help… quick…before she kills me too!"

"There's no need for profanity, ma'am. Now, tell me calmly…who's trying to kill you?"

Before Kai could give the woman Terelle's name, address and any other fucking bit of information she needed, she glimpsed a female figure. The woman seemed to appear out of nowhere.

Kai's scream resonated through the garage. Hysterical,

she dodged behind her car and began scrambling inside her handbag for the elusive car key. She was no longer willing to place her life in the hands of some 9-1-1 moron. If she were to survive, Kai realized she had to take a chance and get out of the garage. However, despite her desperation, she made a mental note to later deal with that ignoramus who obviously hadn't bothered to read the manual provided for emergency dispatchers. Kai would make sure the inept woman was severely disciplined. Yes, that blithering idiot could just kiss her job goodbye. Kai would personally see to it!

Refusing to stand still and offer herself as an unmoving target for Terelle, whom she perceived as a trigger-happy thug-girl with nothing to lose, Kai miraculously retrieved her car key; and jumped inside her car. The woman she assumed to be Terelle was now running toward her. Flooring it, Kai reversed out of the narrow parking spot.

The female parking attendant who had run to the scene with a male security guard close behind became winded. She bent over to catch her breath and let out a chilling scream. She covered her face in horror as she witnessed a black Benz back out of a parking spot and deliberately crush a disabled man.

Kai grimaced at the appalling crunching sound made when she accidentally rolled over Marquise's legs. That mishap, however, did not deter her speedy get-away from the woman she believed to be Terelle.

Chapter Fifty-One

Saleema pulled up in front of Terelle's apartment building. Saleema's nerves were so shot, she wasn't sure if she could safely drive home. From her peripheral vision she could see Terelle staring straight ahead, looking like a wild-eyed lunatic.

Sobbing one minute and laughing crazily the next, Terelle seemed to be losing it, but Saleema was too frazzled by the entire ordeal to be of further assistance. As far as she was concerned, Terelle had pushed their friendship to the limit. She didn't really know whether Marquise was dead or alive, but she realized that without a doubt, it was time to get ghost. In fact, the trip to Aruba offered by one of her johns, was starting to sound like damn good idea. Saleema didn't want to see or hear another word about Marquise Whitsett for a long, long time.

"You're home, Terelle. Go ahead in. I'll talk to you later."

"You comin' up?" Terelle asked in an annoying whimper.

Saleema screwed up her lips and shook her head no.

Terelle sucked her teeth, sighed and slowly departed the SUV.

Saleema didn't wait for Terelle to open the front door. With tires screeching, she sped away, leaving long black skid marks down Kingsessing Avenue.

✿✿✿

Upstairs in her apartment, Terelle walked in circles as she tried to figure out what to do. Which hospital was near Columbus Boulevard? Hannemann? Yeah, Hannemann University Hospital was probably the closest to Dave & Buster's. But then again, they may have taken Marquise to Thomas Jefferson University Hospital. Deciding to call Hannemann first, she reached for the phone. When it occurred to her that she was probably a suspect in the shooting, she quickly withdrew her hand. Of course, he'd only been grazed, but nevertheless, a gun was involved and she'd be questioned—interrogated. No, it wasn't a good idea to call the hospital.

She glanced at the phone and noticed the blinking message light. Seized by a sense of forlorn and filled with a premonition that bad news loomed, she refused to retrieve the messages. Terelle stumbled backwards, away from the phone.

The phone rang. The sudden sound of its peal caused Terelle's heart to pump.

"Hello?" she said, sounding frightened.

"Terelle, this is Aunt Bennie." Aunt Bennie's voice sounded like the voice of doom. Terelle's stomach clenched. *Dear Lord, please don't let her say anything about Marquise.*

Aunt Bennie spoke each word softly and slowly as if a higher pitch and faster pace might cause physical pain. "I know you aren't prepared for this..." she continued in that horribly droning tone.

"What? What's wrong, Aunt Bennie? Tell me," Terelle shouted. She needed to know what had happened to Marquise right now!

"Your grandmother passed today. I've been trying to reach you for hours."

With great relief, Terelle exhaled. If Gran was dead, then Marquise had to be alive. It was impossible for two people whom she loved to die on the same day. God wouldn't do that; he'd never be that cruel.

Relieved that she could stop worrying about Marquise, Terelle was suddenly animated. "I'll be right over, Aunt Bennie. You holding up okay? Want me to pick up anything from the store?"

"I'm okay for now. I guess it hasn't settled in yet. No, I don't need anything but you. You get here as fast as you can." Aunt Bennie's tone changed to an even lower volume. "Cassy's here." Then, in a voice barely above a whisper she said, "Your mother looks bad, Terelle. Skinny as a rail. And she's taking Mom's death so hard, me and Sheila are thinking about taking her over to the emergency room at Presbyterian to see if the doctor can give her something to calm her down."

Terelle's thoughts shifted to Marquise. Had he been taken to Presbyterian? If that were a possibility she'd insist on taking her mother to Presbyterian just so she could check on Marquise. But no…Marquise had gotten hurt near Penn's Landing and that was some distance from West Philly.

"How's Keeta?" Terelle asked, refusing to show compassion for her mother.

"She's fine. Watching cartoons, eating snacks…you know. She's too young to understand any of this. But she's been crying for you…and every now and then she cries for Quise." Terelle's heart dropped.

"Okay, Aunt Bennie, I'm on my way." Terelle hung up feeling sad for Markeeta, but was cheered in the knowing that she, Markeeta and Marquise would soon be reunited as the family they were destined to be. Marquise was alive! She could feel it. As soon as she'd paid her respects to Aunt Bennie and any other family members who turned up, she would scoop up Markeeta and be out!

Despite everything, even what she'd seen with her own eyes, Terelle knew that Marquise didn't want Kai. That social worker had some kind of hold on him. But not for long. Terelle intended to reclaim her man tonight!

Comforted by the reverie, Terelle went to her bureau drawer, pulled out her engagement ring, put it on and held out her hand in admiration. She happily bounded the stairs of her apartment building and set off to walk to Woodland Avenue to catch the 11 trolley.

While walking, she told herself that the first thing she had to do was contact Ayanna. By now, Ayanna had to know something. Damn, she wished she had a cell phone! She stopped briefly in front of the pay phone on the Avenue, but she knew the damn thing only worked when it wanted to. Only fools risked putting money into that tricked-up equipment.

Terelle moved on. Brainstorming, her musings turned back to Ayanna. Surely, Ayanna's boyfriend, Jalil would know something and he would have shared that information with Ayanna. She would call Ayanna the second she arrived at Aunt Bennie's house.

Bouncing along Woodland Avenue, Terelle fantasized a scenario where she screamed hysterically the moment Ayanna spoke the words *shot* and *Marquise* in the same sentence. *"They don't know who did it; but the good thing is...he ain't hurt bad,"* she imagined Ayanna saying, *"The bullet just grazed 'em, but girl, whatchu waitin' for? You better get over to the hospital, Jalil said that yella hussy is up in there takin' over and tryin' to act like she's Marquise's wife."*

His wife, my ass! Terelle though with indignation as she reached the trolley stop. She'd see about that shit! There'd be a showdown in the hospital room. She twisted her engagement ring around; its presence would convince the hospital staff that she was his fiancée and soon-to-be wife. She knew that once Marquise saw her face, he'd come to his senses and send that half-white bitch packing.

Visualizing Kai getting booted out of Marquise's room brought a smile to Terelle's face. The smile, however, swiftly changed to a perplexed scowl when it dawned on her that she still had no idea of Marquise's condition or his whereabouts. She stopped in her tracks, as if the answer would elude her if she continued moving. Which hospital, she wondered again? Which trolley or bus would get her there? Maybe she should call Saleema for a ride, she mused as she resumed walking. No, Saleema's nerves were shot! Terelle didn't dare ask her girl for any more favors for a while. Hell, she would walk to the hospital if she had to. Grow wings and fly—whatever. Terelle threw her head back and laughed as she imagined herself flying. It was loud raucous, inappropriate laughter. People stared, but she truly didn't care. The thought of showering Marquise with kisses caused Terelle to scream in sheer delight. Passers-by looked at her strangely, but Terelle stared right back and muttered, "*What's your fuckin' problem?*"

She knew with all her heart that everything was okay. Marquise was okay. She also knew that despite Saleema's anger toward Marquise, her girl would be pleased to see him and Terelle back together. This near tragedy would bring Saleema and Marquise closer—they'd finally let go of the past and become friends. Terelle giggled at the thought of the three of them chillin' together without anyone making sarcastic or hurtful remarks. Ah! Life was so good.

Terelle reached the trolley stop and briefly stood still to wait for the 11. But, troubling thoughts swirled in her head. What would she do if Marquise ever found out she was responsible for his pain? Frowning and mumbling, Terelle shook her head and began pacing back and forth. A group of people who were also waiting for the trolley murmured in confusion and inched away from Terelle. Oblivious to the scowls and quizzical glances of her fellow travelers, Terelle commenced to carrying on a one-sided conversation. *Quise knows I'm scared to death of guns; Not a soul on this earth would be able to convince him that I pulled the trigger of that gun. Shit, he'll probably think somebody from his past shot him. Yeah, he'll blame this mess on some old drug debt he owes.*

She silently asked God to forgive her. Then, a warm feeling moved through her body and she knew He had forgiven her.

Thank you, Lord, she cried as she fell to her knees and held her hands in prayer. There was a startled and collective cry of disbelief as passengers waiting for the trolley cautiously moved further away from Terelle; some walked to the curb anxiously searching for the trolley while craning their necks back at the crazy woman on her knees in prayer.

Finishing her prayer, Terelle stood and brushed the dirt off her knees, comforted by the thought: *God doesn't give you more than you can bear.*

[illegible] strength or hint of [illegible] and [illegible] to go [illegible]

Finally reached the motel [illegible] stood still [illegible] everything [illegible] in her head. What would [illegible] but she was [illegible] and [illegible] anything [illegible] her head [illegible] for [illegible] and [illegible] Obvious [illegible] and physical changes [illegible] correct [illegible] [illegible]

She [illegible] called God [illegible] body [illegible] had [illegible]

[illegible] and held her [illegible] There was [illegible] waiting for the [illegible] walked [illegible] for the [illegible] on her [illegible]

[illegible] the [illegible]

Chapter Fifty-Two

"Oh Jesus!" Aunt Bennie cried out when she opened the door and saw Terelle. Terelle was filthy, like an auto mechanic after a hard day's work. Dried mucus stained her oil-streaked face. Terelle, unaware of her startling appearance, opened her arms to embrace Aunt Bennie.

"I'm so sorry, baby," Aunt Bennie said in a choked voice. "We knew you were gonna take it real hard that's why we didn't want you to find out until you got here." Aunt Bennie hugged Terelle tight. "I want you to know your family...and your mother too..." Aunt Bennie said as she cut a worried eye at Terelle's mother who was standing in the background, clutching her hands together nervously and wearing a grim expression. "We're all gonna see you through this. Ain't that right, Cassy?" Cassandra nodded quickly and attempted to cast a loving gaze in Terelle's direction.

Terelle ignored her and turned her attention back to Aunt Bennie. "Why y'all acting so strange? I'm glad you told me about Gran. I got here as fast as I could so

I can help out with the funeral arrangements and everything. Where's Keeta?"

Markeeta came running from the kitchen. "Mommy!" Markeeta ran excitedly toward her mother, but took one curious look and backed away. "Mommy dirty," Markeeta said, wrinkling her nose.

Terelle looked down, appraised the condition of her clothing and shrugged. "Come here, girl. Mommy was in such a rush to get here; I didn't have time to change my clothes. Give me a kiss!"

Markeeta shook her head no. Laughing, she ran toward Aunt Bennie.

"Come here, Keeta. Come sit on Grandma's lap," Cassandra offered.

"I'll take care of Keeta, Bennie. You deal with Terelle," Cassandra said as she lifted Markeeta onto her scrawny lap. "I want to talk to my daughter in private—later."

Terelle shot a look of pure hatred at her mother. "You ain't got shit to say to me."

Cassandra's mouth fell open. Embarrassed and at a lost for words, Cassandra closed her mouth and bounced Markeeta on her knee. Markeeta squirmed. "You wanna watch cartoons or something, Keeta?" Cassandra asked

"No, I wanna watch Daddy on TV," Markeeta replied.

"What did you say, Keeta? What did you say about Daddy?" Terelle wanted to know.

"Terelle this is a time when families gotta come together; I want you to listen to what your mother has to say. It might help."

"Whatever," Terelle said, jerking her body to show her disgust.

"You heard her, Bennie; she don't wanna talk to me."

"You're her mother!" Aunt Bennie exploded. "Get up and talk to her! Can't you see she's in shock?"

"I'm not in shock. What's wrong with y'all?"

Finally stepping up to the plate, Cassandra stood up took Terelle's hand and led her into Gran's bedroom. Aunt Bennie solemnly nodded, urging Terelle to go talk to her mother.

They sat on Gran's old-fashioned four-poster bed. With both hands, Cassandra lightly grasped Terelle's. Looking into her daughter's eyes intently she said:

"I've been a terrible mother..."

"I know that's right," Terelle said defiantly.

Cassandra sighed and pressed on. "I've done things that I know you'll never forgive or forget, but I've always loved you Terelle."

"Hmph! You gotta strange way of showing it, Mom." Tears began streaming down Terelle's cheeks.

"I know, baby. I'm so sorry. But this addiction..."

"Yeah, whatever...you finished?" Terelle stood up.

"No, Cassandra whispered, urging Terelle with a tug to sit back down.

Terelle reluctantly complied. She lowered her head, refusing to meet her mother's gaze, afraid that if she looked into her eyes the love she'd always felt would come pouring out in torrents. Her mother didn't deserve her love, so she kept her head down.

"The worst thing I ever did was to tell you that big lie about Marquise."

Her interest piqued, Terelle raised her head. "What lie?"

"Marquise never made me perform oral sex. Never! When he first started hustlin' he wouldn't even sell me drugs…outta respect to you. But when he found out I was doing whatever I had to do with his squad and anybody else who had ten dollars, he started giving me money and drugs. He was embarrassed that his girl's mom was out there freakin' for drugs. To get high, I'd sell my body in cars, abandoned houses, alleyways… you name it. And Marquise thought if he gave me drugs I wouldn't have to trick anymore. But what he gave me wasn't enough for my addiction." Cassandra gave a heavy sigh.

"I figured out where he kept his stash—and I took it…all of it. A big-ass duffel bag filled with blow. It hadn't even been cooked-up yet." The memory seemed to make Cassandra's eyes glaze over in ecstasy. Terelle felt like killing her, but wanting to hear the rest of the story, she restrained herself.

"After that, the big boys came through—lookin' for him. They fucked him up real bad and then gave him two days to get their money. "

Terelle's mind raced back to the time Marquise had a busted lip and sore ribs. She regarded her mother with loathing. "Mom! How could you do that to Quise?"

"It wasn't personal. I..."

"What happened next?" Terelle cut her mother off mid sentence.

"I heard that his friend, Jalil fronted him a couple hundred worth of weed and some wet. But you know how slow that shit moves. Marquise was on his grind day and night. He wasn't gittin' no sleep. Tired and not on top of his game, he made a mistake and sold a couple dime bags to a narc."

Terelle remembered that night well. After the narc had identified himself, Marquise had tried to ditch the rest of the weed and the wet he had stashed in his pockets and tucked in secret compartments inside his boots.

"Marquise went to jail because I stole one of his packages," Cassandra confessed. "After he found out that I took his shit, he came after me. But on the strength that I'm your mother, he gave me twenty-four hours to get his money. I tried, but I couldn't get it. Then, when the big boys came back looking for him...he got scared and started taking all kinds of risks. That's why he slipped up and sold that weed to a cop."

Terelle sobbed. "If you knew you caused Quise to get knocked, why did you talk so bad about him the whole time he was locked up? You acted like you hated him."

"I hated myself," Cassandra said sadly. "Still do... and now that he's gone, I'm gonna get myself clean once and for all. I have to...for Quise."

"WHAT!" Terelle sprang up from the bed. "He's what? Don't play with me, you bitch!" Looking like a madwoman, with eyes blazing, Terelle got up in her mother's face.

"He's dead, Terelle..." Cassandra shrank back, cowering from her daughter's raised fist.

Having heard the commotion, Aunt Bennie and Sheila with Markeeta toddling on their heels, ran screaming into the bedroom. Cassandra was on the floor, curled into a knot. Terelle, looking like a raving lunatic, was stomping her mother senseless.

"Stop it, Terelle!" Aunt Bennie cried. Both Aunt Bennie and Sheila tried to pull Terelle away, but Terelle had the strength of three burly men.

"Quise...ain't...dead!" Terelle screamed. Each word was accompanied by a kick in her mother's ribs.

"He's dead, Terelle," Aunt Bennie screamed as she desperately tried to pull Terelle away from Cassandra. "We thought you knew. Figured you'd found out before you got here...and your grief...well, we thought your clothes were all messed up because um...maybe you went crazy or something when you found out." Aunt Bennie looked for some support from her lover, but Sheila, stunned into silence, was mute. She was apparently unwilling to speak a word that might set off the crazed young woman.

"Some woman killed Marquise," Aunt Bennie went on. "She shot 'em and then ran over him with her car and tried to leave the scene of the crime, but two witnesses saw the whole thing and the police caught up with her somewhere near Penn's Landing. It's been on the news for the last couple hours."

"Quise ain't dead!" Terelle insisted. Her angry fist aimed for her aunt. Aunt Bennie ducked. She and Sheila tried to restrain her, but Terelle easily broke free from their feeble grasp.

Needing to hurt someone, Terelle took a few steps backward and then assaulted her mother with a running kick in the ribs. Unconscious, Cassandra jerked and groaned from the blow. Markeeta, Aunt Bennie, and Sheila all screamed.

Terelle had to be stopped before she killed Cassandra. Not knowing what else to do, Aunt Bennie leaped on Terelle's back and sank her teeth deep into her niece's shoulder.

Terelle welcomed the pain. Like a wounded animal, she bared her teeth, threw her head back and howled Marquise's name.

Chapter Fifty-Three

Though completely unaware, Terelle was quite the celebrity at the mental health facility where she'd been transported by ambulance in restraints.

Given enough psychotropic drugs to sedate an elephant, Terelle was oblivious to the frenzied atmosphere within the facility where doctors, nurses, and support staff had their faces buried in the newspapers and glued to the TV screen as they followed the media coverage of the murder of Marquise Whitsett.

For the past two days, Kai Montgomery, photographed in handcuffs, had been making the headlines in all the local newspapers. *The Daily News* had given her *The Thug Princess* moniker and portrayed her as a spoiled Mainline debutante who had everything money could buy, but needing a new thrill, had dallied with a convicted criminal merely for the excitement.

An *Action News* snippet stated: *Two employees of a parking garage on Columbus Boulevard fingered Kai Montgomery. Ms. Montgomery is accused of shooting Marquise Whitsett in cold blood and then maliciously crushing him under the wheels of her late-model Mercedes Benz. Her fingerprints were found on the gun. Considered a flight risk, Kai Montgomery is being held without bail.*

The media portrayed Terelle Chambers as the second victim, who upon learning that her fiancé had been viciously murdered, had succumbed to a mental breakdown.

✿✿✿

Saleema climbed the stairs to Terelle's apartment feeling mad at the world. She should have been chillin' in the Caribbean, sipping an exotic drink and puffing on a big-ass Bob Marley-sized blunt. She should have been so twisted that she was damn near amnesic when it came to flashing back to what really had happened to Marquise.

But instead of escaping to a tropical paradise, she was saddled with the responsibility of clearing out Terelle's apartment. Miss Bennie was overwhelmed with funeral arrangements for her mother and was also trying to put together a memorial service for Marquise. Terelle's mother wasn't capable of helping with shit. Saleema rolled her eyes thinking about how that very morning, after visiting Terelle at the crazy house, she had stopped by to see Miss Bennie to pay her condolences. Miss Cassy was there. Covered with bruises; her cracked ribs bandaged, she looked a hot mess. Saleema would have given anything to have seen the ass whoopin' Terelle had put on her. Miss Cassy was trying to get sympathy by walking around all bent over, looking sad and decrepit. She had the nerve to ask Saleema for ten dollars—talking about she needed some money to pay for her pain medication. Yeah, right! The skinny bitch wanted to get high so bad she didn't give a damn that her daughter had had a nervous breakdown, her own mother was dead, and her newly orphaned granddaughter was crying for her parents. She was willing to shirk all responsibility, run out and get high. As far as Saleema was concerned, the ass whooping Miss Cassy had gotten from Terelle was a long time in coming.

Saleema's anger kept her grief at bay. However, as she stuck Terelle's key in the lock, tears clouded her vision, then poured down her cheeks. She opened the door remembering how hard Terelle had worked to acquire the apartment and how happy she'd been to finally have a home for her and Marquise. For Terelle, this dump of an apartment had been a dream come true. And all her girl had ever asked was for Marquise to treat her half-ass decent and be a father to their child.

Now was that too much to ask from the man she'd devoted her entire life to? How many women could honestly say that they'd had sex with only one man in their whole damn life? Well, Terelle could make that claim. When it came to sex, Terelle didn't mess around and Marquise knew it. But that didn't stop him from whoring around and breaking her heart until she couldn't take it anymore.

Infused with renewed anger directed at the deceased Marquise, Saleema wiped away her tears. She thought about her visit this morning with Terelle. Poor Terelle was sitting in a goddamn wheelchair—too doped up to walk. She was drooling and looking crazy as a bedbug from taking all that medication. It was hard to imagine that Terelle would ever come back around. And none of this shit would have happened if Marquise had just kept his dick in his pants. What a fuckin' mess!

And the mess had spilled over into Saleema's life—big time. It looked like she was going to have to take care of Markeeta until Terelle got better. Miss Cassy wasn't worth a fuck and Miss Bennie...well, she was nice and everything, but Saleema would be damned if she'd let two Lesbos raise her godbaby. Hell no!

Inside the apartment, Saleema walked from room to room, in a quandary as to where to begin. Okay, she'd sort through and pack Markeeta's things first. Oh! She'd better call her john to let him know the trip they'd postponed would now have to be cancelled. She doubted if he'd want a young child tagging along.

The flashing light at the base of the phone caught her attention. She might as well listen to messages and try to tie up all Terelle's loose ends. Saleema dug into the secret compartment in her wallet and pulled out the code that Terelle had entrusted her with along with an extra set of keys back when she first had moved in.

She turned up the volume and began loading up green trash bags with Markeeta's toys. The first two messages were from Miss Bennie, telling Terelle that her grandmother was slipping fast. The next message was from the nursing home, informing Terelle that she'd been terminated and should call the Human Resources Department to make arrangements to turn in her employee ID in order to get her final paycheck. Saleema sucked her teeth and gave the phone her middle finger.

In the midst of sorting through Markeeta's toy box, the next message sent a chill up Saleema's spine. Stunned, she dropped a crate of wooden alphabet blocks, slid down the wall and sat in a corner on the floor.

Yo, Terelle! This is Quise. I know you mad, babe. You got every right to be. But believe me I got a good explanation for all the bullshit I done put you through. Babe... look...this is the deal. I got involved with this crazy jawn. She's rich...but scattered like a muthafucker. I'm talkin' fatal attraction crazy. She been threatenin' to have both of us locked up. She been talkin' all kinds of crazy shit 'bout that damn watch. Yeah, I lied about the watch. I told you the Jamaicans gave it to me. But check this...she think she can buy me. So, I'm gonna run some game and act like I'm wit it. Tonight we gonna pick up this fly-ass truck I talked her into buyin' for me. I woulda had it yesterday, but it wasn't ready. She paid for it in cash and I made sure she put it in my name. I want you to pack up yours and Keeta's shit 'cause after I git the keys to the truck...we gon' be the fuck out. We can drive down South somewhere and start all over. Fuck Philly. Philly don't offer a nigga nothin' but jail time or death. I'm tired of bein' a fuck-up; I'm through lyin' and cheatin' on you. It's a wrap, babe; count on it. I'm a family man now—I'm through wit the streets. You hear me, babe? I said it's a wrap; I swear on my life. I love you. But you know me...I can show you better than I can tell you. Put on something sexy, aiight? I'll be home tonight."

Listening to Marquise lying to Terelle from the grave made Saleema weep for her friend. Saleema knew that if Terelle ever recovered and heard the message, she'd easily believe that once again, Marquise had become a changed man. The horror of being responsible for ending his life and interrupting their happy future together would definitely send her girl back to oblivion. Thus, sniffling and wiping her eyes, Saleema erased the tape.

Chapter Fifty-Four

For Kai, the past thirteen months had been a progressive descent into hell. She had experienced unrelentingly horrendous events during this period, beginning with her arrest and concluding with her present loathsome reality: life behind bars. Kai shuddered as she recalled the first time she'd felt the cold embrace of metal handcuffs around her dainty wrists instead of the comfort of her 3-carat diamond tennis bracelet and Versace mother of pearl wristwatch.

Her eyes wandered around her new home—a prison cell the size of her former walk-in closet. She felt like a trapped animal. Flooded by a feeling of despair, Kai dropped her head into her hands. The atmosphere was cold. In fact, everything inside the cell was cold… and hard: the cement walls, the metal sink, the toilet, the bolted-down stool, the tabletop, which was connected to the wall. The metal bed frame, covered by something plastic, seemed more like an exercise mat than a mattress. The temperature felt below zero. She shivered as she recalled the cold shower she'd been expected to take earlier that day. Taking a shower in full view of a horde of ugly, foul-smelling women was bad enough but when cold water shot out from the overhead nozzle, stinging her body like crushed ice pellets, Kai yelped and leaped away from the assault without so much as even unwrapping the bar of prison-issued soap.

Kai brushed falling hair from her face and absently inspected a tendril. Her hair was brittle and in desperate need of a trim. Considering her options, she quickly decided she would hack it off herself before she'd allow any of the jailhouse beauticians to get their unlicensed hands in her hair. She began frantically twisting her hair around her finger. *This situation is fucking tragic! I'm innocent, dammit.* She shook her head pitifully. She wanted to scream to the top of her lungs. But realized screaming was useless. She'd been screaming for the past year to no avail. Hell, the judge had banished her from the courtroom for screaming out her innocence.

According to her inept yet high-priced attorney, that particular stunt had sealed her fate. After her public temper tantrum, the jury, who already despised her for exhibiting an arrogant air of entitlement and for possessing both beauty and wealth, happily delivered a guilty verdict. Even the judge hated her. It appeared to Kai that the judge had struggled to suppress a smile when she sentenced her to life in prison. *Life in fucking prison!* And now this! She raised her head and reached for the letter. Her hands trembled as she reread for the thousandth time that day the letter from her defense attorney. It seemed ludicrous that such expensive, richly embossed paper could bear such bad news. Her attorney, the shyster her parents held in such high esteem, whose weak defense had landed her in prison, had the audacity to inform her that he was rescinding his initial offer to begin the appeal process.

With the mountain of evidence against you and without benefit of a credible witness or an alibi, it is unlikely that we could expect anything other than another guilty verdict, a portion of the letter read. Kai ripped the letter to shreds. *Good riddance to bad rubbish and fuck you, too, dickhead!*

She'd find her own damn attorney—one with some balls. She'd hire someone who honestly believed she was innocent and who would point an accusing finger at the real murderer, Terelle Chambers. The name rang in Kai's mind, taunting her. The whole world, it seemed, sympathized with Terelle, considered her a victim; they were all duped by her crazy-as-a-bedbug routine.

Kai had definitely underestimated Terelle. How could she have allowed someone so ill bred and ignorant to bring her life to such ruin? Kai had ended up convicted of first-degree murder and abuse of corpse, while that hairy ignoramus claiming to be too crazy to testify had gotten away with murder. Maybe if she too had pretended to be *touched by an angel*, she'd be serving a minimal amount of time in some cushy mental facility.

With an insanity defense, there would have been the prospect of an early release—there would have been hope, but now...

Tears of anger began to well, but Kai fought the urge to cry. Crying would be an admission of defeat. Her inept attorney had given up...Jeeze, even her own parents had given up. But, Kai refused to give up.

Her father had traveled to the women's prison only once; her mother didn't accompany him using the excuse that she couldn't bear to see her daughter behind bars. What nonsense! The bitch hated Kai. Always had. And Kai knew why. Miranda Montgomery was barren and Kai was the living evidence of Philip Montgomery's infidelity. The unethical bastard knocked up one of his charity patients and covered his tracks by pretending to be a do-gooder who was willing to give an unfortunate mulatto child a better life.

Though there was no tangible evidence that Philip Montgomery was her natural father, Kai was convinced that he was. Those black people in Chester took one look at her and knew the truth. For the life of her, Kai would never understand how the white community had never questioned her parents' fabricated story. Without question, she was Philip Montgomery's natural child; the resemblance between them was astonishing—she had her father's thin lips, sharp nose, and dark brown eyes.

When this nightmare ended—when Terelle was

brought to justice, Kai's family would have to pay. And that included her biological bitch of a mother whom she planned to hunt to the end of the earth to dispense the appropriate justice.

The jangle of keys broke into Kai's delicious thoughts of revenge. She looked up as two male guards entered her cell. Their leering expressions made her stomach churn with disgust. Sexual misconduct by the staff, she'd overheard through the prison grapevine, was a routine occurrence.

Judging by their predatory gazes, Kai supposed they viewed her as fresh meat, ripe for ravaging and expected her to tremble with fear. She was annoyed, but most definitely unafraid of the two correctional officers. Hell, they didn't have to rape her; she'd give them what they wanted. After all, getting dicked down by two men was an unfulfilled fantasy and it made perfect sense to seize this opportunity to take care of her carnal needs.

Quickly abandoning all thoughts of legal problems and ponderings of revenge, she cast a lingering look that traveled from their faces and down to each man's crotch. She'd deal with her problems some other time. Right now, she could use some stiff dick to relieve thirteen months of pent-up stress. Kai had been yearning for a real orgasm; the weak release she'd been achieving with her fingers only added to her frustration

She sized up the guards and decided it would definitely take two dicks to replace the big one Marquise had possessed.

Kai threw her head back and licked her lips, slowly parted her legs and greeted the two wanna-be rapists with an inviting smile and a sultry, "Hello."

The two prison guards looked at each other in bewilderment, their lustful expressions quickly changed to a no-nonsense glower.

"You have a visitor," barked the short correctional officer.

The second guard who was about a foot taller than his cohort and who had obviously been pumping way too much iron, stood with his thick legs spread and beefy arms folded. "Get moving," the beefy guard said, jerking his head toward the open cell door.

✿✿✿

Though the guards didn't provide Kai with the name of her visitor, she assumed it was her father. No one else had bothered to visit. Kai entered the visitors' area and glanced around the crowded room. Taking in the zoo-like atmosphere, she sucked her teeth and muttered under her breath contemptuously. The place was swarming with pathetically poor people who despite the dismal environment wore wide grins, whooped and hollered with glee as they embraced their incarcerated loved ones. *Jeeze!*

There was a multitude of babies and young children—

brats of every nationality who created a cacophony of sound that was certain to bring on a migraine.

Kai sniffed at the air, her face contorted as if she'd been force-fed an entire lemon. What was that stench? An unpleasant musky odor hung in the air. It smelled like a combination of sour milk, sweaty armpits, and funky vaginas.

She sure hoped her father had some goods news regarding a new appellate attorney because she didn't know how much longer she could survive this nightmare.

With brows knitted in agitation, Kai looked around the visitor's room again. Where the hell was her asshole of a father? It should have been easy to spot him considering that aside from the few Caucasian correctional officers positioned like sentries at various posts, there were no other Caucasian men in the room.

Eyes narrowed, she scanned the room again. He wasn't there. Had someone screwed up and brought her down to the visitors' room by mistake or was this some sort of prank? With her hand pressed against her head as if overcome by a terrific headache, she wondered if her life could get any worse?

Kai turned and motioned for the nearest guard. Being escorted back to her suffocating cell was better than mingling with this pack of happy heathens. Just as the guard acknowledged her, a feminine voice called her name. Kai jerked around.

A rather flashy black woman—late thirties, early forties—whom Kai did not recognize sat alone at one of the tables in the rear. She waved happily at Kai. Kai shrugged; she didn't know any black women besides her parents' housekeeper, the nurses and other staff at the nursing home and she certainly didn't associate with or consider any of them as friends. Squinting in confusion, Kai took tentative steps forward.

Smiling knowingly, the woman beckoned Kai with fluttering talon-like fingers.

The smile was vaguely familiar, but Kai still couldn't place her. She inched closer, and inexplicably her heart began to pound.

"Come on over here, baby!" The woman spoke authoritatively and gestured impatiently.

Baby! Kai was offended by the familiarity in the woman's tone and simultaneously scared out of her wits. She froze and began to tremble.

As if on queue, the stranger arose and rushed toward Kai. "Come on, sweetie; get yourself together," she said softly, yet firmly as she directed Kai toward the table. "It took me damn near three hours to get here; let's not give these people a reason to terminate my visit."

Kai bristled; her limbs became rigid. She desperately wanted to resist, but was unable to. With inappropriate self-assurance, the stranger took her hand and guided her stiffened body to the unoccupied table. Though the distance was short, it was the longest walk Kai had ever taken. She crept along as if she were made of crystal—a crystal figurine so fragile that any abrupt movement might shatter her into a million pieces.

Chapter Fifty-Five

"You know who I am, right?" the woman asked as she eased her willowy body into the hard chair. She flashed another knowing smile as she leaned forward and awaited Kai's response.

Kai knew exactly who she was, but was so unprepared to be seated across from the person she hated most in the world, her stomach twisted into a tight knot. Hit with a surge of panic, Kai attempted to appear calm as she looked the woman in the eye. She refused to allow her gaze to waver. Her quivering hands, however, were a dead giveaway. Unsteady hands were folded and placed in her lap. It was surreal. Here she was, finally looking into the face of the woman who had the leading role in all her murder/revenge fantasies and instead of leaping at her and gouging her eyes out, Kai was confused by dual emotions of intense love and hatred.

She searched the woman's face and beneath the heavy layer of pancake makeup, neon-blue eye shadow and bright orange lipstick, she saw a toffee-colored, older, unrefined and hardened version of herself. The resemblance was so startling, Kai couldn't speak. *This is un-fucking real*, she thought as she looked away from her macabre replica. She felt lightheaded and disoriented. Kai's connection to this confident hussy was powerful and immediate.

"You're my biological mother," Kai said in a cracked whisper. Smiling broadly, the woman bobbed her head in delighted agreement.

Unfolding her trembling hands, Kai reached for a tendril and began nervously twisting it around her finger.

"You do that, too?" the woman asked, amazed.

Too traumatized to speak, Kai nodded.

"Uh-huh, you picked that bad habit up from me. You better quit before you pull out all that pretty hair," she said, then presumptuously pulled Kai's hand away from her hair.

Kai's eyes flicked to the woman's hair. Curly auburn extensions brushed her shoulders. In response to Kai's unasked question, the woman brushed the hair away from her face. Kai cast a furtive glance and noticed that the woman had a bald patch that was three times the size of Kai's quarter-sized bare spot.

Kai quickly looked away. There were too many unpleasant similarities.

"What's your name?"

"Melissa Peterson."

"Was my last name, uh, Peterson...at birth?"

"Look, I'm gonna answer all your questions in due time, honey, but..."

"No, you look!" Kai interrupted, her voice raised. "My entire life has been a charade. Do you have any idea how it feels not knowing your true identity? If you didn't come here with a long overdue apology for abandoning me and to tell me the truth about my identity, why the hell are you here?"

"Oh, I see you got my temper, too," Melissa said calmly, then chuckled. "No, sweetie, Peterson's my second husband's name and that joker's not worth the breath it would take to tell you about his sorry ass."

"I'm not interested in your second husband," Kai said sharply. "What's the story?" Kai's voice softened; her eyes became misty. "What's *my* story?"

"Well, let's see...where should I start. First of all, I didn't name you Kai. I named you LaQuisha Chardonnay Maxwell," Melissa said proudly, then her face clouded. "But Doc changed it to Kai. Kai sounds all right, I guess. Plain, but it's all right," Melissa said with a shrug.

Kai felt overwhelming gratitude to her father for sparing her *that* name. "Is Philip Montgomery my biological father?"

Melissa squirmed, studied her tacky acrylic nails and began picking her cuticles. "Girl, I know you have a lot of questions, but I don't have a whole lot of time to explain everything. They only let me have a half-hour visit 'cause I couldn't prove I'm an out-of-town relative, but I'll straighten that out and make better arrangements the next time I make this long-ass trip. I can probably get a three-hour visit if you sign something stating that I'm your mother from New York."

Still dancing around Kai's questions, Melissa talked fast and gesticulated with her long glittery talons. Kai's eyes were riveted to the woman's lengthy curled-over fingernails, which were painted a gaudy gold and dotted with rhinestones. She had never tried to visualize what her mother might look like. It was too frightening to even think about what a black mother might look like. However, if she were forced to describe how she imagined her biological mother, she'd have to admit the images leaned toward a more matronly and humble woman, someone passive, and contrite. Never would she have conjured up an image of this unrepentant, self-absorbed, cheap-looking floozy who sat across from her.

Kai felt anger building. She didn't care if they only had a half-hour to visit. How dare this biological bitch waltz into her life after being MIA for twenty-four years and then have the audacity to withhold the one thing she could give: the truth.

"Look, my parents flat out refuse to divulge any information pertaining to my birth and adoption. Those callous white devils even had the records sealed. So, if you think I'm going to sit here and have a polite chat with the likes of you, you're sadly mistaken." Kai stood up, indicating the visit was officially over.

"All right, sweetie. Come on and sit yourself back down," Melissa cajoled. "Now, what do you want to know?"

Kai sat down. "Why did you allow my own father to adopt me?" Kai asked accusingly, her bottom lip protruded.

Melissa cocked her head to the side. "That's what Doc told you?"

"No, he denied being my natural father, but I heard some gossip about him getting one of his charity patients pregnant and then adopting her child."

Melissa propped her elbow on the arm of the chair and rested her chin on her fist. "They gave you a life sentence, huh?" she said, skillfully changing the subject. "That's rough." She frowned and shook her head. Then, repositioning herself in the chair, she pointed a finger. "But don't you worry, honey. We're gonna get you out of this mess. Let's concentrate on getting your freedom for the time being, okay?"

Momentarily distracted, a light of hope shone in Kai's eyes. Desperately needing to believe that someone cared enough to help her fight this unjust imprisonment, Kai stared hopefully at the woman who was her mother and decided to not press for more answers—at least not right now.

"Now, the reason I came all this way to see you is

because your father contacted me through his lawyer…"

Kai was all ears, and nodded for Melissa to continue.

"I wish I had the letter, but they wouldn't let me bring nothin' in here." Melissa sighed. "It took all my will power not to cuss them female guards out. Them dyke bitches patted me down and searched me like *I'm* some damn criminal…" She rolled her eyes hard as she recollected the violation. Snapping out of her indignant interlude, Melissa continued, "Anyway, his lawyer said something about Doc losin' a whole lot of money from his practice due to you being in the news for killin' that boy…"

"I didn't kill Marq…"

"It don't matter, baby girl," Melissa interjected and patted Kai's hand condescendingly. "What matters is that that slimy bastard is trying to break our legal contract and hightail it out to California."

"What contract? Don't tell me you *sold* me to my parents!" Kai's voice was loud and high-pitched. On alert, one of the guards shot a disapproving glance at Kai and Melissa.

"Be quiet," Melissa hissed, then she quickly sent the guard an alluring smile. The guard blushed and lowered his gaze. Melissa turned fiery eyes on Kai. "What the hell is wrong with you, girl? Do you want them to throw me outta here before I get a chance to give you the 4-1-1?" she asked in an angry whisper. She glanced up at the big institutional clock. "Now look, I only have fifteen more minutes. Would you please shut your damn mouth and listen to what I'm tryin' to tell you?"

A zillion sarcastic remarks flitted through Kai's mind, but she held her tongue, pursed her lips and nodded obediently. She'd met her match in this crude, overbearing poor excuse of a mother and felt truly powerless in Melissa's presence. In fact, she was slightly afraid of her.

"All right, look...you're a big girl, so I'm gonna give it to you straight, but you better not interrupt me," Melissa warned as she wagged a long finger in Kai's face.

"No problem," Kai muttered with a touch of attitude.

Melissa shifted her position and swallowed. "When I got pregnant, Doc promised to take care of me for the rest of my life if I kept my mouth shut and didn't put his name on the birth certificate."

"Were you one of his patients?" Kai interrupted.

Melissa gave her a sidelong glance, then said, "Hell no! He was doing some kind of charity work at a clinic in Chester. But, every night after the clinic closed, Doc used to come over and party with the girls at my Aunt Addie Mae's house."

"My father frequented a house of ill repute? A whorehouse? In Chester?" The story was getting progressively worse; Kai felt nauseous.

"He sure did. Doc used to get his drink on, too. Anyway, I was just sixteen years old back in 1980, just a country girl from North Carolina trying to earn a couple bucks over the summer. I used to help my auntie keep the place clean while her sportin' girls entertained the 'Johns.' I poured liquor, changed bed linen, ran to the store...all sorts of odd jobs in addition to cleaning the place like a damn slave for hardly no money. One day when my auntie wasn't around, the girls let me make some money. Dr. Philip Montgomery was my very first customer." Melissa beamed. "But he damn sure wasn't my last." Hunched over, shoulders shaking, Melissa cackled like a witch.

"You're a prostitute?"

"No, I wouldn't put it that way," she said, pulling her self together and taking on a serious tone. "I like to think of myself as a businesswoman." Melissa gave a snort and cut her eye at the clock. "Look, I told you I'm pressed for time, so listen up and stop buttin' in."

Though Kai thoroughly disapproved of Melissa's tone she couldn't afford to piss the bitch off just yet, so she kept her thoughts to herself. "Sorry, what were you saying?"

"Hell if I know; you made me lose my train of thought. Anyway...when I turned up pregnant, there was no way Aunt Addie Mae was gonna send me back home to my momma knocked up. At first, she was going to take care of the pregnancy, if you know what I mean. But when she found out, I'd been trickin' with the doctor, she changed her mind because she figured there was some money to be made. Oh, my auntie was a crafty old fox, God rest her soul," Melissa said with laughter. "She had her lawyer draw up some papers for Doc to sign admittin' that he knocked me up. He agreed to pay my auntie a certain amount for my room and board and for keeping her mouth shut. Plus, he had to pay for my prenatal care, and he paid me ten thousand dollars—cash money to keep his name off the birth certificate. Your original birth certificate says: *Father Unknown*.

"All through that pregnancy, my momma thought I was going to Chester High School!" Melissa laughed and slapped her thigh.

"Well, if my father paid for his anonymity, how'd he end up raising me?"

"That's the funny part," Melissa said with a chuckle.

Kai winced. "I find nothing funny about any part of this sordid story."

"Oh girl, stop being so sensitive; where's your sense of humor?"

Kai shrugged hopelessly. The insensitive harlot didn't give a damn about her, never had and never would.

"So, like I was sayin'...I planned to put you up for adoption, but Doc had to have a look at you first. And boy-oh-boy, what did he do that for?" Melissa shook her head. "That man fell head over heels in love with you..."

"Really?" Kai's face lit up.

"Uh-huh. And I have to admit it, you were one beautiful baby. You had a head full of beautiful curly reddish-colored hair..." Melissa glanced at Kai's hair. "It's not as red as it used to be," she said, scowling at Kai's dull and damaged hair. "But, girl, you know white people don't have babies as pretty as we do. Anyway, he pulled a fast one and tricked his stupid white wife into thinking they were adopting somebody else's half-breed. Well, quite naturally, my auntie took advantage of that situation, too. After she threatened to spill the beans to his stupid wife, Doc paid her a hefty sum and promised to take care of me for the rest of my life. And he took real good care of me... for a while."

Melissa checked the time, leaned back and took a deep breath, apparently exhausted from recounting the long tale. "Damn, I sure could use a stiff drink and a cigarette right about now." She looked around as if there was the remote possibility that someone in the room might be able to help her out.

Ignoring her mother's idiotic cravings, Kai ventured, "So, bring me up to date. What were you saying about my parents moving to California? My father hasn't mentioned anything like that. He's supposed to be finding an appellate attorney to represent me."

"Hmph. Trust me, him and that wife of his are cuttin' out of there. Probably gone already. His practice sure is shut down tighter than a virgin's...well I won't go there. Let's just say he's out of business."

Kai shot her a look of disbelief.

"Call the number; you'll see."

"I can't. The office number isn't an authorized number on my phone list; I call my parents at home...collect," Kai said, then gazed off into space, obviously distressed.

"We've got five minutes, so listen up." Melissa leaned in close and began speaking in a whispery tone. "When that DNA mess came out, your father took it upon his self to go get y'all tested.You must have been about nine or ten years old at the time. Well, it turns out, he ain't even your father!" Melissa folded her arms, sucked her teeth and gave Kai a look that suggested *she'd* been hoodwinked. "After that, he just left me hangin', never paid me another dime. Quite frankly, he tried to pawn you off on me, but I wasn't having it. I told 'em a deal is a deal, goddamit!"

Thinking back, Kai remembered how the closeness between her and her father had ceased abruptly. She used to be a daddy's girl, but at some point during puberty, he became withdrawn and standoffish, pushing her off his lap, tearing her arms from around his neck, telling her to behave like a young lady. Now, she finally understood why. A lump formed in her throat. She struggled to get a grip, but gave up, covered her face and wept into her hands.

"Hush up, sweetie. It's all good. I made the right decision. I made him honor his commitment to me and to you. Uh-huh, I sure did. Listen to how good you talk, and all that fancy education you got out of the deal." Melissa patted Kai's arm. "If I don't know nothing else, I know how to work a man to get what I want. Don't worry, I might not have been there for you when you was little; but I'm here now, and I'm gonna get you outta this situation. But I'm gonna need your trust fund money to do what I gotta do."

Kai gave Melissa a look of incomprehension.

"Doc's trying to keep that money for his damn self, talking some bull crap about the DNA test terminates your right to your trust fund," Melissa said, talking fast. "But, I say fuck a DNA test; he owes you that money, and he can't go back on a legal document. Hmph! Baby, trust me...Doc ain't thinking about doing nothing else for you. It's just you and me now. So, work with me on this. You can't do much of nothing for yourself sitting behind bars...Now, I can help you beat this case, but I'm gonna need some kind of cash."

Kai felt undiluted hatred for her scheming birth mother. She took her hands away from her face and wiped her eyes. "Who *is* my father?" she demanded through sniffles.

Melissa wrinkled her nose. "Girl, that was so long ago, how the hell do I know? I had about three or four white customers, but Doc was the only one with any kinda money. Trust me...you wouldn't want to claim any of those other losers. But If I recall correctly, there was an insurance salesman...um, one of 'em worked the assembly line at Sun Ship, and there was that long and lanky red-headed trick who sold water ice from a truck..." Melissa's voice trailed off as she squinted in thought.

"Time's up, ladies. Visiting hours are now over," announced one of the guards in a booming voice.

"Damn, you had me running my mouth so much, we didn't get a chance to take care of any business," Melissa grumbled. "Look here, I'm gonna send you some forms to sign. Like I said, I can fight your case on the outside better than you can handle it from in here. You'll be hearing from me real soon...okay, baby?" Melissa blew Kai kisses and gave her a final reassuring smile.

Chapter Fifty-Six

"Single file, ladies...up against the wall," the correctional officer commanded the female prisoners as they streamed out of the visitors' room. Dazed, Kai trudged to the end of a long line of women clad in garish orange jumpsuits.

It had all happened so quickly...the unexpected visit from her birth mother and the devastating news she'd imparted. Kai's entire life, it turned out, had been a complete sham, a cruel joke. She, Kai Montgomery, was not the biological daughter of an affluent Main-line surgeon as she'd always believed.

She was nothing...a nobody.

In truth, she was the spawn of a cheap, conniving hooker and quite possibly a fucking water ice man! Making matters worse, her adoptive parents had abandoned her, leaving her behind with that despicable creature posing as a mother. If that fast-talking schemer was the only person she could depend on, Kai knew she could just kiss all hope of freedom goodbye.

She was utterly alone.

Overtaken by agonizing despair, tears clouded her vision.

As they waited in line, the woman in front of Kai shifted impatiently from foot to foot, and then turned around. There was a raw jagged scar on the woman's right cheek. No doubt, a knife wound. Kai grimaced.

"I hate it when they make us stand around like this," the scarred inmate complained. "All it takes is for just one knucklehead to get caught tryin' to sneak somethin' in here and the next thing you know, they got us all on lockdown." She twisted her lips in disgust.

Repelled, Kai shrank from the woman's intimidating presence, nodded her head and then quickly looked away. Making eye contact might encourage this revolting convict to try to engage her in more jailhouse conversation.

Then, quite suddenly, an awareness of a more profound truth overwhelmed Kai.

The power of the revelation took all the breath from her body.

If her entire life had been a lie, then everything she believed about class distinction must also have been a lie. Thus, she had to accept that she was no different than this disfigured, common criminal or any of the other disadvantaged people she had looked upon with such contempt.

Feeling lightheaded and grieving the abrupt loss of her former well-to-do identity, Kai's knees buckled and she began to slide down the wall.

Grabbing Kai around the waist, the inmate broke her fall.

Kai looked into the woman's eyes and what she saw shook her to her very core.

She saw centuries of pain and suffering, strength and endurance, triumph and failure, compassion...hope... and love.

This woman whose worth she'd been so willing to disregard just a moment ago, was now gazing upon Kai with unconditional love and sisterhood. And in that instant, she knew that her incarceration and life sentence for a crime she did not commit was retribution for all the hatred she'd felt and the pain she'd inflicted upon so many innocent people. Feeling deeply ashamed, Kai shuddered as the emotional catharsis traveled through every cell in her body.

"Hey, you okay? Do you need to go to the infirmary?" the inmate asked.

"No, I'm okay. I'm fine; I just need to get back to my cell and lie down."

"Girl, you almost passed out. Now, you know this ain't the time to be going off by yourself. You're new here, right?"

Kai nodded.

"Girl, you can't make it in this place without a friend. You need somebody to look out for you. Oh, check me out...I'm just runnin' my mouth and I ain't even introduced myself. My name's Shanita, but they call me Neet."

"Hi, Neet, it's a pleasure to meet you," Kai said, in an uncharacteristically kind and sincere voice. "My name's Kai and I'd be honored to be your friend."

"*Honored!* Damn, girl. It's all good and everything, but you ain't gotta put yourself out there like that," Neet said, laughing. Kai joined in the laughter.

"Quiet down, ladies," the correctional officer boomed.

Kai girlishly covered her mouth, stifling more laughter. Her former life had been filled with the finest of everything from European vacations, haute couture fashions, luxury cars, and daddy's inexhaustible funds, but none of those things had ever given her as much joy or gratitude as this woman's timely offer of friendship.

"You wanna hang out in my crib for a while—play cards or watch a little TV?" Neet whispered.

Kai didn't even bat a condemning eye when Neet referred to her cell as her "crib." Nodding her head enthusiastically, Kai accepted Neet's offer by mouthing the word, "*Okay.*"

"All right, ladies, move it!" commanded the correctional officer.

✿✿✿

In the day room, clusters of women wearing serious expression engaged in card games, checkers, backgammon, and chess. The TV was dark and silent. No television until four in the afternoon. If an inmate wanted to enjoy TV before that time, she had to purchase her own.

"That's my crew back there." Neet pointed to a group of women hunched over a huge piece of fabric. A sewing group. Their facial features were relaxed, their chatter sounded upbeat—more energetic than the other women in the day room.

"Whassup, y'all? This is my new friend, Kai," Neet said. "She's gonna be hangin' with us now."

They looked up from their work, curious. They'd all heard about Kai—the callous murder she'd committed, but there were no judgmental sidelong glances, no utterances of disapproval.

"How you doin' Kai," said an elderly black woman. "My name's Selma."

"Whassup, girl?" asked a hardened white woman who sounded black. "They call me Pinky. Don't ask me why 'cause ain't nothin' on me pink no more. Not even my gums." Pinky, obviously a heavy cigarette smoker, laughed and coughed simultaneously.

"So, what's your story?" asked a young Hispanic woman.

"Um...I don't," Kai stammered and began twirling a dry ringlet. "I really don't know where to begin."

"Well, don't even worry about it," said Selma. "Sit down and join us. We all got a story and we're telling our stories through this quilt."

Kai looked at the quilt, which was sewn together

with fabric remnants that represented different aspects of a woman's life. With bits of material from baby clothes to prison garb, the women were telling their stories.

"Ain't nothing but time in here," Neet offered. "Talk when you're ready. In the meantime, you might want express yourself on this quilt."

Kai had never sewn a thing in her life, and was too ashamed to admit it.

"Heard you was rich," Selma said, shaking her head sadly. "Can't sew, can you?"

Kai shook her head.

"We'll teach you," Neet chimed in. "Like I said, ain't nothin' but time up in here."

Smiling hopefully, Kai hugged herself. She'd taken the first step toward healing the self loathing and alienation that had haunted her entire life. This feeling of acceptance and belonging was a soothing balm.

But there was still work to be done. Forgiveness. She had to learn to forgive herself. She hoped God would forgive her and consider her unjust incarceration as debt paid in full.

Chapter Fifty-Seven

Most days Terelle was left alone in bed in her room with minimal stimulation, but due to the possibility of an impromptu state inspection of the facility, the nurses had gotten her out of bed and situated her in a Geri-recliner in the sun room.

Terelle's body was twisted into a rigid, bizarre fetal position. She lay motionless, eyes wide open, but unseeing. There was no reaction to her surroundings; she was uncommunicative. Clinical and support staff swept past Terelle as if she were an inanimate object.

Family and friends had sadly accepted that she'd had a nervous breakdown; snapped under pressure, which forced a break from reality, a disconnection from life. In essence, a living death.

For almost a year, those who loved her had been trying through prayer and vigilance to bring Terelle back to life. Recently, their visits to the facility had become painful and unrewarding, dwindling down to just once or twice a month.

The term, *nervous breakdown*, was no longer used by

health care professionals. Terelle's condition was diagnosed as Catatonic Schizophrenia. She was treated with antipsychotic medication and antidepressants. Nothing worked. There was little hope for recovery. She had become a forgotten person who was provided only basic care. Terelle was hand-fed by unenthusiastic nursing assistants, rarely washed, and her adult diapers were only changed when the stench became unbearable to the staff.

Thus, the tiny whimpers she emitted as well as the slight shift in her position had gone virtually unnoticed all day.

Until the whimpers became a scream.

It was a long and loud, blood-curdling, God-awful, bone-chilling scream that sent staff scurrying in the direction from whence it came.

Startled into awareness, Terelle heard the scream, too. *Turn it off!* her muddled mind demanded. *Somebody, please turn it off!* But the scream blared persistently. Oddly, she could feel it vibrating inside her. The horrible sound, she now realized, came from her own widely stretched mouth. *But why?* What could possibly cause her to produce such a gut-wrenching sound?

Panting and winded, staff stampeded into the sun room and surrounded her. Worried faces peered down at her. Attempting to take vital signs and checking for injuries, the nurses prodded and probed the screaming and thrashing woman named Terelle.

Now frightened and confused, she pleaded with her eyes for them to make it stop. *Make it stop! Make me stop!* She shouted in her mind as her wrists were being restrained.

Then suddenly, the restraints reminded her of something. But what?

Handcuffs! Oh my God! Someone was handcuffed. There were handcuffs on television—on the news. On Kai! Then the memories flooded her mind.

Now the scream took the form of a word—a name.

"Marquiiiise!" she screamed in a tortured voice. Her eyes, once beautiful, were now tormented and wild. "Oh God...Marquise...I killed him. Marquiiiise."

"She's delusional!" the charge nurse said as she quickly injected a needle into Terelle's arm.

Terelle tried to fight the drug; she had to make them understand it had been a terrible accident. She didn't mean to kill Marquise; she loved him. From the depths of her soul, she loved him. Then she felt herself sinking into the drug-induced void, but she fought to hold on to herself. She fought to hold onto the realization of who she was and the terrible thing she had done, but to no avail.

Her screams dissolved into a muted wail as she sank deeper and deeper into nothingness.

All that was left of her revelation was a single tear streaming down her face.

And then came sweet oblivion. At least for a while.

About the Author

Allison Hobbs is the author of *Pandora's Box*, *Dangerously in Love* and *Double Dippin'*. She lives in Philadelphia. Her next novel, *The Enchantress*, will be released in the fall. Visit the author at www.allisonhobbs.com.

Excerpt from

Pandora's Box

By Allison Hobbs

The handsome young black guy wearing a Rocawear jacket, matching knitted cap, and Timberland boots chose Victoria. His equally handsome and well-dressed buddy picked Jonee. The pair resembled urban-wear models, or rappers. Or, as Victoria strongly suspected, drug dealers.

Jonee had been right; their luck had changed. The young man was Victoria's fourth customer and it was only 3:30 a.m.

She wondered why two handsome young men would come out in the middle of the night, in the freezing cold to pay for sex?

The young man introduced himself as Kareem.

"My name is Pleasure," she said with a sincere smile. "How are you, Kareem?" The money in her purse had changed Victoria's mood from somber to gay.

"I'm doin' all right," Kareem said, looking her up and down and nodding with approval as he dug into the pocket of his baggy jeans.

"Two Benjamins should cover it, right?" Kareem grinned confidently as he handed Victoria two one-hundred dollar bills.

"What's the extra hundred for?" Victoria instantly wanted to take back the words that Jonee would certainly frown upon.

"For your pleasure, Pleasure," he said with a wink, which made Victoria blush.

She couldn't get over how long and dark his lashes were. Damn, he was fine! Not at all like the sad-looking patrons she was accustomed to. His good looks influenced her to behave demurely. Speaking softly, Victoria excused herself and took the money to Dominique.

Today's youth were a mystery. The crude street jargon and the thuggish behavior were disgusting. Victoria viewed them as angry, disrespectful hellions, and she made it a point to steer clear of them, avoiding places where they gathered, such as the corner deli in her neighborhood where ten-ounce bottles of malt liquor were the most frequently purchased items. That lack of respect was apparent in the way they dressed and in their music. Profanity had become acceptable speech in rap music—and the way women were referred to as bitches and hoes was unconscionable. To think that her music was deemed unacceptable, dated, non-commercial, while record companies rolled out the red carpet for hoodlums whose music boasted of criminal activities: selling drugs, robberies, killing sprees...

Oh, but let me not go there, she reminded herself. The music industry's lack of good taste was of no concern to her. Not anymore.

Anyway, who was she to pass judgment? she asked herself. It wasn't as if she had room to talk, working in a bordello and all. So Victoria allowed her thoughts to return to the handsome young man who was waiting for her. He seemed different than his contemporaries. Maybe he wasn't a drug dealer. For all she knew, he could be a professional athlete, or...the hell with stereotyping, he could be a medical or law student, a congressman, or senator, a teacher, a preacher or any damn thing he wanted to be. Why, she chastised herself, did she label him a drug dealer?

Victoria avoided the eyes of a surly Reds when she went to the lounge. She gave the money to Dominique and rushed back to her cute customer.

Kareem had stripped down to his boxers. He looked relaxed, as if he were lounging on his own bed. His jacket hung from a hook on the back of the door, his cap dangled from the doorknob. Seeing his cap made Victoria take notice of his hair. It was well groomed, cut close with neat, tiny waves trained to stay in place. The rest of his clothing was folded neatly on the chair. Though she couldn't see the label, Victoria supposed that his jeans sported the Rocawear label also.

Ready to take charge, Victoria said, "So tell me, Kareem, what brings you out in the middle of this cold, wintry night?" Her demure demeanor was gone. She was feeling playful. Flirtatious. Happy!

"I came out in this treacherous weather," Kareem said with a teasing grin, "to meet the woman of my dreams."

Unprepared for his quick comeback, Victoria cast her gaze downward; she felt her face flush.

She recovered and though it was difficult, she looked Kareem in the eye, determined to hold her own.

"Well, I'm glad you did because seeing you has made my night. Look at you! You're so cute..." She paused, enjoying watching him squirm. "With those pretty eyes...and mmm, I love your lips."

It was Kareem's turn to blush. Victoria watched as he involuntarily lowered those long lashes and self-consciously moistened his lips. She had disarmed him!

Her eyes ran the length of his body. His chest and arms were developed. Boldly, she placed a hand on his shoulder and turned him around. Not bad, she thought, blaming Evander Holyfield's beautiful back for her appreciation of a man's posterior view.

"Would you like a massage?" she asked, reaching for the baby oil. She wanted to touch his hard, young body. His taut, smooth chocolate skin looked edible.

"Nah, that's okay. I just want to look at you." Kareem gently pulled Victoria onto the bed.

"Hey, I like that," he said, indicating the red crushed velvet teddy she wore. "Red is definitely your color."

Kareem touched the fabric lightly and ignited a spark. Victoria flinched. Without a word, he drew her into his arms, inhaled her. "You smell good, too," he whispered into her neck. His lips moved up to her face. Victoria stiffened as she recalled one of the top rules of the working girls' code of conduct: never kiss a trick.

But throwing caution to the wind, Victoria offered her lips and clung to him. Her hands, with a will of their own, traveled Kareem's wide, muscular back—caressing, kneading, massaging, and all the while soothing her own aching heart.

The sexual encounter was intense, yet tender. And when it was over, instead of jumping up and darting out the door, Victoria nuzzled next to Kareem. Like lovers, with their bodies entwined, they lay together in the dark. She listened to his even breathing, feeling his chest rise and fall. And for this intimacy, shared with a stranger, Victoria would be eternally grateful.

There were three thumps on the door.

Kareem stirred. Victoria jumped.

"Time's up," Dominique said gruffly.

Victoria felt embarrassed. As if she'd been caught doing something wrong.

Feeling unsure of what had just transpired between them, she smiled weakly at Kareem. She hoped she hadn't made a complete fool of herself.

Victoria noticed that Kareem no longer had the self-assured look he had earlier. There was no way to exit gracefully, so she grabbed a towel and wrapped it around her naked body and began gathering her belongings.

"Thank you, Kareem. I hope you'll come again." Her normal closing spiel sounded awkward and inappropriate.

"Yeah, I'm definitely coming back to see you again." Kareem nodded his head as he spoke, as if to reassure her.

Victoria detected tension when she returned to the lounge. Dominique and Reds mumbled under their breath, and Jonee wore a stony expression that suggested she, too, was in a foul mood.

"What's up, girl?" Victoria asked Jonee, playfully speaking in street vernacular, but enunciating clearly.

"We got some mad hoes up in here tonight," Jonee announced.

"Angry at me?

"Yeah, and I don't blame them. You can't have the room on lockdown for a whole hour. You wouldn't believe how many customers walked out because all the rooms were tied up."

"Was I supposed to kick my customer out to accommodate someone else?" Victoria snapped, rolling her eyes.

Jonee had not been introduced to the feisty side of Victoria and was visibly taken aback.

"And furthermore," Victoria raised her voice, turned and glared at Reds and Dominique, "if a customer is paying, I can spend the entire night in the room if I so desire and I don't need permission from any of you."

The women fell silent. Reds looked as shocked as if she'd just been falsely accused.

Kareem appeared in the doorway of the lounge and beckoned Victoria. The lounge was strictly off-limits to customers, but with her eyes, and wearing one of her Nana's stern expressions, Victoria defied any of the women to say a word.

"Is it possible to see you outside?" Kareem asked as Victoria walked him to the lobby. "Can we go out sometime?"

She wanted to shout an emphatic yes, but realized that an involvement with Kareem could only add more confusion to her already complicated life. Victoria smiled sadly and shook her head no.

"I can respect that," he said. "I understand. So, uh, I guess the only way I'm gonna see you is if I come back here?"

Victoria nodded.

"When are you working again? Will you be here tomorrow?"

"No. This isn't my regular shift. I'll be here Monday night after five," she said, while thinking, *Damn, Kareem must have money to burn.*

"Okay. I'm gonna try and get back on Monday." He brushed his hand across her face. "So tomorrow is your day off?"

"Yes. Why?"

"Just wondering." Kareem touched her chin with his finger. "Wanted to know, just in case you change your mind about going out with me."

"Yo, Kareem," his friend called from the lobby. "Come on, man. Let's roll. I've been out here freezing my ass off while you're in there trying to fall in love."

Kareem laughed and kissed Victoria on the cheek. She watched as he and his friend disappeared out the door.

Victoria made careful steps as she returned to the lounge. Trying to stay grounded wasn't easy for someone who was walking on air.